THE
GLADIATOR'S
MISTRESS

THE GLADIATOR'S MISTRESS

CHAMPIONS OF ROME SERIES

JENNIFER D. BOKAL

Published by Montlake Romance, Seattle

www.apub.com

Amazon, the Amazon logo, and Montlake Romance are trademarks of Amazon.com, Inc., or its affiliates.

ISBN-13: 9781503944589

ISBN-10: 1503944581

Cover design by Regina Wamba

Printed in the United States of America

To the memory of two fabulous and fierce women—
my grandmother Thelma Marcus, for teaching me to
always love a good romance, and my mother, Elizabeth
O'Finan, whose counsel and company I miss now more
than ever.
For John. While traveling life's peaks and valleys, I'm
glad that you're by my side.

Chapter 1

Rome

Year of the consulship of Marius and Fimbria
650 years after the founding of Rome (104 BC)

Valens

Torches surrounded the soft sand of the makeshift arena. Long shadows reached into the garden and stretched high on the walls of the surrounding villa. Light glinted off the blade as it arced toward Valens. The other gladiator, eager to fight, knew little of defense and left his chest open and unguarded. Raising his sword to block the blow, Valens ignored the easy target.

Lunging right, Valens aimed to the left of the man's shoulder, the cold steel blade passing so near that his knuckles grazed skin. Dropping low, he spun around and slammed the pommel of his sword into his opponent's back.

As one, the crowd gasped and began chanting his name. "Valens. Valens. Valens."

Emboldened by the cheers and cries, he whirled to the right, leaving his challenger unsure of where to move next. His opponent came in again. Valens blocked the blow. The two men circled and locked swords, their shields pressed together. Applause and cheers came from all parts of the garden.

Valens fought several times a year at private fights like this one. More than the coin earned, Valens enjoyed displaying his flawless agility and understanding of the crowd's craving for entertainment.

Nearly one hundred people filled the garden in which he fought. Some stood and watched from open doors while others lined the gravel path that wove in and out of trees, flower beds, and trimmed bushes. The oval filled with sand worked for fighting better than most places he found at private parties—often just a drained pool or a cramped atrium.

All large villas, like this one, shared a similar layout. They rose up only a single level, and a large garden was cut into the middle of the larger rectangular villa. Almost every room opened to the family's personal paradise. A high, thick wall, meant to keep out unwanted plebs, surrounded the entire property.

Sprawling out across the Palatine Hill, these villas meant for single families could have luxuriously housed dozens of less ostentatious plebs or freemen. The waste of space in such a crowded city irritated Valens. He struck three successive blows on his opponent's shield, bringing the other man to his knees.

It was not just the homes that shared a slavish devotion to similarity. The people did as well. Thin women, their faces bright with cosmetics, wore even brighter wigs of spiraling curls. Jewels gleamed at every throat, wrist, and ear. Gowns of silk shimmered in the torchlight. White togas denoted the men's place in the Senate. A few others wore expensive tunics in a variety of colors, the edges embroidered with golden thread.

These wealthy men and women, the privileged elite of Rome, used any excuse to come together for feasting and drinking. And fights like this one served to satisfy the Roman lust for blood. Tonight, however, they gathered not for a typical party, but rather a wedding banquet.

Senator Phaedrus Scaeva Didius had requested Valens by name. Valens had accepted, since it paid well. But gladiator fights at a wedding banquet? Even he, a mere gladiator, felt that blood and combat boded ill for a married couple. Valens also figured the entrails read by the augurs that morning had been green and smelled of death. The bride, Senator Scaeva's daughter, turned her body away from her husband, as if hoping for a chance to flee. The groom, an elderly senator, seemed to take no note.

Marriage was not for gladiators. So he did not question the groom's disinterest. All the same, Valens could not help but think that if the bride were his wife, he would speak to her and try to put her at ease.

His opponent lunged again. This time the blade came closer than Valens anticipated, and he returned his focus to the fight. The sound of steel on steel echoed in the garden as he attacked. Slice, slice, thrust. Push, push, slice.

They maneuvered to the base of a terrace from which the bride and her new-old groom looked down. Beside them stood Senator Scaeva, Consul Fimbria, and another man whom Valens did not know. Tall porticoes rose up at their backs, the uppermost scrollwork lost to the dusk. The other gladiator came in at a run, his head lowered, ready to butt Valens in the middle. Wait. Wait. Valens swiveled to the side an instant before impact. He stuck out his foot as his opponent passed, and Valens slammed the hilt of his sword between the man's shoulder blades.

The gladiator took two more steps and collapsed in the sand. He remained on the ground for a moment and then rose unsteadily to his feet.

The crowd cheered. Valens extended his arms and turned in a circle. He glanced at the bride. A deep-red, sheer bridal veil draped over her shoulders and down her back, covering her dark hair. The gown of ivory silk skimmed her lithe body, its neckline draping low over her high breasts perfectly. The short sleeves of her gown were gathered

3

at the shoulders, held in place by silver and ruby pins, her only jewels. Compared to the other women with their gaudy clothes and hair, Valens thought that her natural beauty made her the most exquisite woman at the party.

Bouncing on the balls of her feet, the bride clapped her hands. Compared to the rest of Rome's elite, where every movement was studied and done deliberately to impress, the bride's response seemed candid. Valens remembered not the last time he had known anyone willing to be sincere.

He blocked a blow that came in low and stole another glance at the bride. Her hand worked at the wedding knot at her waist, the same one her husband would untie later once they retired to their marital bed. What was she thinking about now? The beautiful bride did not appear overly affectionate toward her old goat of a husband. She could not be looking forward to their first night as man and wife.

For a moment Valens felt a certain level of kinship with this young woman. He was no good at feigning emotions he did not feel, either.

The other gladiator rushed in again. Valens paid little heed to the newest assault until the flat of a cold blade slapped his torso. He stopped thinking of the woman and brought his attention back to the fight. It would not do to lose, even at a private party where they fought only to first blood.

Valens knew little of his opponent except that he had been newly admitted into his gladiator troupe and wanted to prove himself. That much was evident in the way he locked swords with Valens at every chance, not giving either of them room to move and entertain the crowd with combat.

Without momentum, the other man stumbled, too intent on finding a way to make steel meet flesh. Valens lifted his sword to strike him on the shoulder while also giving the new gladiator time to block the blow.

He again glimpsed the bride standing on the terrace. Drawn into his movements, she watched him. In all his years as a gladiator, Valens had become adept at reading his opponents. Facial expressions, shoulder placement, shuffling feet, and twitching fingers—all of it told something.

Outside of the arena it allowed him to quickly take the measure of a person. In his estimation, the bride was honest. Maybe too honest for a senator's wife. Had she been more attuned with social conventions, her eyes would have been lined with thick kohl until her blue irises blazed like sapphires in the light. She would have also been more careful of her stance next to her husband. Even now the space between the two told Valens, and the rest of the world, that she would rather be with anyone else than with him.

Yet she seemed to enjoy the fight. Maybe through feats of combat he could distract her, at least for a moment. It seemed the least he could do for the last honest woman in Rome.

Chapter 2

Phaedra

The gladiators came together, their swords locked. A thin sheen of sweat covered the tight ridges of their backs and the strong muscles of their arms. Phaedra watched with an eagerness she never would have predicted. She found the intensity of the struggle infectious. She gripped the woolen belt encircling her waist as if it held the power to control the outcome of the contest. Her trembling fingers traced the Herculean Knot, the one to be untied later by her new groom, Marcus Rullus Servilia.

The notion that she was now a married woman left her lightheaded. The wedding had been far from ideal, at least for her. Whoever heard of the wedding feast taking place at the bride's home and not the groom's? Making matters worse, and more embarrassing, were the gladiators hired by her father. She had begged him not to make fights part of the evening's entertainment. Gladiator contests were for funerals, not weddings.

Despite her arguments and pleas, her father had insisted. Consul Fimbria, the head of the Senate, planned to attend the wedding, and he held an extreme fondness for the games. In order to impress the consul, and make a new senatorial ally, her father would go to any length. Besides, her father said this would make her wedding banquet all the more memorable. In that regard, he had been right. For most of the guests, the excitement of seeing Valens Secundus, Rome's champion, fight in such a small and intimate setting overrode the importance of her union. And for Phaedra, that was fine. The less attention paid to her marriage, the better.

Although she had seen her husband, Marcus, many times before becoming his betrothed, she had spoken to him only once. After her mother's death, he had offered her his sympathies. To the then eight-year-old Phaedra, it was a shocking thing to be spoken to by an adult, as an adult, and his words had offered her no comfort. Instead, he had terrified her.

What was she, a young girl, to say to an adult man? Instead of accepting his condolences, she had burst into tears and run from the room. Knowing that her mother had seen her shameful behavior from Elysium, Phaedra sobbed for days. From her deathbed, her mother had left Phaedra with a single piece of advice: "Mind your tears and do as your father tells you. As your father, he is your lord and master." The next day, Phaedra had broken her mother's first rule, and in front of an important friend of her father, no less.

And now she was married to the man.

Glancing over, she caught a glimpse of her husband. Like all senators, Marcus wore a brilliantly white toga. He kept his silver-tinted hair cut short, and his beard was neatly trimmed. He was her father's mentor in the Senate. A man with enough coin to afford a million sesterces for his own Senate seat and plenty left over to loan her father a million more to keep his. Marcus had never asked for a dowry, and Phaedra understood the kindness of his gesture.

Until now she had had no marriage proposals. Her meager dowry had kept away any serious suitors of her own age. Many called Marcus the First Man of the Senate, an unofficial title that spoke of his importance in the Roman republic. Besides, at twenty annums, Phaedra knew it was important that she be wedded and bedded, so in some ways this union suited her.

She returned her attention to the gladiators, a wholly different kind of man. They separated, circling one another, their breath coming short and ragged. The famous one, Valens Secundus, stepped back and then came at his opponent again. The thick muscles in his back and shoulders tensed. Sweat dampened his hair. It curled and the ends swept out to the side. His dark, well-formed brows drew together in concentration. He pressed his lips together, the bottom fuller than the top. She wondered what he looked like when he smiled. Perhaps he always wore the same scowl of focus and ferocity.

The gladiators wore loincloths. Tied at the waist, drawn through the legs, a wide leather belt held them in place. The muscles of their powerful thighs quivered with exertion; their calves stood out bold and stark in the torchlight that danced around the garden. As the two men crashed into each other, their swords ringing out, Phaedra held her breath and prayed for Valens to come away victorious. She wondered for a moment why she prayed for this stranger, and not—with a guilty afterthought—her new husband?

Valens attacked, driving the other gladiator back to the edge of the sandpit. Three days before, two olive trees with waxy leaves, a rosebush with blooms of red and white, and a marble bench had filled this space. But her father had ordered it all removed so her wedding banquet might become a grand spectacle. He had made his point, she thought. Grand and virile, the gladiators were a spectacle in themselves.

The power and strength of the gladiators—especially that of Valens—registered in Phaedra's middle, causing it to tighten in the most intimate way. The fight shifted, and Valens came to face Phaedra. The combatants paused, their bodies taut with anticipation. The air around them vibrated with unrepentant masculinity.

Phaedra's skin tingled, hot and flushed at once. The scent of male sweat, leather, and steel mixed together and became more intoxicating than a cup of strong wine.

The fight continued, yet Phaedra stopped watching the back-and-forth of combat and focused only on Valens. His concentration, his drive, and his passion lured Phaedra's gaze, capturing it completely.

What would it be like to have a man such as Valens Secundus focus upon her with the same intensity as he did the fight?

For a moment their eyes met. Then the corners of Valens's mouth twitched up, and he winked so quickly that Phaedra wondered if it had not been her imagination. He rushed his opponent again. This time, when the other man tried to deflect the blow, Valens's sword connected with his wrist. A thin line of red appeared where the blade met flesh.

"First blood," her father cheered.

Voices filled the garden as the guests chanted, "First blood. First blood. First blood."

Her father lumbered down the wide stairs, dragging his left foot, swollen from gout. He gripped tight to the marble railing. The edges of the garden were lined with couches where guests reclined. Small tables laden with food and drink were tucked out of sight near bushes and in the shadows closest to the villa. Slaves stood nearby and waited to serve.

Still clapping, her father stopped in the middle of the newly constructed sandpit. He clasped Valens by the wrist. Holding their arms high, he said, "The victor and most famous gladiator in all of Rome. Your presence brings good omens to my daughter's marriage. You must remain and join us in the feast."

The guests cheered as her father, still holding on to the gladiator, turned in a slow circle. They stopped, facing the terrace upon which Phaedra stood.

"I offer congratulations on your wedding," the gladiator said. He spoke to Marcus, of course, but Phaedra felt Valens's eyes upon her, his gaze like a caress.

"Your congratulations are gladly received, Valens Secundus. You honor us with your well-earned fame on this, a most important day," said her husband.

Marcus slipped his hand around Phaedra's waist. The thin muscles in his arm felt unmistakably solid. At least her husband had not gone to fat like her father. Still, she wondered how the gladiator's touch might feel. Warm, with hands both strong and soft, a powerful grip mixed with sweet embraces. She shivered at the thought, and Marcus placed a kiss upon her temple. She smiled at him and tried to imagine her life filled with some sense of joy or hope. Perhaps she would have children. Yes, even a single child would bring her happiness and purpose.

Marcus held out his hand. With one last look at Valens, Phaedra allowed herself to be led into the villa. A table covered in a white cloth sat atop a dais in the triclinium, the largest dining room. A platter full of meats, four bowls filled with green olives, and a plate of steamed pears were laid out, along with several jugs of wine. Five empty chairs stood behind place settings. Marcus took the seat in the middle with Phaedra at his left. Phaedra's father sat next to Marcus, with Consul Fimbria next to him. Acestes, the son of Marcus's sister, occupied the seat to her left. With the two men on either side of her, Phaedra saw a striking family resemblance. Both had the same square jaw and full lips. Thin, dark brows arched over eyes the color of slate.

Yes, in his youth, Marcus must have been a very handsome man. For the first time, Phaedra realized that his stateliness held its own appeal. She hoped he was kind, or perhaps learned. They had shared few words up till now, so she knew not what to make of him. Even here, at their wedding banquet, he leaned away from Phaedra and spoke to her father and Consul Fimbria about the upcoming magisterial elections in the provinces. They discussed whom they favored and why. Phaedra tried to listen but soon grew bored.

Acestes smiled at her. Phaedra smiled back but kept her eyes down. She wanted to appear neither rude nor encouraging. To balance between the two was to walk the sword's edge, one wrong step fatal.

"You make a lovely bride," Acestes said.

"Thank you." She shifted her veil so it draped like a curtain between them. He should not speak to her so, not here, not ever.

Acestes laughed. "You never need to hide from me, or my compliment."

She wished that Marcus would intervene on her behalf. He sat next to her, his elbow so close that if she stretched out her finger she could touch him. Yet he spoke to the other men—senators and knights of the republic—ignoring her as if she were not there at all.

With her face still hidden behind the safety of the veil, Phaedra said, "I thank you for your kind words."

She surveyed the room. It was filled with people—laughing, talking, eating, and drinking. Some wandered about, a plate or cup in hand, while others lounged on sofas. Without a doubt, it was the most guests she recalled ever having in her home.

And they had all come for her.

No, she reminded herself, very few were in attendance for Phaedra. Most had come for her father or Marcus. A few might have attended only to see the famous Valens Secundus fight.

Yet to see her triclinium packed with people made it look like a different place altogether. And certainly not the quiet room where Phaedra often came to read histories of philosophy.

It was not as if she never left the villa, not that she knew no one. She did leave, and often, too. Whenever her father needed her to attend a state dinner, Phaedra went. There were also the times he wanted to make better friends with a certain senator or wealthy Roman. Phaedra was then dispatched to call upon that senator's daughter or wife.

Many of those women were in attendance. Phaedra wondered if Marcus would require her to continue those friendships or if she would need to nurture new ones. She liked the ladies well enough. Yet there was but one person for whom she felt true friendship.

Her best friend and matron of honor, Fortunada, stood near the door, goblet in hand. Their eyes met and she lifted her cup in salute. Phaedra lifted hers as well. Just seeing her friend lifted Phaedra's spirits. From behind, Fortunada's husband approached. He placed a hand upon his wife's shoulder and lifted his goblet to Phaedra as well. Again, she returned the gesture. But neither Fortunada nor her husband saw. They stood close and spoke only to each other.

There was no place in their love for Phaedra. She did not begrudge her friend a happy marriage. On the contrary, she longed for a husband of her own who also loved her to distraction.

"A friend of yours?" asked Acestes.

"She is," said Phaedra.

"Good and true friends are a rare commodity in Rome."

"I believe you are right. I am sure that is why my father chose your uncle as husband to me."

Acestes looked beyond Phaedra to Marcus and the conversation about politics. "They are all very intent on running the republic. Friendship plays but a minor role," he said in a voice not much above a whisper.

She knew enough not to speak ill of her husband, even if he did ignore her. "All of them are important men, to be sure."

"I plan to leave for North Africa with the legion by month's end," Acestes said.

"It seems as though I am surrounded by important men."

"I plan to be consul myself one day. That is all I have ever wanted."

"May Fortune smile on your ambitions." Phaedra tucked the veil behind her shoulder.

Acestes sipped dark-red wine from a golden goblet and watched Phaedra over the rim. He took a long swallow and set his drink aside. "I feel as though I am well prepared to assume my position in politics. Being a patrician provides me with the opportunity to take a seat in the Senate. My father left some money, but I will get more during my time in North Africa. Upon my return I will be of age to run for consul, leaving me in need of a wife from a politically connected family."

"Your life seems so clear."

He shrugged and took another drink. "You must have your life planned out as well."

"Of course I do. I now have the marriage I wanted, and soon, the gods willing, we will make a child."

Phaedra looked at her husband and smiled. He glanced away from his conversation. Catching her chin in his hand, Marcus gave her an affectionate squeeze before turning away to greet another senator. Phaedra bit her lip. What did it foretell of their future if Marcus paid her scant attention at their wedding banquet? Did Phaedra matter so little that she warranted a quick pat on the head in passing, much like affection given to a dog or trained monkey?

Acestes leaned in close, his breath hot on her shoulder. "He never told you, did he?"

"Tell me what?"

"He has had two wives."

"I know that," she said.

"And no children," Acestes added.

What was Acestes implying? Phaedra looked at Marcus and his strong Roman profile. A handsome man, she decided, one that women must desire. "I find it hard to believe that your uncle never tried to make a child."

"Trying is not the problem."

"What of the other wives?"

"They cannot both be barren, now can they?"

"Why would you say such a vile thing? You are jealous of your uncle and his position in Rome."

Acestes leaned in closer. "Lower your voice."

Phaedra took a long swallow of wine. It tasted like vinegar and slanderous tales told by envious men. She stood and turned to Marcus. "I think I shall refresh myself and then retire."

Marcus stood, also, and pressed dry, paper-thin lips to her temple. "Of course, my dear. This has been a long day for us all. I will be along directly. I need to speak a bit more to the consul, and that will give you time, as well."

Phaedra's childhood nurse—now her maid, Terenita—stepped from a shadow behind the table. She wore, as she always did, a cream-colored turban and a shapeless, buff-hued tunic that fell to the floor. For the festive evening, the maid had tied a belt at her waist, accentuating her womanly curves.

Terenita followed Phaedra from the dining room. Torches in the garden smoldered on their stakes, the sharp scent of pitch unmistakable. A half-moon hung in a clear sky, and thousands of stars shone down. The sandpit gleamed white in the darkness. In the distance Phaedra heard the low gurgle of the fountain. Tomorrow she would leave her father's villa for Marcus's huge estate that sprawled across the very top of the Palatine Hill. Hot tears stung her eyes, surprising her. She had not expected to be sad about leaving her father's home.

"Go back to my rooms," she said to Terenita, with a squeeze to her hand. "I will be there in a moment."

"Whatever pleases you, my lady."

Phaedra wandered to the back of the garden, near the grove of orange trees. The tang of citrus hung in the air. She removed her bridal veil and wrapped it around her wrist. Tighter and tighter she wound it, trying to choke Acestes's hint that Marcus might not give her a child. The sound of water splashing called to her, and she moved toward the fountain at the far wall. She decided to stay a moment or two. Long enough to shed her tears and regain her composure before returning to her rooms and waiting for her husband.

Chapter 3

Valens

How did a bastard born on a wooden floor in a stinking apartment in the Suburra ever find himself as a senator's wedding guest? Valens knew not how to talk to men of quality, although he had bedded quite a few of their wives. They never wanted to talk to him, either—content just to pay him for the use of his body and the pleasure he gave them.

After such a fight he was in no state to remain in Senator Scaeva's dining room. The senator had been good enough to send guards back to the ludus where Valens lived and trained as a gladiator. They had returned with his finest tunic. Scaeva had even offered the use of a bath. Valens had washed, dressed, and then spent a few awkward moments standing in the dining room. Neither a slave on display nor an invited guest, his discomfort drove him into the garden to wait for his escort back to the gladiator school.

He stretched out on a marble bench, its stone still warm from the day's heat. The water from a nearby fountain shone silver with moonlight. He watched it, transfixed.

As always when Valens had no other thoughts to occupy his mind, the faces of gladiators he had defeated came to him. Like an infected tooth, the guilt for having slain so many was always with him. At times, the ache was not so great and could be easily ignored. Other times the discomfort threatened to split his skull in two. It was during quiet moments, like this one, when the pain was at its worst. He imagined the Gaul with yellow-white hair who died after Valens severed his jugular, along with the large African, a happy fellow with a wide smile, who died after a leg wound festered and days later the poison spread through his blood.

More faces came to him unbidden.

He shoved them from his mind and looked again at the water spraying from the fountain. He concentrated on the mystery of the unending water. How could that be? Water rose from a single pipe hidden in the fountain's base and was somehow diverted into two separate sprays. Each of those landed in two large marble bowls that spilled over into a pool and became part of the arc again.

The feat amazed Valens. He wondered what his life might have been if he had become an engineer, trained by a Greek, instead of a gladiator taught at a ludus. But to be an engineer was not his lot, and life as a gladiator provided him with far more than Fortune might have bestowed otherwise.

Beneath the gurgling water he heard her—faint but unmistakable came the sound of a woman's sobs. He sat up and looked into the darkened garden, finding her at once. She no longer wore the crimson veil, but he recognized the bride, Phaedra Rullus Servilia, at once. Valens thought of sneaking away through the shrubbery surrounding the fountain. He shifted on the bench. She stopped crying and looked toward him. She gasped, a small "Oh" of surprise on her lips.

"Apologies, my lady," he said. "I came to the garden for some air."

She swiped a hand under each eye and stood taller. "I accept your apologies."

Valens scooted to the edge of the bench. He should not be talking to this woman in a darkened garden, alone. True, they were behind the walls of her father's home and her father had invited him to stay. But patrician men did not want gladiators around their wives or daughters, and Valens knew he would be the one to bear the punishment if anyone saw them together.

He tensed his thighs, ready to stand. The bride could not contain herself and sobbed again, her shoulders convulsing. Then, wide-eyed, she clamped a hand over her mouth and stared at Valens. It was as he had feared—she had not wanted this marriage. Without thought he stood and moved to her side. He placed his palm on her shoulder. Her skin, soft and warm, with a hint of lean muscle underneath, enticed him to touch her more. Her silken gown draped over her collarbone and dipped low, allowing Valens a view of the valley between her breasts. Maybe she had requested him at her wedding. Like so many aristocratic women, the bride might want him as her bedmate.

Did she purposely tempt him by appearing upset and then allowing him to offer comfort? He had been seduced in worse ways by worse women. His cock stirred and he breathed Phaedra's scent, light and clean. She smelled of lavender and something else. Aloe, he decided.

She looked at his hand, the point where their flesh joined, and then to his face. Her eyes were light blue, and he read sadness in them, not desire. The need to ease her suffering hit him like a fist. He stepped away. His hand fell to his side, damp and chilled in the balmy night.

"Apologies," he said, feeling more like an oaf than a god of the arena. "Allow me to take my leave."

"Stay, Gladiator. I need to return to the party."

As a slave, he was bound to do the bidding of all patricians, the bride included. He nodded and waited for her to walk away.

She did not.

She drew her bottom lip between her teeth, and his mouth went dry. Valens imagined pulling the bride to him, kissing her lip free, and exploring her mouth with his tongue. His cock jumped again.

"Gladiator?" she said, ending his momentary fantasy.

"My lady?"

"Might I ask a question of you?" She did not wait for him to give his permission. "What thought you of fighting at a wedding banquet? Do you fight at them often?"

"This was my first," he said.

She chewed on her lip again. "I thought that it might be so."

"Did it please you?" he asked hesitantly. "The fight?"

"I enjoyed it more than I anticipated."

Warmth started in his middle and spread outward. It took a moment for Valens to recognize the feeling as joy. "I was honored to fight for you." Valens pushed his fist hard into his leg. This woman was not his to protect or make happy.

"Thank you, Gladiator," she said. "I will let you return to your air, and I shall return to my duties."

She turned to walk away, as she should, out of his life forever. "Valens," he said, just to see if she would remain for one moment more. "My name is not Gladiator. It is Valens Secundus."

She stopped and turned back to face him. He should never have called out to her. The wife of a senator, the daughter of one as well, would not want to be corrected by a mere gladiator.

"Apologies, Valens Secundus."

She looked into the darkness and he followed her gaze. The lights from the house were visible through the surrounding foliage, yet the fountain drowned out the sounds of music and laughter. She looked back at him. Somehow she had aged years in a few seconds.

"I think I shall remain here for a moment," she said as she took a seat on the bench and smoothed her gown over her lap.

That was it. She had dismissed Valens. He should not be surprised or injured, and yet he was. "Of course," he said. "I should return to the party."

"Stay, Valens Secundus," she said as he turned to leave. "I would have a word with you."

Chapter 4

Phaedra

Why had she just asked the gladiator to stay? Perhaps it had nothing to do with his hazel eyes or the strength in his shoulders, or that his green tunic turned his skin a deeper shade of bronze. Perhaps she only wanted the company of a single person on a day when a room full of people overwhelmed her.

Yet why him? Why not Fortunada? Phaedra knew that answer. Fortunada's perfect marriage clearly illustrated the imperfections in Phaedra's own. Her father, another person to whom she could speak, saw only the advantages of her union, leaving no room to understand her disappointment.

Besides, Valens Secundus had come to the garden for solace. It was what she had sought, and during this moment they shared a need.

Whatever the reason, Phaedra knew that remaining with the gladiator in the garden would be considered improper, if not wrong. She should not put him in such a position, nor open herself to a possible scandal. But no one knew they were alone together. Phaedra's husband assumed she waited in her room. Had anyone even noticed where the gladiator had gone?

Valens stood before her with his hands clasped behind his back. His tunic fell just below his knees. Her gaze traveled from his well-muscled chest down to the woven belt resting on his flat stomach. The fabric draped over the juncture between his legs, and she wondered about his phallus. Phaedra had never seen a real one, of course, just those on statues. But all her married friends had told her what to expect on her wedding night. And the phallus was of the greatest importance.

At the juncture of his thighs, the fabric of the tunic stretched a bit, as if the phallus had moved. Moved! Phaedra looked up. He stared at her with eyes wide, as she knew hers must be. Had his phallus never moved before? Phaedra understood that with the correct attention it became firm and rigid. But she had never been told that it might twitch.

"Did you know—" she began. Yet the courage to finish her question evaded her. With any luck, Valens did not know exactly what she had begun to ask. A minute too late, she realized that she was pointing. She lowered her arm and averted her gaze.

He shifted, rotating his hips so the fabric once again draped smoothly over his thighs. "My lady, you wanted a word."

Phaedra's face flamed red and hot with embarrassment. She unwound the bridal veil from her wrist, slowly, hoping that she might think of something to say. She smoothed the fabric over her lap. "Tell me of your life. You have much fame. Even I, a person who never follows the games, knows of Valens Secundus."

"I am a gladiator, my lady."

"Have you no purpose beyond being a gladiator?"

"For me, there is no other."

Phaedra suddenly realized that she had endowed the gladiator with attributes desirous to her, but ones he could not possess. For a brief instant she had imagined that he enjoyed a variety of interests and was a man with great intellectual and emotional depth who also just happened to possess the physique of a god. Phaedra's chest tightened as she realized she had only fooled herself.

She lined up the corners of her veil and folded it into a square. His dissatisfying answer echoed in her mind. Perhaps it would be better if he returned to the party and left her a moment to collect her thoughts.

She had a wedding night to endure, after all, and her maidenhead to offer her husband.

"I have kept you too long," she said. "You may go."

Valens continued to stand, his hands at his sides, his palms facing forward, with fingers slightly curled. "My job is to entertain with feats of combat. I show the Roman disdain for death and the virtue of courage in the face of adversity. Above all, I bring honor to my ludus, the gladiator school that trains me, and the place I have called home for the last eight years. I know nothing else, my lady. I see in your eyes that my answer disappoints."

Phaedra did not deny his words. Yet he spoke with conviction and passion. What if his attention was set to other tasks? What might he accomplish then? "You sound as though you see yourself as little more than a trained beast, and that is your mistake. You are a man, capable of great achievements, greater even than your accomplishments in the arena."

Valens dropped his gaze from hers. "I am not."

"How can you not see who you are? What you have? You possess fame. Anything you ask for would be given to you, freely, gladly. You will never be forced to marry for money." Phaedra pressed her lips together. She had not meant to engage in such a conversation.

"As a patrician you have a power all your own," he said. "This city is bound to do your bidding."

"As a woman I have no power of my own. Much like you, a slave with a master, I am the property of my family. It is almost as if I am invisible, unless my father needs something."

"How can anyone not see you? For me," said Valens, "you are like the brightest star in the sky."

"You flatter me," she said with a quick laugh, "and jest."

Valens came to stand next to her; his body radiated heat. "See that," he said. She lined up her gaze with his outstretched finger. He pointed to the single brightest star. "It is known as Polaris and is a fixed point in the sky. It shall be yours. Anytime you look at it from anywhere, you will know that you are seen."

This man was a stranger to Phaedra, yet he had given her the most valuable gift she had ever received. In this moment, she existed. Yet she could think of nothing to say that would express her deep gratitude. "How is it that you know of stars?" she asked. Phaedra mentally groaned. Oh, the gods preserve her, that was the least charming thing said in the history of language.

"A sea captain told me of Polaris when I traveled aboard his vessel bound for Alexandria."

"I have read of Alexandria and its white-pillared library, filled with more scrolls than one mind can comprehend. Did you see that during your travels?"

"There are many buildings such as you described. One of them may very well be the library. Yet I would not know."

Of course. She doubted that Valens even knew how to read. He had gone to Egypt for fighting, not learning. Regardless of the reason, he had been! "It must have been thrilling—to travel, I mean."

"I enjoy leaving Rome," he said. "Has your father never taken you?"

"No," said Phaedra, "I have yet to know the pleasure of leaving the city."

"Perhaps one day you will sail to Egypt, and then you can tell me which one of the grand buildings is the library."

"If my husband allows it," she said. The delight of travels not yet taken disappeared like the dream they were. For Marcus, Phaedra might be nothing. She certainly was not the brightest star in the sky. The realization came crashing down upon her with all the force of the heavens. "I have enjoyed this moment with you, Valens Secundus. Thank you for the gift of Polaris. I think I will remember you long after this night has ended."

"And I, you," he said.

"I really should return," she said. Like a tether around her middle, her duty to family and honor pulled her back to the villa. "Once you have gotten enough air, I hope you return to the party and enjoy the food and company."

"This is a grand party," said Valens. "I have attended many. Your father must love you very much. He spent a great deal of coin in simply hiring me."

"My father loves a party; my marriage is secondary," Phaedra said. "To him and to me." Heat rose in her cheeks. She must stop sharing such details with the gladiator.

"You could ask to choose your own husband next time," Valens said.

Phaedra knew he meant if she outlived Marcus. If she became a young widow, her father might try to marry her to an even more ancient man for even more money. But what if she asked for assurances for a marriage of her choice? Could she? Should she? The idea of asserting some control over her life by choosing her husband left her breathless. At the same time it made so much sense that Phaedra could hardly believe she had not thought to bargain with her father already.

In Rome, marriage defined a woman's life. A married woman held the keys to the villa. She managed all the servants and slaves. Married women handled the household accounts. Even the clothes married women wore differed from those worn by unmarried women, divorced women, widows, or prostitutes. The matron's stolla was the one piece of clothing every girl child aspired to wear. The long cloth was draped over her shoulder with the tail wrapped over her arm. Phaedra had already selected a shimmering silver stolla for tomorrow. But more than being a wife for all to see, Phaedra wanted a partner who loved and respected her. How different would this night be if her groom adored her? How might she view the rest of her life if she truly cared for her husband?

"You give me much to think on, Valens Secundus," she said. "What of you? What would you do to change your fate?"

"Fortune smiles upon me already, my lady."

Phaedra waved her veil at him. "That is far too safe an answer for a man who just now spoke of my new husband's death. There must be something you want."

"If I could, I would learn to read and write."

"Why do you not? Then the next time you travel to Alexandria you could see the library for yourself."

"There is no one at the ludus to teach me," Valens said.

"The school's owner, or his steward, must know how to read."

He shrugged. "I might consider asking one of them for instructions."

Valens had given her a rare and valuable gift. He deserved one in return. Yet she had nothing to give beyond her encouragement. Rising to her feet, Phaedra reached out her hand. "We shall bind ourselves to one another in a pledge to challenge the Fates." She clasped Valens around the wrist and he gripped her in return. Her flesh tingled where his fingers wrapped around her arm. Phaedra's pulse raced, fluttering at the base of her throat, and for a moment she forgot to breathe. "I shall ask for a choice in husbands should there come a time when I might marry again, and you shall ask for a tutor to teach you to read and write."

Valens threw back his head and laughed. "When I fought earlier today, I worried for you, a lamb among wolves. You have a keen mind, my lady, and a larger set of balls than Jupiter himself. Pardon my language."

"You worried for me when you fought?"

"I did. I saw you upon the terrace, a fresh and unformed flower among the withered sticks. Now I see my mistake."

Phaedra tightened her grip on Valens's arm and pulled. He hesitated a moment and then let her draw him closer. "It was you who suggested that I bargain for my next husband. I would never think of such a thing on my own."

He closed the gap between them until they almost touched. "You would have, no doubt."

So, this is desire. Two halves pulled to one another, damn the consequences. Heat collected in the space between their bodies until Phaedra's skin felt too tight. She moved in, closer still. She looked up at Valens. His breath washed over her and she caught the scent of costmary, like balsa wood, mixed with leather, and salt from his skin. With it, an underlying smell Phaedra could not catalog and decided it was the aroma of a fit and virile man.

Valens lifted his hand. He held it a hairsbreadth from her face. He seemed to want to touch her but would not allow himself to do so. Even she, a sheltered patrician daughter, knew that gladiators should not touch aristocratic women, especially married virgins. She also knew that she should not crave his touch. Yet she did. More than a want, it was a need, like a need to draw breath. Leaning toward him just a bit, she placed her cheek in his palm.

He leaned toward her, his mouth close to hers. She ached to take this man inside her. It welled up from a primal place that existed before Phaedra, or Valens, or this garden, or even Rome herself. She longed to hold him, to caress him, to taste him, and to learn of all the ways men and women were different and yet complemented each other.

Phaedra hesitated. Outside of this place, and this moment, she belonged to Marcus. True, her husband had done nothing to deserve her affection or loyalty beyond providing her father with financial security. At the same time, he had done nothing to warrant an unfaithful wife, either. Could she dishonor their union as soon as it had begun?

In the darkened garden with the music of the fountain, who would know if she let the gladiator steal a kiss?

She would remember. She would know.

Phaedra stepped back, releasing Valens's wrist. She ignored the veil as it slipped from her fingers and fell to the ground. "We are bound now to change our fate."

He blinked at her several times, as if adjusting his eyes to a bright light. "Yes, my lady."

"Since we are so bound"—she kept her voice bright and light, belying the sense of absolute loss within—"you must call me Phaedra."

"Phaedra," he said, his voice hoarse and smooth, deep as thunder.

She shuddered at the loneliness she heard there. Or perhaps it was the echo of her isolation.

"There you are." A man's voice came from behind them.

Phaedra and Valens took several steps apart as Acestes walked into the clearing by the fountain. "I have looked everywhere for you since you left the banquet. I fear I offended you by what I said." He looked at Valens. "What are you doing here alone with her?"

Valens clasped his hands behind his back and lowered his eyes. The stance transformed him from a man with the desire to read and write and understand the inner workings of a fountain to a slave. Which, of course, he was. She felt the hot rush of anger at Acestes for bringing them back to reality.

"We met by accident while I walked through the garden," she said, answering for them both. "Did you know that he has never fought at a wedding before? Do you think that will make my wedding better or worse? Better if it becomes the fashion, worse if it does not."

Phaedra could not stop herself from rambling. Better that Acestes think her a fool than untrue. Thank the gods she had not given in to the temptation to kiss Valens. If she had, then Acestes would have discovered them in an embrace. Even her thoughts were so tangled together she could hardly parse one from the next.

"The gladiator does not belong here," Acestes said.

Valens lifted his eyes. His look flashed with the same razor-sharp edge as his sword. Acestes saw it, too, and stepped back. Lifting his chest, Valens stood tall, his legs spread and braced. "Apologies if my presence offends."

Phaedra knew that Valens did not feel the least sorry.

"Go to the kitchens, Gladiator," Acestes said. "Have someone fetch guards from your ludus. It is time you returned home."

"Only if the lady wishes it so. I need to see to her safety."

"I am her family, one of her kind." Acestes leaned toward the gladiator.

The air in the garden crackled with hostility. Phaedra could not allow an altercation. Acestes was a patrician. If Valens did him harm, he would violate one of Rome's oldest and most sacred laws. Regardless of the reason or outcome of any fight, for Valens, a slave—property and not a man—the consequences would be severe. He would suffer torture, maiming, followed by a slow and agonizing death.

Lifting her hand to the left, Phaedra said, "The kitchens are over there."

Valens looked at her once and then lowered his eyes. "Gratitude, my lady."

Acestes placed his hand on Phaedra's elbow and steered her back to the party. "You and I need to talk," he said.

She glanced over her shoulder at the gladiator as they walked away. "Thank you," she said.

Valens faded into the shadow of an orange tree, his figure a black form within the darkness. But even though she could no longer see his features, Phaedra glimpsed him holding her crimson bridal veil. Slowly, carefully he wrapped it around his wrist, covering the place she had held him when they bound themselves to one another and swore to change their fates.

Acestes said nothing as they walked through the garden and away from Valens. Once the lights of the house and the jumbled voices of her father's guests poured onto the terrace, he stopped and turned to face her.

"What were you doing with the gladiator?" Acestes asked.

Phaedra's mouth went dry. She had not kissed Valens, but she had encouraged him to hold her and had returned the embrace. That alone might cause her ruin. "I told you already." She had hoped to sound annoyed with the question, or at least weary of the asking. Instead her voice came out too high and trembled slightly. She breathed in deeply and emptied her lungs slowly. "He was just about to leave when you arrived. I needed some time alone."

"Alone? You were with the gladiator. Did you arrange to meet him?"

"I would never dishonor your uncle or myself in such a way," she said. She put the sharp edge of outrage in her voice, and still she could not deny to herself that a part of her still craved the gladiator's touch.

"Many women take gladiators as lovers. You would not be the first."

Phaedra felt the argument shifting to her benefit. Surely Acestes would have accused her of wrongdoing if he had actually seen anything. "I am not many women. I tire of your insults and will once again take my leave."

"Phaedra, wait." Acestes placed his hand on her shoulder as she turned to go. "I have offended. I do not know what to say, because you intrigue me."

"You cannot speak to me thus," she said. Her heart beat fast in her chest. Phaedra had never dealt with a man of rank before. Her father had kept her hidden away behind the walls of the villa, allowing her to have a circle of suitable patrician girls for friends. For the first time she understood her disadvantage. She wanted to be rid of Acestes's indictments and accusations and the very maleness of him. She slipped away from his grasp. Avoiding the villa and her drunken guests, she ran along the outer colonnade to her room, leaving Acestes standing alone.

Terenita sat on a stool, a single oil lamp burning on a table nearby. She stood when Phaedra entered. "My lady, I had begun to worry."

"Thank you for your concern," she said as she leaned her head onto Terenita's shoulder. The maid stiffened under Phaedra's touch. Terenita was a kind and gentle woman, but she kept a physical distance from everyone. As a child Phaedra was never offered an embrace upon waking or a hug that followed a skinned knee. Above all else, it was this lack of touch that kept Phaedra mindful of her position as mistress and of Terenita's as slave. Phaedra stepped away, realizing that she had been foolish to expect that somehow her maid had suddenly become demonstrative. "I was overwhelmed and went for a walk in the garden," she said. "Did you know that there is a fixed star in the heavens? Polaris, it is called. Sailors use it to navigate the seas."

"I believe that the stars are really the spirits of our ancestors looking down upon us. But if you want me to believe that they are not, I shall."

"No, Terenita. You can believe whatever you want," Phaedra said with a small smile. She sat at her cosmetics table and rested her face upon the cool marble top.

Phaedra's room had changed little since her childhood. A single bed, with a curved head and footboard, took up its middle. A table with a basin and pitcher for washing sat in one corner, with a reclining sofa covered in red silk at another. In order to make use of the bright Mediterranean sun, her cosmetics table and chair sat next to the door that opened onto the garden. A cabinet that usually held her clothes and jewels stood on one side of the door that led to the villa, with a small altar on the other. Clay figures of various goddesses and one of Phaedra's mother sat atop the wooden altar. Candles burned in sconces high on the wall, bathing the room in a weak golden light.

"Shall I take down your hair, my lady?" Terenita asked. "The board holding your bun in place must be pulling by now."

"Thank you," Phaedra said as she lifted her head. Picking up a palm frond, she slowly fanned her face as the maid unwound her hair. Even in the scant light, she saw the flowers arranged on the small tables set throughout her room, rose petals on her bed, and a large basket of fruit near her reclining sofa. At least her chamber had been decorated correctly with symbols of fertility. Perhaps when Marcus arrived they would participate in the ritual of touching fire and water while pledging to be together through every extremity.

"My room looks beautiful," she said to Terenita.

"I hoped it would please you, my lady. Without you having either mother or aunt, I took the liberty to make sure you were treated like the lovely bride you are."

"You are mother and aunt to me," Phaedra said. The words came out thin as a thread, emotion having all but stolen her voice. She wiped away a tear and remembered that Terenita loved her for who she really was, even if no one else cared for her beyond what she might give, or be, for them.

"I almost forgot," said Terenita. "Your father came looking for you earlier. He will be back directly."

Phaedra's throat closed. "What did he want?"

Before Terenita could answer, three loud knocks came from the closed bedchamber door. It opened without invitation. Her father stood on the threshold, his white toga gleaming in the candlelight. "Where have you been?" he asked.

Had Acestes, the serpent, told her father about finding Phaedra alone with Valens? Or had someone else spied them? That thought made her ill. Phaedra gripped tighter to the armrests. "Where do you think I have been?" she asked, deciding instead to see what her father knew.

"You were at the table one moment. I left to relieve myself and you were gone when I returned."

Phaedra sighed. Her head throbbed and she laid her cheek upon the stone top of her cosmetics table. "I needed some air," she said.

"This has been a momentous day for you."

"It has."

"Terenita, fetch the matron of honor. I would like to have a moment alone with my daughter."

Once the maid left, her father pulled a chair next to hers and eased down, shifting slightly to fit his corpulent frame onto the seat. "I must tell you, my dear, that I am not obtuse to your plight."

Gods save her, *did* he know about the gladiator? Had he only wanted Terenita gone so she did not bear witness to Phaedra's shame? "Father, allow me to explain."

He held up a hand and she stopped speaking. "I married your mother for love. My father let me choose my own wife. At the time I did not realize the gift he had given me. To truly love your spouse is to know that you will never be alone. I never remarried after she died because no one would be for me what she had been."

She had heard her father say much the same to her before. This time she wondered what her parents' match had to do with Valens. Had the same silent and powerful attraction that had drawn her to the gladiator also brought her mother and father together?

"And now I have you," he said. "I always had hoped to give you the same gift—a spouse that you love. I cannot and that pains me. Marcus is fond of you. He will treat you well. You will be one of the wealthiest women in Rome. While not a love match, I have found that ample coin can bring great happiness, too."

Phaedra's tight shoulders relaxed. He knew nothing of Valens, thank the gods. "I understand, Father."

"You are more precious to me than all the sesterces in the world. By marrying Marcus, you saved us both from financial ruin. Had this marriage not taken place, I would have had to sell some property. Not long ago I received a generous offer for Terenita."

Terenita? Phaedra gasped. "I could not live without her."

"I thought as much. In fact, I have given her to Marcus as a wedding gift to you."

"Thank you," she said.

Her father shrugged. "I think it is what your mother would have suggested."

Phaedra leaned forward and kissed her father's cheek. Much of her indignation at being forced into a marriage faded away. Yet she wondered what might have become of them all if the lifestyle of patrician and senator had not defined their lives.

"I wish Mother were here," she said.

"Do you recall much of her?"

"Her voice. She liked to sing."

"You are very much like your mother, with her dark hair and blue eyes. Both of you are the quintessential Roman woman—agreeable and always willing to do your duty. She would be proud of you today," he said.

"I hope so. Maybe she watches us from Elysium." Her mother's final words to obey her father rang again in Phaedra's ears. "I want her to be proud."

He squeezed her chin. "I am sure she is. I do wish she would send me a sign. I feel as though I should say something to prepare you for your first night as wife."

"I have friends who have told me what to expect."

He seemed relieved. "Good. I should go, then, my dear." Her father braced his large hands on his knees and hefted out of the chair. "Fortunada should be waiting to say the final blessing."

Phaedra rubbed her wrist at the same place that Valens had held on to her earlier. Knowing that in his melancholy mood her father would refuse her nothing, she did not hesitate. "Father, wait. Can I ask something very important of you?"

Her father lowered himself back into the chair.

"If I ever find that I am no longer married," she said, "will you allow me to choose my next husband?"

"You mean if you become a widow, not if Marcus divorces you?"

Phaedra shrugged. "I have no ill wish for my husband, but he is older even than you."

"And that makes him almost ancient." Her father's eyes twinkled, but looked sad, too.

"I did not mean to imply that."

"Yes, my dear, you did. But I agree. If you outlive Marcus, then you will marry next when it is your choice."

"And to a man of my choice," she said.

"To a man of your choice," he said, "providing that you are an honest and true wife now."

Her father was what? Forty-three annums, maybe forty-four. That made Marcus fifty, give or take a year. Too old for her, and yet he might live for another decade. A few robust souls even lived until their seventh decade. That would make Phaedra a widow at the same age as her father was now.

Valens.

His face, his body, his voice all returned to her. Was she willing to lose her chance at picking her next husband for a man she had met once?

No, Phaedra decided, she was not.

"I agree to your demands, Father."

Chapter 5

Valens

Every day Valens looked upon the two hills reserved for the homes of Rome's wealthiest citizens. The Palatine and Aventine hills were together known as the Capitoline. Most of the patricians lived upon the Palatine, and those with less distinguished lineage upon the Aventine. The busiest marketplace in the republic ran along the base of the two hills. Among the shops, taverns, and stalls sat the ludus, or gladiator school, in which Valens lived and trained.

Like many slaves, Valens had taken the last name of his master as his own. With his loyalty, renown, and the most winning record of any gladiator, Valens was treated with the deference of a prince, even though he was in reality a slave. Other slaves brought in to serve the gladiators were told to obey Valens without question. The lanista often introduced him to foreign dignitaries and wealthy visitors. If Valens requested to leave the ludus, he could, although his wanting do that happened rarely. In fact, there was but a single reminder of his status as a slave—the guards who accompanied him wherever he went.

Even though he accepted them as fact, their presence rankled as they walked away from Senator Scaeva's villa, and Phaedra. Surrounded by four armed men, he trudged down the steep street that wound back and forth across the Palatine Hill. Their footfalls on the worn cobbles echoed off the high walls of the surrounding villas. Each guard carried a short sword and wore a leather breastplate and a bronze helmet. He watched as the sword swung in the scabbard and hit the thigh of the one who carried a torch aloft. Valens could grab the blade and drive it into the hollow of the guard's armpit, then slay the others before they fell upon him like ravenous wolves. But to what end? So he could walk home alone and think about the beautiful and keen-minded bride?

The Forum Boarium, the sometime gladiatorial arena and often-times cattle market, lay a short distance from the ludus. At this hour of the night, without the crowds, Valens saw the spindly outline of the temporary wooden stands erected for a series of games scheduled for later in the week. He would not fight, not this time, and Valens thanked the Fates for keeping him alive, at least for now. The round wooden-roofed monument to Hercules Victor rose up to the left of the ludus. Long and low, the Temple of Portunus stretched out to the right. In the distance the Tiber wound its way to the Mediterranean. Moonlight glinted off the darkened waters until the river looked serpentine, as if it were a living thing, waiting to devour them all.

"The lanista wishes to speak to you," said the guard with the torch as they walked through the empty marketplace.

Valens nodded. "I will see him in the morning before training."

"No. He wants to see you now."

"Now? Why?"

The guard shrugged.

Paullus most likely wanted to offer congratulations on another successful fight. But it was late, and if Valens were to train tomorrow, he needed his sleep tonight. Tired gladiators fought in a sloppy manner.

Valens was never sloppy.

Unless this meeting had to do with what had happened after the party with Phaedra. While nothing *had* happened, speaking privately in a garden while they stood close to one another had the power to ruin them both.

Adulterous women were not treated kindly, often thrown to the arena where they were fed to starving beasts. Valens wagered that

Phaedra's maidenhead was still intact, and therefore she was likely to suffer only disgrace.

He, on the other hand, could be executed for any reason. Valens considered his options. He looked at the short sword the guard still wore at his side. A quick flick of the blade, one more life gone, and Valens could slip away into the night.

Murdering the guard was the coward's way out, though, and Valens refused to be a coward. Besides, everyone died sometime. Death was Rome's great equalizer.

"Take me to the lanista," Valens said.

They approached the shared compound of the gladiator school and the home of Paullus Secundus and his family. Rather than bang on the large wooden gates leading to the training grounds and cells where Valens and the other gladiators lived, the guard escorted him around the corner to the front door of the house.

Valens unwound the veil from his wrist and tucked it under the belt at his waist. No need to bring attention to the fact that he had been alone with Phaedra. And yet the veil served to remind him that he had the power to change his destiny, or so she believed.

He cast a quick glance upward and found Polaris in an instant. The immovable object in the sky steeled his resolve at once. He was Valens Secundus, Champion of Rome. There was nothing he could not achieve, even if it was mastering words and written language. Perhaps one day he could win his freedom.

Valens followed the guard through the atrium. The ceiling had been cut away to let in rain with a shallow pool underneath to collect the water. To his right, a blue canvas curtain hung over a doorway, obscuring the tablinum where Paullus conducted all his business. The guard pulled aside the curtain and Valens stepped through.

Paullus Secundus sat behind his large wooden desk, surrounded by a halo of light. An oil lamp burned at his elbow, and a fat candle spluttered in a holder on the wall. Aside from the desk, there was scant space for anything else in the room. A small shelf to the left of the desk held several scrolls, neatly stacked. Alongside were a few wooden boxes that contained waxen tablets. Two chairs sat in front of the desk. The lanista raked his hand through a shock of white hair as he scratched a stylus over a tablet. Valens let out a polite cough after entering, and Paullus looked up.

"You made a fine impression tonight," Paullus said with a wide and easy smile.

The tension slipped from his shoulders as Valens said, "I fight to honor you and this ludus."

"Sit." Paullus gestured to a chair opposite the desk. "I would have a word with you."

Valens sat and waited for his master to begin.

"What did you think of the gladiator you fought?"

"He is eager," said Valens, "but fights with little grace and no thought to the entertainment he provides."

"He is an auctoratus."

"A volunteer, like me?"

"Yes and no," said Paullus. "He is a volunteer, but no normal man. He is an equestrian."

"A knight of the Roman republic? Has he any military experience?"

"Some."

"That explains his aggressive fighting style," said Valens. "An equestrian turned gladiator will draw large crowds. Romans will love watching one from their own upper class fight in the arena."

"I mean for him to be more than a novelty, and I want him trained quickly and well. He refuses a complete conscription and will only fight for six years. But in him I see the spark of greatness, and I want him as Rome's new champion."

Valens sat back, the air sucked from his lungs. "If he is champion, what does that make me?"

"I recall the first day you came to the ludus. I had been watching the gladiators practice when my steward told me that a conscript wished to join. I expected to see that a man had volunteered. Instead, I walked in to this office and found a thin boy. You could not have been more than fifteen or sixteen annums."

"I know not. My mother never reckoned my age."

"In your eyes I saw a hunger that had more to do with glory than food," said Paullus. "Although you behaved like a starved pup would and ate more than enough for two boys in those first few weeks."

Valens did recall that day. For three weeks his younger sister, Antonice, had been ill. She had stopped eating and drinking. Her lips were cracked and they bled. There was no money for food, much less a physician. His mother thought to throw the child, only five annums, over the cliffs and end her suffering with minimal cost. Before his mother acted, Valens had come to the gladiator school and had sworn to be loyal and brave for the rest of his days in order to earn a wage and help keep his mother and sister alive.

For Antonice's life he had willingly traded his freedom. Taking the gladiator's oath—*Uri, Vinciri, Vererari, Ferroque, Necari*—Valens had sworn to endure being burned, bound, and beaten, and to die by the sword. He had taken Paullus's brand, now just a small silver scar on the front of his shoulder. It was a promise worth making. Antonice and his mother lived well. He had been given a purpose beyond an impoverished life in the Suburra. Eight years had passed since then, and from that day to this, Valens had kept his promise.

"You are in top form now, but you are getting older," said Paullus. "How long can you continue to win? Would you not prefer to leave competition as a champion? You could have a long life as a trainer."

Ah, so that was it. Valens had never considered what Paullus might do when he stopped being useful. Profitable. No one had ever stayed in the arena as long as Valens. Most of the men who had joined the gladiator troupe with him had died long ago. A select few had gained their freedom when they became too old to fight. Was now Valens's time?

"I will train your new gladiator," Valens said, "but I ask two things of you."

"Of course."

"First, the equestrian will teach me to read and write if I teach him to fight."

Paullus looked surprised, but nodded. "What is your second request?"

"To be set free."

Paullus had begun to rise from his seat but fell back hard. "Free? This is your home. The gladiators are your family. I am your family. Why leave?"

"My sister and mother live in the Suburra. I would be with them more."

"You can visit them now all you want."

Phaedra's face flashed in his mind. Valens wanted to wed a woman like her and call her his own. "I would take a wife."

"Most gladiators live at the ludus, true. But exceptions can be made. Jupiter knows you are a wealthy man. Buy a villa and take a wife. I will let you live wherever you want."

"As a freeman the choice would belong to me, not you."

Paullus sighed and rubbed his forehead. "The equestrian can teach you to read and write. I cannot give you your freedom, but in a few years, when the time is right, perhaps. For now you will remain with the ludus. You may not fight much longer, but you must remain a part of the troupe and mold new gladiators in your image. Valens Secundus: The Maker of Champions. The title fits, does it not?"

Disappointment roiled in his stomach. It coated his tongue. He wanted to spit. "Yes, it does," he lied.

"I will allow you to come and go as you please, so long as you continue to train."

"Without guards?" Valens asked.

"You are worth too much to let you out unattended."

"Is it my worth, or do you doubt my return?"

Paullus moved to the front of his desk. He leaned on it, clasping his hands before him. "There is no one I trust more, Valens. If you desire to leave the ludus unattended, then you may."

"Thank you," Valens said. "Do you require more of me?"

"No. Sleep well. In the morning you begin working with the new gladiator."

A guard stood in the atrium waiting to escort Valens to the barracks attached to the house. Although weary of body, mind, and spirit, Valens doubted he would sleep much. He had found a tutor for his reading and writing. With literacy he could cross the line separating man from beast. There was also the possibility that one day he might gain his freedom. Valens Secundus, freeman. Ah, now there was a title that fit. Yet right now he was still a slave, and the one thing he truly wanted could never be his. Phaedra.

The guard unlocked the door to Valens's cell and stepped aside to let him enter. The small square room sat in darkness. There were no windows to let in moonlight at night, sunlight during the day, or even give the room a breath of fresh air. The only illumination came from a torch the guard still held. Using instinct more than sight, Valens made his way to a small table and found a candle. He brought it back to the guard and touched the taper to the flame.

Flickering candlelight chased away the gloom, but just barely. No, Valens thought as his eyes adjusted to the dimness. This would not do, not anymore. He wanted more than a single bed crammed into a corner alongside a table and lone chair.

"Is there anything else you need?" the guard asked.

"Leave the door unlocked."

The guard shook his head. "I cannot do that."

"The lanista promised to let me come and go as I please," said Valens.

"He did not tell me, and I hold the key." The guard slammed the door and locked it, the iron jamb hitting the bars with a clang that reverberated in Valens's chest.

Chapter 6

Phaedra

Phaedra's best friend and matron of honor, Fortunada, came into the bedchamber. Dressed in silver, Fortunada looked every bit the embodiment of Pronuba, the goddess of marriage. The back of her gown trailed across the floor and caught rose petals as she passed. Her sleeves were sheer and hung loose at the wrists. Under the fabric, Fortunada had woven silver cords in a crisscross pattern up and down her arms. The same silver cord had been wound in and out of her flaxen hair. Large silver hoops hung from her ears, and she shimmered with each movement.

"Come," Fortunada said as she held out her hand to Phaedra. Together they knelt before the bed. "Wise and gentle goddess, please take your daughter Phaedra unto you on her wedding night," said Fortunada. "Keep her always faithful to her husband, and make her fertile to bear many children."

"Wise and gentle goddess," Phaedra repeated, hoping the goddess Pronuba was listening. "Take me unto you on this, my wedding night. Keep me always faithful to my husband, Marcus, and make us fertile to bear many children."

When they were girls, countless times in this very room, at this very bed, she and Fortunada each had pretended to be the bride and the other her matron of honor, with all the accompanying sacred rituals. Now that she was actually saying those prayers for the reason they were intended, the supplications felt hollow. Was it because the groom did not love Phaedra the way she had always hoped? Or perhaps it was because Valens's scent still clung to her skin.

They moved to the small wooden altar. Phaedra first fastened her gaze upon the clay likeness of her mother. Then, as an offering to the goddess, she poured olive oil and dropped bits of dates onto a candle flame.

"Time to put you in bed," said Fortunada. She peeled back the blankets and Phaedra scooted across the mattress. "You are well prepared for your wedding night?"

Phaedra rested her back against the carved wooden headboard. Again, Valens came to mind. "Yes," said Phaedra, "I remember in great detail what you told me of your wedding night."

Embarrassed and giddy, they both laughed.

"Marcus is older. He may need more attention to become aroused."

"I have been warned to be very aware of the phallus."

"Phallus?" Fortunada sat at the foot of the bed. "Sometimes I think it is unhealthy for you to have been so sheltered. Cock. Call it a cock."

"Cock," Phaedra said, laughing nervously.

"You may have to kiss him," said Fortunada, "and not just on the lips."

"You mean his neck," said Phaedra, although she knew what her friend meant.

"Lower."

"I thought you would say that."

"Take him in your mouth. Lick and suck as if you are getting juices from your fingers. Do not use your teeth."

Phaedra considered these new instructions, and warmth spread down to the juncture of her thighs. She wanted to become a woman in every way. Without her even willing it, the face and body of Valens came to mind. She replaced him with Marcus and the image of having a lover lost its power.

"I will do as you suggest," said Phaedra.

"I would have you know something else. When he enters you, there will be some pain and blood. Do not fear either. The pain will subside and the blood will show him you are untouched."

Phaedra knew all of this already, having heard of wedding nights from other friends. Certain that Fortunada wanted to take her role as matron of honor seriously, she listened without interruption. "Thank you for the warning and the words of wisdom."

"Hard-won wisdom, I assure you." Fortunada stood. "Shall I send in Marcus?"

Again Phaedra's cheeks grew hot, and she fought the urge to smile. She had dreamed of this moment. Now, finally, the time had arrived.

As was customary, Marcus would come to her and ask to get into the bed. She would refuse, also the custom. He would then speak words of undying love and call her *wife*. After that, she would call him *husband* and invite him to join her under the covers. "Yes," she said to Fortunada, "invite him in."

Fortunada walked to the door and looked into the hallway. She stepped out farther, looking both left and right. "He is not there," she said. "I am sure he just stepped away for a moment."

Phaedra tried to ignore the unmistakable look of confusion from Fortunada, who went off to find the wayward groom. Maybe Phaedra had somehow angered the goddess. Had Pronuba seen into her heart and found Valens residing there? Had she chased away Marcus with a full bladder, or the need for another glass of wine as punishment?

Another, much worse, possibility occurred to her. What if Pronuba was giving no thought to Phaedra's marriage at all? Marcus was not waiting in the hallway because he had never come to her room. The bride had left the banquet, as had the matron of honor. But all the while, the groom remained in the dining room, more interested in discussing politics than doing his duty as husband.

Phaedra tried to calm down. Fortunada would find him. Soon Marcus would come to Phaedra's bed. As husband and wife, they would join and become one flesh. In fervent silence she prayed to Pronuba and promised to be a good wife, an honest wife. To show her sincerity, she pledged to remain awake until Marcus came to her.

Phaedra stretched out under the covers. The seconds slid through the hourglass, becoming minutes, and the minutes began to pile higher and higher. Her eyes grew heavy and she closed them for a moment. A soft noise, a shuffling, drew her from the haze of sleep, and she sat up.

"Marcus?"

Her husband sat on a stool, unlacing his sandals. "I am sorry, my dear. I did not mean to wake you."

She rose from the bed, knelt before him, and reached for his foot. "Can I help?"

"No. I am fine. You return to bed."

To bed to sleep, or to bed to be made a wife? She ran her fingers over the belt at her waist. "Do you want some wine?" she asked.

He shook his head. "I had plenty."

Phaedra stood behind Marcus and placed her palms on his shoulders. She moved her hands under the heavy fabric of the toga and tunic beneath. His skin was both warm and dry under her fingers. Her pulse raced and fluttered at the base of her throat. Should she touch her husband without his invitation? Phaedra wanted to show Marcus that, although a virgin, she still welcomed his attention. Her hands slid lower. He gripped her wrist, stilling her explorations.

"My dear, the plentiful wine has unmanned me."

Fortunada had warned her of this exact possibility. Phaedra swallowed her hesitation and kissed Marcus on the cheek. She placed small kisses down to his throat and flicked her tongue over his earlobe. She moved in front of him and knelt again. She ran her hands up his calves, past his knees and to his thighs.

Suck and lick as if getting juices from my fingers.

Marcus sighed and clasped her hands between his. He pulled her to standing and eased Phaedra onto his lap. "You are truly lovely," he said, "and I wish that I were a young man. But I am not. Tonight we must be satisfied with each other's company. You understand?"

In all the disappointments of her life—waiting years to marry, being bartered as a bride for senatorial support—having her husband refuse to love her on her wedding night seemed the cruelest of them all. "Yes," she lied. "I understand."

"There is a good girl. Tomorrow, then?"

He pressed his lips to her palm. She smiled, despite the sour taste of disappointment coating her tongue.

Marcus stripped out of his toga, careful to keep his back to her, and slid between the sheets. Within seconds he snored. She blew out the lamps and undressed in the dark, fumbling with the intricate knot at her waist, undoing the symbol of their union.

Chapter 7

Phaedra

Phaedra awakened alone. A sliver of light shone on the tiled floor. She refused to call for Terenita, loathing the notion that anyone would know she had failed at the singular task set before her—to please her new husband. Pulling the sheets from the mattress, she wadded them into a bundle and threw them into the corridor.

While most of her belongings were already at Marcus's villa, a single gown of pink silk remained with her in her father's home. She held it up and it shone with different colors in the light, reminding her of the inside of a seashell. She dressed and draped the silver-shimmering stolla over her shoulder, all the while wondering if she really should bother at all.

Without the help of servant or slave, Phaedra could fashion only a single hairstyle. She pulled up twin locks from each temple and fastened them in the back with combs before using her fingers to loosen several tendrils to frame her face.

After examining her reflection in a polished bronze disk, Phaedra found that she looked as awful as she felt. Using fine white powder, she covered the dark circles under her eyes before lining her eyes with kohl. Then she applied berry juices to her lips and cheeks.

Phaedra found her father in the small dining room. He sat at a table, like a woman, not reclined on a sofa as the men of Rome usually did when they ate. He stared, bleary-eyed, at a bowl of porridge. His usual ruddy and full cheeks were slackened with a yellowish undertone.

"Good morning, Father."

He pressed the bridge of his nose with thumb and forefinger. "I have too much of a headache for anything to be good."

"You saw me wed—that should lift your spirits."

"That it does."

Phaedra sat next to her father, and a slave brought her a similar bowl of porridge and a container of honeyed dates. She scooped the dates into the porridge and stirred, wondering where Marcus had gone. Maybe in the middle of the night he had changed his mind about being married to her. She imagined him sneaking from the villa before Rome awoke, with sandals in hand.

"Has my husband eaten already?"

"Marcus left for the Senate House before dawn," said her father. "We received word of some problems in Sicily. Slaves working the fields have revolted. Any unrest there will disrupt our grain supply, and it needed immediate attention. My head aches too much or I would be there with him."

"Those are important matters of the republic, both the grain supply and your headache," she said. Her father seemed not to notice her jest. For a moment, Phaedra wished that she was better at making jokes.

"I told Marcus you would understand. Who better to wed a senator than the daughter of a senator?"

"No one, I imagine."

"This is a great union," her father said. He tried to smooth down his disheveled hair. Instead, thin wisps spread to where none should be. "I need a million sesterces to retain my Senate seat. Marcus needs an unwavering ally against those who want the plebs raised up beyond their birth. I care little for his politics, you know. But you needed a husband, and all of this was accomplished in one fortuitous event."

Of course the reasons for her marriage were political and not personal. Still, she hoped that Marcus somehow wanted her, not just her father's support.

"By the way, Marcus will send a litter to take you to his villa by midmorning," her father said. "Then the housekeeper will present you with the keys, and you will become mistress of your own home. That must excite you."

Phaedra stared at her bowl. Fat black dates hung suspended in the lumpy white porridge. She wondered at ever having had an appetite for this unappealing mess. "If it pleases you both," she said.

"I am going back to bed. We all celebrated your happiness far into the night. And now I suffer." He limped from the room.

Alone again, Phaedra tried to take a few bites of porridge. The time from breakfast until midmorning stretched into an interminable length.

A slave entered the dining room. "Pardon, my lady," he said. "General Acestes is here."

General? She had not known of Acestes's rank last night. "Marcus left already this morning, and my father is unavailable for visitors."

"That is why I came to you, my lady. The general would have a word with you in their stead."

"Show him in," she said.

Two reclining sofas, both upholstered in green silk, sat next to each other at the side of the room, flanking a small round table in between. Phaedra moved to one of the sofas and arranged the soft folds of her gown over her ankles.

"Greetings," Acestes said as he approached. He was dressed in military garb, and as did all officers of the legion, wore a leather breastplate with bronze details and a pleated leather skirt over a red tunic. Under his arm he carried a bronze helmet with a bright red plume. Had Marcus served in the legions as well? Phaedra did not know, but she wondered if he looked as dashing as his nephew in the regalia.

"Greetings," Phaedra said. She gestured to the other sofa. "You, like all legionnaires, look splendid."

"I know it is illegal to wear my uniform inside the walls of the sacred city, but I am off to put down a slave uprising within the hour. Since it is the Senate who gives my orders, I doubt they think I will declare war. Still, I must apologize for my attire. I pray it does not offend."

She found it hard not to notice Acestes's long, strong legs as he reclined. After last night's encounter, she knew it was imperative that she behave with the utmost decorum. "Have you eaten yet? I can offer you porridge and dried fruit."

"Gratitude, but I came to say good-bye."

"Father already told me about the events in Sicily. It sounds terribly dangerous."

"Do not tell me you worry for my safety," he said. "You walked away from me twice last night."

As he spoke a slight smile lifted the corner of his mouth, and Phaedra found his looks pleasing. She should not flirt with her new husband's—and now her own—nephew. But since he had teased her first, she felt it impolite not to respond in kind. With a smile of her own, she asked, "Are you always so candid?"

He laughed. "I see no reason not to be. Subterfuge has caused more heartache than it is worth."

She smiled and thought that perhaps she could come to like Acestes.

"It pleases me that we speak alone," he said after they had sat in companionable silence for a moment. "I would be blunt again, if you give me your word not to walk away."

"I promise."

Acestes looked over his shoulder before leaning toward Phaedra. "Marcus and my mother were twins," he whispered.

Twins were unusual and sometimes even considered bad luck, but not so damming that it needed to be kept a secret. "I did not know."

"That is why I look so much like my uncle."

"You do look very much alike."

"All my life I have heard my uncle's previous wives complain to my mother about his lack of interest in the bedroom. Both women also complained that due to his scant attention, they failed to conceive a child. When neither provided an heir, he divorced them."

"I see," said Phaedra. If Marcus had not been a virile man in his youth, he certainly would be lacking in ardor since he had aged. If she understood correctly, it was because the phallus of older men tired more easily. In a way it came as a relief that their failure to consummate the marriage had been Marcus's and not hers.

"I could get you with child," said Acestes.

"You cannot think that I would want you as a lover," she said. "You are my husband's nephew."

"I do not come to you looking for an affair, or even a tryst. By rights, Marcus should name me his heir. He has not. It is because I am the son of his sister, not his brother. Also, he wants a child of his own. He will not get one with you unless his passions have grown stronger over the years, which is not likely when you consider his advancing age."

So he did not actually want her, either. The realization that no one really desired her was humiliating. Her face burned and tears stung her eyes.

"If you were to give him a baby, that child would inherit," said Acestes. "If you bore my son, then he would inherit."

Phaedra turned to look at Acestes. The bronze of his breastplate and the gold of his hair glowed in the morning light. "I cannot," she said, her voice small. "I am his wife."

"He does not love you. You know he married you for a political alliance. You do not owe him anything. Besides, if you do not give him a child, he will divorce you, as well."

Without question she knew Marcus would set her aside if she stopped being useful. But if she bore his child, or a child he believed to be his, she would always be bound to him. By engaging in the act of love, something she had longed to do last night, she could secure her future. With a child she would have security and would control his entire fortune should Marcus pass away.

Phaedra wondered if she was capable of passing off one man's child as another's. Even if no one ever questioned the child's parentage, she would never be able to tell that lie.

And what of Acestes? He needed Marcus's wife, and it mattered little who that person might be. Phaedra would serve as a vessel for Acestes's son to come into the world and claim an inheritance he believed belonged to him.

Draping his arm over the back of the sofa, he said, "Think about my offer. After a few months of marriage, you will change your mind."

Phaedra stood quickly. Her head buzzed and her vision grew dim around the edges. "You should go."

Acestes stood and shrugged. "I shall come to you when I return from Sicily."

"Do not seek me out," Phaedra said, her voice dripping with disgust. "I never want to see you again."

Chapter 8

Valens

Before the sun rose, the training ground stood empty. Walls surrounded Valens on all sides. Far from feeling trapped, he felt sheltered. The back wall connected to the house of the lanista by a second-story balcony from which Paullus could watch his gladiators' progress. Behind the wall on the right were the barracks, the kitchens, and the infirmary. The heavily guarded armory hid behind a barred metal door. A set of high gates bisected the final wall, and those gates, the only way in or out of the ludus, led to the forum.

Even with the forum so near, Valens heard no noises, save for the call of a bird and the crunch of his footfalls on the sand. The new trainee should come out any moment, and he disliked having to share this solitude with someone else, especially someone meant to replace him as Rome's champion.

In the center of the training ground a platform stood taller than the tallest man. Rough wooden beams held it high, although not stable. Later in the day he planned to bring the new gladiator to the platform and teach him about balance and the need to know his perimeter. Several large tree trunks stood upended. Their bark and wood had been hacked away by years of practicing aim and correct swordsmanship. Today he would begin his own training, and the training of the new volunteer, with strokes at a tree.

Valens's first trainer, an ancient and wise man with a limp and scar from chin to brow, had shared an invaluable secret on his first day of training—costmary leaves that were crushed, covered with olive oil, and left for days would increase his fighting ability. When rubbed onto the skin before bathing, it loosened the muscles, and the combination of costmary and steam from the hottest bathwater would make both sight and hearing more acute. In short, costmary helped the gladiator become more than a man of the sword. He became a predator with animal-like reflexes certain to bring victory.

Over the years others had tried to guess what Valens used in his bathing oil. It was one thing he never told. Yet now that *he* was the trainer, he wondered what secrets he might share with the equestrian gladiator, and if costmary would be one of them.

The sun crested over the walls. For a moment it was just a thread of light, the glare so brilliant it turned the whitewashed wall black. A heartbeat later it rose. The brilliance blinded Valens and he blinked. Several racks filled with practice weapons lined one wall. When his eyes adjusted to the light, he selected his favorite wooden sword and went to work.

Slash, slash, thrust, spin, slice.

The movements felt good and pure. His muscles, his mind, his weapon, and his will merged, becoming one and the same. He acted and reacted with purpose and, at the same time, without intent. A barred door clanged open and Valens turned.

The new gladiator stumbled into the light, rubbing away sleep. He and Valens were almost the same size. Valens guessed that the equestrian, fit and devoid of any marks that denoted a hard-lived life, had not yet reached twenty-five annums. He carried himself with the unpracticed grace common to all the upper classes and had the kind of face women found attractive. Yet, there was more to being a gladiator than an athletic physique, a high rank, and a handsome face. A person needed to know much more than how to wield a sword.

Valens decided that he envied the equestrian. Not only did Paullus intend to make this man the next Champion of Rome, as a member of Rome's elite, the new gladiator could marry Phaedra someday if he wanted. On top of it all, the damnable noble had thought to bargain and would be allowed to retire from the arena, assuming he survived the next six years.

Valens wondered if Phaedra had already spoken to her father about choosing her next husband, and if her father had agreed. Assuming she had gotten her way, and assuming that she outlived her current husband, the next time she married it might be to this man.

"You are late," Valens said to the equestrian.

"I thought training began after breakfast," said the man.

Valens drove the hilt of his sword into the man's middle and waited for him to stop wheezing and retching on the ground. "The first lesson you will learn is to not think. You are a gladiator, meant to embody the strength and honor of Rome."

They were not the moving words he had heard on his first day as a gladiator, but this task was different. Valens had entered the ludus as a lump of clay and allowed the master's hands to mold and shape him. This man before him was already formed. He needed to be broken, crushed to dust, and then reassembled.

To be a gladiator, a man of the sword, one needed to learn to fight even as his bowels turned to water. He needed to stay and face an opponent when any sane man would run. He had to struggle through the pain and the blood while the crowd chanted his opponent's name and called for his own death. To be a gladiator one must endure all of this for the glory of Rome, although his position remained that of a slave.

How could Valens put all that in words? How could he explain the discipline needed, the strength, the perseverance, to a man for whom life always provided the best of everything?

"The second lesson you will learn," said Valens, "is that I am your new god. I have complete control over your fate. You will train when I tell you, and eat, sleep, and shit when I feel you have earned the privilege."

The new gladiator stooped over, his hands resting on his knees, as he took a heavy, panting breath. "Who are you to strike me without warning?"

What was the equestrian expecting from a gladiator school? To be tickled? Better to learn the harsh realities now than to have his dead body dragged from the arena by a slave dressed as Charon, the ferryman. With a loose grip on the wooden sword, Valens brought up his fist, connecting with the man's chin. The new recruit fell backward, an arc of blood shooting from his mouth like a fountain.

The man lay on the hard-packed earth, blinking. He rolled onto all fours and spit. The dry ground soaked up the blood. Looking up, he opened his mouth and Valens suspected that the equestrian was about to ask another inane question.

"Do not speak," Valens said.

The man opened his mouth wider and sucked in a breath.

Valens knelt and their gazes met. "This is not the life for you." Valens poked the front of the equestrian's shoulder with the tip of his sword. The flesh bore no brand. He had sworn no oath. No matter what the agreement was between the equestrian and the lanista, it was something Valens considered breakable. "I will tell the lanista you do not have the makings of a gladiator. You will be released from any contract."

He stood and motioned for the guards to collect the bruised and bloodied man. As they hooked their arms under the equestrian's shoulders and dragged him to his feet, Valens wondered how much of his relief came from the fact that he would remain champion of the ludus and of Rome. True, he had lost the person designated to teach him to read and write. So be it. He could find another tutor.

"No." The man struggled with the guards. "I do have what it takes."

Valens did not even bother to look up as he called out to the man. "Go back to your home. Tell your friends that you fought Valens Secundus at a private party. Tell them that Consul Fimbria attended. It will make a great story that can grow grander in the retelling." Valens returned to his drills.

Slash, stab, slice, thrust, spin, duck.

"I have no home." The equestrian said as the guards dragged him toward the arena's edge. "I have nothing."

A homeless equestrian? Now he had seen everything. Valens knew the desperation that came from not having a place in the world. He had never known his own father, or even the name of a possible sire. A fatherless son never belongs. Valens stopped and held up one hand. The guards let the man go. "You have a story. I would hear it."

"My wife left me for an Egyptian trader. She took all my coin, sold my villa. Everything went with her, even my dog." The equestrian shook his head. "I still miss the dog."

Valens snorted. What a waste of a man to let a woman take all while he sat back and did nothing. "You had no notion to stop her?"

"It happened while I served with Gaius Marias in North Africa. I had no idea she had left, much less stolen anything."

"Your people did not stop her, either?"

"My family hails from Padua and I live in Rome. She sold my steward first so he could not warn me of what happened."

Padua, what a dung hole. Yet this man and his story piqued Valens's interest. "Why become a gladiator? Why not buy a tavern or something else a disgraced equestrian might do?"

"First, I have no coin. Have you not been listening? Second, I know of no better way to regain my fortune or reputation than in the arena. I am good with a sword and not afraid to die."

Valens grabbed another practice sword from a rack near the wall and dropped it in front of the equestrian. "Come after me, if you think that is all it will take."

The new gladiator picked up the sword. He whirled it across his body to the right and then to the left before balancing the blade on the side of his hand, twirling it around his wrist and catching the grip.

"That is a nice trick," said Valens. "It will make all the women in the stands wet. Now come at me."

With sword raised high, the equestrian rushed forward. Before he connected, Valens struck him twice, once to the solar plexus and the other at his gut. The new gladiator bent double and retched on the ground.

"Too open," Valens said. "Try again."

Lowering his sword, the equestrian rushed in, ready to slash. Valens stepped aside and delivered a hit to his back as he passed. The other man stumbled forward only a few steps before dropping his sword on the ground.

"You fight like a child of privilege that no one dare strike." Valens picked up both swords, threw them high across his body, and caught each in the opposite hand. Then he whirled the wooden blades above his head and ran around screaming. Valens knew he looked ridiculous, but he taught a lesson with his antics.

"I do not look that foolish."

Valens shrugged. Maybe, maybe not. "You lack control."

"I always trained with the sword, and my instructors rarely landed blows."

"Your instructors knew enough to make you feel like a superior fighter. You would not have paid for their services if they had beaten you." Valens held out the sword. "Come at me again."

The equestrian gripped the hilt and let the sword hang down. He crouched and held the wooden blade at the ready. With the other hand he motioned to Valens. "You come at me."

Valens smiled. Maybe this new man showed some promise after all. "Attack only when necessary. You learned this lesson quickly. Have you a name?"

"Spurius Mummius Baro. Most people call me Baro."

"Baro, you need to know much, much more." Valens picked up a broken spear and drew a square in the sand. "Establish a space.

Defend your space. Study your opponents, learn their limitations. Know your own limitations. Then you can attack. Always remember, our job is to entertain."

He surprised Valens by nodding. "I will think on what you have said."

Valens held out his arm. Baro took it and the two grasped each other's wrists. "Welcome to the brotherhood of gladiators. I would have a word with you about something else." Valens scratched the side of his ear. Sometimes, he decided, one had to leave the safety of the known and directly assault a problem. "I desire to read and write. Paullus said if I trained you then you would tutor me."

"A fair trade." Baro took the broken spear from Valens and traced symbols in the dirt. "This is your name," he said and pointed to each figure. "V-A-L-E-N-S."

Valens studied the letters and nodded his head. "Go and break your fast. We will continue after we have eaten."

After Baro left, Valens traced the letters until his arm knew the feel of them and his mind would forever know what each one meant.

Chapter 9

Valens

The sun reached its zenith, and all the gladiators went indoors to eat and escape the midday heat. Having trained since before dawn, Valens decided to leave the ludus and explore Rome alone. He walked to the front gate and stood before a guard.

The guard knocked on the heavy wooden door, and it opened. Without a word, Valens slipped into the crowd that moved through the Capitoline Market. For the first time since his adolescence, he was unencumbered by the orders of another. Expectantly he held his breath, hoping the world was somehow different now that he was no longer surrounded by guards. Breathing in, he found that the air smelled the same. The bright white sun shone down on the forum just as it had in the ludus. He trod on the exact same gray paving stones as always, slightly uneven in height, but perfectly fitted together.

Like a snake, the responsibility that came with freedom coiled around his heart and constricted. He looked back at the gate, eight feet tall, with steel beams reinforcing the wood. He thought of going back to the ludus, making a joke that even without guards, Rome still smelled like dung.

Valens could not return, not yet. He faced men in the arena. Men with swords who meant to do him ill. That never bothered him. Since when did walking on the streets become frightening? He supposed it was because the last time he had been free, he had been coming *to* the ludus.

No. He would not be a coward, even if only he knew of his cowardice. But where should he go?

To his right stood the Palatine Hill and the villa in which Phaedra resided. That was where he wanted to go, but he should not. He knew that he should never see her again. Perhaps one day a litter would pass by and he would catch a glimpse of her profile. Just then, two litters approached. He craned his neck to see inside of each one. She rode in neither. Valens struggled to quell his craving for the woman. It did not work.

His mother and sister lived close by, and he decided to visit them. He turned left, away from Phaedra and her villa and its high walls that kept her hidden within, and him alone and without.

After two years as a gladiator, Valens had earned enough money to buy his mother and sister a home in any part of the city he chose. His mother, born and raised in the Suburra, cried at the thought of leaving her friends. Valens suspected she feared that a higher class of people would never accept her.

Hoping to make her happy, Valens had bought her an apartment in a cleaner section of the Suburra. The four rooms took up a quarter of the building's third floor. Most of the residents were former slaves who had bought their freedom after learning a trade. His mother spent much of her time at the restaurant that occupied the whole of the ground floor, while his sister, Antonice, played in the streets, as did all the local children. Valens hoped Antonice was happy. She seemed happy, at least.

Valens entered the apartment building through a side door and walked up the two flights of stairs. He knocked. A sweaty man with long hair answered. "Yes?" the man said.

Without a doubt, it was another one of his mother's male friends. As each year passed, his mother's companions seemed less fit, less kind, less everything good.

Valens had hoped to find his mother and sister at home and alone. Still, the man could be sent on his way soon enough. Without acknowledging the man with glance or word, Valens tried to walk past.

"You cannot barge in here."

"Get out of my way," Valens said as he bumped into him.

The man staggered and righted himself. Narrowing his piggy eyes, he glared. "Who are you? You do not belong here. Go away."

Bile rose in the back of Valens's throat, and his vision narrowed. Over the man's shoulder, Valens saw into the apartment. The table he had purchased for his mother filled the middle of the room. Bowls someone had given him when he fought in Capernaum—that he then had gifted to his mother—sat on top of the table. Spices circled the room, tied in bundles that hung from the ceiling near the shelf Valens had paid for.

"Who am I?" Valens shoved a finger into the man's flabby chest. "Who are you?"

Antonice came from her bedroom. Taller than he remembered, with dark brown hair that fell loose around her shoulders and down her back. How long had it been since his last visit? A week? A month? No, a whole season had passed. For the first time, he noticed the slight and subtle changes that transformed her from a little girl to young woman. What was the sweaty, flabby man doing in the apartment alone with his sister?

Antonice rushed past the man and threw her arms around Valens, lifting herself off the ground by the force of her own embrace. "It is so good to see you. Where are your guards? We would have made you dinner if we knew you were coming. How are you? It has been so long. Too long." She let him go and dropped back to the floor. "It is good that you are home."

"You are quite the chirping little bird," said Valens as an unaccustomed glow of contentment spread through him. "Where is Mother?"

"She is in her room resting," said Flabby.

Valens ignored him, and he noticed with satisfaction that Antonice did, too.

"Mama," she called. "Valens is home."

Straightening her disheveled tunic and smoothing hair away from her face, their mother emerged from her room. She looked older, too. A thin webbing of lines surrounded her eyes. Deeper creases were etched into the sides of her mouth. More than a few gray hairs were visible within her dark locks. He vowed to come home more often, to be more involved. The appearance of his mother and sister should not be a surprise. Flabby should not assume he was the man of the house in Valens's absence.

His mother tried to fasten a silver comb in her hair. "Oh, there you are! Whatever brings you here?"

"So, you are Valens Secundus, the famous gladiator," said Flabby.

Valens refused to look at the man and instead spoke to his mother. "I thought to take you and Antonice to dinner."

His mother moved to her male friend and wound her arm around his sweaty, fleshy middle. "Maybe you could take Antonice. I need some more rest."

Flabby nuzzled his mother's neck. "Good idea."

Valens clenched his fist. One hit and the man would die. An elbow strike to the nose and his miserable life would end. "I am to become a trainer," Valens said, still ignoring the man. As always, he was hoping for a moment of his mother's interest. "I train one gladiator for now. With some work, he might be another champion."

Flabby whispered something to Valens's mother, who laughed.

"What did you say?" Valens finally addressed the man directly.

"Nothing," said his mother. "He said nothing."

"I said I thought you would be taller," the man said as he kissed Valens's mother on the cheek.

That was it. Valens grabbed Flabby by his stained and stinking tunic with such energy that neither stopped until they slammed into the wall. The man let out a satisfying whoosh and doubled over. Although Valens had made his point, he loathed the thought of this worthless piece of garbage touching his mother. With as much force as he could muster, Valens drove his knee into Flabby's crotch. The stinking man dropped to the floor, where he lay, curled in around himself, whimpering and smelling of piss.

Valens bent low, his mouth near Flabby's ear. "Try fucking my mother now," he said.

Antonice grabbed Valens by the hand and led him to the door. "He is sorry, Mother," she said. "You should warn your friends about how sensitive Valens can become."

Neither Valens nor his sister spoke until they took seats at a scarred wooden table in the restaurant on the ground floor.

"He is new," said Antonice. "You know how Mother gets when she first meets them."

The tavern keep brought them two jugs, one filled with water and the other, wine. Valens ignored the water and filled his cup with sour red wine. He emptied it in one swallow. He drank a second and third cup before speaking. "I do know."

"He is not as bad as some of the others."

The others. No matter what Valens gave his mother—a new apartment, money, expensive furniture—she never changed. She always chased one waste of a man after another. He knew that to be a fact, and yet hated himself for knowing. He would never change her, but he could keep his sister from the same fate. In order to save Antonice, he needed to get her out of the Suburra.

"Paullus said I could move from the ludus. Maybe I could buy a villa for us all on the Aventine."

"She would bring whoever was her favorite at the moment with her, you know that."

The men, always the men.

"What am I to do?" he asked. "I cannot leave you here."

"There is no need for you to worry. I have friends. I spend a lot of time at their houses. Besides, everyone knows I am your sister, so no one bothers me."

"Maybe it is time I find you a husband." He thought about Phaedra and her forced marriage. "I will find a young man you like. How old are you now, fourteen annums?"

"Twelve. I turn thirteen at the harvest."

"Too young for marriage," he said.

"I agree."

"You promise me that you are fine."

She smiled. "I am. Now tell me about your new gladiator."

They ate and talked, and by the time Valens walked Antonice back to her apartment, Flabby had departed, hopefully for good. His mother pouted until he gave her a few silver denarii to buy a new rug to replace the one that smelled of fat, sweaty men and urine. Before evening came, he left his mother's apartment. Turning his face to the setting sun, he walked toward the ludus, the place that had given him a life and at the same time stolen his ability to live.

Chapter 10

Phaedra

With the sun setting over the Tiber River, a cramped litter with a soiled gold cushion carried Phaedra to her new home, one of the largest villas in Rome. The stars had yet to come out. Would Polaris be there, as Valens had said?

Ascending the Palatine Hill, she saw the Capitoline Market and merchants disassembling colorful awnings at the end of the day. Wooden stands sat atop a grassy bank and overlooked the long, oval dirt track for chariot racing at the Circus Maximus. She heard they meant to construct permanent stands of stone, but knew not when. Close to the Circus Maximus sat the round Forum Boarium, where most of the gladiatorial games were held. Like the chariot track, wooden stands surrounded the sandy cattle market, although she knew those were erected temporarily for games and taken down when they ended.

Would Valens fight in the next series of games? Perhaps Marcus might attend and take Phaedra with him. They could sit in the box seats reserved for senators and drink sweet wine as they watched Valens win in splendid fashion.

In the far distance to the north, the Via Appia wound toward the city. Travelers trying to reach the city gates before they closed looked like small brown specks upon the white stone road.

At the villa, Marcus greeted Phaedra on the street. His housekeeper, Jovita, a thin-lipped woman, gave Phaedra the keys and pronounced her *domina*, mistress of the house. The housekeeper and Marcus took Phaedra on a tour. Moving from the atrium with its open ceiling and large tiled pool below to a cavernous triclinium, she figured that her father's entire home could fit into this building's garden.

Still, the villa had an unkempt air. Once-vibrant blue curtains, now faded to gray, hung in one of four dining rooms. The reclining sofa in a guest room had a wide tear in the upholstery. Dust floated by in clouds and gathered in piles at the corner. A peacock and his peahen wandered unimpeded, eating bugs off the floor and fruit off the table with gusto. Their excrement stained the cracked and chipped mosaics upon which they all trod, bird and human alike.

"What think you of your home?" Marcus asked.

The house reminded Phaedra of a beautiful woman with a dirty face and tattered dress. As domina of this villa, she could bring order. Marcus was a busy and important man. He had no time to worry about the cleanliness of his home. But *she* could, and by taking care of her husband, he would come to love her and need her.

"The villa is splendid," she said.

Marcus led Phaedra through the corridors to her new room, or rather, rooms. There was one for sleeping, another for dressing, yet another for eating, and a final room in which she could entertain guests. Like the rest of the villa, her rooms seemed poorly tended. She noticed an unpleasantly sour smell in her private dining room, as if someone had spilled a dish that had not been properly cleaned up. Or perhaps it was many dishes. Marcus seemed not to notice, so Phaedra said nothing.

Her bedroom was by far the nicest. Sheer white curtains hung in front of the door that led to the garden and moved lazily with the breeze. Her large bed had wooden posts at each corner, with four beams atop that connected them all. Silken white curtains hung from each post and were tied back with golden rope. A mosaic of the sea and great silvery fish covered her floor.

She and Marcus were alone. They stood near the door that opened to the garden, close to each other but not touching. A breeze blew and the curtains rose and fell like a sigh. The bed was nearby. Was now the time? "This room is breathtaking," she said for want of something to say.

The color rose in Marcus's cheeks. "I had hoped you would like it," he said.

Phaedra came to understand that her husband had taken time to make her feel welcome, and she was filled with affection and hope. "Thank you."

"Apologies," Marcus said as he shifted from foot to foot, "for making you wait all day. Dealing with the slave uprising in Sicily is taking longer than I anticipated. I could have sent the litter to retrieve you earlier, but I wanted to be here myself when you entered your new home."

"It pleases me that you were here," she said. True, Phaedra had spent much of the day distraught, pacing and wondering when she might be summoned to her new home. But to know that her husband had wanted to personally welcome her relieved her worry.

"I would share dinner with you tonight, but I have more meetings. The Sicilian slaves do not respond to the usual encouragement and have stopped working altogether. The time of planting has just ended, and we need them to tend the fields or the entire republic will starve."

"I understand," she said, although she felt keenly dissatisfied again.

"Your father said you would be most accommodating. I do not want to disappoint you, my dear. We can get to know each other better after we leave the city."

"You planned a wedding trip? I am shocked and flattered."

"Oh, we can call it that if you wish. I always retire to Pompeii before the hot season arrives and stay until the rains return to Rome."

"That means we will be gone for months," she said.

"We will."

Many of Rome's wealthiest citizens owned homes in coastal Mediterranean towns like Pompeii or Herculaneum. There they escaped the summer's heat, the noise, and the rancid air that rolled off Rome's wharves, carrying diseases. Phaedra's family did not have one of these homes. What little money her father had went to the trappings of an aristocratic Roman lifestyle—furnishings, food, wine, parties, and clothes. She had always wanted to travel to one of the beachside towns so popular with other patricians. But not like this. A season away from her father and friends with an indifferent husband for company sounded less like a holiday and more like a punishment.

"Make sure you have everything you need," said Marcus. "Silks, cosmetics, jewelry. We will attend parties most every night, and I would have you looking magnificent. Go to the Capitoline Market tomorrow and have the purchases delivered to the villa. The quality of the goods found in Pompeii is equal to what you find in Rome, but the prices . . ." Marcus shook his head and rolled his eyes. Phaedra took his gesture to mean that costs were higher than even one of the richest men in the republic was willing to pay.

Her father had never allowed her to go to the market, even with a guard and an attendant. She had never bought anything, or even made the final decision on a single purchase. Her pulse roared in her ears. Sweat dripped down her back and pooled under her arms. She was sure that she would have no idea how to conduct herself in the market, yet Marcus expected her to be comfortable in that setting.

Breathe.

Inhaling, she chanced being honest. "I do not frequent the market."

He paused, suddenly understanding. "Have you never been to the market at all?"

Phaedra looked down and said nothing, her silence answering for her.

"It is not difficult. You decide what you want and send your maid to make the purchase. I shall provide you with two guards and enough coin for anything."

"I tell Terenita what I want," she said, "and she makes the purchases for me. I can do that, I think."

Marcus placed his hand on her shoulder. "I am sorry if this frightens you. Anytime you do something for the first time it will frighten you. You will see that going to the market is simple, and after your first visit, it will become commonplace."

She looked at him. His gray eyes were full of understanding and compassion. "I trust you," she said.

"Good. That pleases me." With a quick brush of his lips to Phaedra's cheek, Marcus left to attend another meeting.

Phaedra and Terenita spent the evening organizing belongings and making a list of things to buy before leaving for Pompeii. She wondered if Marcus might come to her bed when his guests left.

After all her gowns, sandals, and jewels had been laid out and the candle burned down to a nub, Phaedra stopped wondering. She knew the answer. She stepped out into the garden and cast her gaze upon the heavens. Polaris looked down upon her as it also must on Valens. With a weary sigh, she turned back to the villa. Alone, she climbed under the blankets of her musty bed and tried to sleep.

Chapter 11

Valens

The next day Valens woke at dawn and began to train. As the sun reached its zenith, he decided to venture into the city again. Maybe this would become his pattern—train in the morning, leave the ludus for the afternoon, and return in the evening. He liked the idea, even without a notion of where he might go.

The Capitoline Market sprawled out in front of the gates, and he decided to lose a few hours wandering by the stands and shops. Bright awnings of yellow, orange, and green shaded the vendors and their goods. Fruit sat in wooden bins and meats hung from hooks. People called to each other, speaking in every language of the republic. Merchants held out their wares as he passed, bowls filled with brownish-red cinnamon, ripe yellow melons. Others displayed fabrics of every hue, some rough as wood and others smooth as the surface of a still pool.

Men loitered on street corners. They nudged each other as he passed and asked, "Was that Valens Secundus?"

"I think not. He is blond and hails from Gaul."

Women stood in doorways and offered to please Valens for free. At least they recognized him. Their ample breasts spilled from necklines cut low and tight. Garish red colored their cheeks and lips. Powders of blues and greens covered their eyelids. All of it melted in the heat and their sweat until they appeared to have cried multicolored tears.

He ignored it all.

Ahead he saw the stall of a silk merchant. Squares of different colors floated in the slight breeze, one of them the exact crimson of Phaedra's bridal veil. Had she bought the fabric here? Was he standing in the same place she had stood a few weeks before the wedding, selecting the perfect shade?

Coming from the opposite direction, in the midst of the throngs of people, he saw her. Two thickly muscled guards stood nearby, and she had a maid at her side. His gut twisted with excitement and indecision. He wanted to speak to her again and tell her that he was no longer a stupid beast and could now read and write, if only a little. Yet he knew that he should not.

Before Valens could slip away into the crowd, he spied her walking near a blind beggar. The old man sat in a doorway. A grimy rag was tied round his eyes, his hand upheld in want and waiting. Did she see not the man? What if he was not right about the head? He could be dangerous. Valens moved forward. The world around him slipped away, and he saw only Phaedra.

She stopped before the beggar, bent low, and seemed to speak to him. What had the man said to draw her attention? Valens increased his pace. Phaedra turned to one of the guards, who held a leather pouch. From it, he withdrew a few coins that he dropped into the palm of the beggar. Hand on hip, Phaedra looked back at the guard, who then produced several more coins.

Valens could not help but laugh aloud. Poor cloistered Phaedra had stood up to the brutish guard for the sake of a lone blind beggar.

She turned. Their gazes held. The hairs at the nape of his neck stood on end. He breathed in her perfume, clean aloe and the soft lightness of lavender. Valens hoped to hold her scent forever.

"Greetings, Valens Secundus," said Phaedra. "What brings you to a silk merchant?"

Valens froze. She was as beautiful as she had been on the night of her wedding, maybe more so. Finally one word tumbled from his lips. "Greetings," he said.

"I purchased the fabric for my wedding veil from this merchant. His colors are so vibrant. Best in the republic, I would wager."

Valens's eye found Phaedra's color among the others once again, but he chose to lie. "I had not noticed your exact fabric." He could hardly admit that he had thought of little save her for the past two days, or that he had wrapped her veil around his wrist time and again since he had last seen her.

Valens very much wanted to run his fingers through her hair, which hung loose over her shoulder. Or better yet, kiss her on the cheek. But even he, a stupid bastard from the Suburra, knew he would never be allowed to touch an aristocratic woman in public. He balled his hands into fists and held them to his sides in case they betrayed his need to reach out and touch Phaedra.

"How do you fare?" he asked.

Phaedra examined the cloth on display. Running her hand over a length of blue silk, she shrugged. "Have you found a tutor yet?"

"I have," he said. His hand tingled with both the memory of writing and the excitement in sharing his newfound knowledge. "Come." Using his finger, Valens traced the one word he knew on a dusty wall—V-A-L-E-N-S. "I know it is not much, but it is me. That is my name."

Phaedra's eyes shone with pride. "That is marvelous. Who taught you to write?"

"The gladiator I fought at your wedding, Spurius Mummius Baro, volunteered at my ludus. He knows how to read and write. I am his trainer now and he is my tutor."

"So you train as well as fight? I never knew. Then again, I do not follow the games, so there is much about gladiators I do not know."

"Baro is my first trainee. The lanista means to make him the next Champion of Rome."

"What will become of you, Valens Secundus? What will you be, if not the champion?"

"The trainer of champions," he said. The title tasted of lead, cold and hard.

"It does not suit you, if you do not mind me saying so."

Valens laughed. Ah, at least someone was willing to be honest. "I could not agree more."

"It pleases me that you have learned to write your name. The next time we meet perhaps you will have read Plato, and we can discuss whether Rome is the ideal state."

"Will there be a next time?"

He wanted to see her again, and for a moment thought she might want to see him, too. Phaedra looked away and chewed on her bottom lip. He felt that he had said too much, pushed too hard, and she wanted to be rid of him.

In silent answer to his question, she shook her head. After a moment, she added, "In the morning I leave for Pompeii. I came here to buy fabrics, jewelry, everything I need."

As if suddenly punched in the stomach, Valens lost his breath. Yet, why? Why Phaedra? There were other beautiful women in Rome, agreeable women who desired him. What did he need with one person when the rest of the republic worshipped him?

Until that moment Valens had thought of his attraction to her as only physical. But it was more than that. It was her willingness to speak candidly and to be kind that drew her to him. The desire to read and the courage to leave the ludus came from his longing to become good enough for her. If he never saw Phaedra again, then who would know if he became a better man?

"Safe travels," he said after realizing that he had stood too long without speaking.

Phaedra smiled and Valens died a little.

"Thank you," she said.

The guards approached Phaedra. Valens turned away and began to examine a piece of silk. He stared until the fabric became a combination of parts and was no longer a whole. He found each individual thread, finer than a baby's hair. At first glance the color appeared uniform. Then he saw that it varied by degrees—bright blue in the middle, and by the time the eye traveled to the edges, the color had lost its luster.

"I have more purchases to make," Phaedra said. Her guard gave the silk merchant a handful of coins and exchanged a few words about delivering the order that day.

Valens said nothing.

She spoke to a female attendant with a voice so bright and happy that his head ached. Did she feel nothing for him? She did not. She could not. He was a slave and she a patrician, the wife of Rome's wealthiest man and the daughter of its most popular senator. He needed to let Phaedra go.

"Farewell, Valens Secundus," she said.

"Farewell," he said, still looking at the silk.

The air around him ceased to vibrate, and the soft scent of Phaedra evaporated. Without looking up, Valens knew she was gone. He stood at the silk merchant's stand for several moments after Phaedra had gone.

"Can I help you with something?" the merchant asked.

"No." Valens looked once more at the silk that hung in rows, his eye finding the familiar crimson of Phaedra's bridal veil. "There is nothing here for me," he said, and walked away.

Intent on returning to the ludus, Valens made his way through the crowded marketplace, ignoring the whispers and stares of passersby. When mud walls that had been painted white rose up before him, surrounding the ludus and the training ground, Valens thought but one word: *home.*

Weary of spirit and foul of mood, he slammed an open palm on the wooden doors thrice before a guard pulled them open.

"What took you so long?" he snapped at the guard as he shoved his way past.

The training ground stood empty and silent. All of the practice weapons sat on their racks. A group of men stood together in the shade of a wall, laughing and enjoying a moment of rest.

Valens nodded toward the group of men. None returned his wordless greeting, or even noted his arrival, causing his temper to flare. As he had learned to do long ago, Valens turned his anger into force that he would save for his next fight. Turning his back on the group, he began to scan the training ground for his new trainee.

He did not consider the new gladiator a friend. But Baro had taught Valens how to write his name. That kindness deserved to be returned. The first days of gladiatorial training were meant to be brutal and frightening. While Valens did not want to make the trainee weak, he also felt some responsibility for this young charge.

After a moment of thought, Valens walked toward the kitchen. It seemed reasonable that Baro sought respite in the darkened quiet of the dining hall. Valens had done so himself when he first had arrived at the ludus. Baro was already singled out to be Rome's new champion. Who better than Valens knew how lonely was the journey to the apex of greatness?

It was then that the men laughed again. Without thought, Valens turned. Standing in the middle of the group was Baro. He held the bowl of water shared by the gladiators during training, a sure sign that he had been accepted by the troupe. He apparently had just said something that everyone found hilarious.

Like a candle quickly snuffed, Valens's feelings of kindness disappeared. They were replaced by an emotion he felt much more comfortable with. Rage.

Valens had never been a member of the brotherhood of gladiators. Oh, yes, he had been a gladiator for over eight years, but he
had never been one of them. At first, none of the others had taken
notice of Valens because he was so young and inexperienced. He hid
in obscurity, eating alone and training hard. When Paullus rewarded
the men with wine and female company, Valens avoided the party. So
clear was his vision of greatness that he saw it all as a distraction. When
he stepped onto the sands for the first time, he showed himself to be a
champion in the making.

Everyone saw it. Everyone knew.

Now, without thinking, Valens grabbed a dulled metal sword
from the rack of training weapons. Moving quickly, he came upon
the group of men. He struck Baro's shoulder from behind. The others,
so jovial a moment before, backed up with eyes wide as the equestrian
crumpled to the ground. Although the blade was not sharp enough to
slice flesh, it was heavy enough to crush bone. Valens focused on the
knobby ridge of backbone at the base of the neck. He lifted his sword
high, ready to strike.

"Halt."

The one word pierced his fury, and the blade stopped a hairsbreadth away from making contact.

Upon the balcony of the house, overlooking the entire training ground, stood the lanista. How long had Paullus been watching? Had he witnessed all the events, or just stepped out at the
right moment? The sword dropped to the ground as Valens's hand
trembled with shame.

"Both of you," said Paullus, "come to my tablinum. The rest of you
get back to work."

The trainer organized men into rows to practice drills as a guard
led Valens and Baro through the villa. Paullus was already seated at
his desk when they arrived. He did not, Valens noticed, offer either

of them a chair. Baro held his injured shoulder and glowered, while Valens did his best to ignore him.

"You attacked Baro," said Paullus. "Why?"

Valens shook his head. He knew that saying, *He has made friends*, was not a worthy excuse, even if it was the reason.

"Do you know why he attacked you?" Paullus asked of Baro.

"You saw it all yourself," Baro said. "I did nothing to provoke him. I demand severe punishment."

Paullus held up his hand and Baro stopped speaking. "You are no longer a freeman, Equestrian. You cannot a demand a thing. This is a ludus. Do you understand?"

"I do not think that I do," Baro said.

"If I feel the men need to be entertained, I will hire actors," said Paullus. "You do not need to amuse them with stories."

"It is my nature to make people laugh and make friends."

"There can be only one champion in the arena. Men fear the champion. He inspires them. If you want to make people laugh, learn to juggle. You are dismissed."

Both Valens and Baro turned to leave the room.

"Not you, Valens," said Paullus. "Just the equestrian."

Valens stood before the desk as Baro and the guards left the room.

"That man is my property and I will not see him destroyed by your whims," said Paullus. His nostrils flared, and Valens thought of a horse, too angry to be ridden or controlled. "I have always gone easy on you, Valens. You are the champion and therefore treated differently than the rest of the men. Never have you given me reason to punish you. But this"—he pointed to the door of his tablinum—"I will not tolerate. Tell me now. Why did you attack?"

He could not lie to Paullus. The sickening feeling of guilt began again and set his arm trembling. Valens clasped both hands behind his back. "I did not attack the equestrian to teach him a lesson, but because I was jealous of his easy way with the men."

"Listen to yourself. You were jealous. Are you an old woman?"

"I'm not sure of what I am. Not anymore."

"You are a gladiator and still Rome's champion. You can only be champion a little longer. If you continue to fight, someone will eventually beat you. Or you can retire from the arena in your own time, become a trainer, and always remain undefeated."

Valens shook his head. He thought of his mother and all her men. He thought of Phaedra sailing to Pompeii and living her life without him. Not for the first time, Valens wondered about his own father. Did the man even know that he had sired a famous son? "I have no one who cares for me. That is why I attacked."

"You have Rome. The entire world knows your name. They all love you. Is that not enough?"

"No. It is not. Yet it seems as if that is all I shall have."

"It is more than most," said Paullus.

Valens shrugged. He no longer cared to have this discussion. "Am I dismissed?"

Paullus raked his hands through his hair and sighed. "You are."

Nodding, Valens left the tablinum. In the atrium he met a guard who led him to the locked and barred door that separated ludus from home.

On the other side of the door, they found Baro waiting.

The guard fumbled with the key while working to make it fit into the lock. Valens saw that the guard was nervous and unsure of how to handle a brawl between two gladiators. Finally, the door swung open and Valens stepped through.

"Stop staring at me as if I convinced Jupiter to piss in your porridge," he said to Baro. "I would hear your complaint."

"I do not accept the lanista's reasoning. You did not attack me to teach me a lesson. He said that only to save you from a punishment you richly deserve."

Valens lifted one shoulder and let it drop. "Have you a point?"

Open-mouthed, Baro gaped. "I would have the real reason."

Valens scratched the side of his ear and tried to find the words to explain such a violent reaction he barely understood himself. "I am the Champion of Rome. I am the most famous gladiator in the world, and yet, I am not one of them." Valens hitched his chin toward the training ground where the rest of the troupe practiced drills. "As a champion, I am not a normal man."

"You are angry at me for being the one meant to take your place."

"Not entirely," said Valens. He paused. He did not owe this man an explanation. Yet he sensed that Baro sincerely wanted to understand, and Valens longed to be understood. "I do not know how to be a normal man, and you do."

Baro leaned against the wall. He winced and righted himself, holding his shoulder. "So we are to teach each other more than just swordplay and letters. I will teach you how to be a normal man. Maybe I can even teach you how to be charming. At the same time, you will teach me how to be a champion. So when the time comes, we might switch roles."

Valens paused, unsure of what to feel or how to react. His first inclination, of course, was to put this equestrian in his place. He was Valens Secundus, the undefeated Champion of Rome. Everyone loved Valens. He did not need to be charming.

And yet, Baro had found the words Valens wanted to speak. "Yes," he said, "that is it."

"Good," said Baro. "We are understood."

"We are." Valens knew what he wanted to say this time, although he now lacked the courage. He inhaled fully. "I am sorry for striking you unawares."

"I accept your apology," said Baro. He touched his bruised flesh with his fingertips. "Do you think I should visit the medicus?"

Valens shook his head. "Your shoulder is not broken. Besides, if you want to be champion, you must first learn to ignore pain."

Baro scowled. "If you want to be a normal man, you must forget everything you have taught yourself about being champion."

"Then it seems we both have many miles to travel together first."

"So it seems."

Valens felt the corner of his lips twitch and found that it led to a smile. Baro glared for a moment longer before beginning to laugh quietly. The laugh proved infectious and Valens began to laugh, too. The trainer turned from his drills to watch. Baro nudged Valens, who stopped laughing, but found that a snort of amusement broke free. Baro laughed again and Valens soon followed.

"Both of you," said the trainer, "get in line for drills."

Valens did not have to take orders from anyone at the ludus beyond the lanista. Yet this time he obeyed. After retrieving two practice swords, one for himself and the other for Baro, he began to strike, sweep, and thrust, following the order for each. He caught a glance from Baro, who then rolled his eyes skyward. Valens took it as a sign that they were traveling the miles together.

They were not quite friends, and yet Valens felt that he was no longer alone.

Chapter 12

Phaedra

With a heady feeling of indestructibility for having conquered the market, Phaedra returned to the villa. The housekeeper met Phaedra, Terenita, and the guards in the atrium. "My lady, the dominus wishes to see you in his rooms."

Phaedra's mouth went dry. Was this the moment? Would her husband now take her and make her a woman? Did he really desire her? The thought of Marcus wanting her was a salve to her wounded pride after her disappointing encounter with Valens. Her pulse sped and blood flowed to each part of her body, leaving her flushed with equal amounts of trepidation and excitement.

She nodded toward Jovita, the only sign that she had registered the invitation to Marcus's bedchamber. "This way, my lady," she said, as she gestured to a hallway.

As they walked, Phaedra's thoughts went to Valens. At the market, he had dismissed her. She had done the same thing hundreds, if not thousands of times before. If the eye contact was withdrawn, then the personal connection ended as well. She wanted to feel furious. Who was this slave, this whore of combat, to reject her?

Yet Phaedra managed only a flicker of anger before misery snuffed it out. Valens's rebuff should not have come as a shock. In the garden they had developed an affinity, a familiarity. They were not quite friends, but not strangers, either. Allies, perhaps. Yes, they had become allies when they had made a pact to change their individual fates. Except in reality they were not.

The thought was truly humbling.

"Here we are, my lady." Jovita stopped in front of a closed door and knocked.

A male voice bade them enter. Marcus.

Phaedra vowed to clear her mind of Valens. To her, the gladiator must be nothing. Her mother, she knew, would see Phaedra's marriage to Marcus as a great success. The connection with the gladiator was a waste of her energies.

Lifting the latch, the housekeeper stepped aside. Phaedra wiped her sweat-damp palms in the folds of her gown, swept clear all thoughts of Valens, and crossed the threshold.

She entered a large chamber that had the well-used look of belonging to a busy and important man. An unmade bed sat against one wall. A latticework of shelves filled another entire wall from floor to ceiling. Stacks of scrolls filled each and every compartment. A desk, larger than the bed, filled the middle of the room. Bundles of papyrus covered the desk. More scrolls tilted drunkenly against the walls, while stacks of waxen tablets huddled in corners. A few loose sheets of papyrus lay about the floor, as if dropped while being read and then not picked up again.

Marcus sat in one of two chairs that flanked an unlit brazier. He wore a dark green tunic with embroidery of gold at the collar and cuffs. The deep hue of the tunic brought out color in his cheeks, and she thought him to look healthy and handsome.

"Come to me, Wife," Marcus said. Although he did not rise from his seat, he held out his hand to her.

She had longed for her husband's attention, and now she had it. The victory felt hollow as Valens's face came to her mind. She swallowed her reservations and walked toward Marcus, holding out her hand. She drew close enough that they might touch, and he moved his hand away, indicating the chair next to him. She sat and a hard kernel of disappointment lodged in her throat. Determined to love her husband, she pushed aside her frustration.

In her mind she listed his attributes, the reasons she might one day love him. He was, of course, wealthy. Very wealthy, in fact, and he would provide her with a life free of want. Marcus was highly respected, learned, and well traveled. Phaedra again reminded herself that as the wife of such an important man, she became important, too.

"Tell me of your adventures at the market," he said. "Did you find everything you needed?"

"I did," she said. Then she thought to add, "I thank you for your words of encouragement."

He nodded. A slight smile drew upon his lips. "You are very young and inexperienced," he said. "I will not forget that."

"I turned twenty annums two months past. That is not so young."

"At your age, twenty is quite worldly, I am sure. At my age it makes you barely old enough to be away from a nursemaid."

He laughed at his joke. Wanting to please her husband, Phaedra laughed with him, even though she thought his words unkind. They felt all the more callous because Marcus spoke the truth—Terenita had been her nursemaid until just three years ago.

A horrible thought then occurred to Phaedra. The marriage that had been forced on her was one that Marcus had been forced to make as well. He needed her father's support, not her. She was secondary, interchangeable with anyone else who might have provided him with senatorial votes. She could think of nothing to say beyond, "I had hoped to please you."

"Many men my age take younger wives," he said. "It is my belief that they somehow think to reclaim their youth through a young wife. I had no such ridiculous preconceptions when I married you."

Why was it that no one ever wanted Phaedra? Was there something wrong with her? She imagined herself to have pleasing looks. But was she actually hideous? Or maybe, hopefully, she was not the problem. Perhaps it was that all men were conniving? Acestes wanted her to bear his child so Marcus would think that it was his own, and therefore allow it to inherit. Valens wanted her, but only if the seduction were simple. And now Marcus did not want her at all. Hot tears stung her eyes and spilled over her cheeks before she could blink them away. She broke one of her mother's only rules—to mind her tears—which made Phaedra's humiliation complete.

Marcus tut-tutted and held out a cloth to Phaedra. She took it and swiped at each eye. "Dry your tears and calm your emotions. You know why I wed you. Your father has an easy way that draws men to him. He is liked and respected in the Senate and elsewhere. I need his support and wanted more assurances than just a simple exchange of coin provides."

Phaedra took a long, slow breath in and let it out again. This was the life she had been brought up to expect, but she still had hoped for something different. Something more. "I know," she said. "I just thought . . ." A single tear slid down her cheek. Marcus caught the tear-drop with the side of his finger. They both watched as it trailed around his knuckle and finally dropped onto the folds of his tunic, disappearing forever. "I do not know what I thought."

"You are young," Marcus said. "You want to be passionately in love with your husband. You want him to love you in return. I understand, truly I do."

She doubted Marcus understood anything about love, and yet she dutifully said, "Thank you."

"Our marriage will not be one of passion, but neither will I expect you to make me something I am not—a young man. This does not mean that our life together will be unsuccessful."

How could Marcus think that his words might bring her some comfort? The life he described offered nothing that she hoped for. Phaedra wanted love and romance. She wanted children and a husband who cared for and protected them all. Knowing that none of that was to be hers took her to a place beyond despair. Phaedra wanted to scream and beat upon her breast and throw something of value, just to watch it shatter. Yet that would not do. Not now. Not ever.

Sitting taller, she lifted her chin and hoped that by appearing to be aloof she would somehow care less. Phaedra found that she could not help but ask, "What kind of life will we have?"

"I will not live forever," he said. "But with a child I will live on. Not only will you bear the right kind of child, one with pure patrician blood, you are also a lovely, lovely young woman. My vigor has lessened over the years, but I will be pleased to couple with you."

At least he planned to show her the sheets of a marital bed at some point. "I appreciate your honesty."

"My two other marriages failed miserably for many reasons. Let us just say that I have learned that honesty is paramount."

"I am glad to know what you expect of me," she said.

Marcus nodded slowly. "In return for what you give me, I can show you things, Phaedra, and take you to every corner of the republic, if you like. It is not the romantic joining I sense you want, but it is a joining nonetheless."

For the first time since her father had told Phaedra that he planned for her to marry Marcus, she was pleased. No, not pleased, exactly, but relieved. Her marriage would not be what she had hoped for, but life with Marcus would be far from unbearable. He *was* kind and wise and respected. Why had she feared him as a child? He could, as he said, show her things and take her places. For a person who had lived her whole life behind the high walls of a villa, the promise of seeing all parts of the republic held an allure of its own.

As he had pointed out, Marcus would not live forever. With her father's promise to allow her to choose her next husband still so fresh in her memory, Phaedra relaxed. Her next marriage could be one of love and passion. Her current marriage would be one of friendship, freedom, and exploration.

Still, she could not completely quiet her desire for romantic love. Their marriage was new and perhaps they would come to love one another. Marcus had spoken of a child. Was now the time he intended to make one? Phaedra looked at her husband, who watched her still.

Their gazes held a moment. He cleared his throat, then picked up a scroll and began to read.

Their conversation was at an end. Phaedra stood before he had a chance to send her away. "If you have nothing else, I should let you return to your work while I complete my packing."

"We set sail tomorrow with the morning tide. You may employ anyone in the villa to make sure you are ready."

"I will," she said. "Thank you."

As she reached the door, Marcus called out to her. "Might I have one more word?"

She turned to face him. "You may have as many words as you like."

He chuckled, although she had not meant to be humorous. "I hope that by my speaking the truth you have not been injured. That was not my intent. You are a lovely young woman. While you cannot do miracles and change my age, you do make me wish I were a younger man."

"I understand," she said, and thought that she might.

Marcus returned his attention to the scroll. She waited for a moment to see if he would say something else. He did not. Without another word, Phaedra slipped from the room.

Chapter 13

Year of the consulship of Marius and Flaccus
654 years after the founding of Rome (100 BC)

Phaedra

From the galley's deck, Phaedra stood at the prow and watched as the brown urban sprawl that was Rome came into view. She had left four years before as a young bride, and in all that time had never found a compelling reason to return. Yet here she was—home.

So close to the waterfront were they that the sails had been lowered and the oarsmen belowdecks propelled them forward. Someone beat upon a drum, marking the time for each stroke. But to Phaedra it seemed as though the ship had a heartbeat of its own.

While away from Rome, Phaedra had seen much. In her first year of marriage, she had sailed around the Hellespont. Since then, she had climbed the steep stairs to the Parthenon—the seat of commerce in Athens. Over land she had traveled to the base of the Alps and watched with wonder as the jagged mountain faces turned purple with the setting sun. A galley, much like this one, had carried her to Sicily, where she stood atop lush green hills that ended in cliffs leading to white sand beaches. And her final trip, the one she had longed to take from the beginning, brought her across the Mediterranean Sea to Alexandria. Phaedra had been standing on the steps of the famed library when Marcus first coughed up blood.

At first her husband had said he wanted to return home to recover. But as she watched his strength and vitality slip away a little each day, Phaedra came to understand that Marcus wanted to die in Rome.

Their ship approached the harbor. The oarsmen ceased their strokes as the drumbeat from the bowels of the ship died away. Several ropes were thrown ashore, and they were pulled up to the docks. Phaedra ducked under the awning where Marcus dozed on the deck, a sofa having been brought aboard for his comfort.

She gave his arm a slight squeeze.

Marcus opened his eyes with a start. "Phaedra," he said. "Have we arrived in Rome?"

"We have." She helped Marcus to stand. The boat shuddered underfoot as it was moored.

"Smell that?" Marcus breathed in and began to wheeze. "No wonder I cough blood. The stink of the city is enough to burn anyone's lungs."

Phaedra smiled and thanked the gods that her husband retained a sense of humor about his weakening body. They walked down the plank arm in arm, their journey complete.

Two litters awaited them at the docks, along with several carts for their belongings. Phaedra helped Marcus recline in the cushioned litter and tried to ignore his raspy breathing, his too-thin arms, and the dried blood that clung to the corner of his mouth.

She settled herself among the cushions of the second litter and looked at the city as it passed. She tried to see the Rome of her youth among the never-ending building projects sponsored by the Senate. The lines between old and new were so hazy that she barely recognized her childhood home.

New statues stood at a familiar intersection, and they passed a large fountain that she did not recall at all. Scaffolding climbed up the outside of a building that was being enlarged. Men wheeled carts and carried loads on their shoulders—it was a hive of busyness. The streets seemed noisier and more crowded than she remembered. Or perhaps they had always been thus, and she was now seeing them in juxtaposition to the wide lanes of Pompeii.

They made their way through the Capitoline Market, hectic with late-morning shoppers. Through the sheer curtains of her litter, Phaedra studied each face that passed. She strained to see if she could find the stall of a particular silk merchant. Or the broad shoulders and wavy brown hair of a gladiator she had known long ago and for an all-too-brief moment.

Valens. He had been with her each night as she looked at the sky and found Polaris. He visited her in dreams, and she saw him in the men she passed on the street. Excited and nervous, she would be positive that *this* time she saw him. But as the man came close, Phaedra would realize that it was not Valens and, once again, her mind had tricked her.

The litter stopped on the street in front of the villa. "Senator Scaeva waits for you in the dining room," the housekeeper, Jovita, said to Phaedra. Two male slaves helped Marcus alight from the litter.

"Call for a physician," said Phaedra. She bit her lip, not knowing which doctor to request. She had been gone so long, far too long.

"Your father has seen to it already, my lady."

Phaedra was unsure if she should be relieved or offended that her father had taken charge in such a way. She was no longer his to order about, nor was it his place to make decisions for her. Yet, if it helped Marcus heal, then she would allow his interference this once. "Make sure to see to all the comforts of the dominus," she said to Jovita before leaving to find her father.

The villa had four dining rooms, although Phaedra had not lived in the house long enough to commit even a single room to her memory. By Fortune's grace alone, she stumbled upon the smallest triclinium, reserved for the family. Her father reclined on a sofa, a plate of stewed meat resting on his ample stomach.

Phaedra's father had been a guest at the Pompeian villa on several occasions. Why was it that she was now nervous to see him? Was it because Marcus was so gravely ill? Or rather, because in Pompeii, Phaedra was the mistress of her villa and a grown woman, but here in Rome, and especially with her father, she felt like a child again.

"How fares your husband?"

Phaedra wiped her damp palms on the sides of her gown and sat. A whirl of dust rose up around her. Her eyes itched and watered. "He is unwell."

"It is hard to imagine the Senate without him," said her father. "He will be sorely missed."

Had her father nothing else to say? Marcus had been a close friend and mentor. Did his inevitable passing not warrant more emotions?

"He will be sorely missed by more than the Senate," she said.

Nodding, her father chewed another piece of meat. "I wish you two had made a child," he said around his food.

Phaedra reached for a slice of orange from a tray of fruit sitting on a table next to her father. "There are many things that I wish were different. A child is just one."

"Has he named an heir?" her father asked.

She shook her head. "He wanted to return to Rome first."

The housekeeper stood at the door. "Pardon, the dominus wishes to see you both."

Phaedra held her father's arm and followed the housekeeper to Marcus's chamber. Her husband lay on a bed surrounded by pillows. His once full mane of hair was now sparse, and his skin had faded to the color of a dove's wing. Two short, dark men stood nearby. They spoke in Greek, and although Phaedra understood little of what they said, she surmised that these were the doctors.

Marcus held up his hand. "My wife. My friend. Come to me, both of you."

Phaedra sat on the edge of the bed and held Marcus's frail hand in hers.

Her father leaned in and spoke overly loudly. "We are here. Whatever you need, just ask."

"I need to name an heir," Marcus said, his voice hoarse. Speaking the few words consumed his energy. He sank deeper into the pillows and breathed his raspy, rattling breath.

Phaedra's father reached around her and grasped Marcus's other hand. "We will honor any and all of your wishes."

"You have been a good friend, Scaeva," Marcus said. He tried to smile, and his purple gums showed. "You gave me one of my greatest treasures—your daughter."

A treasure? His treasure? Phaedra's throat constricted and her chest tightened. Marcus was dying. She had known this for more than a week. But until now, she had been so focused upon their return to Rome that she had never thought of him as dead. Gone.

"You do me a great honor," her father said.

"I regret we never had children, Phaedra. Out of all my wives, you would have made the best mother."

"I love you," she said.

"And I love you. Are the physicians close?" Marcus asked. "Bring them close so they may bear witness to what I say. I leave my money and lands to a member of my family. My nephew, Acestes, proved himself a leader in Sicily, and now he serves Rome well in Africa."

"Acestes? Is he your heir?" asked Phaedra's father.

"I have no one else," said Marcus.

Phaedra could feel the tension emanating from her father.

"But surely I have been more your son than father-in-law!"

How could her father make such a demand of Marcus on his deathbed? She could not allow her father to push her ill husband in this way.

"Not now," she hissed.

"If not now, then when?"

She turned to glare at her father, shocked to find his features as guileless as a baby's. Was he so focused on gaining Marcus's fortune that he did not understand how wrong his actions were? "Father, do you think of no one other than yourself?"

"Please do not quarrel now," said Marcus. "I need to sleep. When I wake, we can discuss my choice of heir. Of course, if the law allowed, I would leave my fortune to you, Phaedra."

"You could still leave your fortune to her," said her father, "by leaving it to me."

Marcus answered by closing his eyes.

There was much Phaedra wanted to say to her father, yet for her husband and his well-being, she would keep her peace. Still, her face burned with shame at her father's blatant opportunism. "Let him rest. I find your single-mindedness disturbing. This is my husband, your friend, who is dying." She mouthed the last word, afraid that speaking it out loud would bring about the inevitable all the faster.

"You do not know how dire things have become." Her father's eyes were moist, with a pleading look.

Although he slept, Phaedra patted Marcus's hand before leading her father to the far side of the room where they might speak without disturbing her husband's rest. "Dire how?"

"My accounts are near empty."

"Four years ago, on my wedding day, Marcus gave you one million sesterces, a dowry in reverse. Four years?" She paced, trying to expel the anger, which filled her with its venom. "You squandered a fortune, Father. How can that be? My husband made you a very rich man."

"I wish you understood all the pressure upon me. There are so many expenses. Food, clothes"—he held up a fold of his tunic. The woven cloth shimmered and flowed with liquidlike movement. Phaedra reckoned it cost several thousand denarii, more than a pleb might ever see during his life.

"Marcus would be a fool to name you his heir. You would spend all his money in a decade, maybe less."

"Let us not quarrel. What has been done has been done. Yet, you need to ask yourself this question: When Marcus dies, who will care for *you*?"

She knew the answer. Paterfamilias dictated that Phaedra once again became her father's property. If her father did not have coin enough for his own care and well-being, he would never have enough to provide for her. So that was his game. She was unable to look her father in the eye.

"I see that you understand the predicament."

A chill settled on Phaedra, and she folded her arms over her chest to conserve any warmth.

"Convince him to change his mind," her father said.

"Pardon," said one of the Greek doctors. Both Phaedra and her father turned to look. "My sympathies," the physician said. "He is gone."

Marcus lay on the bed in the same posture they had left him. He no longer breathed. Since he had died in his sleep, she did not need to close his eyes. Still, she slipped her fingers over his lids and placed a final kiss on his lips. "Marcus," she called to his spirit. "Marcus. Marcus. Marcus." How many times did she need to say his name before his soul found the portal to the River Styx? "Marcus," she said once more.

Her father nodded and she stopped.

The doctors placed Marcus's body on the ground. They washed him in water mixed with special oils. Afterward they redressed him, and Phaedra placed a single silver denarius on his lips. She overpaid Charon, the ferryman, in hopes that through her generosity Marcus might be treated well during the ferry ride that would end in the paradise of Elysium.

Phaedra looked around the room. Everything spoke of her husband. Shelves filled with wax tablets and scrolls lined one wall. A desk, cluttered with sheets of papyrus, sat near the door to the garden. Dark leather chairs flanked a tarnished brazier in the middle of the floor.

She imagined Marcus in this very room, working until late at night. Phaedra turned to the doctors. "Please send word to General Acestes that his uncle has passed and named him as heir."

Then she addressed her father. "We need to make arrangements for the funeral procession."

Her father held up one finger to the physicians and pulled Phaedra to the door leading to the gardens. "You cannot give up this money. You heard Marcus—he changed his mind."

Her husband had said nothing of the sort. Her father understood the truth as well as she did, and so did the doctors who had witnessed the whole scene. Yet he grabbed for a fortune that did not belong to him.

She refused to give in to her father's schemes. Shaking her head, Phaedra said, "His mind was set. We all four heard it."

Her father glanced at the Greeks and leaned in closer. She knew what he was thinking.

"Do not even suggest it," she said before he spoke a word. "I will not steal from my late husband, nor will I bribe or hurt innocent men to hide that sin."

Senator Scaeva stood taller. "I was not going to suggest anything of the kind. I will go to Marcus's tablinum and write a missive to General Acestes personally. I will also have the announcement read in the forum. That will be the easiest way to notify everyone."

His easy acceptance of her defiance puzzled Phaedra. Yet she dutifully kissed her father's full cheek, and he left the room. The physicians placed Marcus on a sheet in order to carry the body to the atrium. With his feet pointed toward the door, he would remain in the house for the full eight days of mourning. On the eighth day a funeral procession would wind through the streets and end with his cremation outside of the city.

And then what?

Then he would be gone. Truly gone. The simple fact left Phaedra heavy and gritty, as if she were not flesh and blood but a dried skin filled with sand. She wandered to the garden. Like a damp and dirty blanket, a low gray sky lay over Rome. Fine mist hung suspended in the air and trapped a chill. She took the stolla from her head and wrapped it over her shoulders.

Her husband was dead. The notion left her numb. At the edge of her emotions, Phaedra sensed an unending sadness. Since she had become his wife, Marcus had served as her protector, her benefactor, and her teacher. True, their union had never been a perfect romantic joining. But life with Marcus had enabled Phaedra to change from a naive girl to a composed and competent woman. She wondered whom she would become without him.

Chapter 14

Valens

Valens sat in a tavern near the Senate building. People wrapped in cloaks against the light drizzle hurried past the open window. Women and girls held baskets and pots under their arms, and men stored scrolls in the folds of their clothing. A low fire hissed and sizzled in a brazier in the middle of the room and gave off more smoke than heat. Since winning his freedom two years past, Valens had spent many days enjoying a glass of wine and a meal in a tavern with people who still remembered his name and wanted to hear firsthand of his feats of heroism in the arena.

Aside from Valens, a handful of patrons sat at similar wooden tables. No one seemed to notice him. *So goes the way of fame.* He threw down a few coins and ate his last two olives, bitter from being harvested too early, and washed them down with dregs of wine. He stood and the wine rushed to his head. He held on to the table until the unsteadiness passed, then waved to the tavern keep as he opened the door to leave.

Sometimes he thought of buying a tavern of his own. Once his sister, Antonice, married, he would have more time. She was now sixteen annums. A troubled time in anyone's life, made all the worse because it was she who had discovered their mother's mutilated body in the apartment the two women shared.

After their mother died, Valens had asked for his freedom. His sister was young and needed the kind of guidance only a family member could provide. Paullus was a reasonable man, a good man, and had agreed to let Valens retire provided that he defeated his personal trainee, Baro, in the arena. It had been billed as a battle between the titans, and was with certainty Valens's most famous fight. Even now, Valens suspected that Baro had let him win the match.

The last time Valens visited the arena, he had sat in the stands and watched as his mother's murderer, and her former lover, had died *ad beastium*, torn apart by an African lion. He still blamed himself for not having taken better care of his mother. The apartment and money upon which to live was not enough. He should have known the men with whom she had spent her time. Perhaps if he had, he would have known that this man flew into deadly rages. At least Antonice had not been home at the time, lest she had become a victim as well.

Once outside, Valens wrapped his cloak closer to his body. The Senate crier came from the white-pillared chamber and began to climb to the rostra, a wooden podium set outside for public announcements. The crier slipped on the rungs, slick with water, and cursed before reaching the dais and calling for all to attend him. Valens cared little for politics, but with nothing else to do on this dreary day, he joined the small crowd and listened.

"Hear me well," the man said. His deep, clear voice carried to all parts of the forum. "The Fates have cut the string that tethered the esteemed senator Marcus Rullus Servilia to this life. He arrived in Rome this morning after completing an official senatorial visit to Alexandria in Egypt. He died not long after his arrival from a prolonged illness. The funeral procession will begin at his house on the eighth day and end outside the sacred walls of the city. The Senate declares all of Rome to be in mourning."

Phaedra's husband. Dead.

Over the years he had tried to forget her, but could not. Or was it as he feared on lonely and dark nights as he stared into the heavens at Polaris—that he simply did not want to forget Phaedra? In the garden, on the night of her wedding, she had spoken *to* him. Not at him, or about him, as if he was not even in the room at all. For Phaedra, Valens had been a man, not a lowly slave or a famous gladiator. After he had met her, no other woman could ever rise to the measure she set.

The plebs of Rome loved to talk about the aristocracy. Although Phaedra was never the focus of a scandal, Valens had heard her name mentioned just the same. Having left Rome after her wedding, she never returned, although Valens was fairly certain that her husband had come back when the Senate held sessions.

Now Phaedra was in Rome. She had to be. Valens could not imagine the loyal bride he had wanted to kiss in the garden on her wedding night becoming the kind of woman who sent her ailing husband on a voyage from Egypt to Rome without her care.

The senatorial crier ambled down the steep wooden steps of the rostra and made for the wide marble ones of the Senate chamber. Valens intercepted the man. "Halt," he said.

The crier stopped and looked at Valens.

"I fought at the wedding of Marcus Rullus Servilia," he said, not completely sure why it was important for him to share this news with anyone, and most especially the Senate crier.

"Ah, Valens Secundus. I attended that wedding. At the time we did not realize we were watching the two titans of Rome, Valens and Baro. I did not recognize you among the crowd just now. Apologies."

"Most people imagine gladiators in nothing other than armor. I wore it for a while after retiring, but it chafed my arms."

The crier stared at him for a moment and then began to laugh with a deep, clear voice. A flock of birds took flight, screaming as they rose into the dull gray sky. "Armor chafed his arms. That *is* very funny."

"What do you know of Senator Rullus and his death?"

"Nothing more than what I just announced. He and his wife arrived in Rome earlier today, and the senator died within an hour of returning to his villa. He must have been holding on to life until he reached home."

Phaedra was back.

The drizzle turned to rain, and both Valens and the crier shielded their heads with their hands. "Gratitude for the news," Valens said.

"Armor chafes, ha," the crier said as he climbed the Senate stairs.

Rain came down in sheets, and soon Valens found it nearly impossible to see the buildings at the other side of the forum. He returned to the tavern and settled at the same table he had left a few moments before. The barkeep glanced at him as he entered. Valens held up one finger, and a serving girl delivered a cup full of wine. None of the other patrons bothered to look up. His anonymity pleased him this time.

He wanted a moment alone to think.

Chapter 15

Phaedra

For two days Phaedra remained in her rooms and saw no one except for Terenita. She slept much, ate little, and allowed time to pass in a fog. On the third day, she woke before the dawn and ate a full meal. Somehow the continual rest had not only renewed her tired body but also filled the empty place in her heart and eased the heavy burden of grief.

After eating she pushed away her cleared plate and said to no one in particular, "Now I must wash." Terenita stepped forward and clapped her hands as a signal that the domina needed a bath. Phaedra led the way through the warren of hallways until she found the baths.

Like all Roman baths, there were three pools—cold, warm, and hot. Scant light came in through the high and narrow windows, so tapers burned in their holders along the brightly painted wall. At the far end of the room, steam hovered over the surface of the hottest pool. Without waiting to be massaged, scraped, or rinsed, Phaedra disrobed and submerged into the final pool up to her neck. Pinpricks of heat stung the soles of her feet and her palms. She held her breath and waited for the discomfort to subside. Closing her eyes, she lay back in the water and floated just beneath the surface. The cool air caressed the peaks of her body like a lover's kiss, and the face of Valens came to mind.

To think of another before her eight days of mourning ended shamed Phaedra and her husband's memory. She cleared her mind of any thoughts, especially those that included lips on her flesh.

Marcus had taken the greatest care of her. Their match had not been of a passionate nature, nor had it taken on the ease of an intimate friendship. But for years it had been her life, and it had been far from unpleasant.

"Send a message to Fortunada inviting her here for the midday meal." Amplified by the water, Phaedra's words sounded too loud. She righted herself and sat on a stone ledge of the pool. Her face felt too hot, and it seemed as though she continued to float. She stood, and a moment later her senses returned entirely.

"Of course, my lady," said Terenita. "I will see to everything."

Five days of official mourning still remained. Yet it could hardly be considered disrespectful to meet with her dearest friend, especially if she stayed safely hidden behind the walls of her villa. Besides, Marcus, his death and his life, were what she wanted—no, needed—to speak of.

After her bath, Phaedra had her hair arranged with silver combs and then dressed in a gown of violet. Both seemed appropriately somber.

A small white sun hung high in a cloudless sky of soft blue. The air, unseasonably warm, was pleasant enough that Phaedra decided they should eat in the garden. A table, inlaid with golden wood depicting a wild cat of some sort, was brought out to a patio near the small dining room. Two sofas followed, one orange and the other green. The colors, so bright and vibrant, irritated her. Marcus was dead and everything should be dour. Or at the very least, they should match.

"Wait," Phaedra said to the slaves as they prepared to leave. "Take these away and bring back two sofas that are the same color."

"The housekeeper said to use these," one of the slaves said. "There are no matching sofas, and these are in the best repair."

Phaedra placed her hand on the back of the green sofa. It had been so like Marcus to not care at all about the color of the sofa upon which he sat, or if the seams had come loose or the fabric was ripped or had faded. "I suppose these will have to do," she said, dismissing the slave.

Phaedra had not seen her friend since her wedding night. Over the years they had written to one another, but letters often took weeks if not months to reach their destination. By then, the news they carried was old.

Phaedra worried that their friendship was not strong enough to survive a prolonged separation. Yet the four years mattered not at all—upon Fortunada's arrival, the flame of lifelong friendship sprang to life immediately. After embracing and crying tears of joy, both reclined on a sofa as a slave poured weak wine into goblets.

"You look dreadful," said Fortunada.

Phaedra felt her shoulders tense at her friend's too-honest assessment. "I feel much better than I have since returning to Rome."

Fortunada picked up her goblet and took a sip. "How do you feel, then?"

"Dreadful," said Phaedra, and they both laughed.

A plate of roasted pine nuts sat on the table between them. Phaedra pushed one from the edge to the center before picking it up and chewing slowly. She swallowed. "I miss him."

"Did you ever love him?"

Phaedra lifted one shoulder and let it drop. "How can one help but love the person with whom they live, so long as that person is kind?"

Fortunada reached across the table and grasped Phaedra's hand. "Then I grieve with you. It is a terrible thing to lose one's husband, is it not?"

"It is."

"Has your father spoken to you of another marriage?"

"On my wedding day my father promised that if I outlived Marcus, then I could choose my next husband," Phaedra said. A thrill of excitement coursed through her veins and sped up the beating of her heart. She was now a woman who could choose her own path in life, or at least her next spouse.

"I congratulate you on your forethought. That promise may very well save you from a worse marriage than the one you just got out of."

Although Phaedra understood what her friend implied, she still felt the need to defend Marcus. "My marriage was not bad."

"But the next one could be worse," Fortunada said, her tone biting.

"True." She studied her friend. The lines around Fortunada's light eyes spoke of sadness that had hardened into something deeper—anger, or bitterness, maybe. Phaedra knew that her friend's life had been less than perfect while she was away from Rome.

Fortunada's husband, a wealthy man from the knighted equestrian class, had asked for a divorce after six years of marriage and the birth of two children. He then quickly remarried another woman, a patrician with ample coin of her own.

All of this had been shared in letters, and Phaedra had many times offered her heartfelt condolences. Yet this was the first time they had met face-to-face. So focused had she been on her own sorrows that until that moment Phaedra had not thought to ask about Fortunada's well-being. "I grieve with you, as well," she said quickly, hoping it was enough to right the wrong.

Fortunada waved away the concern with a flick of her wrist. "After three years there is nothing to grieve. After my husband cast me aside, I returned to my parents' home. I have my children with me. My father has never taken the family's seat in the Senate, and therefore has no need for allies bound by marriage. I am, as you are, a woman with choices."

"Are you happy?" Phaedra asked.

Fortunada touched the goblet and ran her finger up and down the stem. "I am content," she said finally. "As of yet I have no hope for the future, but I have learned to enjoy today. My attitude about life has greatly improved over the last year. One day I will be happy."

She breathed a sigh of relief. Her friend was not entirely a pessimist and would again bless the sun for its warmth and not curse it for the burn. Phaedra lifted her own goblet. "Then let me propose a toast. We are a rare breed, you and I. Women with the ability to set our own paths."

Fortunada lifted her goblet and touched rim to rim. "To us."

Phaedra drank, and although she still felt sorrow for having lost Marcus, it no longer felt bottomless. She took another sip and thrilled to the realization that she had her whole life to live, and it would be one of her own making.

Chapter 16

The eighth and final day of mourning
for Senator Marcus Rullus Servilia

Phaedra

Phaedra waited in the atrium as a handful of people arrived to walk Marcus's body to the cemetery. Large drops of rain fell through the opening in the ceiling and splashed into the pool below. The water level crept higher and higher. She worried that the pool might overflow before the body was removed. Dead things and disease came calling together, and she feared what the water might carry throughout the villa.

The designator, the man hired to organize the funeral, stood at the front of the procession and organized the rest of those gathered. Next in line were the actors who wore waxen masks of Marcus's notable ancestors. Then came the musicians and after them the praeficae, or mourning women. All of them wore black. Since Marcus had no children and his named heir, Acestes, had not yet returned to Rome, Phaedra's father took the next place in line reserved for a male heir. Like the son of the deceased, Senator Scaeva draped a dark cloth over his head.

After the hired mourners and the heir, any freed slaves would have come next. Marcus had died with the single directive to make Acestes his heir, so no slaves joined the procession. Next were the influential men of the city, the current consul, Flaccus, and a few other senators Phaedra did not know. After them, a small group of wealthy men gathered, made up of the sons of patrician households. Phaedra lined up with a few other women. As his wife, not the mother of his child, she had no real place in his funeral. She did insist that Terenita join her. Fortunada, a dear and true friend, also came to lend support.

Such a small group for such an important man.

Thunder rumbled and lightning split the sky in two. The rain fell harder, heavier. If it was not for the weather, she imagined that hundreds, if not thousands, of people would now be lining the streets to show their final respects to Marcus. Her father could stop the procession from taking place today, she knew. But what of the body and the diseases it might attract? No. Better to deal with the cremation now. Eight days was long enough.

The doors to the villa opened, and everyone filed out in their assigned order. Marcus's body, now wrapped in black cloth, lay upon an open litter. Four hired mourners held on to poles at the corners. As Phaedra passed she saw Marcus's face through the gauze. The denarius she had placed on his mouth had been wedged tightly between his lips. *Good. The ferryman's fee will not get lost.*

Phaedra and Fortunada stood under a square parasol held by Terenita. They took their place near the end of the woefully short line. The bright red silk, meant only to block the harshest rays of the sun, soon leaked and provided no protection from the rain. Phaedra gripped Fortunada's arm all the tighter as they walked, sliding precariously over the wet paving stones. No one stood on the streets waiting for Marcus Rullus Servilia to pass. No one called out blessings on him or his family. The musicians played. Their wailing instruments sounded much too loud for the empty streets. The mourning women wept. Holding up a waxen imprint of Marcus, the designator lauded Phaedra's late husband and his considerable life accomplishments.

Befitting a man of Marcus's importance, the funeral procession made its way through the forum. Her father climbed the rostra and waited. Slaves carried the couch with Marcus's body up to the platform.

"The family of Marcus Rullus Servilia," said her father, "is descended from kings by his mother, and on his father's side from the immortal gods all the way to Saturn. His stock has the sanctity of royalty, and at the same time the supreme power that the gods hold over men. He served the republic of Rome as a soldier, a magistrate, and as one of the most respected members of the Senate. To the gods of the netherworld, we ask that you spread your favors on this, a great man."

Marcus and his sofa were then taken from the rostra, and Phaedra's father followed. The procession wound through the deserted streets and out of the city gates.

Rivulets of rain flowed from the upper cliffs of the ceremonial grounds used for cremations and burials. Thin creeks of brown water ran across the dirt, making shallow pools and murky puddles. Mud clung to the bottom of Phaedra's shoes and stained the hem of her dress. The crowd gathered around a stack of heavy limbs arranged in a mound. Someone had thought to throw a large sheet of canvas over the wood to keep it dry. The designator removed the sheet and threw oil on the wood. The body was placed atop the unlit pyre. It must burn wholly and quickly or else his soul might be trapped forever on the earthly plane. A torch was thrown as the women hired to lament screamed and clawed at their faces.

Hungry red flames spit, threw sparks, and licked at the black shroud. The flesh burned. Phaedra held her stolla over her nose and mouth to mask the stench of rotted meat being cooked. Her stomach threatened to revolt, and her eyes watered. Phaedra knew that she must remain emotionless and composed but found that she could not. She cried tears borne of grief, frustration, and the fear of her uncertain future. She also cried for the loss of her husband and her companion. She bit the inside of her lip. The pain quelled her urge to cry.

The wood charred, turning black and then gray with white edges. The pall disintegrated and the body with it. At the outer ring of the gathered mourners, a rider approached on a great black stallion. The man sat tall and proud. A crimson cape hung from the shoulders of a bronze-and-leather breastplate. The rain wet his golden hair until it fit his skull like a helmet, and his gray eyes matched the stormy clouds. The group separated as the man and his horse approached. The nose, the eyes, and the angles of the chin all looked so familiar. The gods preserve her—it was Marcus, reincarnated, but not as a babe. He had returned to the world of the living as a grown man.

He grew near and nodded at Phaedra as he passed. Her legs trembled and she clung to Fortunada's arm for support. Phaedra's father stepped forward and the man stopped. It was then that she saw the differences between this man and her late husband, subtle but present. The tilt of the man's head was not right. The branding of a Roman legionnaire stood out on his forearm. SPQR—Senate and People of Rome.

"Greetings," her father said. "We grieve with you, General."

Acestes had returned.

Chapter 17

Valens

Valens stood under a dripping tree and watched the funeral procession as it entered the cemetery. He found Phaedra at once and his mouth went dry. She was beautiful still. Gone was the long angular shape of youth, in its place the curves that only a woman could possess. Her dark hair made her creamy skin look more delicate—as if she had been wrought by the hands of the gods and created just so Valens would have something worth protecting.

She held on to the arm of a blonde woman. Both wore unadorned dark tunics of deep blue. Phaedra stood at the back of the group, a black stolla over her head, and watched as the fire consumed the shroud and the body within. The pyre burned high, despite the wet—a sure sign that Marcus had already ventured across the River Styx.

Phaedra did not cry. Just like a proud patrician to be without emotion. He almost believed her to be insensitive to her husband's passing, but every now and then she lifted her hand to her eye and wiped away a single tear.

Not a day during the last four years had passed without Valens imagining this moment. Phaedra, free of marital claims, being reunited with Valens, now a free man. He had wanted to learn to read and write. She had wanted to choose her own husband. Valens had gotten his wish. Had Phaedra gotten hers?

Valens needed to speak to her again and find out. Perhaps he could ask a wealthy enthusiast of the gladiatorial games to make an introduction. He began to think of those he knew who might also know Phaedra, but stopped as a man on horseback approached.

The man wore the long red cloak and leather breastplate of a legionnaire officer. Valens guessed that the man was a relative arriving in the last moments of the funeral. Then he remembered him from the night of Phaedra's wedding; he was the man who had found them in the garden just seconds after Phaedra had stepped away from their embrace. The man had treated her with great propriety, resting his hand protectively on her elbow.

After the man passed, Valens slipped away. He walked through the gates of the city as the rain slowed and then stopped. The sun peeked from behind voluminous white clouds. The air warmed, and steam rose from the ground. By the time Valens reached his home on the Aventine Hill, his rain-wet tunic had dried and was once again soaked, this time with sweat.

There were many grand homes in Rome, sprawling villas with private baths and gardens where exotic animals wandered free. He had seen such homes while fighting at parties behind their high walls. Then there were the nights that husbands were away and the woman of the house paid him for an entirely different service.

Yes, the Palatine and Aventine hills were filled with opulent and beautiful houses, the likes of which most people living in the Suburra never imagined. While Valens's own home was not among the residential showplaces of the city, it brought him enormous pride.

Its single story surrounded a formal garden. All the rooms had doors that led to that garden; he woke each morning to birdsong and the scent of flowers in bloom. He liked the gentleness of his new life, although he would never discuss in the company of men a liking for birdsong or fragrant flowers.

The front door opened to a proper atrium tiled in gold and red. A rectangular gap had been cut into its ceiling. A shallow pool, meant to catch rainwater for use in the kitchens, sat underneath. Opposite the front door was the tablinum, the room where Valens conducted his business. Twin hallways branched off from the atrium. Valens lived in a suite of three rooms on the left side of the house, which also held the dining room. Antonice had a similar suite on the right side of the villa, closer to the kitchen.

Modest by some standards and grand by others, but it was all paid for by Valens alone. Enough coin remained to keep a housekeeper *and* a few other servants. He had hired a former trainer to manage affairs as his steward.

"Greetings, dominus," said his housekeeper, Leto, as Valens walked into his house.

"Greetings."

Valens scooped a handful of water from the pool and washed the back of his neck.

"Have you a moment?" she asked.

Whenever he saw the housekeeper, he thought of a happy ball. Leto, round of hip and face, possessed an easy laugh and an easier smile. A freewoman born in an Italian province, she had moved to Rome with her husband, who had had the bad fortune to die shortly after. Valens had hired her in the hopes that her jovial manner might ease some of Antonice's suffering. It had worked at first, but now Antonice preferred the company of a spoiled neighbor, Damian, to that of anyone else. His sister cried or screamed whenever Valens suggested she find other friends.

"Such is the way with girls and love," Leto had said many times before.

Valens knew little of such matters, yet nodded as if he did.

On this day, he guessed that Leto wanted to discuss his sister's behavior yet again. "You may have more than a moment, if you need," he said.

"It is Antonice."

Valens stood and shook water from his hands. "I assumed as much."

"I found this in her room." The housekeeper held out a long pearl necklace that Valens had never seen before.

"You asked her about it?"

"I did. At first she said she bought it with her own coin. Then she said you gave her the money. Later she said it was a gift."

"Not a gift from me."

"I did not think so."

"From Damian?"

"That was my thought."

"Where is she now?" Valens asked.

"I sent her to her room, but she cursed me for being a fool and left."

"How long ago?"

"Less than an hour. I sent the steward to look for her. He has not returned, either."

Valens had hoped to change from his damp and stained tunic, but he needed to find his sister first. He knew to look in the most obvious place—Damian's home.

Lucky for Valens, Damian lived close by, higher up on the Aventine Hill. During his career as a gladiator, Valens had fought all over the Italian peninsula. In that time he came to recognize that as the republic expanded its borders, it arranged cities on a grid. The forum and government buildings were placed in the center with a large marketplace nearby. Streets ran straight with perpendicular intersections. Why, then, did the city of Rome, the shining jewel of the known world, have so many wandering streets that twisted and turned, coming back on one another, while others ended at a wall? After all these years, Rome still confounded him, although he would never admit to being lost or stop to ask for directions.

Most patricians lived on the Palatine Hill, but Damian's family resided on the Aventine in a villa modest by aristocratic standards. No guards stood outside the door, waiting to turn away unwanted visitors or announce guests. Valens struck the front door with the side of his fist. An old man with a crooked back answered. "I came for my sister, Antonice," said Valens. "Retrieve her for me."

The old man stepped aside, allowing Valens to enter the atrium.

"Wait here for Lady Fortunada," said the old man before shuffling away.

Valens did not like being left in the atrium when proper manners demanded that he be shown to either a dining room or tablinum. Nor did he wish to see the lady of the house when the master held the power.

A moment passed before a slender blonde woman entered the atrium. She was too young to be Damian's mother, Valens was certain. And something about her looked familiar. She wore a pale silk tunic cinched under her breasts with a golden belt. Wet hair flowed over her shoulders. Valens was too focused on finding his sister to wonder where he might have met her before.

"Greetings," the woman said. "I assume you are Valens Secundus. I am Fortunada, sister to Damian. My mother tells me that your sister, Antonice, is a favorite of my brother."

"So I understand." At least Damian's mother and sister knew of Antonice and her frequent visits. The finer points of decorum still evaded Valens. But even he knew that young people needed supervision and that a mother served as the best kind of chaperone.

"The steward said you wished to see your sister. I am sorry," said Fortunada, "but she is not here."

"I will speak to your brother, then."

"He is not here, either."

"Where is he?"

"I am the sole member of my family in the villa at the moment and just returned from a funeral procession."

Yes. That was where he had seen Fortunada. She was Phaedra's companion. "Marcus Rullus Servilia," he said. He had not meant to speak aloud.

"You knew Marcus?"

Valens shrugged. "I fought at his wedding."

"Ah, that is right. Phaedra, the bride, or now the widow, is a dear friend of mine."

"How is your friend?"

"Phaedra? Saddened, I am sure. Do you know her?"

"I spoke to her at the wedding," he said. "She seemed a kind person."

"I shall tell her that you asked after her well-being."

A slave with a jug entered the atrium and filled it with water from the pool. She slipped away as quietly as she had come. In that moment, Valens thought of asking Fortunada to reintroduce him to Phaedra. Still, that favor would have to wait. Right now, he wanted to find his sister.

"Have you any idea where Damian might be? I am certain my sister is with him."

"Father arranged for him to work with the army's quartermaster assigned in Rome. He might be there."

Someone knocked on the door. Valens stepped aside as Fortunada opened a wooden slit and peered into the street. "Mystery solved," she said as she worked the bolt loose.

Damian entered. In one arm he held a basket. The other one was wrapped around Antonice's waist. Damian and Antonice were laughing, not bothering to look at anyone beyond each other. She turned to find Valens standing in Damian's home, and all her merriment ceased.

Antonice clenched her teeth. "What are you doing here?"

Valens flinched at her cutting tone and wondered where his sweet sister had gone. "I could ask you the same thing."

"Damian took me shopping."

"More jewelry?"

"Yes," said Antonice.

"Give it back."

"I will not," Antonice said, "and you cannot make me."

"That is where you are wrong." Valens jerked the basket away.

"That is not yours." Damian's eyes flashed with anger as he spoke.

Valens stared a minute before the youth lowered his gaze and shuffled backward a pace or two. In the basket Valens found a length of fine linen wrapped around a golden chain of coins. How much did either cost? More than any gift Antonice should accept. Valens placed the items back in the basket and shoved it into Damian's gut.

"You both hear me well. There will be no more gifts. Do you understand?"

Damian nodded as his ruddy cheeks turned a deeper shade of red. The shamed look on the youth's face pleased Valens. Yet Antonice was not so easily embarrassed.

"You cannot tell me what to do. You do not control my life."

Valens grabbed her arm with a grip he knew she would take seriously. "You are wrong again. I am your brother. Without a father, the law gives me full right to decide about anything you do or do not do. We will take our leave." Still holding Antonice by the arm, Valens turned to Fortunada. "Excuse the intrusion."

Fortunada inclined her head. Without a word, she opened the door. Valens led Antonice from the villa and walked toward their house. A sullen silence hung so thick about his sister that Valens imagined he saw a mist.

"You cannot marry him. He is a patrician and you are a pleb. The laws will not allow your union," Valens said.

"We never planned to marry."

A cold sweat collected at the nape of Valens's neck. Antonice understood the law, and still she accepted expensive gifts from Damian. Far from the naive child being led astray, his sister now played the role of the tempting seductress. "I do not know if you toy with him or he with you. This relationship must end."

"You are jealous that I have someone to love and you do not."

Valens released Antonice's arm lest he squeeze and squeeze until he marked her flesh. "You cannot see him again."

Antonice lifted one shoulder with more defiance than a curse and walked off, unspoken expletives trailing in her wake. What was he to do with an incorrigible sister? Let her go? Throw her over his shoulder and carry her to the house?

How easy life would be if it followed the simple structure of gladiatorial combat—two opponents fighting with strictly enforced rules that determined a single victor.

Valens decided to follow his sister at a close distance. The Fates smiled on them both when Antonice locked herself away in her room before either had a chance to say something else to regret.

Chapter 18

Phaedra

Few mourners stayed until the body had cooled enough for the designator to shovel the ashes into a brass urn. Once the funeral was completely over, Acestes announced that he planned to hold a series of gladiatorial games lasting five days in honor of his uncle. According to Acestes, it would be the grandest spectacle in the history of Rome.

Everyone remaining agreed that Marcus deserved such a remembrance. Then each one offered final condolences and left the cemetery. Acestes remained with Phaedra and her father. Terenita stood nearby.

"I think that went well," Acestes said as he stroked his horse's neck.

"Very well indeed." Her father reached out to touch the horse's nose. It whickered and tossed its mane. Senator Scaeva withdrew his hand and stepped away, clearly frightened by the large warhorse. "Your offer to host gladiatorial games is most generous."

"My uncle deserves such a tribute."

Phaedra's father nodded. "I agree."

Acestes turned to Phaedra. "I am sure your father will not mind if I ask you to take me to my uncle's villa."

"Nothing pleases me more than to have Phaedra show you your new home," said her father. "But you must make sure she is safely seen to my home later."

"Of course." Acestes rummaged in a leather bag hanging from his saddle and pulled out a buff-colored tunic. He shook it twice and hung it from the pommel of his saddle. "I must change out of my uniform.

"I will leave you both, then." Her father limped away, his foot once again swollen and purple with gout, and from standing too long.

Phaedra's palms grew clammy. She had not seen Acestes since the day after her wedding, when he had asked her to bear his child and pass it off as Marcus's in order to secure a family inheritance. Although she had never spoken of the shameful and humiliating incident, she thought of it often. The passage of time had only served to turn Acestes into a monster of sorts in Phaedra's mind. Yet, as he stood before her now, she saw that he was simply a man. Perhaps the enmity she had harbored toward him was unjust, although it mattered little. He still made her nervous, and Phaedra did not want to be left alone with him, especially as he disrobed. She wondered at her father's suddenly conciliatory attitude toward Acestes, too.

"Father, wait," she said and stepped forward.

Her father continued to walk onward, never bothering to turn around. "There is much for you to discuss," he said with a backward wave.

Had she been so terse with her father after Marcus's death that he refused to help her now when she needed him? Did he hope that she would return to the villa meek and chastened, only to live mildly by his rules once more? Or was the reason her father had left much simpler? She wondered if her father wanted her to marry Acestes. In leaving them alone, with only Terenita as guard, perhaps he hoped that a romance would develop. A romance with Acestes? Not damned likely.

Acestes moved toward Phaedra and instinctively she tensed.

"I assume that everything is in order in my villa," he said.

It was then that the gravity of the situation hit Phaedra. Having given everything to Acestes upon his death, Marcus had left Phaedra with nothing. The villas, both in Rome and Pompeii, now belonged to Acestes, as did her dishes, her clothes, and even her cosmetics. Over the years Marcus had gifted Phaedra a small fortune in jewelry alone. She should have been shrewd and sold some of the more expensive items in the days following Marcus's death. With the profit, she and her father could have lived in relative comfort a little longer. Instead, she had spent eight days cocooned in darkened rooms as grief swirled around her like dead leaves caught in the gale. Now it was too late.

"I assumed you would write to my father and tell him when you planned to arrive. Since we had not heard from you, you were not expected," she said to Acestes. "Still, you shall find everything as your uncle left it."

"I traveled faster than any rider with a missive would have," Acestes said.

"Was your journey long and tiring?"

"Yes to both," he said while lifting his arm. "Now, be good and help me untie this."

Phaedra dutifully pushed his scarlet cloak aside to reveal a series of canvas ties at the side that held the molded leather breastplate in place. She worked knots, stiff with dirt and sweat, loose. The muscles in Acestes's back and shoulders were unmistakable under his fine woolen tunic. Heat radiated from his skin. Far from repelling Phaedra, the warmth drew her in. At the same time, she hated the betrayal of her own flesh's carnal reaction.

Acestes stepped away from his armor without warning, and Phaedra held the weight alone. She staggered to stay upright. Terenita stepped forward with arms outstretched to accept the load. Phaedra shook her head and continued to hold the armor. Her shoulders ached, yet she refused to hand over the burden and have Acestes view her as weak.

"I usually have men who travel with me," Acestes said, taking no note that she continued to hold his breastplate. "In order to make it to Rome on time for the funeral, I needed to travel faster than I could with a retinue."

"Even so, I am glad you made it in time to accept his ashes," Phaedra said, shifting to balance the armor on her hip. "Certainly, your uncle looks down from Elysium, proud that you arrived looking splendid in your uniform and humbled by how much trouble you took on his behalf."

"I hope that more people than my uncle saw my efforts. What a small and disappointing crowd. I imagine word will spread. I almost missed my chance to arrive in such grand fashion. The rains actually slowed my travel today."

Phaedra waited for a moment, unsure if she had heard Acestes correctly. She had, had she not? "You planned your arrival for this moment?"

Acestes wiped a hand across the back of his neck as he shook his head. "You are still so naive. I camped nearby last night. I actually hoped to arrive in time to meet the parade in the streets. Imagine my surprise when a swollen creek delayed me by an hour."

Yes, when they first met, Phaedra had been a naive girl, and Acestes's bluntness had intimidated her. Now she was a woman with a mind of her own. Far from being frightened of the powerful general, she was outraged. "You degrade Marcus's memory with your theatrics."

"In order to court the plebs for the vote and impress the patricians, one must always remain aware of appearances. I had little love for my uncle, you must recall." He reached out and traced her jaw with a featherlight finger. Phaedra's insides tightened and her breath caught in her throat. "Just think. If you had accepted the offer I made to provide you with a child of my loins, I never would have inherited. I thank you for being such a loyal wife."

Phaedra shoved the armor at Acestes. He flexed backward and gave off a satisfying *oomph*. "Swine," she said.

"A swine, am I?"

She shrugged.

Acestes easily lifted the breastplate onto his saddle. "I pay you the highest compliment, my dear. A loyal woman is rarely found."

"I am not your dear, and what know you of loyalty? Nothing. You know nothing."

"I disagree," Acestes said. "Since childhood I have been single-minded. I mean to be consul, and I will be. In this life, I have been nothing if not loyal to that goal."

"I see," said Phaedra. Acestes's ambitions were like a knife blade—exacting, pointed, and all the more dangerous because of it. With his lofty goals, she also saw that he was not one with whom she wanted to quarrel. She needed to endure his company only a little while longer, and then she could be rid of him forever.

Acestes pulled the short red tunic worn by all Roman legionnaires over his head and used it to wipe down his arms. Phaedra tried not to stare at his well-muscled chest or his long, strong legs. It took even more willpower to ignore the fact that he wore no loincloth. She looked away, but not quickly enough.

"I have thought of you, you know," he said.

She refused to look back at him. "You never crossed my mind. Not once."

"Liar," he said. "By the way, I am dressed now. You can speak to me instead of to the horse's ass."

"Oh, I had not noticed a difference."

Acestes laughed. "Why so skittish? It is not like you never looked upon a naked man before. Unless you have not, and if that is the case, I should have taken my time in dressing."

Phaedra knew what he implied, but in fact, during her four years of marriage, Marcus had lain with her sixteen times. Once a season he plowed Phaedra as if she were a field, both hoping that he had planted something fruitful.

"I have," she said.

"Just not often, I would wager."

"That is where you would be wrong."

"That is the second lie you told me today. Do you know how I can tell?" He did not wait for an answer. "You grip the side of your gown." He held his tunic between thumb and forefinger.

Phaedra eased her right hand from the fabric she held. "My, you have become astute," she said. "But tell me: Why do you insist on forcing your company upon me? You must realize that I do not want to become reacquainted with you."

"You are doing it again."

Phaedra turned to Terenita. "Come, let us take our leave." Both women began moving from ground that still smoldered and air that still smelled of death.

"Wait," he called after her. "You cannot walk away from me forever."

She ignored the delicious desire to yell something horrible at Acestes.

"You cannot leave me to find my way back to the villa," he said. "What will become of your possessions once the house belongs to me?"

Ah, but she could leave Acestes to enter Rome alone. Her pots of cream be damned.

"Pity if I claimed something you value, like your maid."

Phaedra stopped. Damn him. Terenita had been given to Marcus as a gift for Phaedra. By rights of the law, she *did* belong to Acestes. For her sake, for Terenita's sake, she would endure a few more hours of Acestes's company. She held her hands in front, folding them together lest her twitching fingers betray her thoughts. "Of course," she said. "We can leave as soon as you are ready."

He held the horse by the reins and came to stand next to her. "Might we start over? I have often thought about seeing you again. Each time the encounter is different, but this, well, this was never what I envisioned."

"You should not think of me," she said.

"But I did. I do still. You unnerve me, Phaedra. With you I speak foolishly. Act rashly."

"And make improper propositions," she added.

"Marcus owed me this inheritance. At the time I worried he would not honor his family. Just think about this. If you agreed to my offer, you would not be a barren widow, but the mother of a child everyone assumed to be your husband's and a very rich woman."

"I have been used by my father. He saw me wed to your uncle for enough coin to maintain his position in the Senate. Your uncle took the bargain to ensure my father's support. My father then brought the other moderate senators over to Marcus's side. Apologies, General Acestes, but when it is my choice, I refuse to be a means to someone else's end."

"Well, we all did the right thing. You refused to bear my child and pass it off as my uncle's. My uncle honored his family and named me heir."

"Yes, we all behaved very admirably." She hated Acestes, and at the same time found him inexplicably compelling. The gods save her—she must resist finding him handsome, too.

They walked toward the city and began to climb the Palatine Hill. Soon they stood at the doors to Marcus's villa. Phaedra knocked and a small flap in the wood opened. A pair of eyes peered out.

"See to the beast," she said, "and to the general's belongings."

The heavy wooden door opened. Two slaves in short brown tunics came out. One wrested the bags from the saddle, and the other led the horse away.

"Alert Jovita that I have arrived with the new dominus," Phaedra said to another slave. They entered the atrium where Marcus's body had lain for eight days, the faint scents of death remaining. Pungent herbs mixed with flowers dried and then crushed, and the underlying smell of decay.

Acestes touched her elbow and brought her back to the moment.

"He will see the housekeeper in"—she paused, not sure where to introduce a new master to his staff—"the small dining room. Bring wine and food."

"Yes, my lady," the slave said before leaving to do her bidding.

She gave Terenita a few orders about packing their belongings. Tonight Phaedra must return to her father's home, and she meant to take as many things as possible.

Acestes ran his hand over a table near the door. "I see the villa is as untidy as ever."

"Marcus never did care much for trivial comforts. Almost sanitary seemed good enough for him." She shook her head, not quite believing he was gone. She led Acestes through the garden, the shortest way to the family dining room from the front door. "I kept the Pompeii villa in order, but I never came back to Rome the entire time we were married. Marcus came to the city for matters of the Senate. A short stay here, a month there. I doubt he ever noticed the dust."

"Do you miss him?"

"Yes."

"Did you love him?"

"In my way."

"For your loss, I grieve," he said, "sincerely." Acestes kept his gaze on the white gravel of the garden path.

"I thank you for your heartfelt sorrow."

Phaedra had never told Marcus of Acestes's advances to her. She did not want to upset her husband and cause a rift between the two men, or so she told herself. In those early days she had not known how Marcus might react, and Phaedra had feared her husband would side with his nephew and accuse her of wrongdoing. Sighing, Phaedra realized that if she had told the truth about Acestes, her father might well have inherited Marcus's fortune. There was nothing to be done about it now, but the knowledge brought back some of her former animosity toward Acestes.

"What will you do now?" he asked.

"Return to my father's home."

"Not for long. I imagine that Senator Scaeva is planning another high-profit marriage for you right now."

Phaedra shook her head. "I choose my next husband."

"Have you chosen him already?"

She said nothing as they entered the smallest dining room. A tray of fruit and cheeses already awaited them on a table. Phaedra reclined on a sofa and picked up a fig. She ate without speaking.

"It is my belief," said Acestes, his voice ending the uncomfortable silence, "that the law gives your father the right to choose for you in order to keep you from making an unwise decision."

"With your uncle," she said, "I visited a people in Africa ruled by a queen. Your antiquated Roman notion of a woman's place bores me," she said. She refused to live within a box ever again.

"And yet, here we are in Rome, with Roman laws. Not in some barbaric hinterland where women have not the decency to cover their breasts as they walk among the people," Acestes said.

Phaedra looked away. There would be no fighting with this man, especially since he spoke the truth. Her father was once again her lord. She was his to do with what he saw fit. The only way to shed her father's yoke was to marry. Yet, in taking a husband, she traded one master for another.

Before Phaedra could respond, Jovita entered the dining room. With hands clasped in front of her, she kept her gaze on the floor.

"General," said Phaedra, "you recall your uncle's housekeeper, Jovita."

"Of course! You have been with Marcus longer than I have been alive. How do you fare?"

"Well, dominus," she said.

"No aches in your knees, or pains in your back?"

"No, dominus. I am still fit."

"The household staff, are they relics from my childhood, too?"

"No, dominus. Most are young, all hardworking."

"Good. I want this villa cleaned from top to bottom." He turned to Phaedra. "I have lived too long in army camps and squalid cities. I will not reside in a fine villa that resembles either." Then to the housekeeper, "You may go."

Phaedra waited until the old woman left before speaking. "Marcus is rather fond of Jovita. I doubt he would like you speaking to her as you just did."

"Was," said Acestes. "Marcus *was* many things. He is *not* anything, not anymore."

She stood. "I dislike both your attitude and tone. I must make sure Terenita has collected all my belongings so I may take my leave."

"I wish you would not walk away from me every time I open my mouth."

"I wish you would either think before you speak or, better yet, keep your mouth closed."

"Earlier I said you unnerved me, Phaedra." Acestes stood and moved until they were so close they almost touched. "The truth is I unnerve you, too."

Her skin prickled. She shuddered as she breathed in his scent of leather and horse.

"Stay," he said.

It would be so easy if she could just relax and lean into him. If she could allow this man—with his face and voice so familiar, yet his scent and touch so foreign—to love her at least for the night.

He moved closer and pressed his lips to her temple. "Stay," he said again, the word a kiss on her skin.

Yes. Her mind, her heart, her flesh, all said, *yes.* Yet Phaedra remained mute.

"Stay here," Acestes said, "tonight and always. You never need leave. Keep this as your home, with me."

One word, spoken aloud, would solve all her problems.

Yes.

Her father's overspending and increasing debts would never cloud her life again. She could stay in the villa in Rome or move back to the one in Pompeii.

"Stay here, with me, in comfort. You never need to feel the pressures that come with decisions, or the responsibilities that come with them."

Acestes was offering her a gilded life, free of worry. She pressed her palms into his warm chest. *Say it. Say yes.* She opened her mouth, ready to speak, but found that the word did not come off her tongue. Marcus's old pet peacock wandered into the room. His beautiful tail dragged across the floor. The once glossy and colorful feathers had grown tattered and dull with age. He cocked his head, looking at Phaedra. In his small black eyes she saw the light of understanding. After a moment she realized she saw a reflection and not an illumination of the mind. Would that be Phaedra's fate? To wander the grand villa until her beauty ebbed and faded, never thinking, waiting for something to be given to her?

Acestes wrapped his arms around her waist and drew her to him. She wanted his hard muscles to excite her, or his warm skin to soothe her. They did neither. Instead, she felt confined, even smothered.

His mouth came closer and Phaedra pushed away. "No," she said.

Acestes stopped, his lips almost touching hers. "No?"

She pushed him again, this time harder. He released her waist. "No. I cannot," she said.

"You cannot?"

Phaedra shook her head.

"This seems sudden to you, I am sure," he said. "While you have been married to my uncle, I have been thinking of you."

Had he really been thinking of her, or was this another tactic to get what he wanted? Her father's political connections would be important to someone so focused on becoming consul one day.

"I cannot," Phaedra said again, a little less sure this time.

Acestes pressed his lips on the top of her head. "I understand."

"Do you?"

"You still grieve. Given time, the reflexive loyalty you feel for my uncle will pass."

Phaedra heard the truth in his words, but she doubted they spoke of *her* truth. Her reluctance to accept Acestes's offer did not come from grief. Rather, it came from her need to live life as she saw fit, never fashioning it blindly after another's wishes. "I will think on what you said. Now I should go. Father will be looking for me."

"Tell me you do not leave in anger."

"I do not."

Acestes lifted her chin and studied her face. She saw more differences between the man who now stood before her and her late husband. True, both men had the same gray eyes, but Acestes's color darkened toward the pupil and had no flecks of blue.

"Tonight I will see to any army business that needs tending, and tomorrow I need to start making arrangements for the games honoring my uncle," he said. "But I would call on you after, if I might."

Phaedra hesitated. Acestes now had her home, her servants, her wealth. There was nothing more for them to discuss. Yet he wanted to see her. Phaedra found Acestes attractive. And still, she did not desire him, although she knew that she should. Her mother, she imagined, would have found Acestes a suitable husband. Perhaps Phaedra's affections would grow if given time. "You may," she said finally.

"Thank you." He let go of her chin. "You can stay here as my honored guest, you know. Remain in your own suite. There is plenty of room in this old villa."

The simplicity of the word returned to her. *Yes.* But in agreeing to Acestes's offer, she would be saying no to any other future she might have. Then again, what kind of future could she expect? Neither poverty through overspending nor jewel-encrusted captivity appealed to her.

"I must return," she said.

"I will call on you tomorrow, then."

Little good it would do to refuse Acestes. Phaedra, once again, had no power of her own.

Chapter 19

Valens

Sleep never claimed Valens. Clear childhood memories came to him of his mother. He remembered dancing through their one-room apartment, both of them laughing and singing. He also recalled being awakened in the middle of the night to the sounds of his mother's rutting in the next bed. She was desperate for the love of a man—even as a small boy he had understood that. In her last paramour, his mother thought she had found it. Yet that man had taken her life.

All of his regrets circled back to Antonice. She was a puzzle of her own. Charming when she wanted something, spiteful if denied anything. So far, the only young man she had associated with was Damian. Yet, now that Valens had ended that relationship, what would Antonice do? Next time, what kind of man would she choose?

The room was shrouded in dark as he rose from bed. Lighting a taper, he sat at a table that overlooked the garden. He unrolled a scroll of writings by the recently deceased Gaius Lucilius. It was one of his earlier works, written after the Numantine War fifty years prior. Yet, like all of Lucilius's work, it was a scathing commentary on all tiers of Roman society. Valens hoped for some inspiration of what might be best for Antonice and found only one answer: marriage.

True, Antonice could not marry Damian or any other patrician. But Valens planned to offer a generous dowry when the time came for her to marry. Enough coin would help attract reasonable suitors.

Although Valens had always imagined her wedding taking place in the future, now timing seemed of the essence.

The sun had been up less than an hour when a knock sounded at his door. "Come in," he said.

The steward entered. "Begging your pardon, dominus. You have a visitor."

Valens's eyes burned from lack of sleep. His neck ached from having sat in a chair all night. He smelled of sweat and mud and ash. Perhaps it was Damian, the patrician turd.

"Tell whomever it is that I am indisposed," he said as he rose to his feet and stretched.

"I tried," said the steward, "but he will not be dissuaded. It is General Acestes, newly returned to Rome. He waits for you in the tablinum."

Valens gave a weary sigh. The meeting with General Acestes was a nuisance and would follow a predictable pattern. Most likely Acestes had seen Valens defeat another gladiator in Padua or Capua or Carthage or Rome. The general would ask many questions about how it had felt or what he thought during a particular fight.

It happened all the time.

Valens hoped he recalled something of the specific match and could add to the conversation. Otherwise he would have to rely on some well-practiced lies he had developed over time.

I thought of how blessed I have been by the Fates to have such an opportunity to entertain the crowds of the republic and celebrate the glory of Rome.

He would never tell the truth. He would never say, *I wondered who forced this poor, dumb bastard into the arena with me. If he were any sort of man, he would be in here and not in the stands screaming for blood. For that matter, if you were a man, you would have been in the arena, too. Real men do their own killing. What is your excuse?*

Valens entered the office from the garden door. A man he assumed to be the general sat behind the table Valens used as a desk, his sandaled feet propped up on the wood. The man's bearing seemed familiar, although Valens did not remember meeting the great General Acestes. He had heard his name used many times in connection with the harsh and decisive treatment meted out during the Sicilian slave uprising a few years past.

Then Valens recalled.

On another night, in another lifetime, he had first seen this man. Yes, it was the same aristocratic bastard who had come upon him in the garden on the night of Phaedra's wedding. He was also the same arrogant man who had arrived on horseback at Marcus's funeral.

Acestes looked over his shoulder and waved a lazy hand. "I want no food or drink. Go and tell that ancient steward to hurry up and fetch your master."

For too many years Valens had lived as a slave and an instinctual, "Yes, my lord," nearly escaped his lips. Instead, he stopped the words before they tumbled out of his mouth. Without obviously moving, he clenched his fists so tight that his fingernails dug into his palms. He breathed in and out, releasing first his fists and then all other tension as well.

Acestes looked again. "Did you not hear me?"

"I heard you. Now get out of my chair."

The general swiveled around and narrowed his eyes. "Ah, it is you. It is a funny thing to see Valens Secundus and not recognize him. You were famous once."

"You are in my home and asked to see me."

Acestes turned his back to Valens. "We met once, a few years ago. I doubt you recall."

"Your uncle's wedding," said Valens. "I recall."

Glancing over his shoulder, Acestes said, "Come to the front of the desk. I shall injure my neck for trying to speak to you while you lurk behind me."

Valens thought of lifting the chair and dumping the general on his ass, but he hesitated. Until he knew why the general wanted to see him, he decided cordiality was the best stratagem. He moved as requested, and for a moment he was not quite sure whether to sit or lean on the desk.

He decided instead to adopt a stance he had used many times before fights in the arena. Legs spread, braced against the floor to engage the thigh muscles. He kept his arms at his side, but chest and back taut. The result was a figure that looked imposing, if not menacing. Until he knew what Acestes wanted, appearing a bit dangerous seemed like a good stratagem, too.

"You recall my uncle's wedding, do you?"

"I fought at a single wedding—his."

"Then you may have heard my Uncle Marcus went to his reward in Elysium not long ago."

Valens nodded. "Along with all of Rome, I grieve with you."

"A man as great as he deserves to have a grand set of fights to honor his life."

Ah, so that was what the general wanted. Valens had been asked before, many times, to return to the arena. *Just this once.* The coin offered would be ample. Yet he knew, without even hearing the amount, what his answer would be. Never would enough coins be minted or enough gold mined to entice him back to the games.

After he won his freedom, Valens had decided to live an honorable life as a tribute to all the men he had slain. Going back into the arena, for any reason, would cheapen the sacrifice made by them all.

"I plan to sponsor those games," said the general. "That is why I have come to see you."

"I see."

Acestes said nothing for a moment. He rested his elbows on the desk and clasped his hands together. "Your sister, Antonice, lives with you."

The question, too obscure to be random, chilled Valens. Gooseflesh sprang up on his arms. "What do you want?" he asked.

"I returned to Rome yesterday," the general said.

"How does that concern me and my sister?"

"There has been an upsetting development. It deals with a friend of your sister's, Damian."

Valens said nothing. What had the two of them done? His fingers trembled and he clasped his hands behind his back.

"Damian serves the republic by working with the legionary offices in Rome," said Acestes.

"The quartermaster's clerk, if I recall."

Acestes nodded. "For some time the quartermaster has noticed his coffers coming up short. Not by much, but enough. Accounting mistakes happen and a certain loss is to be expected. But this happened consistently, and only when Damian had access. Then the quartermaster heard about some jewelry Damian had purchased for your sister. I was informed of this last evening, not long after I arrived in the city."

Valens's legs began to shake. Acestes had not come to ask him to return to the arena. He had come to take Antonice into custody. Reaching for a chair, Valens sat down hard. He should have wondered where Damian had found coin for such expensive gifts. If he had been a better brother, he would have asked. In his ignorance, Valens had failed.

"You are here," said Valens as he fought to remain in control of his emotions, "to arrest my sister." Thievery was a capital offense, punishable by death during the next set of gladiatorial games. Over the course of his career, Valens had witnessed horrible executions—criminals tied to the backs of raging bulls or torn apart by starving lions. Sometimes the condemned fought one another, the victor being forced to fight battle after battle until he finally died. Valens understood that merciless sentences carried out for all to see provided public lessons in lawlessness and obedience. Still, it was incomprehensible that Antonice would become such an example.

The world might know him as Valens Secundus, Rome's champion, but he was a just a man with no other family beyond his sister. Without her, he would be alone.

As he had done before, he would save her. But how? She surely would not be spared if he stood by, frozen with indecision.

Valens needed to fight for his sister, preferring the option of pummeling the general to arguing with him. But laying hands upon one of the patrician class was also a capital offense, and it would do his sister little good if he were executed, too.

"What does my sister have to do with Damian's deed?" he asked. "How could she have known where the money came from? Is Damian to be executed in the arena, too?"

Acestes shook his head. "His father and I made an arrangement. Damian swears that the money he took was ill-gotten by the quartermaster, although the guilty usually lie to save themselves. Damian left this morning for the legions. If he survives seven years in the wilds of Germania, he will be a changed man."

"You take my sister to die, and he has a chance at life and redemption? She did not even steal anything, ill-gotten or not."

"The law is clear. Anyone involved is guilty, and Damian's father has sworn that he stole at her behest."

"Damian is young. But he is a man, not a child goaded into sneaking a sweet from the kitchens. I cannot believe that he would be so susceptible to anyone else's influence."

"I have found that beautiful women can be quite convincing."

Valens could think of nothing to say.

"I have always admired you and your career," Acestes continued. "I am sorry it had to come to this."

"If you are sorry, let her go. She is a child."

"I cannot allow your sister to go free since I already granted a pardon to Damian. I plan to run for co-consul, and people expect to see justice."

Justice? Acestes allowed Damian, the thief, to join the legions while sending Antonice, the accomplice, to the arena. Where was the justice in that?

Valens despised all patricians. Damian's lineage determined his fate, just as Antonice's family determined hers. Valens had little to offer in return for his sister's life. He had money, but not enough. Even if he gave the general his last coin, it would not be enough.

"It pains me to do this. But I am the highest-ranking officer in Rome now. This is an army matter, and as I said, I must consider how all of this looks to the voters."

Of course, courting the voters mattered more to Acestes than the life of a single person.

Acestes stood. He squeezed Valens on the shoulder and walked to the door.

"Wait." Valens moved toward the general before realizing he had even gotten up. "I will fight in your opening primus. The crowd still loves me, and they will love you for bringing me back to them."

Acestes stopped and stood for a moment with his back to Valens. "These games will last five days. The plebs would forget you by the end. One fight would not suffice. I am sorry."

Funeral games, like the one Acestes planned to sponsor, might last only a day or two. The grander, more expensive games sometimes lasted for more than a week. In that time several fights would take place each and every day. Lesser gladiators fought in the morning. Executions took place at noon. More experienced gladiators fought in the afternoon, saving the main fight, or primus, for the end of the day. Most gladiators fought only once during a series of games due to the physicality and brutality of each combat. Oftentimes injuries received were severe and could require months of medical attention. If by chance a gladiator remained unscathed, he was exhausted. Either way, it was impossible to rest and recover in time to face another challenger in just a few days.

Yet he would be fighting for his sister. What did Valens care about a few more bruises compared to saving her life?

"Three times," said Valens. "I will fight for you three times. I can take to the arena on opening day, sometime in the middle of the games, and on the final day."

Acestes turned to face Valens. "You are saying that I can bring Valens Secundus back to the arena for three fights?" He pressed his thumbnail onto his lips. Valens imagined that the general tabulated how many votes he would lose for allowing a thief to go free compared to how many he would gain for bringing back Rome's champion. At length, the general said, "All the fights will be to the death, not just to first blood, or winner chosen for exceptional valor or skill. You must win thrice. If you die, then I will have no choice but to enforce your sister's execution."

Valens wanted to argue. But he had no advantage. All he could do was defend, maintain, and hope that perseverance saw him through, as it had so many other times before. "Agreed."

"I decide whom you fight and under what conditions," said Acestes.

Valens hesitated. He had witnessed many cruel and uneven fights in his life. "As long as I am armed; equally matched; and my opponent is not a lion, bull, or some other type of starving beast."

Acestes sighed and Valens wondered what twisted combat the general might have planned. "Agreed."

"You must also leave my sister in my care. I refuse to fight if she is taken from this home."

"How do I know that you will not remove her from the city?"

"How do I know that you plan to keep your word and set her free later?"

"Pity you are only a pleb," Acestes said as he held out his hand. "You have a good bit of a deal-making politician in you."

"There is one thing more. Antonice's part in all of this must be kept secret." Accusations such as this had the power to ruin her reputation, her life.

Acestes withdrew his hand. "That is a stipulation to which I cannot agree. In order to make this arrangement work for me, I must appear benevolent and shrewd."

"But Antonice will suffer her entire life from this stain."

"I have but two things to say to you. First, she should have thought of the consequences before committing the crime. Second, I sincerely do not care what happens to your sister. If you want to save her life, this will be public. If you do not, the reason why she is executed will be known as well."

Valens could not recall hating a person more than he hated Acestes at that moment. Yet all of the sordid details being made public could work to Valens's advantage. If all of Rome knew their bargain, then Acestes would be forced to keep his word and set Antonice free if Valens, indeed, won.

"We are agreed, then?" asked Acestes.

The two men grabbed each other's wrists.

"We are agreed," said Valens.

Chapter 20

Phaedra

Phaedra sat at her cosmetics table and listened as the bells marking the hour rang out ten times. The morning, not half-gone, and already she was weary of the day. Phaedra had spent the last four years as a wife and the domina of her own villa in Pompeii. She loved that city with its clean, fresh air and waves that lapped the shoreline. Here, in her father's villa and in Rome, nothing interested her. Most of her girlhood friends had a child or two, making their lives very different from hers. Besides, Phaedra felt her own lack of offspring keenly enough without spending time with living, breathing reminders.

"Excuse me, my lady," said Terenita. "You have a visitor. General Acestes is here to see you."

Like a thick gray fog, melancholia swirled around Phaedra. She had done little with her day and was still overtired. If Acestes asked her for anything, would she have the strength to refuse? "Tell him I am unwell."

"Your father sends me, my lady, and requires you meet the general in the garden."

"I suppose it would do no good to tell Father that I am unwell, also," she said.

"I think not, my lady," said Terenita. "It is a beautiful day. The sunshine might help to improve your mood."

"It might," she said, although Phaedra doubted it very much.

A patio of white stone and mortar spread out from the villa's garden door to its dining room, a new addition since she had lived in her father's villa last. In the middle of the patio, as if it sprang from the rock itself, stood a fragrant tree. Acestes sat on a bench, also new, in the shade of the tree. He made room for Phaedra as she approached.

Once settled, she looked around the garden. No servant stood nearby waiting to bring them a chalice of water or a plate of bread. No slave trimmed the roses back so they might bloom again this year. Her father had arranged this moment of privacy, no doubt. Yet she spied him inside the villa, resting on a reclining sofa that sat near an open set of doors. So Phaedra and Acestes were not exactly alone.

"I spent my morning arranging the games I am sponsoring to honor my uncle. They begin in less than a week," Acestes said as a way of greeting.

Marcus had cared little for the games. Still, she said, "He would be pleased."

"Do the games please you?"

"I have not seen a fight since my wedding day. Watching men bludgeon each other for sport clouds my conscience."

"Then perhaps I have something you might find more pleasing." Acestes retrieved a small wooden box from the folds of his tunic. "Open it," Acestes said. "I bought it for you."

"I should not."

"I insist," said Acestes. He held the box toward her.

Phaedra kept her hands in her lap.

"May I?" he asked after they had sat a moment too long. He opened the lid.

Inside the box lay a necklace on a silk cushion. An emerald the size of a grape hung from several entwined chains. The thick strands of gold and silver captured the morning sun, projecting it throughout her father's garden, its refraction leaving her all but blind. It was stunning and yet Phaedra knew that by accepting the gift, she also accepted Acestes as her next husband.

"I first saw this emerald in a North African market," said Acestes, "and I wondered which was the more beautiful, you or the stone."

"It is lovely," she said. "Thank you for the compliment and for bringing the necklace here for me to see."

Acestes undid the pins that held the necklace in place and held it up. "This is yours, Phaedra, if you would have it."

"You do me great honor, but I cannot accept such a generous gift."

His eyes narrowed and the muscle in his cheek flexed. Phaedra felt rage rolling off him like heat from a fire, and yet when he spoke, his voice was without enmity. "I hate to think that you would refuse a gift from me. I might take the rejection personally."

A spurned suitor made the worst kind of enemy. Phaedra, who cared little for politics and intrigue, still knew enough to handle him with care. He clasped his large hand around hers. Both of them held the jewel, and Phaedra no longer saw her own fingers. She tried to pull her hand away, but he held tight. A sparrow fluttered above her head, taking shelter in a gap between two broken roof tiles. Ah, to be the bird and fly away or take refuge in a small, hidden place.

Her father rose from his reclining sofa and limped toward them, dragging his swollen left foot. Gout stretched the flesh, turning it yellow and then purple as the sandal's thongs bit into his skin. "What have you, my dear?"

His question fooled no one. He had heard every word and had watched every moment. Her father had come to intervene before the conversation became a quarrel. And most likely to lend his support to Acestes.

Acestes let go and Phaedra found herself holding the necklace.

"Nothing, Father," she said. "Acestes has shown me a piece of jewelry."

"Senator Scaeva, I am actually trying to give this necklace to your daughter as a gift. I hope she will agree to wear it at the gladiatorial games I am sponsoring in my uncle's honor."

"It has been so long since I have seen any decent gladiators," said her father. "Valens Secundus—now there is a true man of the sword."

Phaedra's pulse resonated at the base of her throat, and her stomach tightened at the mention of Valens's name.

"Funny you should mention him," Acestes said. "I am planning a surprise that you might very well like, then."

"What kind of surprise?" she asked, although she knew better than to show any interest in Valens when Acestes might notice.

Acestes lifted one eyebrow. "You need to attend if you want to find out."

"There is no way we could miss the games, is there, my dear? Especially ones which honor Marcus," said her father.

The thought of Valens wavered and vanished. As she feared, her father had chosen Acestes's side over hers. She bristled at his disloyalty to family. But Phaedra could not fight her father, Acestes, and the laws of Rome all at once. Forcing a pleasant smile on to her face, Phaedra responded, "If it is for my late husband's memory, then I must attend."

"Good. And you will accept my gift?"

"I simply could not." She held it out again, offering it to Acestes. He drew his brows together and took the necklace.

Her father moved closer and sniffed as if the jewel gave off a scent. "It is beautiful, Phaedra, my dear. I am sure it cost Acestes a good bit of coin. The least you can do is to let him see it on you."

"Father, I should not."

"No argument. Turn." He drew a circle in the air with his finger.

Phaedra twisted in her seat, leaving her unprotected back to Acestes. He slipped the necklace around her neck. Somehow it felt heavier than it had in her hand, and colder, too.

Acestes clasped the ends together and rested his palms on her shoulders. "You are the more beautiful of the two."

"To whom do you speak?" She asked as she turned to face him, "Me or the emerald?"

"You must know that I am fond of you, Phaedra." Acestes reached for her hand. She did not pull away. He stroked her wrist with the tips of his fingers. "Marry me."

This man was a master of manipulation. By proposing in front of her father, Acestes was certain to secure her agreement. Both men stared at Phaedra as they waited for her answer. She knew what they expected her to say, and yet she found that she could not.

"My official eight days of mourning ended only yesterday. I cannot make such a decision. Not now."

"I understand," said Acestes. "But nothing prevents your father from deciding for you."

Her father nodded in approval. "You are used to being in charge of your own home. Besides, it is time that you have a husband with whom you can have a child."

"Is it done, then?" she asked. "Have you accepted a proposal without consulting me?"

"Do not cast your father into the fires of Tarsus," said Acestes. "I had spoken to him about my offer of marriage. He explained that you have the right to choose your next husband, just as you told me last night."

At least her father had remembered his promise.

"But I urge you to take this proposal very seriously," her father said. "This marriage is to your advantage."

Her advantage? Being forced into marriage was never to a woman's advantage. Having a powerful general for a son-in-law, being related to the consul, would certainly benefit her father.

True, as the wife of a consul, Phaedra would be one of the most celebrated women in Rome. Still, if she were to have that life, it would be of her own choosing.

Phaedra shook her head. "I cannot."

"Cannot marry me, or cannot decide?" Acestes asked.

"I am not sure."

Acestes stood, his eyes narrowed, his jaw clenched. "I should go. The preparations for the games are pressing."

Her father held up his hands and stepped in front of Acestes. "Be patient, please. Let me talk to her. My daughter became fond of your uncle, and she still grieves."

"Patience may be considered a virtue, but it is not one I value."

Phaedra unclasped the necklace. "Here, this is yours."

"Keep it. I will never let the silly emotions of women keep me from what I want. You will be my wife, Phaedra. I expect you to attend the games. Wear the necklace then."

"She will," said her father. "And will be honored to do so."

"At least one of you shows some sense." Acestes's tone was cold as he walked out of the garden. The golden embroidery edging his tunic shimmered as he departed.

Her father eased down onto the bench. "That could have gone better."

"You should have warned me."

"I thought you would be pleased to accept him. You get to keep your house, your servants, and your money. Acestes is a handsome man. He is much younger than Marcus."

"He is my nephew."

"Phaedra, be reasonable. He is not your nephew. You did not watch him grow from babe to boy to man. He is not your kin. You need to marry someone again, and soon. The Senate needs proof that I have a million sesterces before the sessions begin next year. If I do not have it, then they will take my seat from me."

Phaedra closed her eyes against the sun and the sky and the reality of her life. "I understand that it is my duty to remarry in order to see to your comforts, Father. But if I must remarry now, then at least let me pick one of the other men to whom you have spoken."

"No one else is interested, my dear. Four years without a child is a long time. They fear you are barren, or worse, frigid."

Phaedra bristled at the notion. "I am neither barren nor frigid. My husband had two wives before me, and none of them ever gave him a child. We cannot all be barren. Therefore, the problem lies with the common factor."

"People have forgotten the others and see you."

"What if I know of a man whom I want to marry?"

"Can he afford to allow you to live in comfort?"

At least her father had not asked the real question: *Can he afford to pay for my Senate seat?*

"I have not met him, not yet. But if I do?"

Her father laughed. "Marriage to Marcus turned you into quite the deal maker. It is to be expected, I suppose. He was a rare politician."

"You are changing the subject, Father. I need you to give your word."

"I promise to consider all suitors," he said with a sigh.

"Thank you."

Holding up his hand, her father said, "Do not thank me too much. Acestes is a powerful man, and someone I think neither of us wants to displease."

Phaedra sighed. "He plans to be consul one day, when he is old enough to take his family's seat in the Senate. He will be powerful one day, Father. It is just not today."

"I know you care little for politics and power, my dear," her father said. The fact that he spoke the words slowly, as if she could not understand these deep subjects, set her teeth on edge. "But Acestes was wealthy even before he inherited Marcus's money. Acestes also has an army to ensure that his will is done, and a ruthlessness that shows how little he cares for those who get in his way. You would be wise to remember that."

"His army is in Germania," said Phaedra, although as she spoke, she understood that mattered little. People would do what Acestes wanted because having an army gave him power, and having money brought him influence. Everyone would want to befriend Acestes. She tried another tactic. "You do not plan to keep your word, do you, Father?"

He sat taller, his chest expanding with indignation. "I told the great general that you were allowed to choose your own husband. You yourself heard him say as much."

"That you did, Father. I am sorry," she said, although she did not feel entirely in the wrong for her question.

"We shall strike another bargain," he said. "Acestes will be busy with these funeral games. They will not start for several days. You must find another husband before they end or be ready to accept Acestes's proposal."

"You cannot be serious."

"I am. You have one week to find another suitable husband."

One week. It was all she had to change her fate.

Chapter 21

Valens

Somewhere near the forum, bells rang out to mark the eleventh hour. After his meeting with the general, Valens had sat in this tablinum for over two hours, numb with shock, trying to comprehend all that had happened. At least Acestes had allowed Antonice to stay at home.

Oh, what heartache his sister had caused. He wanted to throttle her, but Valens knew he would never raise a hand to Antonice. He could yell, however, and at the moment it seemed the best place to start.

"Leto," he called to the housekeeper. "Bring Antonice to me at once."

Leto returned a moment later. "Apologies, dominus. Your sister is still abed."

Anger flooded his veins. Valens stood so quickly that his chair toppled backward, clattering as it hit the floor. He kicked it and it skittered toward the wall. His shin throbbed where it had connected with the wood. The pain felt pure, real. The red rage that now consumed him was better than the numbness that had enveloped him during the morning.

Valens did not stop to think on his actions or try to develop a stratagem for dealing with his sister. He stormed to her side of the house, upending tables and scattering urns and pitchers as he went.

I am here. The debris spoke for him. *I have been here. You cannot ignore the bits of pottery and shards of glass. You cannot ignore me.*

Without knocking, Valens pushed open his sister's door. Curtains pulled against the daylight left the room in shadow. Even in the dimness he saw her. Antonice lay curled up with a blanket pulled to her chin and partly over her head. She looked so like a mouse in its hole that some of Valens's fury slipped away—although not enough to blunt his temper.

"What have you done?" He yanked the curtains opened and light filled the room.

Antonice sat up. Dark hair fell loose over her shoulders, and her eyes opened wide. She looked much as she had as a young child. Valens nearly sobbed aloud despite his wrath.

"What have you done? Tell me you did not know how Damian found the coin to pay for your jewels."

Antonice stared at her brother and said nothing. Yet the tears that slipped down her cheeks spoke volumes. She had known and, with that knowledge, had been complicit in the crime.

He wanted to shake her. For her, he would be returning to prove himself in the one place he had sworn never to go again. He swung his arm across her cosmetics table, scattering perfumes and powders. The cloying scent of jasmine and a fine, shimmering dust hung in the air. With a force that rattled his very bones, Valens pushed out of the room and slammed her door.

"She does not leave this villa," he said to Leto. "Send the steward to hire guards. Do you understand?" He stormed from the house.

Only as he wound his way down the crowded streets of the Aventine did Valens register his housekeeper's silent response of tears and a nodding head.

He had failed his sister. If Valens had been more attentive to Antonice's activities when she was younger and their mother alive, this—this goat rope of a problem—might have been avoided. Even years ago, Valens had known he needed to do more, to *be* more. Instead he had done nothing beyond give them coin. His pace slowed as he entered the Capitoline Market. The temples to Hercules Victor and Portunus flanked a ludus. *His* ludus.

As a child Valens had possessed the courage to enter these doors in order to save Antonice. Now he stood at the door to Paullus's house and lifted his fist to knock, instead resting his knuckles on the wood without making a sound. Why? Did he so loathe the idea of killing, even if that death allowed his sister to live? Or was it that if he reentered the ludus, the Fates might cut the thread tethering him to the earth, and the only way he would leave again was by dying?

Valens knocked. A slave opened the door. A guard stood nearby. "State your business," the slave said.

"I am here to see the lanista."

He did not wait to be invited in or be led through the atrium. Valens immediately walked past the stunned guard, knowing the way well enough. He found his former master sitting behind a desk with scrolls and tablets strewn about.

Paullus looked very much as he always had. In the familiarity of the situation, some of the tension Valens felt left. Yet in its place came a worse thought. *What if nothing has changed? What if I am still the same man, a bastard who cheated death and poverty by capitalizing on my willingness to kill?*

"Ah, my friend." Paullus moved to the front of the desk and clapped Valens on the shoulder. "You should have told me you were coming. I would have been better prepared."

"I need a favor," said Valens.

Paullus gestured to a chair and Valens sat. "Anything you need is yours."

"I need the German to train me. I am going to return to the arena."

Paullus laughed. "For a moment I thought you serious. No, really, what do you need?"

"I wish I were joking. Antonice has gotten herself into some trouble with the army. In order to have the charges dropped, I agreed to fight again."

"Tell me you jest."

Valens shook his head.

"Did she do what she was accused of? You could hire a solicitor to argue her case. As a freeman you have that right, you know."

"She is in the wrong. I am certain of it," said Valens.

"How long do you have to train?"

"The games take place in a few days. Over the course of five days, I have to fight three times to the death in order to set Antonice free."

"Three fights in one week? Impossible." Paullus raked his hands through his hair, and white tufts stood on end. He looked Valens up and down, appraising him. "I fear for you, my friend. You have gotten so soft."

"Soft?" Valens flexed his arm muscles. "I am not soft."

"What have you done since leaving the ludus? Eat, sleep, enjoy your fame, spend some money, and bed a few women."

Valens shrugged. He had earned his easier life.

"I know what you have not done," said Paullus. "You have not trained."

"I tried running up and down the Aventine carrying a tree trunk, but the neighbors stared."

Paullus shook his head. "Always a smart comment with you."

Valens shrugged again.

"I never fight a gladiator without training him for at least six months. Otherwise it is suicide."

"I trained for eight years," said Valens. "I do not need six months for my skills to return."

"You need longer than you have. Besides, winning three fights in a series of games is impossible. Even if you fought to first blood, or if the winner was determined by referee, the task is too difficult. Is there no other way?"

"I can think of nothing. My sister has been accused of thievery. She encouraged her favorite, an aristocrat named Damian, to steal. The boy's father arranged for him to join the legion and serve in Germania to pay for his deed. I have no family connection, but I do have my reputation as a gladiator."

"So, it is the arena for you or death for her?"

"At least I have a chance of surviving."

Paullus raked his hands through his hair again and sighed. "I love you like a son, Valens. That means I must love Antonice like a daughter. You became a gladiator to save her life. After cheating death for so long, are you willing to return with these impossible odds in order to save her once more?"

"I have no choice. She is my family, my responsibility. Antonice is all I have."

"I wonder if she appreciates what you are doing for her."

"She does not even know."

"Go home tonight. Get your affairs in order. Come back in the morning. You will need to live at the ludus and become a gladiator again if you want to win."

"To save my sister, I must win," said Valens.

Before leaving the ludus, there was one last thing Valens needed to do—find a way to get Antonice from the city. If she were not in Rome, then she could not be taken into custody when—or if—he died. His former trainee, Baro, had family in Padua. Baro owed Valens nothing, yet options for removing his sister from Rome were limited. With an imperfect plan, Valens sought his former trainee.

Baro practiced in the middle of the arena, fighting two gladiators at once. Valens saw the eventual outcome well before the final blow fell. Without question the student had surpassed the master. Valens's chest swelled with pride, and at the same instant contracted with shame.

Pride that Baro had become an exquisite fighter, shame that Valens no longer possessed those skills himself.

"Hail, Valens Secundus," said Baro as he walked away from opponents who limped, gripping their backs and sides. "I heard interesting news about you. Is it true, then? Are you returning to the games?"

"I wish it were interesting news and nothing more."

"Are you daft, man? Why?"

Valens shrugged. "Might I have a private word?"

Baro accepted a clay cup of water from a slave and nodded his head to the far wall. They stood in the shade for a moment before Valens spoke. "I need a favor for my sister."

"For the pretty Antonice, you can ask anything."

"She is in trouble. I need her out of the city."

"What kind of trouble?"

"It is the kind that makes it necessary for me to return to the arena in order to keep her out of it. Do you still have family in Padua?"

"I do. My aunt just birthed her seventh babe. Seven children, can you imagine?"

"With all those children, your aunt might need help," said Valens.

"I could write to her and ask," said Baro. "I assume you want this kept private."

"Be as silent as the dead."

"How will I find you when they reply?"

"Simple," said Valens. "I am not just returning to the arena. I am going to live in the ludus again, too."

Chapter 22

Phaedra

The walls surrounding the villa closed in upon Phaedra. The noonday sun, a great white ball in a cloudless sky, heated the garden. Near a bench grew an orange tree; a single shriveled piece of fruit clung to its stunted branches. Oppressed, she sought the cool and the dark of her rooms and stared outside.

She recalled the events of the morning—Acestes and his formal proposal of marriage, her refusal to answer, and her father's encouragement to accept. Phaedra shifted on the sofa, the silk gown clinging to her sweat-damp skin. Her father was right about one thing: she had grown accustomed to living as her own mistress, and residing in his house no longer suited her.

Life with Marcus had been full of freedoms. She traveled often with him, but there were times when he was in Rome and she, Pompeii. During those times she answered to no one. As a daughter in her father's home, he controlled her every move again. Or did he? Could she simply walk to the market and purchase, say, an orange and tear through its dimpled skin, releasing a spray of citrus into the air?

Well, why not? Her father had not forbidden her to leave the villa. Rules had not been established since her return as a widow. The air pressed down on her skin. She sat up.

The Capitoline Market sprawled out at the base of the hill, close enough to walk with just Terenita as her escort. She could avoid calling for a litter and guards, making her trip much less likely to draw her father's attention.

Phaedra stood. "Terenita, I would have an orange."

"Yes, my lady." The maid clapped her hands, and another slave entered the room.

"No," said Phaedra, "not from the kitchens. We shall go to the Capitoline Market and buy one."

Terenita hesitated. "Whatever pleases you, my lady."

Leaving the claustrophobic villa pleased her very much. They walked to the front door without encountering anyone else. A guard outside dozed in the shade. He opened his eyes and stood taller as she shut the door. He did not stop her or try to keep her from leaving. It was his job to keep people *out* of her home, not in.

Terenita held a silk parasol overhead, and their footfalls echoed on the quiet streets. No vendors pushed carts up and down the hill, calling out for people to buy their wares. No slaves washed the high walls or swept in front of red-roofed villas. Everyone had been, like Phaedra, hiding away to escape the midday heat.

As she descended the Palatine Hill, the houses became less opulent, and the drowsy spell lifted. Lower mud-brown walls surrounded smaller homes. A few people milled about on the uneven, narrow lanes. A woman tossed a bucket's worth of refuse into the gutters before shutting a wooden door with a loud crack. Two thin dogs snarled at each other as they ate whatever the woman had just thrown away. Phaedra crossed the street, not wanting to be too close to the mongrels or the bucket's contents. Too late she saw a group of men huddled on a shaded corner. They stopped talking as she passed. Sweat trickled down Phaedra's back, and her pulse beat fast. She should have been content to eat an orange from the kitchen.

Just as she decided to return home, the avenue widened and the market stretched out in front of her. Wooden stalls with roofs and walls of colorful cloth spread out before her. Singular voices mingled until they became one sound—no longer words, just noise. She caught the spicy scent of cinnamon and the heavy fragrance of fennel mixed with the seductive undertones of jasmine. Phaedra did not know what to see, smell, or listen to first.

At that moment Phaedra realized why she had wanted to come to the market. She did not care about the orange or the freedom to roam at will. She wanted to find out about Valens Secundus. Perhaps she would hear a pleb mention his name as they passed, or spy a tattered and weather-worn bulletin announcing his next game. What she most wanted was to see him in the flesh. She scanned the market and saw faces, thousands of faces, in all skin tones. But she did not see Valens with his hazel eyes. She gave a passing thought to finding his ludus. She discarded it quickly. Even though Phaedra had seen most of the civilized world, she was still not bold enough to seek out the company of a gladiator at his ludus.

Today she would settle for a memory.

"Terenita," she said, "can you find the silk merchant I used before my wedding?"

Chapter 23

Valens

Valens left the ludus unsure of even a single victory, much less his ability to win all three matches. Was he prepared to die in the arena? During his time as a gladiator, Valens had glimpsed his demise many times over. But life during the past two years had been gentle and kind, if a little less than exciting, and he loathed the notion of leaving the world just yet.

What would fulfill him on this day, his last day of freedom? Her name came to him as easily as a breath. Phaedra. He wanted to see her once more and to let her know that her challenge to change their fates had held the power to change his life.

How could Valens see Phaedra again? He doubted any slave would let him enter her villa even if he asked for her. Senator Scaeva might grant an audience. He had, after all, hired Valens for his daughter's wedding. What kind of excuse could he give to the senator?

Damian's sister knew Phaedra, yet after what had happened, Valens doubted his welcome there as well.

As Valens strolled through the market, he realized that he might have to be satisfied with a memory. His feet had carried him halfway to the silk merchant's stall before he could acknowledge to himself that he wanted to go there.

It still sat in the same place. Squares of color hung on a string and fluttered in the breeze. He spied the exact shade of red Phaedra had worn on her wedding night. He still had her veil and secretly looked at it often, so his eye knew the color well.

Several wealthy, well-dressed women stood near the stall talking to each other. With a slight lift of the chin or a raised eyebrow, they summoned their female slaves. A quick nod of the head and the slaves were dispatched to the merchant to haggle over prices.

So well trained were the slaves that their aristocratic or noble mistresses never needed to voice a desire for anything or agree to pay a price. All communication happened with subtle changes of the face and stance. The noncommerce of the patricians and equestrians amused and confounded Valens. The powerful of the republic spent fortunes without ever buying a thing.

He looked at each and every face and did not find the one he sought. He had been foolish to think that, in a city of a million people, he might find her here, yet he felt ill with disappointment all the same.

He turned from the silk merchant and caught a glimpse of something, someone. Was there a similarity in the curve of the chin or the deep brown shade of hair? The hairs at the nape of his neck tingled; his pulse increased and echoed in his ears. As his mouth went dry, his palms grew damp. In that moment the noises quieted, the smells grew fainter, and the air surrounded him like a comforting blanket.

"Phaedra," he said.

The woman glanced in his direction, her eyebrows drawn together in a look of questioning and confusion.

She found him and their gazes met.

"Greetings, Valens Secundus," she said. "I had hoped to see you in the market today."

Chapter 24

Phaedra

How could Phaedra have said such a thing and in such a forward manner? In her years away from Rome, she had become accustomed to speaking her piece. Now that she was back in the center of politics and intrigue, she needed to be mindful of her words, and vowed to choose more carefully before she spoke.

"Greetings, Phaedra," Valens said. "I heard of your husband's death and that you had returned to Rome. Accept my sympathies for your loss."

Of course Valens would know of Marcus's passing. She then wondered if he ever thought simply of her. So great was her desire to know that Phaedra feared she would blurt out her question. Instead she said the expected, "I thank you for your sympathies."

"You look well."

"You do, too. I am surprised to see you in the market without guards," she said.

He laughed. "I fought more men in the arena than most soldiers do in their lifetime. I do not need a guard. Besides, I won my freedom two years ago."

Valens's freedom came as news to her. Fearing that she would hear something unpleasant about him, Phaedra had made a point to avoid talk of the games. "I congratulate you."

Valens nodded, smiling but tight-lipped. Then he smiled again, larger and more genuine this time. "I could ask the same of you—where are your guards? Or have you taken up the sword, too?"

"I just wanted a moment away from the villa," she said, fearing again that she had been too honest. "What of your life?"

"I live on the Aventine with my sister."

"Just you and your sister? No wife?" Oh, may the gods preserve her and help control her emotions and the words that follow!

"I never found a woman I wanted to bind myself to," he said.

"Good." Good? Good? Had she just said *good*? What must Valens think of her? "It is good to wait and marry when you find a person you favor, I mean."

"I thought that was what you meant." His eyes twinkled and she looked away, her cheeks feeling flushed.

Phaedra saw other patrician ladies she knew standing near the silk merchant's stall as their maids purchased goods. What would the gossip be tomorrow if Phaedra talked to Valens for much longer? Yet what did she care? Acestes's marriage proposal had not been accepted by either her or her father. She was a widow, not an unmarried virgin. Even though she once again lived with her father and his rules, she did have a certain amount of freedom.

Valens stepped toward her and her skin tingled. She had forgotten how standing close to him brought about a primal need like the drawing of two halves together, as if they were trying to become whole. The first time she felt it, Phaedra had not entirely understood the feelings and emotions. Now she did.

She understood something else as well. Her father meant for her to marry Acestes. True, her father loved her and he wanted her to be happy, but he cared much more for his own comforts and his position. Although he had agreed to consider all suitors, she knew he would not. He had given her a week to find another husband to appear benevolent and nothing more. That left her with seven days in which to enjoy the autonomy she craved. With her newly understood freedom, Phaedra could ask Valens to come to her villa late in the night. It was scandalous, but why not?

Without thinking of the consequences, Phaedra leaned close and said, "Come to my father's villa after the tenth bell this evening. My maid will let you in."

Chapter 25

Phaedra

Somewhere near the forum, the ninth bell rang. Blackness crept across the sky, stealing the day's warmth as the light faltered. Phaedra sat in a small dining room with her father as he read. A single candle sat at his elbow, the glow illuminating a small circle. He rolled up the papyrus with a sigh. "I cannot see a thing," he said, pressing thumb and forefinger to the bridge of his nose. "We need more light. More candles, more oil for lamps."

"Shall I have someone fetch them?"

"No. My accounts are empty. Oil is expensive. Candles are more so." He sighed as he stood. "I am off to bed and will rise with the dawn."

"Splendid idea," said Phaedra. Her pulse raced. As expected, her father planned to take to his bed early. "Perhaps you should send all the slaves to their beds as well."

Her father nodded to the steward who waited nearby, giving a silent order that the villa should be dark. She followed her father through the corridors and entered her dim bedchamber. He lit a taper on her cosmetics table.

"Do not let it burn long," he said.

"Of course not." Phaedra waited until her father was out of earshot before turning to Terenita. "I have a visitor arriving tonight."

"The gladiator," said the maid.

"His name is Valens Secundus. Wait by the door and bring him to me."

"My lady, I must caution you that this is foolish."

"Tonight," said Phaedra, "I care nothing for caution."

"My lady, why do you insist on bringing the gladiator into your life? He is handsome, even I acknowledge that. But General Acestes is pleasing to look upon as well."

It was a valid question. Did Phaedra only want Valens Secundus to prove that she could take a lover? That her father did not control every aspect of her life? No, there was more than that. It was the man. "When Valens looks upon me," she said, "I am seen."

Terenita lowered her eyes. "I understand, my lady."

Phaedra tilted the maid's chin up until they looked into each other's eyes. "Do you sincerely understand?"

"I do, but this gladiator makes me uneasy. You risk much for little gain, and I would not want to see you hurt."

To be seen, and heard, and to exist once more, Phaedra would have risked more than the consequences of an illicit love affair. "I appreciate your concern. But my mind is set. Please bring Valens Secundus to me when he arrives. The regret that would come from wasting this moment would be more injurious to me than the safety that will come from forgoing his company."

"I think I understand," said Terenita with a small smile before she walked silently from the room, which left Phaedra alone to wait. She watched the sands of her hourglass slip from one bulb to the other, thinking, wondering, all the while.

This was the first time she had invited a man to her villa for sex. How did one wait for a lover? Dressed? Naked? Lying across the bed? What if he did not come at all?

She poured a glass of wine and sipped it to warm her insides. Two fat candles burned on a table. They lit a small circle of wood, and the rest of the room remained in shadow. She lifted another taper from its holder and went to light it.

"Phaedra."

He had come.

He moved to her, covering the space between them in a few steps. His lips pressed against hers, his tongue slipped between her lips, and she allowed him to explore. She tasted him in return. Her head spun with Valens's kiss, and every part of her tingled with the nearness of him. As much as she had longed for this moment, as much as she thought about him, and for all the times she had tried not to think of him and failed, Phaedra reminded herself that what she felt now was lust and not love.

His touch skimmed from her shoulders to her arms. Their hands joined, palm to palm, fingers intertwined. Valens moved his lips to her neck as he placed leisurely kisses under her chin and behind her ear. Every part of Phaedra shivered with anticipation.

He cupped her breast. His thumb grazed her nipple through her gown and the linen strips used for binding. Even through both layers of fabric, she responded. Her nipple hardened and she arched her back, pressing herself closer to him. She wanted—no, needed—Valens inside her, to complete her.

Her hands moved down his arms, feeling the contours of his muscles as they shifted each time he changed his grasp. She traced his broad shoulders and tight chest before tugging at his tunic, hoping to get even closer to his flesh. Valens obliged, and slipped his clothes over his head. He did not wear a loincloth, and his erect phallus stood out. He was larger than Phaedra had anticipated, and she gave a fleeting thought about the pain she might feel when he entered her.

Phaedra still wore the same dress she had donned earlier in the day, red silk with a woven belt of golden wool. She tried to untie the belt, but her fingers fumbled, and the knot refused to come loose. Valens encircled her wrists with one hand and raised her arms above her head. His other hand moved to her middle.

Valens's fingers worked the knot free, and the belt slipped to the floor.

Valens held her chin in both his hands. The look of liquid desire in his eyes left her weak in the knees. When he placed his mouth on hers, hungrily now, the kiss possessive, her legs failed to hold her. He held Phaedra tight and pressed her to him. Her softness formed to the rigid angles and planes of his body. She lowered her arms, running her fingers through the silk of his hair.

With him guiding, she walked to the bed. The back of her legs met with the mattress. Once again, he lifted her arms. This time, he pulled her gown over her head. With little trouble he untied the linen strips that held her breasts in place. She stood naked before him. The vulnerability of it all came upon her, and she crossed one arm over her breasts and the other over the juncture of her thighs. Valens placed her wrists at her side. He held up one finger, walked across the room, and brought back a single candle that he placed on a small table near her bed. Light spilled over her, chasing away the shadows that kept her hidden.

"You are beautiful. More than beautiful—you are exquisite. I have long desired you, Phaedra, and I want to see your body and face while we make love," he said.

Her mouth went dry. She wanted to say something, needed to tell him. Yet, tell him what? Words no longer held meaning. She nodded.

His mouth trailed across her skin. He kissed her everywhere—and, it seemed, all at once—from her shoulder to her breasts, her stomach to her fingers. She could not think or reason, only feel. Holding on to his shoulders, she reveled in being touched, kissed, and tasted.

Slipping a hand between her legs, he found her most tender spot, already swollen with desire. He rubbed in a small circle, and a keener hunger awakened. Whimpering, she pressed into his hand. He laid her on the bed.

One of his hands still worked between her legs as the other hand spread her knees. He knelt on the floor and lifted both of her legs on either shoulder. "Come closer," he said.

Phaedra almost fainted with longing. Many times, too many times, she had tended to Marcus with her mouth. Each time she wondered if men did as much to women. She assumed they could, and yet Marcus never did. Phaedra eased down to the end of the bed, and Valens's breath cooled her inner heat.

He kissed her sex in much the same manner he had her mouth. First tenderly, then he spread her folds and explored her. As she panted and neared a climax, he kissed her in a manner meant to claim, with such passion that Phaedra felt herself slipping into the sweet oblivion of release.

Valens ran his tongue up her sweat-coated stomach and rolled her hardened nipples between his fingers. He held himself over her. His eyes—how often had she seen his eyes in her dreams? Or his lips. How many times had Phaedra thought of kissing his lips, never thinking that one day she might?

Situating himself between her legs, Valens spread her open with the wide head of his phallus. The first stroke was tentative; the second used more force. On the third thrust he entered her all the way and she cried out. She wrapped her legs around his back, pulling him closer, wanting him in deeper. She began to climax again, and Phaedra could no longer lie to herself. As unlikely as it seemed, her attraction was more than merely physical. In one evening, under a sky filled with thousands and thousands of stars, Phaedra had fallen in love with Valens Secundus. If all she had with him was this night, Phaedra vowed to make it one worth remembering. Her muscles deep inside clenched as Valens moved back and forth. As her climax reached its peak, she gave voice to her emotions. "I love you."

Chapter 26

Valens

Phaedra's juices remained on his tongue and lips. No matter if he lived a few days more or until he was an aged man, for the rest of his life Valens would always equate the taste of Phaedra to that of the perfect female. He plunged inside of her, harder. He went deeper and deeper and yet never deep enough. He wanted to possess Phaedra, to make her his. He wanted to hear her call out his name as she climaxed and know that he alone brought her rapture. He wanted more of her beyond this night.

Valens had spent years thinking of Phaedra, wondering about her, hoping that the Fates would again bring them together. In his mind he had made love to her several times over, although the fantasy had never compared to the exquisite bliss of reality. In all the times he thought of her, never once did Valens imagine that she would tell him that she loved him. Valens thrilled at the idea.

Another thought came to Valens, a horrible thought. What if Phaedra, like Valens many times before, was physically bedding one person while mentally making love to someone else? He thrust once, hard.

Arching her back, she gasped. Her hands gripped his shoulders. Collecting first one wrist and then the other, he held them over her head and balanced on his elbow.

"Tell me," he said with his nose nuzzled into her hair. "Who do you love?"

She stiffened under him and stopped moving. "Apologies," she said. "I had not meant to speak aloud and offend you."

Damn. He hated the patricians. Valens's hips slowed. Well, it was not the first time a noblewoman had bedded him. If he survived the three fights, it would not be his last. Yet Valens hated the thought of Phaedra not being with him fully. He wondered who had earned her love. Her dead husband? Or—the gods forgive him—that bastard Acestes? Phaedra struggled against being pinned to the bed, and he released her wrists.

She held his face in both hands and placed her lips on his. "I cannot make sense of it, either," she said. "We met twice before today. I understand if you do not feel the same." She stroked her thumb over his chin before letting go of his face. "I am not sure that I understand myself."

The urge to cry came upon Valens with such suddenness that he could not stop the first tear. It landed on her cheek and trailed into her hair. He began to move again and kissed her deeply, wanting to be deeper inside of Phaedra.

"I love you, too," he said.

He wanted to make her climax a third time and maybe a fourth, but the raw ardor he felt for Phaedra left him breathless. Stopping the ocean's tide would take less effort than staying his passion. His cock throbbed and Valens growled with satisfaction as his seed spilled inside Phaedra.

He collapsed on top of her, spent, sure that he had never ejaculated so hard before. His pulse throbbed throughout his body, echoing his pleasure. He wanted to say something affectionate and soothing. He needed to assure her that his declaration of love had not been brought on by his impending orgasm. "I learned to read and write because of you," he said. He sighed, unhappy with his horrible excuse for romantic pillow talk.

She stroked the side of his face from brow to chin. "That pleases me. You won your freedom and have become your own man, Valens Secundus. I knew you would."

Her eyelids fluttered, heavy with sleep. They had taken their pleasure, and now he longed to show her tenderness and caring. He knew of no better way than to kiss her eyelids.

"What of you?" he asked. "Did your father agree to your bargain for a husband of your own choosing?"

"He did," she said.

Valens rolled off her and lay on his back. She curled up beside him, resting her head on his shoulder. Lying together, their arms and legs tangled, felt simple and pure and right. He imagined them years from now like this, assuming he survived the fights. True, they could never marry. Valens was not a patrician, or even a member of the equestrian class, the wealthy of Rome who had not been born aristocratic. He had enough coin to qualify for the honor. Yet he did not have any serious supporters in the Senate who would vote for him when the time came. Even if he overcame all those odds, he still lacked a father, and therefore a clan, an essential piece of becoming an equestrian.

All that mattered little. If Phaedra were free of marital ties, they could be together like this always. Many patrician women kept long-term lovers, and both were accepted as a couple in society. True, any offspring would be considered illegitimate. True, Valens wanted more for Phaedra than to be his mistress. None of that could be helped. All that mattered was that they had found each other again.

Phaedra snuggled more deeply into Valens's arms and let out a sigh that reminded him of a contented cat. He kissed the top of her head, satisfied to hold her as they slept.

"He did agree," she said, her voice hoarse and slow. "Pity that he is not keeping his bargain."

Valens became alert. "What do you mean?"

Phaedra rolled over and placed her chin on Valens's chest. From his vantage point, he saw down her back to her perfectly round bottom. His cock stirred.

"I married to save my father from being removed from the Senate due to his lack of funds. Even though Marcus gave Father enough coin to last several lifetimes, it is all gone. Again I need to make a profitable marriage."

"But your father has not chosen a husband for you yet."

Phaedra's lips blazed a trail across his chest. She rolled her tongue around one nipple while brushing his other nipple with her fingers. His cock lengthened and he rubbed it against the soft curve of her hip.

She placed one final kiss on his collarbone. "I think he has picked out a husband for me. Someone asked to marry me."

"Has he accepted?" Valens asked. "Have you accepted?"

She shook her head and her hair spilled onto his chest. "Not yet. I have one week to find someone I might like better. That is as much of our bargain as Father's willing to keep." She pushed up on her elbows and kissed his lips. He did not kiss her back. "I know that one week is not a very long time, but I would meet you here every night if you are willing."

He was and he was not. "I would love to," he said. "But I cannot."

"You cannot? What is so important? I thought you said . . ." She sat up and combed her hair with her fingers. "I have thought of you often, Valens Secundus. I enjoyed this night. I can see it did not mean the same to you. You may go."

He had wounded her, he knew. That was why he took no offense at being dismissed. Valens ran his fingers over her cool silk sheets and waited for her to acknowledge him. She turned to look and he patted the mattress beside him. "Come to me." She looked away for a moment, and then with an exasperated sigh lay down beside him. She did not rest her head on his chest, but rather leaned her back on his side. He rolled over so his contours fit hers and his hard cock rested in the cleft of her buttocks.

"My life is complicated right now," he said.

"Everyone has complications."

She had a point. He kissed her shoulder. "Make love to me again."

She flipped her hair so it landed across his face. He wrapped the tendrils in his fist and held them up. He placed a kiss at the nape of her neck before smoothing her hair over her shoulder.

"I wish we could be together for the rest of our lives, but we cannot. I cannot marry you, nor can I share you with another man," he said.

"My father will not accept the proposal for another week, so now I belong to no one."

"It will be difficult enough to leave your bed today. A week from now, it will be impossible." He should tell her about returning to the ludus, his sister's thievery, all of it. But pride forbade him from speaking. He could not bear the thought of Phaedra seeing him as anything less than a man worthy of her love. "Make love to me again."

She pressed her round, firm buttocks onto his aching cock. "Just once more and that will be it between us."

"I wish it were different and we could be together always."

She lifted his hand to her lips and kissed his palm. "So do I."

Valens knelt behind Phaedra while she knelt in front of him. He entered her from behind. He wanted to watch as she closed her eyes, her mouth grew moist, and her cheeks flushed with pleasure. Yet Valens knew if he could see her, then Phaedra could see him . . . and the unmistakable regret etched in every line of his face.

Chapter 27

Phaedra

Phaedra woke alone in her bed. Valens stood at the door and faced the garden. He had not bothered to don his tunic, and the moonlight bathed his well-formed body, making it look as if he were cast in silver. She had not spoken a word, or even moved. Yet Valens somehow sensed she had woken.

"Every night for the past four years I have looked into the sky and found Polaris. It brought you to me," he said. "For so many reasons, I hate to leave you, and yet I must. This cannot be our life. We cannot live upon clandestine meetings, nor will we ever be together legally."

True, making a life together would be hard. She was willing to risk much to be with him, and yet he was not willing to do the same. She said nothing, knowing it was best for them both to let him slip away. The candles had burned out long before, and he rummaged in the dark for his tunic and sandals. Once dressed, he leaned over and kissed her. Not passionately or hungrily as before, but slowly, tenderly, as if he were trying to memorize this very moment. Or perhaps that was what she wished were behind his actions.

"Terenita will show you out of the house," she said. As she spoke, her maid emerged from a room nearby.

Valens stroked the side of her face. She pressed her cheek into his hand. The words *Stay, please,* were on her lips. Yet she did not voice them. Instead she said, "Wherever I go, you will always be with me."

"And you with me."

He followed Terenita from the room. Phaedra lay in the darkness and the silence. Her eyes burned. Her chest felt tight. Yet she did not sob, or even shed a quiet tear. She had no word for what she felt now. A part of her had vanished with Valens, leaving her an unfinished person.

Chapter 28

Valens

Dazed, Valens walked down the empty streets. He avoided the crowded parks and squares where men and women gathered for a late night's entertainment. The voices of the actors and singers carried above the sounds of conversation and laugher. He wondered how anyone anywhere might feel happiness, not to mention joy. Even if he survived the three fights, what would there be for him to live for?

As a gladiator he had never considered taking a wife and making a family, even after Paullus gave his permission. No child should grow up with the blood and gore found in the arena, or so he told himself. Once Valens had won his freedom, his excuse had changed—Antonice needed his undivided attention, although in that, he had failed, too.

All the while Valens knew the real reason he had never taken a wife. Phaedra. She had become the beacon, and the rest of the women he met were the rocky coast.

Yet they could share nothing else beyond tonight. Death in the arena, sword in hand, with the cheers of the crowd, seemed a sweet release. His feet carried him to his neighborhood. He rounded the corner and his villa came into sight. He was reminded immediately that he did have something else. He had Antonice. He could not give up, because if he did, then she would die.

A slave opened his front door.

"Can I bring you wine or food, dominus?" the slave asked.

In a few short hours, Valens would no longer be the master. Even though he would not be a slave, he needed to become accustomed to taking care of his own needs again. "Thank you, no," he said, and then he dismissed the slave for the night.

Alone in the atrium, Valens knelt by the pool. Cupping his hand, he brought water to his lips and drank. He rubbed the back of his neck with a wet palm. He should sleep. The dawn drew near and the day would be more tolerable with some rest.

He went to his room and lay down on the bed, once comfortable, now too cold and too big. He should not have left Phaedra.

Staring into the darkness, he saw nothing. He dared not close his eyes, for when he did the faces of gladiators defeated long ago floated before him. Did they beckon him to Elysium? Had their fate really been meant for him? Intermixed with the visions and worries, he thought of Phaedra. Always Phaedra.

Knowing that sleep would continue to elude him, Valens rose. He found his canvas sack packed with a few tunics and a jar of bathing oil. Without benefit of taper or torch, he felt his way through the darkened corridors and found Antonice's room.

She lay with the blankets pulled up around her head, so nothing more than her nose showed. He sat on her bed. She shifted, whimpering in her sleep. What nightmares came to Antonice?

He shook her shoulder. She opened her eyes and gasped. "Valens?"

"I did not mean to frighten you."

Antonice pulled the blankets tighter overhead. "I am fine."

"I have come to say good-bye."

"Why? Where are you sending me?"

Valens patted the top of her head. "Nowhere now. I am the one to leave. I am returning to the arena. Just a little more than a week and I will be back. Leto will care for you, although I have told her you are not to leave the villa at all."

Antonice sat up and the blanket fell to her shoulders. "Do not leave me," she said. "I promise to be good."

"I know you will." Earlier he had decided not to tell his sister why he was returning to the ludus and his fights. What good would come from upsetting her and making her feel responsible? But then he never would have guessed that Antonice might view his leaving as abandonment. Besides, word would spread, and Valens could not protect Antonice from gossip. "Damian taking money is serious business," he said. "Thievery is a capital offense."

"I took nothing," she said. "Besides, he said it was stolen already."

"No charges were brought against the quartermaster. You, on the other hand—" His words pained him, and Valens could say no more. He breathed deeply and tucked his emotions away. "Charges were brought against you and Damian. Damian's father arranged for him to serve with the legions in Germania."

"And me?" Tears clung to her lashes.

He pulled her to him, wrapping his arms around her. Instead of returning his embrace, she folded her arms tighter across his chest. "I will keep you safe," he said.

"That is why you are fighting."

He nodded. "Yes, three times in a series of games. I will be at the ludus if you need me. Send word and I can come home."

Antonice started to tremble and her teeth chattered. "Thrice? You mean to fight thrice? You never fought in the arena more than once a season. You said gladiators who did not know their limits were the ones who lost."

Had he said that? It sounded like wisdom he might have spouted during his time as Champion of Rome, but Valens did not recall ever speaking those exact words. "There is no other way," he said. "If you receive word to leave the city, go without question. I want to keep you and Leto together." He hugged her tighter. She wrapped her arms around his middle.

"I love you." Antonice buried her face into his chest and sobbed. "You are all I have."

"I will return to you. When I do, I will be a better brother."

"What if you do not come home?"

Ah, now she asked the hard question. What would happen to her if he died in the arena? "I will come back to you," he said.

"I am so sorry," she said. Or at least that was what Valens assumed she said through all the sobs and snivels.

"I must go." Valens stood. "Behave for Leto. We are not her children, but she loves us both better than our own mother did."

"I know. I am so sorry for the trouble. Please say you forgive me."

Did he forgive Antonice? Because of her he found himself returning to the arena and a life he had sworn to leave behind. Phaedra had just a single week to give to Valens, yet he could not be with her because of Antonice. Aside from spending every night making love to Phaedra, Valens would have devoted every day to finding a way for them to remain together. Despite all that, Antonice was his sister. They shared the same blood and bone and history. Did he forgive her? In all honesty, he had never blamed her in the first place. It was his failings, his lack of involvement in her life—both before and after their mother's death—that had allowed Antonice to fall so far. "There is nothing to forgive," he said.

She nodded and wiped her eyes. "I pray that the gods keep you, Brother."

"I pray they keep you as well."

Without looking back, Valens grabbed his canvas sack from the floor and left his sister's chamber. He did not stop to wake the steward or speak to the housekeeper. A strip of pink shone on the horizon, bringing some color to a colorless world. With his back to the rising sun, Valens descended the Aventine Hill and left behind all he held dear.

Chapter 29

Phaedra

Phaedra lay in bed and looked out at the garden. A bird hopped along the stones of the patio. Picking up seeds, it cracked them between its beak and rocks.

Tap-tap. Tap-tap.

Val-ens. Val-ens.

Last night Phaedra had not been ill used—after all, she had invited Valens to her villa. Her one night with him had given her more pleasure, more connection, more passion than four years of marriage ever had. Then why was she so melancholy? Was it because she would never hold Valens again, or because another undesirable marriage awaited her?

Her father knocked on her chamber door. "You look dreadful," he said as he entered the room. "I missed you at breakfast."

She ignored his first comment. For in truth Phaedra felt much more than dreadful. "I have no appetite."

"Maybe you should go out."

"There is nowhere I wish to go."

"Visit Fortunada. I heard her brother left for the army."

"Damian? He is far too soft to join the legions."

"I thought that, too. Word in the Senate is that he left under suspicious circumstances. I would be interested to know why."

"You want me to attend my best friend and spy?"

"Not spy, visit. Talk like you ladies do. Just let me know if you learn anything useful."

"Why do you care, Father?" Phaedra asked.

"The two most valuable things in Rome are coin and information. Since I have little of the first, I need an abundance of the latter. Do not make me order you."

Once again, Phaedra knew better than to fight her role as a dutiful daughter. Standing tall, she stretched her arms overhead. "I suppose a visit never hurt anyone."

"A litter is waiting outside, as are guards." Her father paused. "Unlike yesterday, you may leave the villa only with an escort and my permission."

Blood cooled in her veins. Her father knew of her trip to the market with Terenita. Did he also know that Valens had come to her bed last night? And what if he did? As a widow a certain amount of freedom was allowed, unless he did not care to give her any. Phaedra lowered her eyes. "Yes, Father."

After bathing and dressing, Phaedra was carried in a litter from her home to Fortunada's. As girls, the two had shared everything and played together almost every day. They had sworn, as many fast friends do, to be together always and live inseparable lives. Neither had known at the time the truth in their vow. Now both Phaedra and Fortunada were women without husbands, living once again under their parents' roofs.

The litter stopped in front of Fortunada's home. One of the guards announced Phaedra. The villa door opened and all six slaves who carried the litter set it down in a single, fluid motion. From the side of the litter, a slave folded down a set of steps, and Phaedra alighted. Terenita, who had walked beside the litter, followed Phaedra into the villa. In the atrium Phaedra was bidden welcome by a female slave who then led her to the smallest triclinium in the villa, where Fortunada waited with her children.

"Kiss your auntie," Fortunada told her son, an active boy of six, and his little sister, a three-year-old blonde who toddled on chubby legs.

Phaedra bent down to accept the wet and sticky kisses from both children. Fortunada then sent them off with a nursemaid after promising that they could join her for the midday meal.

Fortunada's eyes gleamed with pride, love, and regret as the children left the room.

"You are a good mother," Phaedra said as she settled onto a sofa and accepted a goblet of wine.

"I do not know what I would do without them." Fortunada took a seat on a sofa near Phaedra and reclined. She arranged the slightly frayed hem of her deep purple gown over the straps of her sandals. "When my husband first divorced me, I missed him. Now I just miss having a man whom I can love."

Phaedra nodded—she understood. Even though she had made love to Valens last night, she still missed Marcus. She might always miss him. Yet her lips tingled with last night's kisses, and she knew that there always would be a part of her hoping for Valens to return.

"Have you heard the news?" asked Fortunada.

Phaedra sipped her wine, which was surprisingly weak and sour, and shook her head.

"Damian left for Germania. He joined the legions."

"Since the law forbids men from the aristocracy from doing any kind of business, his only opportunities lay in the military," Phaedra said, "or politics. But Rome likes the first to precede the second."

"I wish it were that simple."

"Nothing is ever simple."

"I cannot believe what happened." Fortunada began to weep. "Father arranged for Damian to serve with the army's quartermaster here in the city. They caught him stealing. To save himself from death in the arena, Damian agreed to join the legions for seven years."

Phaedra moved to Fortunada's side and held her friend's shoulders as she wept.

"Your brother can regain his honor and return home as a hero."

"That was what Father said." Fortunada wiped her eyes. "If it were not for that stupid cow Antonice Secundus, Damian never would have taken anything."

"Secundus? Like the gladiator, Valens Secundus?"

"His sister," Fortunada said. "And what do you think her punishment will be for leading my brother astray? Not execution like the law dictates. Your husband's nephew is allowing her brother to fight thrice to the death in the funeral games honoring your late husband. The great General Acestes, who dealt with the Sicilian uprising so harshly, is letting the former Champion of Rome take his sister's place."

Phaedra tried not to react to the news, but found that she sat taller and leaned forward. Now she knew why Valens could not spend any more time with her. He had volunteered to fight in the games sponsored by Acestes to save his sister's life. Why would Acestes trade a justified execution for the Champion of Rome returning from retirement? The answer, so simple, came to Phaedra, and she spoke it aloud to Fortunada.

"Acestes wants votes. He plans to run for consul. The mob will vote for him if he entertains them with the return of Valens Secundus. By letting your brother serve Rome in the legions and Valens's sister go free, he also appears merciful. He might be a swine, but he is a brilliant swine."

Fortunada sipped her wine. "A brilliant swine that looks handsome on horseback. I noticed the way he watched you as he arrived at Marcus's funeral."

"Father wants me to marry Acestes. He presented his suit already."

"Aside from the fact that I hate him for taking away my brother, he would be a fine husband. Better to be the wife of the consul than an aged senator."

"I cannot love Acestes," Phaedra said firmly. "I do not want to marry him."

"Sometimes you love your husband, and in the end it does not matter much." Fortunada sighed. "It is not like you love someone else."

"Of course not," said Phaedra. Her gaze dropped to the floor.

Fortunada pursed her lips into an *O* of surprise. "You *are* in love. With whom? Where did you meet him? You must tell me everything."

"I did not say that I love anyone. All I have done is to tell you whom I do not love."

"You are a horrible liar," said Fortunada. "When you lie, you grip the side of your gown. Now give me some good news. Give me the name of the man who earned your love."

"I would rather not," said Phaedra. She and Valens had only the one night to share. Telling others, even her best friend, of their single tryst would complicate both their lives further. "It is not all that simple."

"Nothing is ever simple—is that not what you said to me about Damian?"

"I hate it when I have to listen to my own advice."

Fortunada laughed. "At least I can tell when you are not lying."

Phaedra laughed with her. It felt better than regret or grief or nothingness.

"He came to the villa last night after everyone went to bed," Phaedra said, knowing she told some important information while keeping the true secret hidden.

"He did? You need not be ashamed, you know. You are a widow and a little tryst now and then is expected. Does he love you?"

"I think he might."

"So, what is his name?"

"It matters not. I doubt we will ever see each other again. He is a pleb, so there can never be anything more than a night or two, especially if I marry soon."

"Pity."

Fortunada held up her goblet and a slave filled it with murky red wine. Phaedra looked into her cup and saw silt and bits of unfiltered grape floating near the bottom of the glass. Perhaps money was tighter for Fortunada's family than she had guessed.

Phaedra spent the rest of the visit reliving childhood memories and learning different tidbits about the lives of the other girls, now women, with whom she had grown up. As the litter took her home, Phaedra prayed her father would not ask too many questions. He might want information to barter for power, but if Phaedra said anything, she would betray her friend and their friendship.

Aside from the reason Damian had left Rome, she had learned another important truth—Valens had not used Phaedra for one night of unrestrained but unfeeling sex. Rather, he had spent his last free night with her when he could have been anyplace else.

Chapter 30

Valens

Sweat trickled down Valens's brow and stung his eyes. His arms throbbed, his back ached, and his hand had all but gone numb. When had wielding a sword become so difficult?

Block, block, thrust, cross, block.

The movements, once instinctual, now were slow and laborious. He had lost not only his physical edge but his mental one as well. His trainer was a large red-haired man called the German. Over the years he had sparred with this trainer many times. Valens always had been able to predict the German's next move. Now the fighting style of someone he had known so well was a mystery to him.

At noon the gladiators stopped to rest and eat. Valens sat on the ground with his back against a wall, in much the same place and in the same way he had done for over a decade. The uneven mud wall and the sunbaked earth felt welcoming. He wondered if Phaedra had heard of his return to the arena yet. Again, he chastised himself for not having told her when they were together. What might she think when she heard? Would she be proud that he fought to save his sister? Or did it simply demonstrate to her that his lone skill was to fight, and therefore not a skill at all?

"Greetings," said Baro. He stood above Valens and held out a bowl. "Care for some porridge with a little pork? Its taste depends on your hunger."

Valens took the bowl and scooped out a large bite. "Delicious," he said.

"You must be starving."

Valens ate three more bites before saying, "Famished."

"Your training appears to be going well."

Valens waved his spoon at Baro. "Do not lie to your friends. I am old. I am tired. If I do not win, my sister will die."

With the toe of his sandal, Baro drew a square in the dirt. "Defending," he said, "is all you need to do."

Valens recalled that he had drawn a similar square on Baro's first day as a gladiator. "How do I win by defending and nothing else?"

Baro scratched his cheek and chuckled. "I think I asked the same of you."

"And what did I say?"

"That I will never win if I am run through in the first few minutes of a match."

"Sound advice," said Valens. "Did I have any other words of wisdom for you?"

"Lots, but I ignored most of them."

Valens laughed. The muscles of his stomach contracted, and he groaned.

"You also said to know my strengths."

Valens took a bite of the porridge, now tepid and too salty. "I have no strengths. I am the weaker gladiator."

"You are a legend," said Baro. "No other person who steps into the arena will be a god, a titan, except you. Use the legend you created. The crowd will love you no matter what."

"Unless I lose. Then I am dead and so is Antonice."

Baro sat beside Valens and rested his back on the wall. "Might I share with you a trick of mine? Before I fight, I prepare here"—he gripped his bicep—"and here." He touched his temple. "Breathe. Imagine the editor of the game lifting your arm in victory. Believe you will win and you will."

Valens snorted. "You think I can wish myself to three victories?"

"Believing is the first step. How it happens is immaterial. Also, if you believe that the task is too difficult and victory is impossible, then you have already ensured your loss."

"I like to know the *how* of things."

"Then imagine each and every thing you must do in order to win. It matters little what works for me. What works for you is all that is important."

Valens closed his eyes and tilted his head back. In his mind he pictured the German as he brought his sword in close. Valens blocked the blow. Again the German attacked, and again Valens defended. This went on until Valens found an unprotected side he struck with the wooden sword. "Victory," he said aloud. "Can it be that easy?"

"Nothing is ever that easy, but if you prepare in all ways, you give yourself a better chance."

Valens nodded, understanding the truth in the other man's words. "Costmary," he said. "I mix leaves of costmary with olive oil for bathing. That is my secret and I now share it with you."

Baro stood and dusted the seat of his tunic. "I am honored."

"Have you heard from your aunt in Padua?"

"Not yet, but I shall let you know the moment I do."

They clasped wrists. "Thank you, my friend."

The German approached with two wooden swords in hand.

"Rest time is over," he said in his thick accent.

Valens took a sword and they walked to the middle of the practice arena. Valens inhaled, capturing a breath in his lungs. He played the winning moves in his head once more. Exhaling, he lifted the sword and nodded to the trainer.

The German attacked; Valens defended. Again and again. The sun beat down, scorching the earth and drying the sweat on Valens's brow. In his periphery he saw the other gladiators who gathered to watch. Valens turned his mind from their faces and their cheers and looked for the open side he knew would appear. The German whirled to the right, startling Valens with his change in direction. Yet the movement opened up the trainer from armpit to waist. Valens struck with his sword.

"Victory to Valens Secundus, still the Champion of Rome," said Baro, who had been among those watching from the sidelines.

Valens lifted his arms and cheered with his fellow gladiators. For all his years in the ludus, he had kept himself apart from the other gladiators. But now they were with him. For them, for his sister, he would win. Perhaps in winning he could find a way to claim Phaedra as his prize.

Chapter 31

Phaedra

After visiting Fortunada's house, Phaedra knew that living in dignified poverty would not suit her. Since the law forbade either she or her father from adopting a trade, she needed to marry in order to maintain a comfortable life. As an eligible patrician woman, she was certain that another man besides Acestes would want to marry her at some point. Yet if she married for financial security, then the groom mattered little, and Acestes served as well as anyone else. While all this was true, she also knew that after having spent the night with Valens, any other union would feel hollow.

The litter stopped in front of her father's villa. A guard held the door open. Phaedra entered and found the steward waiting in the atrium.

"Begging your pardon, my lady. Your father wishes that I inform you of his absence."

"Thank you." At least Phaedra did not have to face her father and his questions about Damian right now.

"I must also inform you that General Acestes waits for you in the garden."

Her father being gone when Acestes happened to stop by was a trap, meant to get her alone with the general. Phaedra saw no way to escape. "Bring some wine and water," she called over her shoulder as she walked toward the garden.

The villa's walls threw long shadows over the garden. Acestes stood under a tree, his broad back to Phaedra. He wore a dark blue tunic with a silver toga of silk draped over his shoulder and wrapped around his arm. She noted that he had donned a fine outfit for a casual visit. Perhaps he had just come from an important meeting or he planned to dine somewhere else later.

In a flash of memory not yet lived, she saw her future with him—the entertainment and parties they attended together as living testament to the glory of Rome, their children, although loved, a perpetuation of their parents and a way of life. Yes, she saw it all as clearly as she saw the garden. Yet it lacked the vibrancy and color she craved, the passion and reason for living she needed. She sighed. Her resignation toward it all crushed her spirit. Acestes turned and smiled. She wanted—prayed to her mother—to be warmed by his face and his happiness. Her prayers went unanswered and her soul remained bare.

If she had learned anything in her first marriage, it was that her happiness depended more upon herself than her spouse. It was a lesson she could put to use with Acestes, could she not?

"There you are," Acestes said. His smile remained and Phaedra felt a twinge of an unnamed emotion. She decided it must be guilt for not returning his affections.

"I called upon my friend Fortunada," she said, "and have just returned."

Acestes crossed his arms over his chest and nodded. "It is a pity about her brother's troubles with the quartermaster. I am glad that Damian saw the advantage in joining the legions."

"I am sure he also saw the advantage in not dying in the arena."

Acestes chuckled. "There is that, too."

"My father wants to know why Damian left."

"I spoke to him already and gave him all the details. He went to the forum soon after to share what he knew. I agreed to stay here and make sure you arrived home safely."

"What you mean is that you gave my father information so he agreed to let you spend time alone with me."

He laughed. "I like your spirited nature."

"Well, at least I will not need to betray Fortunada for my father's sake. I suppose this worked well for all of us."

"There is something I wish to discuss with you. It is about the gladiatorial games I am sponsoring." Acestes gestured to a bench.

Phaedra sat and smoothed her skirts over her legs, hoping that her casual gesture hid her frayed nerves. "Aside from the news about Damian, I learned that you have convinced Valens Secundus to return to the arena."

Her heartbeat thrummed, the pulse echoing in the base of her throat. Did Acestes notice? She should not have mentioned Valens, yet she could not help herself. She wanted to speak his name, to know everything about him. For Phaedra, Valens was the soft breeze that blew through the garden, the cooling cloud that crossed the sun, and the blood that flowed in her veins.

"News travels fast in Rome," Acestes said. "Soon everyone in the republic will know that I am bringing Rome's champion back to the arena. And if he falls, then I can still execute his sister. What a drama that would be."

"You have her in custody?"

Acestes stretched out his hand and examined his fingernails. "I had to leave her at her home," he said. "It was part of the bargain."

"Is it not possible that the gladiator will move his sister out of the city before the games? Then, even if he falls in combat, your plan will not work." Although Acestes's failure would come at too high a price, she hoped that somehow his scheme unraveled.

"I have thought of that," Acestes said, "and have stationed two legionnaires in plain clothes near the Secundus villa. If she leaves, they are to follow. If she tries to exit the city gates, they are to bring her to me."

Like a golden coin, Phaedra held on to Acestes's plan. She full well knew its value and that soon it might be needed by Valens. "Is that what you came to tell me?" she asked, hoping to sound bored and disdainful. "That you have soldiers spying on little girls?"

Acestes laughed. "You are far too determined to make me fight to win your affections. But no, that is not what I came to talk to you about." He stood and held out his hand. "Walk with me."

Phaedra placed her fingertips in his palm and allowed him to help her up. They walked without talking. She heard the sound of splashing water a moment before the fountain came into her field of vision. Did Acestes guess he led them to the same place where she had first met Valens? Likely not. She started to relax into the recollection of meeting the gladiator on her wedding night. She let the memory of Valens's lovemaking the night before wash over her in the cool droplets of fountain water caught in the wind.

"This is an important place, is it not?" Acestes said.

Phaedra loathed the notion that this almost sacred spot in her life held any meaning for Acestes. "I do not see how my father's garden could hold any importance to you."

Acestes gripped his chest as if it pained him. "You wound me," he said, even though Phaedra knew she did not. "I came looking for you on your wedding night. I found you here. I wanted to tell you then that you enchanted me, but my words came out wrong."

He closed his eyes and turned his face to the fountain. The sun shone behind the water, creating sparkling jewels of the spray. Even with his handsome face and his obvious attraction to Phaedra, she knew that she could never love this man. Acestes was like a highly polished silver disk that seemed bright, but in truth only reflected the light. Life would be easier if she could find some way to care, but she knew she could not.

"Can I ask you a question about the night you wed my uncle?"

Phaedra did not answer. She knew that Acestes would ask his question without permission.

"I found you with the gladiator, Valens Secundus," he said. "In the moment I felt as if I had interrupted something. Was he your lover then?"

"No," said Phaedra. She did not add, *not then.*

"I thought he might be. That was one of the reasons I offered to get you with child." He paused. "It matters little what I thought then, although there seemed to be something between the two of you."

Phaedra considered lying, telling Acestes that he had mistaken it all. Yet, she found that she could not completely deny Valens and decided that a certain version of the truth might be told instead. "Marriage to your uncle overwhelmed me at first, especially at the wedding. The gladiator came upon me as I was getting my bearings. I felt I should be polite. Besides, Valens Secundus is a handsome man. I know ladies are not supposed to notice if men are attractive or not, but he is pleasing to look upon. I asked him if he had fought at a wedding before."

She stopped speaking, knowing that her manners and mood could give away her deep regret. Oh, what a long and lonely life she would lead with Acestes. His keen eyes saw everything, and to protect her secrets she would need to live inside herself.

"You swear to me that the gladiator means nothing to you."

She must lie to Acestes. But what twitching eyelid or fidgeting finger would tell Acestes the truth? And if he knew, what then? He might take back his offer of marriage. Or he might marry her still and be a cruel husband. Worst of all, he could accuse her of betraying Marcus in adultery. While affairs for men were an expected part of life, married women who took lovers were often executed in the arena.

Hoping that Acestes would be satisfied with an indirect answer, Phaedra responded carefully. "I was as much a virgin on the night I married Marcus as the day I was born."

"And I imagine you were in the same virginal state in the morning as well."

"You warned me of your uncle's cool ardor, albeit a day too late."

Acestes laughed. Phaedra allowed a small smile. The whole situation had been so complicated it bordered on the absurd.

"Tomorrow evening there will be a party at my villa to celebrate the games that will begin the following day," said Acestes. He was moving on to another topic, and Phaedra breathed an internal sigh of relief. "Some important men from the Senate will be in attendance—your father, for one. I would have you attend as well. I would also like for you to greet guests with me as they arrive."

If she were seen helping Acestes greet his guests, all of Rome would view them as a couple. This was why her father had given them time alone, Phaedra knew. If she agreed to be his hostess, then she surrendered to their plans for her.

He continued to talk, speaking of who would attend the event— knights of the republic, magistrates, other senators and patricians, the gladiators who would fight. Valens. Valens might attend the party. No, he must. He was the Champion of Rome returning to the arena for the first time in two years.

Valens.

Yes, she would see him again and tell him everything she had meant to say during their one night together. She loved him now and would love him always. It mattered not that he had been a slave or poor or born fatherless in a society that worshipped patriarchs.

She wanted to tell Valens what he meant to her. During their night together, she had allowed pride to keep her silent. Tomorrow night might be her single chance to right that wrong. She knew that meeting with Valens in Acestes's villa without arousing suspicion would be tricky, if not dangerous. Yet Phaedra saw no other options.

"Say you will attend the banquet," Acestes said.

"Yes," said Phaedra. "There is no place I would rather be."

Chapter 32

Valens

The sun slipped below the horizon on Valens's final day of training.

Sore of body and weary of mind, Valens placed his wooden sword on a rack with the practice weaponry. Most of the shelves were filled with more wooden swords. Spears with the tips blunted and tridents with their prongs wrapped in fabric also stood close at hand.

Earlier in the day a slave had fitted him with a gladiator's kit. Leather greaves covered his legs and a small, round shield had been strapped to his left forearm. A leather and brass manica protected him from fingertips to shoulder. The last piece of his kit, his helmet, had a metal mesh that hung over his face. It was the same type of outfit he had worn during his career. But the sword itself was the same exact one he had wielded on his way to numerous victories.

Paullus had kept Valens's sword as a memento. At first it seemed a sentimental gesture. But holding the well-used weapon rekindled Valens's sense of invincibility, like an echo from another life.

His gear, along with that of every other gladiator scheduled to fight the next day, was locked up in the armory. In the morning a slave would come to his cell and help him get ready. Tonight he wanted to rest. He walked with the rest of the gladiators filing through the door that led from the practice field to the barracks.

Baro clapped Valens on the shoulder. "Are you ready to attend the banquet celebrating the beginning of the games?"

"I am not going."

"Not going? You have to. We all have to."

Valens shook off Baro's hand. "I am no slave, and I will be damned before Paullus orders me to go anywhere."

"Who pissed in your porridge this morning?"

"Jupiter himself."

Baro snorted.

"I am tired. I am sore. Baro, I worry about tomorrow. The Fates can only watch me win so often before getting bored."

"Not just the Fates. Everyone had gotten bored watching you win."

This time Valens let go a real laugh. "I am no good for a party. The patricians will miss their chance to meet the former Champion of Rome and be forced to meet her current one." Valens flexed his biceps, trying for a Herculean pose. His arm cramped at once. "If I survive this, Antonice will never want for anything."

"It is not your fault. What your sister did, she did. Not you."

"I should have done more for Antonice, or at least tried to get her away from the Suburra earlier. You should have seen all the men who were in and out of my mother's apartment." Valens shook his head. "In a way I think my sister's always been lost. Have you heard from your aunt?"

"Not in the two hours since you asked last." Baro slapped Valens on the shoulder. "Soak in the hot bath. Have a slave rub your sore muscles and come to the party. A night of good food and better company is what you need. If you do not show yourself, then the bastard General Acestes will think that you are sore and tired and whiny."

"I *am* sore and tired and whiny."

Baro laughed. Valens had not meant it as a joke.

"Here is something you might find interesting," said Baro. "The funeral games in which we fight honor his uncle, Marcus Rullus."

"I know. Everyone knows."

"The first time we fought each other was at Senator Rullus's wedding. Do you remember that, too?"

Valens nodded. He could not trust himself to speak. Despite all the honesty between them, he found it hard to confess his love for the late senator's wife to his friend. He wanted to give voice to his anger and sadness that he and Phaedra would never be together, but Valens could not find those words, either.

"Interesting how it all circles around. Like a snake eating its tail." Baro drew a circle in the air.

"Do you think she will be there, the bride?"

"You mean the widow? I assume so. I heard she plans to marry her dead husband's nephew, General Acestes. Keep all the money in the family."

The news hit Valens like a fist to the solar plexus. Phaedra had said her father wanted her to marry again, that he had already selected the next husband. She had never said whom he had chosen. She had never told him that she planned to marry the same bastard who had ruined his life by threatening his sister and forcing Valens to fight in the arena once again.

But then, he had never told her that he planned to fight again at all.

Did she hate him for keeping his counsel? Did he hate *her* for keeping hers?

A guard unlocked the door to the barracks and stood aside as the gladiators filed through. Valens followed Baro down the corridor and toward the baths.

"When do you fight?" Valens asked.

"I have the primus on the second-to-the-last day unless the schedule changes."

"You mean unless I am dead by then, which means you fight on the final day."

Still shuffling along the corridor, not even bothering to turn around, Baro lifted one shoulder and let it drop. Of course Paullus needed a plan if Valens could not do the impossible and win all three matches. Everyone understood the business of it all. Still, knowing his friends discussed his demise in terms of scheduling galled. If Valens had not been so sore, he would have punched Baro.

Valens went through the process of bathing while focusing on victory and honor, discarding the distractions of fear and doubt—and Phaedra. Why did she always come to mind? In truth, Valens knew that she never left his thoughts.

He decided to attend the party, if only to see Phaedra. He knew not what to expect from their encounter. Her forgiveness? An apology? Another night in her arms? Perhaps he wanted all of that, but what he wanted most of all was to see her one last time.

Chapter 33

Phaedra

Phaedra and her father arrived at what had once been her home with Marcus an hour before the party began. It was odd being here and knowing that Acestes was now the dominus. A life-size bronze donkey, supporting two wicker baskets, sat in the atrium. One basket held black olives and the other green. Dozens of pitchers were filled with gallons of sweet wine mixed with honey. Slaves stood by, ready to give a goblet filled with honeyed wine to guests as they arrived. Phaedra accepted a cup before wandering through the old villa. Acestes had planned the party without any help, and she would see how he had fared.

In the main triclinium a roasted wild boar surrounded by fruit and greens lay atop a silver platter. There were also two of Phaedra's favorites amid all the other dishes. One was a salad made of coriander, mint, parsley, and fresh salted cheese that was covered with vinegar and olive oil. On a nearby platter, crusts of white bread that had been soaked in milk and then fried now swam in a honey sauce. Dozens of reclining sofas sat along the edges of the big room.

In the medium-size dining room, tables and chairs were made available for any ladies who wanted to dine with only female company. In that room, one table held nothing but tarts. Phaedra took a pine-nut tart as she walked past.

The musicians and dancers hired for the night's entertainment set up on the patio, in the space where villa and garden became one. She watched from the doorway as the dancers rehearsed. Acestes entered and stood behind her.

"This is all very impressive," said Phaedra. "People will speak of this party for a long time."

"Good," he said. "I spared no expense. I am glad that it is to your liking."

Ah, so this was what a party could be when enough coin was spent. "It will be to everyone's liking."

Phaedra still wore her golden wrap over her gown. Acestes ran his fingers between her skin and the cloth. "Can I help you remove this?"

"Of course," she said. She stepped forward and left Acestes holding her wrap. "I am not cold and guests will be arriving soon." Phaedra turned to face him lest he touch her back again.

"Are you certain you are not chilled? Your neck is covered in gooseflesh."

It was. She hated that Acestes brought out a reaction in her at all. "I am fine," she said.

"You are more than fine," he said. "You look beautiful."

"I appreciate your compliment," Phaedra said. And she did. She had spent extra time on her appearance and felt beautiful. For the evening, she had chosen a silk gown of emerald green. Terenita had wound gold-and-silver ribbon through the curls of Phaedra's hair. She had taken such care not for Acestes or the other patricians, but for Valens. She had done it all for Valens.

"You wear the necklace I gave you."

"My father insisted," she said.

"I am glad he did." Acestes led her to the atrium. To prove that he had not been offended by her rude comment, he added, "I am also pleased that you listened to your father. Perhaps you will start listening to his advice on other matters as well."

"Perhaps," she said. "But I doubt it."

Acestes laughed. "You plan to greet my guests with me, of course."

"I have thought about that," she said, irritated that he took her rebukes as part of a game. "I find that I must decline. I want the elite of Rome to focus upon you and your splendid party. I would only serve as a distraction."

"As widow to Marcus, you should be beside me. It is your right to have a place of honor. Of course, I could speak to your father." Acestes continued, "He would see that I am right and insist. Or you could see what is right on your own and stop being an obstinate donkey."

Had he spoken to her thus? The nerve! Well, she would never, ever give Acestes what he wanted. Phaedra looked away. She spied the statue of a donkey, standing in the corner, ridiculously holding baskets of olives. Was she also ridiculous and stubborn?

In the end it would matter little. If she continued to refuse, Acestes would follow up on his threat and involve her father. With a long and weary sigh, she said, "If you wish."

"Thank you," said Acestes. "There is no one else with whom I would rather greet my guests."

Phaedra hated herself for acquiescing. Not only did Acestes now assume she was agreeing to much more than she ever wanted to give him, but once again she had failed to be the strong, decisive woman she had become during her years away from Rome.

For more than twenty minutes, Phaedra stood at Acestes's side and greeted one prominent Roman citizen after another. Many offered her their condolences. For the first time in many days, her grief for Marcus resurfaced. He had been a good man, a wise man, and Phaedra wondered what advice he might give her now.

She was speaking to the wife of a senator, a matron long known to Phaedra, when the air in the room changed. It became heavier, softer. Her pulse quickened. Without seeing Valens, she sensed his presence. She glanced at the line of waiting guests and saw him at once.

A dozen people back, a group of muscular men stood together. They shuffled from foot to foot, ill at ease with their new surroundings.

Valens did not. He stood tall, with his shoulders back. His chest rose and fell with breath—his only discernible movement. He kept his gaze trained on Phaedra. And yet his eyes gave away nothing.

Did he hate her for standing and welcoming guests with Acestes? Or did he care at all? Of the two she preferred his anger to his apathy.

She spoke to the people who separated them but heard little of what they said. Her heartbeat thrummed in her ears and fluttered at the base of her neck. Before long he stood in front of her, and her pulse crashed in her head like waves upon the shore. What did she expect from Valens? What did she want? Wanting and having were two different things, and he greeted her without giving away the intimacy they had shared a few nights past.

His hand touched hers and a spark, like the striking of flint, shot through her arm. Valens must have felt it, too.

She tried to meet his gaze, to somehow show Valens that he still lived in her heart and her mind, always. Now that they were close, Valens never looked directly at Phaedra. She blinked away tears of desperation and regret.

A fit man, a part of the group of gladiators, approached Phaedra. "I fought at your wedding," he said.

"You? I could have sworn my father hired Valens Secundus."

Valens turned her way. Still, she read nothing of importance in his expression. "He did, my lady, but I could hardly fight myself."

The other gladiators laughed, not meanly, but Phaedra felt the heat of color rise in her cheeks. An older man with white hair stepped forward. "I am Paullus Secundus, Lanista, and these are my gladiators. You recall Valens Secundus, I see."

Phaedra inclined her head to Valens in greeting.

"And this is Spurius Mummius Baro, the current Champion of Rome, who also fought at your wedding. We did not know at the time that the two titans of the arena would meet in your garden that night. The Fates must have been smiling upon you, my lady."

She studied Valens in profile. A sprinkling of black hair on his jaw made her think he had shaved that morning and not since. "I do believe you are right, Paullus." She turned her gaze back to the lanista. "The Fates were with me on my wedding night."

The group moved to speak to Acestes. Phaedra watched as they passed. Valens looked over his shoulder and winked so quickly she thought she might be mistaken. He had done that on her wedding night, too. Still a girl, she had stood next to Marcus and watched in awe at the strength and power of Valens. He had seen her, sensed her, and had made that simple and yet lasting connection. If he had not, then she never would have spoken to him later that evening all those years ago.

Without his wink, she would have never met the man Valens Secundus, never loved him.

Without Valens having encouraged her to bargain for her next husband the night of her wedding, she would never have found the courage to speak to her father. That first step, to acknowledge that she too mattered, was the greatest she had yet to take.

She greeted a few late-arriving guests. Still by Acestes's side, she made her way to the main triclinium, where everyone stood about with cups of wine as slaves passed by with trays of food and drink. Phaedra accepted a cup of wine and stood near her father and Acestes as they talked to a conservative senator about plans to renovate the building where the tax collector was housed.

Fortunada approached and linked her arm through Phaedra's. "Tell me what you know of the gladiator who fought at your wedding."

How had Fortunada guessed about her night with Valens? Although Phaedra should not have been surprised at her lifelong friend's perceptiveness. "Valens Secundus? What do you think I know of him?"

"Not him. The other one. His looks please me."

"To be honest I did not recognize him at all. His name is Baro, or some such."

"He is the new Champion of Rome."

"Or so his lanista says."

"So everyone says."

It gave Phaedra joy to see Fortunada excited about something. She looked around the room, hoping to find the gladiator who pleased her friend so well. A banquet before funeral games was the only time that gladiators were welcome guests in the homes of Rome's elite. As the sponsor, Acestes held an obligation to meet the men who might die for his entertainment and provide them with one last meal.

Aside from the important men of the republic and their wives, Phaedra noticed quite a few patrician widows. Not the ancient kind of widow, either, but younger women who would want to spend time with a virile man. She assumed those women attended to make lovers out of the gladiators. It seemed as though Fortunada wanted that, as well. For a moment Phaedra felt disdain for the women, her friend included. For love, she and Valens had defied convention. Perhaps in knowing that they loved one another, she felt superior. Then the reality of her situation came to her, and she realized that she was no better than they. Or perhaps she was worse, for Phaedra wanted to be with Valens always. The other women simply wanted a companion for a night, a much more sensible desire.

In the corner she saw the lanista, Paullus Secundus. Their eyes met for a moment, and he inclined his head. "Come," said Phaedra, "let us see what we can learn about your pleasing gladiator."

"Lanista," Phaedra said as they approached, "you must tell me your secret to having such winning gladiators."

"My lady, I did not know the games interested you."

"They do not, but my friend here"—she pulled Fortunada forward—"says that you have had two champions at your ludus. One champion sounds impressive, but there must be more to it for you to have trained two such successes."

"I think my gladiators fight well for me because I respect them as people, my lady. I know all of Rome looks upon gladiators as being in the lowest profession. At the same time it idolizes these men. At my ludus they are trained to fight and win. That is all."

Phaedra had not really been looking for a serious answer to the question, but to give them something polite to discuss. Yet it comforted her to know that Valens had been treated with respect even when he was a slave. "How do you think your Valens will do in his three fights? They are all to the death, and my understanding is that this is unusual."

"He is not my gladiator, not anymore, although I allowed him to return to the ludus to train. No one has ever tried to fight three times in one week, so I cannot answer your question. No one beat Valens during his career, but he retired two years ago. No one can win forever."

Phaedra's palms grew clammy. She gripped the sides of her gown to still her trembling hands. A world without Valens seemed not a place to live, only to survive. "You said he trained with you. Is he not still an accomplished fighter?"

"He is," said the lanista, "but he trained only a few days. He needs months."

"He will make a fine showing," she said, more to ease her own fears than anything else. Paullus answered anyway.

"These fights are to the death. There is no fine showing, only winning and dying," he said.

"Still, I wager he will win."

Paullus shrugged both shoulders. "The odds are against him, my lady."

"Odds? Real wagers are made on these contests?"

"Even after all your travels, in many ways you are so naive," said Fortunada. "Of course people bet on gladiator fights."

Phaedra ignored her friend's rude comment. "Just out of curiosity, what are the odds on Valens Secundus winning all three fights?"

"One hundred and fifty to one, my lady," said Paullus.

"Someone with coin to spare might make a tidy profit," said Fortunada. "Pity that I have little coin at all."

"Many ladies from your social class use their jewelry to secure a wager," said Paullus.

"Pity that I have even fewer jewels than coin," said Fortunada.

Phaedra forced herself to laugh with the other two, although secretly it distressed her that the odds of Valens winning all three bouts were so low. She noticed Fortunada looking away and followed her gaze to the gladiator Baro. Phaedra agreed that he was pleasing to look upon with his short, dark hair and skin the color of freshly minted copper, although not as pleasing as Valens.

She twined her arm through the lanista's and pulled him toward Baro. "I would have a word with you," she said, "but first we must leave my friend in good company. The dark-skinned gladiator is one of yours, is he not? He said he fought at my wedding."

Paullus began to lead the way. "Baro, come here, I want you to meet someone. I need to discuss business with Lady Phaedra. You will entertain her friend and see that she comes to no harm?"

Baro smiled at Fortunada, his teeth straight and white against his dark skin. "Of course, Lanista. I will do anything to honor the ludus."

Dark, with thick muscles, Baro looked like the opposite of Fortunada, with her light hair, fair skin, and long legs. Yet the two made a matched set, and Phaedra doubted that her friend would miss her as she moved away with Paullus.

"Shall we walk in the garden while there is still some light?" Paullus asked.

Phaedra guided Paullus to the garden. A few other people milled about, enjoying the cool breath of evening. They nodded to each other in passing. Near a statue of Daphne, caught in the moment when flesh turned to wood, the older man paused. Phaedra settled down on a nearby marble bench. "You wish to make a wager," he said. "I know how crude it is for the aristocracy to speak of such things, but I assure you I can handle the details with the greatest discretion."

Phaedra never wagered, had not even when she was married to Marcus and had a vast fortune to command. She started to correct Paullus's mistake, but stopped before she spoke.

She could place a bet. By placing a wager on Valens, she demonstrated a belief in his winning. Like Fortunada, Phaedra had no coin. Perhaps she could persuade her father to place the wager. No, she wanted to personally bet on her lover.

"The necklace you wear must be worth a quarter of a million sesterces," said Paullus.

Phaedra touched the emerald that hung round her neck. The skin under the jewel tingled. "Explain to me how this works."

Paullus stood taller. "You entrust me with what you wish to wager, say, your necklace. I have a jeweler with whom I work. I sell the necklace to him, on your behalf, and then take the coin paid and place a wager. I take care of all the details, and no one need ever know of your involvement."

"If I bet this necklace on Valens winning all of his matches and he won, how much coin would I receive?"

Paullus paused and mumbled to himself for a moment. "More than thirty-seven million sesterces. Call it thirty-four million after my commission for arranging your wager."

Thirty-four million sesterces. The possibility left her dizzy with possibilities. She would never have to worry about money again. True, it was less than Acestes had by tenfold, but it was more than she needed. She reached behind her neck and loosened the clasp. "Bet this on Valens winning all of his games."

"My lady, you understand that no one thinks he can win them all. That is why the odds are so high. He is expected to win his first match. The odds are three to two. You would still make one hundred and twenty-five thousand sesterces after you bought your necklace back. Not a bad investment."

She believed in Valens and his invincibility, because to do anything else was to accept his death. "Take it." She held out the necklace and wondered what Acestes would say when he noticed its absence. Yet if she won, then Phaedra need never care what Acestes thought or noticed again. "I am not very fond of this piece of jewelry."

Paullus took the necklace and slipped it into a cloth sack he wore at his waist. "I shall make the bet first thing in the morning and pray that Fortune smiles upon you."

"I pray for the same thing myself."

"Now, if you will excuse me," said Paullus, "the opulence of villas such as this leaves many of my men ill at ease, and nervous gladiators rarely win. I must return to them."

In the first moments of twilight, the leaves and flowers of the garden were losing some of their vibrancy, but with the sun setting, the heat diminished. Like the villa itself, the garden sprawled in many different directions. Flower beds lined gravel paths. Arbors hung overhead. Trees, heavy with the scents of fruit and flowers, stood nearby. Alcoves formed by the contours of the house lay hidden behind the greenery. Yes, the garden, very much like the villa, was a grand place, or could be, if tended to. But its neglect was evident as spiny weeds poked out of flower beds and gangly flowers fought roses and jasmine for soil. Dead branches reached out from trees that needed pruning.

Phaedra heard footfalls on the gravel path. Without looking up, she knew Valens had come.

"I thought I might find you here," he said.

She turned. Her mouth went dry, yet she smiled because to look upon Valens brought her joy. Muscles created hard planes and deep divides on his arms and legs. His broad shoulders and tall posture showcased his power and vitality.

He wore a short-sleeved tunic of burnt orange. The color brought out coppery strands in his dark brown hair. His eyes showed more green than hazel. His tanned shoulders held the slightest tint of pink, and Phaedra guessed he had spent most of the last two days training out of doors. She noticed a deep purple bruise on his thigh. Phaedra reached out to touch it, but stopped lest she embarrass them both. "You are injured."

"I am a gladiator," he said. After a pause, Valens added, "Again."

"I heard," she said. "I also heard of the circumstances. You are a very brave and noble man, Valens Secundus."

He shook his head. "I failed my sister. That is why she strayed."

"I do not believe you failed her for a moment."

"I wish that were so," he said. He gestured toward the bench on which she sat. "Might I join you?"

"I am not sure that my virtue is safe with you around."

He stared, openmouthed.

Phaedra made room for him on the bench. "It was a joke. Apparently, not a very good one."

Valens chuckled as he sat. "No, it was funny. I just never imagined you to be one to tease."

"It appears that with you I can be convinced to try many new things."

He moved closer. His arm grazed hers and Phaedra's innermost muscles tightened.

"Good," he said. "I worried that you regretted what we had done."

"I will never regret being with you."

He moved closer still. Her flesh tingled in the spots where they touched. Shoulder to shoulder, side of hand to side of hand, knee to knee. In the garden, even in nooks such as where they sat, they might still be visible if someone knew where to look. The heat from his body and his scent of leather and costmary washed over her. She no longer cared who saw or what they thought.

And yet, tomorrow Valens might be dead. If someone saw them tonight, she would be alone and ruined. She hesitated, then moved aside so their shoulders and knees no longer touched. The sides of their hands still rested one by the other. She needed to tell Valens about the guards who watched his home and his sister. Although it was a betrayal of Acestes, Phaedra never considered it dishonest. Her loyalty belonged to Valens.

"There is something you must know. Acestes has two men watching your villa at all times. They have been ordered to follow your sister and arrest her if she tries to leave the city."

"Why do you tell me this?"

"If it were me, I would try to get my sister from Rome and hidden."

Valens shrugged and Phaedra took it to mean that he had been thinking the same thing.

Phaedra shifted so their shoulders once more touched. "You are very brave for saving your sister," she said.

"Antonice," Valens said, "lived with my mother, a woman who enjoyed the company of many men. I should have been in the apartment more, monitored my sister's life more, allowed fewer men into my mother's life. I am the patriarch of my family and never acted like it."

"So, you blame yourself for not beating your mother's suitors."

"Suitors." He snorted. "None ever presented a suit for marriage, trust me."

Phaedra laughed. "Your honest confession scandalizes me. So I will shock you with an honest confession of my own. You men think to control us women, but we have ideas and thoughts, and at times we make up our own mind."

"Like when you decided to marry General Acestes a day after bedding me. Or are you going to blame a man for that as well?"

Chapter 34

Valens

Valens should have kept his mouth closed.

Wide-eyed, Phaedra gaped at him. He swore under his breath and berated himself for his accusation. What could he say now? As impossible as unringing a bell—he knew of no way to take back his words.

Phaedra stood, her hands clenched at her sides. "I should go," she said.

"Wait." He held her closed fist with his fingertips.

Slipping from his grip, she walked along the pathway and deeper into the garden. Valens leaned his elbows on his knees, heavy with shame and regret. For a moment he convinced himself that Phaedra had lied to him. Valens even told himself that his stupid comment was for the best if it severed their relationship completely and irrevocably.

As much as he wanted to, Valens could not believe his own lies. Seeing her with Acestes as they greeted guests pained him more than any wound received in the arena. Phaedra and the general were the same type. They attended the same parties, knew the same people. For all his money and fame, Valens would never be one of them. He would never be able to love Phaedra as he wanted. Instead, he needed to pretend that she did not matter.

He could not do it.

He could not cut Phaedra out of his life. He wanted to be with her even if he had a single day left to live. He needed her. *Especially* if he had a single day to live.

He found her in an alcove, sitting on a bench with her back to the path. An olive tree grew nearby and almost shielded her from view. Her spine lengthened as he approached.

"Apologies," he said.

She looked over her shoulder, regarding him for an instant, before turning away. "You owe me nothing, Gladiator."

Valens surveyed the garden. He neither saw nor heard anyone. Thinking they might escape notice in this secluded spot, he sat beside her and rested his chin on her shoulder. Being close to Phaedra was the best place he had ever been. "Do not call me Gladiator. You know my name."

"But you are a gladiator, are you not? We are all trapped by what we are more than by who we are. I am a daughter of an aristocratic house and cannot escape that any more than you can escape who you are. Sometimes we have to use what we are to help those we love."

"I must fight to save my sister, and you must marry to save your father."

"Exactly," she said.

Her words saddened him. "What happened to the girl I met in the garden who challenged me to change my fate?"

Phaedra shrugged. Her shoulder rose and fell under his chin. "That night she was made to believe that anything was possible. Now she knows better."

"I attended this banquet to see you, to speak to you, not to argue," he said. "I am truly sorry for what I said earlier."

She turned her face to him and her breath tickled his cheek. Valens's cock stirred and he pressed his chest closer to her back.

"I am glad you came," she said. "There is much I wanted to tell you."

"I am here now. I am listening."

She leaned into him. They fit together perfectly. Valens wanted to keep Phaedra near him until he died. He tried not to think that if he lost in the arena tomorrow, the Fates would have granted his final wish.

"I am a better person for having known you," she said. "I wanted you to know."

"In case I die tomorrow," he said.

"I want you to live forever," she said.

"If I survive this, I shall leave Rome," he said. Until that moment Valens had not known he had a plan beyond winning his three fights. "I shall take my sister out of the city and away from all the temptations."

"Away from Rome means away from me," she said. "Or am I the temptation?"

"I cannot watch as you live your life with Acestes, or any man, for that matter."

"I see," she said.

Perhaps she did, but for now he wanted to sit next to her. Her back rested on his chest, and the long shadows of dusk gave way to darkness of night. A few insects chirped as the air cooled.

"I should return," she said as she stood. "I have been gone far too long and must be missed by now. May the gods protect you, Valens Secundus. I will think of you always."

He knew that he should let her go. Yet in letting her leave, he was lost.

"Wait," he said.

She stopped. Valens moved to stand next to Phaedra and placed his palms on her shoulders. His large, callused hands looked too big and clumsy.

Her breath caught in her throat, the sound light and full of air. She had not rejected him. He traced her cheek down to her neck and back up again. He ran his fingers down her arms. His fingers entwined with hers. He pulled her close.

He needed her. He wanted to lose himself and the world inside of Phaedra.

This was a moment meant to be lived.

Valens brought his mouth down on hers. Her tender lips parted and he breathed her in as she mewed. Yes, she wanted him almost as much as he wanted her. His hands traveled to her breasts, and he felt the hard peaks of her nipples through the binding cloth and the silk of her gown. He moved his mouth to her neck, trailing kisses to the point where throat and shoulder met. She wound her fingers through his hair.

Valens's cock throbbed. He needed release. He needed Phaedra to give him that exquisite pain.

He reached between her legs and pulled up her gown fistful by fistful. Her naked thighs tangled with his, and he felt heat coming from her sex even before he touched her. Holding the gown up between their bodies, Valens rubbed her most tender spot.

She gasped. Valens Secundus, Champion of Rome and lover of Phaedra. The titles fit, did they not?

He drew small circles with the pad of his thumb as she pressed against his hand. The power to make the woman he loved breathless with her release left Valens so hard he thought he might fall over. He leaned into her, trapping his cock near her belly. She wiggled against him, as his sensitive tip shuddered with anticipated pleasure.

"I want you," he said.

"Yes," she said. "Take me here. Take me now."

For her, he would risk everything, including discovery. At the same time, he did not want to make life harder for either of them. He hated the thought of Phaedra marrying Acestes. But even he, a dumb bastard from the Suburra, saw the obvious advantages of her union with the general.

Valens looked around and saw no windows or doors or any view to the house. A tree shielded them from the rest of the garden. The darkness hid their movements. Maybe they did have enough privacy. In many ways he wanted the world to know that Phaedra belonged to him, no matter whom she wed. But to be caught in the act would be disastrous for them both. Secure in their limited privacy, Valens lowered his head and kissed her hard, tasting her honeyed breath, taking possession of her for now and always.

Pulling his tunic over his hips, Valens sat on a wall that surrounded a flower bed. He shifted Phaedra onto his lap with her legs on the outside of his own. He entered her all the way in two thrusts. Soft and wet, she surrounded him and massaged his cock with her innermost muscles. Gripping Phaedra's waist, he slid her up and down. He looked between them to the place where he disappeared inside her.

By all the gods, he loved this woman.

He loved the way she smelled, the feel of her kisses, the softness of her skin. He loved that she believed in him. He loved that she was beautiful but seemed unconscious of it. He loved who he was when he was with her, because Valens saw himself through Phaedra's eyes.

The Fates were bitches, horrible hags. An odd thought to have while making love to a woman in a not-very-private garden, he knew. But he could not help but curse them as he entered Phaedra a little bit farther. During his life the Fates had been kind, granting him everything—fame, money, prestige. Never did they see fit to give him a woman to love. Now the hags had brought Phaedra to him for a few fleeting moments. Worse yet, both he and she knew their time was temporary and that soon they would be torn apart. That made these moments more precious, and at the same time, empty.

Phaedra wrapped her legs around Valens's waist, taking his shaft inside her deeper than before. He supported her weight, holding her firm bottom in his hands. Shifting, moving, massaging. He did not want to climax, not yet, but the pressure built and Valens could no longer contain his seed. He spilled inside of her, and his cock throbbed with each beat of his heart.

He promised himself that he would do anything in his power to make her his own. Valens nuzzled his nose into her hair. She smelled of lavender and warmth and their lovemaking. The pounding pulse in his ear slowed and quieted. Far away, but not far enough, he heard Acestes speaking. "You said you saw her come this way." His tone sounded peevish and his words were clipped.

Phaedra heard him, too. She no longer lay against him, her soft and pliable body forming to his own. She sat upright, her back stiff, not moving, not even bothering to breathe.

"You go," she said.

"No, I will never leave you."

"Now is not the time to be stubborn and brave. Acestes has power over us both."

Phaedra was right, although Valens hated to admit it. He let Phaedra slip off of him and sit on the wall. She smoothed her gown over her lap, the silk wrinkled and crushed beyond repair. Valens sneaked behind a tree and rounded to the other side of the flower bed, crouching as low as possible.

Acestes's shadow loomed over the stone and gravel path as he approached. "There you are," he said. His voice changed, growing deeper and slower. Valens imagined that a smile slipped from his face as he spoke. "What happened to you?" he asked. "What happened to my necklace?"

"The clasp broke," Phaedra said. "I did not realize that it dropped."

Valens knew nothing of the necklace. Why had he not thought to gift Phaedra with beautiful jewels?

Acestes cursed. "I will get the slaves to bring torches. Where do you recall having it last?"

Phaedra stood and moved into the shadow cast by a wall. "I found it," she said, "in a flower bed. My father has it now."

"Odd. He never mentioned anything to me, and I spoke to him not five minutes ago."

Her next answer came quicker than the first. "He wanted to save you from the embarrassment of having given a faulty gift, I am sure."

Although Valens greatly disliked the fact that Acestes was gifting Phaedra with anything and that so much attention was being paid to the damned necklace, he could not help but smile. Her last retort would shut the general up, for sure.

"My apologies," Acestes said stiffly.

"I think I shall go back to my old chamber and dispatch someone to fetch me a new gown," said Phaedra as she walked away. "I fear this one is near ruined for having to scramble through your flower beds."

The years had changed Phaedra. She was no longer the innocent bride, easily cowed by Acestes's questions. In the battle of wits, she had held her own. In fact, he might even pronounce her the winner.

With both Phaedra and Acestes gone, Valens stood. Hot blood flowed into his legs, filling his flesh with tiny stings. Without question, he liked the new Phaedra better. Yet he took note—she was now a powerful woman on her own terms.

Chapter 35

Valens

Valens woke before dawn, bathed, broke his fast, and returned to his cell, waiting to be summoned. His form would not improve with a frantic hour of training. With two hours until his fight, he went to the armory. Slaves tied leather greaves over his thighs, a metal band to one wrist, and a leather manica to the other arm. They also fitted him into his leather skirt and bronze breastplate. Aside from the slaves and Valens, Paullus and Baro also took up space in the cramped room.

"Your opponent today is new," said Paullus. "He had some success in Capua. People think since he hails from the birthplace of gladiatorial games, he is somehow blessed."

"I do not want to hear any more," said Valens.

This went against his long-held rule to know everything he could about an opponent before stepping into the arena. Yet he could not view the other gladiator as anything other than an obstacle, just the first task of three.

Paullus and Baro moved to the corner as slaves finished fitting Valens into his kit. No one spoke. The silence provided time for his thoughts to wander. Valens decided to try Baro's trick of thinking about the outcome he wanted. In his mind's eye, he entered the arena and pictured his opponent not as the new gladiator from Capua, but rather a tree. Yes, he much preferred to fight a tree made of bark and wood and sap, not a man of blood and bone and flesh. *The loss of one tree is much the same as the loss of another.*

With less than one hour until the match, Paullus, Baro, and a contingent of six guards led Valens to the Forum Boarium, now free of cattle. Wooden stands circled the stone wall. A large dais stood up at one end of the arena. Even the width of the market away, Valens saw the bright canvas awning stretched tight over the platform providing shade for Acestes, the sponsor of the games, and his guests. Phaedra would be one of those guests.

A crowd had gathered to watch Valens; they screamed and cheered as he passed. Their faces were just as one continual blur, and their words nothing more than a distant rumble. Valens's pulse rose and his palms grew damp with sweat.

Focus.

Fight.

He waited in a stall meant to hold more expensive cattle before auctions. Even though someone had swept the floor clean and put out a stool and a jug of water in a corner, the place still held the grassy smell of cow dung. Valens sat on the stool and shook his head when Paullus held out the jug of water.

Focus.

His mind went black. He saw nothing. He heard nothing.

Paullus touched his arm. Valens stood and followed the white-haired lanista toward a door leading to the arena. Sun slanted over the sponsor's dais, surrounding it with a halo of brilliant white light. Like a lovesick fool, Valens searched for her—one face among many. He squinted under his helmet and tried to make out faces or figures. He saw nothing beyond the shadow of a whole. He turned away, needing to block out everyone but his opponent, his obstacle.

The game's editor, the man responsible for making sure all the rules of conduct were obeyed, moved to the center of the sand. He motioned for both of the gladiators to approach. The other gladiator entered through a door on the opposite side of the arena.

A short man with wide shoulders and black hair that fell down to the middle of his back walked toward Valens. The helmet covered his entire face, having only two holes for eyes. The back of the helmet fanned out, protecting his neck. He wore a leather cuff on each arm, covering from wrist to elbow. He carried two things with him—one hand held a net, and the other a long trident. *Could it get any worse?* Valens wondered.

Both gladiators stood next to the editor as he explained the rules, which were few in a fight such as this. He drew back the baton held between the gladiators as a signal for the contest to begin.

Valens lifted his sword, which suddenly seemed much too heavy and clumsy. The other gladiator moved much more swiftly than Valens had expected and struck Valens's shield with the wooden end of his trident. Valens felt the impact all the way to his shoulder and staggered backward. The crowd booed. The other gladiator struck again and again, sending Valens off-balance. He tried to counter the attack and to guess at his opponent's next move, yet his impulse was to back away in order to remain alive.

Light glinted off the wide visor of the other gladiator's helmet. Through its eyeholes Valens could see the wide-eyed look of unadulterated glee that came with certain and easy victory.

The other gladiator came in from the right. Valens shifted to counter the movement as the other gladiator spun the trident. Three sharp tines shone. His opponent moved left as Valens stepped right. With a stab the trident pieced Valens's shoulder. For half a second, the sounds, sights, and smells of the arena became clear and vibrant: the screaming crowd and the hollow noise of feet stomping on the wooden seats, the colorful awning of the sponsor's box, the dim and dirty tunics of the spectators, the smells of sweat and filth, and the acrid stench of bloodlust.

He saw red as pain rushed from his shoulder to his fingers and echoed back, traveling up his neck. He saw Antonice as a child, her long hair streaming behind her as she raced across a crowded street to greet him. He saw her again as a young woman, laughing in the garden with their housekeeper, Leto, while both women tended the flower beds. Next, he saw his sister being dragged through the same door of the Forum Boarium that Valens had used, tears staining her dirt-covered face. Then he watched as rough slaves tied her to the back of a thick, black bull. His mind could take no more, and his thoughts turned. He saw Phaedra at the door of a villa, a smile of welcome on her lips.

Focus.

Fight.

Valens's world shrank again until he alone existed. If he was in pain, he knew it not. With his sword he meant to rule the heavens and the earth. He swung out once. His sword grazed his opponent's leather arm cuff. Then Valens lowered his attack. His first strike hit the thigh; the second, the knee. The gladiator tumbled to the ground, and Valens drove his sword through the other man's heart.

The editor grasped Valens by the arm, lifting it high.

"Valens Secundus, winner and once again Champion of Rome."

Cheers deafened him. Silver coins rained down from the stands. Women threw roses and tore their gowns, vowing to love him forever. Men wept. Valens turned to Acestes's seats in order to receive the customary praise from the sponsor.

The general moved to the edge of his platform and held his arms up for silence. The crowd ignored him for a moment, but soon even they grew tired of the antics.

"Valens Secundus, you honor us with this great victory," he said.

"I fight to honor your uncle, a great man."

As Valens spoke, saying the words the crowd expected to hear, Acestes looked to his back and extended his arm. When the general faced forward again, he held Phaedra by the waist. His hand rested in the exact place Valens had gripped when they had made love the night before in the garden.

"My uncle's widow thanks you for the honor as well," Acestes said. He emphasized the word *my*.

Valens clenched his sword, ready to strike.

His gaze held Phaedra's for one moment. He read nothing in her eyes that said, *Come to me* or *Good-bye*, or *I love you*.

Then she winked.

Yes, her wink said, *I am yours. Even standing next to this man, I belong to you.*

Yes, her wink said, *we share secrets. We share a history.*

Yes, her wink said, *we have a future together, you and I. Come to me so we can begin our lives.*

In a crowd of thousands, Valens alone knew that she had said anything at all.

He was Valens Secundus, invincible and unstoppable, and champion of the known world. He was loved by a beautiful woman, and no one would keep them apart.

Like a man possessed, he stood in the middle of the arena and laughed.

Chapter 36

Phaedra

Phaedra had spent the afternoon at the games in the sponsor's box with her father, Acestes, and the rest of Rome's elite. The box consisted of a wooden floor covered with lush carpets. A half wall surrounded the entirety, creating more of a visual barrier than an actual one. An awning had been stretched overhead to block out the sun's rays. Sofas and chairs had been brought in for the comfort of those in attendance. Slaves served food and wine all the time, yet Phaedra had eaten little, so concerned had she been for Valens.

Her pulse had not slowed since he had entered the arena. At first, his fighting looked weak. The thought of Valens dying terrified her, and to keep her emotions hidden, she had bitten the inside of her lip until she broke the skin and blood filled her mouth. Then something indescribable changed—Valens had become the embodiment of Mars on earth. She, and everyone else, had seen the transformation.

At the end of the day, Acestes had offered the use of his newest silver litter to take her home. Once at her father's villa, a profound weariness enveloped her, seeping all the way to her bones.

"Tell Father the excitement of the games left me fatigued. I will miss dinner," she said to Terenita.

"Shall I bring a tray to your room, my lady?"

"In a few hours," said Phaedra. "First I need to rest."

She undressed and slid under the cool sheets without first donning either a sleeping gown or robe. She did not even recall closing her eyes before falling into a deep and bottomless sleep.

***

Phaedra woke in a darkened world. She sat up, clutching the covers over her bare breasts. Her pulse hammered and she held her breath. She looked into the darkness and listened for something—she knew not what.

On the table near her bed, a silver tray reflected scant moonlight. She saw the outline of a pitcher, a cup, and a plate filled with bread and fruit. Other than the food, her room looked just as it had when she had first lain down.

She listened to the silence. Something had awakened her. A movement, perhaps. No, a voice, she decided. Had it all been a dream?

In the corner, a shadow shifted.

"Hello," she said into the darkness. Instinctively her chest tightened as she made ready to scream and alert the guards.

"Apologies if I frightened you." Valens had come to her. He stepped from the shadows. Light and dark played across his body as if he were a carefully lighted marble statue.

"How did you get into the villa?"

"I came earlier, but your maid would not let me in. She told me you slept and to come back later. I did. Still, you slept. She said later, so I waited. This time she let me in because she thought maybe I could wake you."

"She could have roused me herself."

"She tried, as did your father. They both feared you had fallen ill."

"Does he know you are here?" She did hate that she had become a daughter once again. Being treated as a child and ordered about angered her.

"No, just your maid. She cares for you, you know."

"Terenita is a good woman."

"But she does not like me," said Valens. "She thinks I will ruin your chances with Acestes."

"She is right. If Acestes knew about our time together, he would make us both pay." She sat up. The covers slid from her body, revealing her nakedness. Valens drew in a sharp breath, and Phaedra smiled to herself. *So, this is what it is to be desired.*

"There is nothing more important in my life than you," Valens said as he stepped toward her.

"I do not worry for myself, and yet I fear for you. Acestes is a powerful man and more influential than I care to think," said Phaedra. "As a patrician, with an army of his own, he could arrange awful things. He might even pit you against two gladiators at once."

"You do not follow the games at all, do you?" The corner of Valens's lip curled into a wry smile. "I am undefeated. In Capua, I faced four opponents during a single fight."

"And you won?"

"Yes, that is what undefeated means."

Phaedra gave a small laugh. "Fighting four men at once sounds impressive."

"Not really. One was blind and two were already dead."

Phaedra laughed. "And the final man?"

"It was a goat that held the sword in his teeth. I knew I had won when he ate the leather grip and could not keep hold any longer."

"My, you are brave to fight two corpses, a blind man, and a goat all in one day."

"You laugh, but the dead put up more of a fight than you imagine."

Phaedra filled a goblet with wine and took a long drink. She settled back on the bed, not bothering to cover her nakedness. Valens moved closer. The darkness stole all the color, but his features were visible. Phaedra focused on his mouth. The remembered feeling of his mouth on her nipples came with such clarity that she almost moaned aloud.

Valens trailed his fingers from her ankle to her knee. The breath caught in her chest.

Yes. Touch me. Taste me. Feel me. Make me yours.

"As soon as I won," said Valens, "I wanted you. The power from the arena is intoxicating. I have never quite found the words for how it feels to prevail or command over death. It always leaves me more alive, and at the same time, less." His fingertips trailed from her knee to her thigh. Phaedra let her legs relax to reveal her sex. Valens moved his gaze to stare at her. A small smile tugged at the corner of his mouth. He slid his fingers higher until they traced the curling hair at the juncture between her legs. "I want to lose myself inside you, Phaedra. Not just now, but always."

She knelt at the edge of the mattress. Drawing Valens to her, she kissed him. His hard length pressed against her, and she stroked him through the coarse fabric of his tunic.

"Tell me how to please you," she said.

"Touch me. Take me in your hand and in your mouth."

Every time she had lain with Marcus, Phaedra had needed to take him in hand and in her mouth in order to awaken his passions. How different to see Valens already aroused. She felt beautiful, and not just an insignificant piece in the game of Roman politics. Together, they wrestled Valens from his tunic.

He pulled her to him, their lips pressed together and their tongues joined. Phaedra reached for his shaft and moved her hand over the silky skin. She traced the enlarged head with a featherlight touch. Valens groaned and she, too, felt the power that came with control over another's sensations.

"Lie back," she said as she pushed him to her bed.

She took Valens in her mouth. Sucking gently, her kisses slid back and forth. Valens combed his fingers through her hair, entangling his fists in the ends.

"By all the gods, you have enchanted me," he said.

Phaedra took him in deeper and faster this time.

He pulled on her hair. The pain aroused her more. "Slow down," he said. "I want to enjoy the feel of being in your mouth. Better yet, swing your bottom up here."

Had she heard Valens correctly? He would, while she did? Was it possible? Of course it was possible, and tonight she was prepared to try. She swirled her tongue around his swollen head once more and moved as he instructed. Valens kissed the top of her sex, sucking and tasting much as she did to him. He slid one finger inside her moist opening and then another. Her muscles tightened as he kissed her and moved his fingers back and forth. Her first climax came with such force that Phaedra buried her face in the side of Valens's leg, lest her cries of pleasure wake her father, the guards, and everyone else in Rome. Running her tongue along the side of his shaft, she panted. Jupiter and Saturn help her, she loved this man and no other. She could no longer imagine her life without Valens.

The thought left her spent and her body relaxed as she continued to lie atop Valens.

"Come here," he said.

She moved to him. His kisses tasted of her pleasure.

"I love you," she said. Her words felt sad and empty. She would never measure their time together in month or years, rather in the few hours or minutes they could steal.

"I love you, too," said Valens, shifting on top of her.

Phaedra wrapped her legs around his waist and he entered her in one stroke. Fitting perfectly, they moved together. Valens lifted up and shifted his shoulders under her legs. She gasped as he moved deeper inside of her, deeper still, as if he could not enter her enough.

Valens and no other.

His pace increased. She clung to his shoulder and touched a piece of cloth she had not noticed before. He had been hurt during the fight, she recalled. She ran her fingers over the bandage's edge and prayed he healed without incident. Yet his injury could not be that bad if he were here now, making hard and passionate love to her.

Valens reared his head back and groaned as his seed spilled inside of her. She untangled her legs and they curled next to each other, her back to his chest.

Hot tears stung her eyes and she stifled a sob. The cruel Fates continually brought Valens and her together and yet forever kept them apart.

"What is the matter?" Valens propped himself on an elbow and looked down at Phaedra.

She wiped a hand across her eyes. "Nothing is the matter."

"Did I hurt you? I always try to be gentle. I find with you I lose control."

She always wanted his loss of control. "I am fine," she said. "In fact, I am much better than fine. This"—she gestured between the two of them—"seems such a waste. I hate the laws that keep us apart. I wish you had a million sesterces so my father could stay in the Senate."

"A million? You know nothing about the games. I am a wealthy man, Phaedra, with more than two million sesterces to my name."

"Really?" She sat up so fast her head swam, and then she remembered that she had eaten nothing since noontime. But hunger and dizziness faded as what Valens said settled on Phaedra. "With half a million sesterces, you can enter the equestrian rank. Then the Senate could allow us to marry."

Valens lay back down and pulled her with him. He lifted her hair and kissed the nape of her neck. "I once thought of becoming an equestrian."

"You did not, though—why?"

"There are three things a man needs to become an equestrian. First is money. I have the money. Second is a senator willing to put his name—my name—forth. No one wants to champion a gladiator. Even if I convinced a senator to present my nomination, how many other senators would vote for a former slave to become a member of their society?"

"Not many," said Phaedra. "Perhaps none. You need someone very influential."

"Aside from an influential senator, I need one other thing that I will always lack. A father."

Phaedra hated to think of Valens being anything other than well pleased with life. Perhaps she could coax him out of his melancholy. She reached up and stroked his face. "You have a father," she said. "Everyone has a father. I thought you understood how all that worked. If not, I can show you again."

Valens kissed her shoulder and Phaedra snuggled deeper into his embrace. "Of course a man lay with my mother and made me. I know not who. I doubt she knew which man, either. Besides, my mother died, so we will never know."

"There has to be a way for us to be together. I feel like the Fates want us to try harder. Then they will reward us," said Phaedra.

"Or flatten us like flies."

"Either one is preferable to being apart." Phaedra's stomach rumbled. Hiding her embarrassment, and before Valens could notice the unladylike sound, she sat up and grabbed a piece of bread and a slice of soft cheese. The heavy oats in the bread complemented the tang of the cheese.

She held out the tray to Valens. "Would you like something to eat?"

Her stomach rumbled again.

"No, I am not hungry. But you are."

"You were injured today. You need your strength to heal."

He reached for his shoulder. "It bled quite a bit, but the trainer patched me up."

She kissed the hand that Valens used to hold his shoulder. "Better?"

"Completely," he said. "Now eat."

"Just one more slice of bread and a little cheese." She followed that slice with two more. Then she ate all the fruit. She washed it down with two cups of wine and lay back, finally sated.

"I love a woman with a hearty appetite."

"I slept through dinner."

"I know. I should tell your maid that you are alive and well."

"She knows already. Terenita stays close by." Phaedra sighed and folded deeper into Valens's embrace. Her mind wandered and she envisioned climbing a mountain to do battle with the Fates. Her only weapons were an influential senator and a man claiming to be Valens's father. She set them both before a trio of disfigured women who shared one eye, in the hopes that they would come up with a solution.

But Phaedra suddenly realized what was needed without the help of the Fates.

"My father and Paullus," she said as she sat up.

Valens rolled onto his back and flopped his arm over his eyes. "Yes. What about them?"

"They are the answer. They can help us stay together. There is no other senator people like more than my father. And if Paullus claimed you as his son, you could become an equestrian and we could marry."

"He is not my real father."

"I know that. You know that. He knows that. But the rest of Rome is none the wiser."

Valens pulled Phaedra down on the bed. "It is a nice idea, Love. But it cannot work."

"Why would it not work? Unless you do not want to marry me, that is."

"Of course I want you. I have wanted you as mine, my wife, since that first time I saw you. But what you suggest is impossible."

She struggled out of his grasp and sat up. "Tell me why."

"No one has agreed to any of this, for one."

"We have yet to speak to them. Once we do, they will agree."

Covering his eyes with his arm again, Valens lay without moving, without breathing. He looked at her from behind his arm. "Do you think your father would agree?"

"If you agree to provide the proof he needs to secure his place in the Senate, he will. But do not give anything to him directly. He will spend it all."

Valens stared at the ceiling. His slow breaths were the only sound in the room. "This might work. Could we actually be together? Could we? Would you love me even if I am not the Champion of Rome?"

"I will. But will you love me when I have turned old and fat and all our children are grown and gone?"

"I will love you all the more then, because we will have gotten old and fat together."

Phaedra kissed him. "If we are to be together, we must make it happen now. I will speak to my father tomorrow. You must speak to Paullus first thing, as well. We will have to act, each of us without knowing if the other is successful or not."

"I will, but with one condition."

She had come to hate conditions and bargains. "Yes?"

"You let me sleep for a while. I worked harder with you than I did in the arena and am now exhausted."

Phaedra agreed and rested back in Valens's arms. He had defeated death today and must certainly do so twice more. They were favored by the gods! Her plan for them to be together would work. She knew it with a certainty she felt in her bones.

Chapter 37

Valens

In the hour before dawn, Terenita awakened Valens. He gave a hasty kiss to a sleepy Phaedra and followed the maid through the house. At the door to the street, the maid stood with her hand resting on the latch.

"You love her," she said.

Valens did not know if she asked a question or made a statement. "Yes, I do," he said.

"Have you not thought to leave her alone? To let her marry Acestes and live a comfortable life?"

"I love Phaedra for who she is, not what she represents, or what she can offer me. I think that is enough."

"How will you support her if she loses the general's favor? Return to the arena full-time?"

"I will do anything I need to make Phaedra happy, including walking away. I would rather start with the two million sesterces I have already. Maybe I can open a tavern. I would like that, and people would pay extra to hear my stories, meet me personally. She warned me that her father has expensive tastes."

"Two million," said the maid. "Not as much as Acestes."

"But it is still enough, and all of it hers."

"I heard your plans," said Terenita. "I hear everything. Do you really love Phaedra, or is she your way into Roman society?"

"I love your mistress so much that I forget where I end and she begins."

"You might be a good man. I have not decided."

"I hope to be a better man for Phaedra," he said. "I do love her."

"I fear for you both. You are playing a dangerous game with a powerful man."

Valens opened his arms as if to embrace the whole world. "I am Valens Secundus, Champion of Rome. None is more powerful than me."

"You jest?"

"A little."

"You do not have the law on your side or an army to command."

"You are right. I have neither."

"Be careful, Valens Secundus," she said. "It is not just your life you chance, but Phaedra's as well."

Terenita lifted the latch and opened the door. Valens inclined his head to the maid and walked out into the street. He headed down the hill to the empty forum and the ludus, just beginning to come to life. Today, the second day of five, Valens planned to rest and train while other gladiators fought. The injury on his shoulder stung, and he decided to see the ludus physician after he spoke to Paullus.

A guard answered his knock on the heavy wooden gates.

"Take me to Paullus," said Valens as he entered the compound.

The guard escorted him to a barred door that led to stairs and the family's home beyond. "I do not think he will like being interrupted this early in the morning and without warning," the guard said as he unfastened the heavy iron lock.

"I care not for what you think," said Valens. "I can find my way from here."

Even before daybreak, Paullus sat behind his desk in the tablinum. Valens knocked on the doorjamb. "Greetings," he said.

Paullus looked up from the scrolls and tablets on his desk. "Greetings. Greetings. Come in, come in. I wanted to speak to you about your fight yesterday. Horrible, eh?"

Valens shrugged. His shoulder hurt. "I won."

"True," said Paullus. "Have you broken your fast? Care for some porridge?"

"I will eat with the men."

"It pleases me to see you embrace the brotherhood of the gladiators."

"Funny you should mention family; that was what I came to discuss."

"Sit down. Is it something about your sister?"

Valens sat and rubbed his shoulder that now throbbed. "It is not my sister, but rather my father."

"Has he come forward? I hate to say this, but I caution you not to believe without proof. A talented liar might be able to ingratiate himself with you, turning into an expense you do not need."

"It is nothing like that, either. I want to marry."

Paullus opened his mouth and Valens raised his hand to stop him, lest they spend the entire morning with a round of guesses, never reaching the actual request.

"Can I at least congratulate you?"

"Not yet. It is complicated."

"How so?" Paullus asked.

"She is a patrician. She is the daughter of Senator Phaedrus Scaeva Didius, widow to Senator Marcus Rullus Servilia."

"You have a sick sense of humor, you know that?"

"This sounds crazy, I know. I have loved Phaedra since the first time I saw her. For her, I wanted to be free. She is the reason I wanted to learn to read and write. I wanted to *be* better for her. I *am* better because of her."

"I am speechless. I know not what to say. I want you happy, my boy, but the law will not allow a marriage between you. Pressing your case will ruin you and her as well."

"A poor bastard born in the Suburra cannot marry a patrician. Even the Champion of Rome cannot marry a lady of aristocratic birth. But an equestrian can." Paullus opened his mouth. Valens kept speaking. "Anyone can become an equestrian, providing they have three things."

"Go on."

"They need money, an influential friend in the Senate, and a family name. I have the money, more than enough. Phaedra thinks her father will sponsor my bid to become an equestrian. He is popular and liked enough to get the votes needed. That leaves a family, a father."

Paullus twirled a stylus on his desk. "Is that the favor? You want me to claim you as mine?"

"I can be the son of no one else."

"There are some problems with your plan or, rather, our part of your plan. Why do I claim you now?"

"Say anything you want, other than I have asked you to lie."

"Always a quick comment with you."

"Said just like an exasperated father."

Paullus twirled the stylus again. "In all seriousness, I must have a reason for claiming you after all these years."

"Say that you lay with my mother and later knew about the child. That is why you accepted me at the ludus when you should have thrown me out into the street. As your bastard son you took me in, trained me well, and let me take your name."

"Why claim you now? Why not claim you when you retired? Or when you first came to the ludus?"

That question proved harder and Valens had no answer. Paullus spun the stylus again and again. As it wobbled, its metal tip scraped the wooden desktop.

Wood. Wooden swords. Metal swords. The answers to all of life's questions came to Valens with a weapon in his hand. "You said yourself I fought poorly yesterday. After all these years, you fear I will die. You cannot let me go to my death without claiming me as your son."

"It might work, but we need to do something grand, something memorable."

"And something soon. If Phaedra's not betrothed to someone else by the end of the games, she will be forced to marry General Acestes."

"This just keeps getting worse and worse, does it not?"

"Excuse me, dominus." A guard stood at the door. "Baro was looking for Valens. He says he has news."

"Tell him I will meet him on the practice field," said Valens.

The guard nodded and left.

"I will claim you as my son today at noon," said Paullus. "It will be the best time, since the morning fights will be done, but the executions will not have yet begun."

Valens was ill at ease with the depth of his emotions. His eyes stung and watered. He could not find his voice. Nodding, he coughed. "I will try to make you proud," he said at last.

"You already do."

Valens rose and they grasped wrists. Paullus slipped his arm around Valens's shoulder in an embrace. It was the sort of thing fathers did with their sons all the time. Yet, for Valens, it was a first.

Paullus was not the man who had created his life, but rather the person who had taught him how to be a man. A father. "I need to see Baro," Valens said, his eyes still leaking.

"Go. Meet me at the eleventh bell. We will walk to the arena together."

Although his shoulder ached, Valens made his way through the villa with unmistakable optimism in his step. He would be with Phaedra, rightly, legally, the way he had always wanted.

Jennifer D. Bokal

On the field of practice, Baro sparred with an upturned tree trunk. Exercises such as this kept gladiators from any accidental injuries, yet it lacked the element of reaction. In any real fight, an instinct to react was paramount.

"Where have you been?" Baro asked without stopping his regime.

"Speaking with Paullus."

"I heard from my aunt in Padua. She would love to have Antonice come and live with them. Your sister can go anytime. Now, even. They live near the marketplace. Ask anyone in Padua and they will give directions to the villa."

Valens moved in to embrace Baro, the awkwardness of it all be damned. Today was a day for embraces. A dull sword swung toward him. Valens ducked, but not quickly enough. The blow landed on his injured shoulder. Blackness filled with tiny pinpricks of light exploded in his vision.

"What are you doing? Trying to get killed? I am practicing, focused on my target. You cannot step in without warning."

Valens gripped his shoulder. Pain radiated outward with each beat of his heart. "I was going to give you a hug."

"Try to hug me again and I will run you through."

"Thank you, my friend. Today could get no better." Valens turned to leave. He needed to visit his villa and tell Antonice the plan. If all went well—and it would—she and Leto could be out of Rome by noon.

"Valens," called Baro. "Your shoulder is bleeding."

"That does not surprise me. It hurts like a whore from Hades. I will see the physician when I return." A guard opened the gate. Valens waved with his uninjured arm and stepped out into the busy marketplace.

236

Chapter 38

Phaedra

"Two million sesterces," Phaedra's father said as if the words themselves tasted awful. "Why would you sell yourself for such a low sum? Acestes inherited all of Marcus's money and already had a fortune of his own. Married to him you would be worth over five hundred million sesterces. Now that is an amount to consider binding yourself to."

Phaedra took in a long, slow breath. She tried, unsuccessfully, to calm her anger. "Listen to what you say, Father. You want me to sell myself, or bind myself, as you say, to a man for money. Am I your daughter to whom you promised to consider all suitable offers of marriage, or a chair to be sold? Or worse yet, do you see me as a prostitute? Do you, Father, do you?"

The jowls on her father's face grew ruddy. He stood and limped toward her. Phaedra feared she had pushed too hard and now might meet the back side of his hand. Her father stopped in front of her and breathed in and out several times, his face returning to a more normal color.

"I do not see you as a chair," he said, "or the other thing."

"I love Valens," she said. "I have loved him from the first moment we met. Even if Paullus refuses to claim Valens as his son, or the Senate does not make him an equestrian, you did promise that I could choose my next husband."

"Yes, yes. I know what I promised. But you might come to love Acestes. Have you considered that?"

"I will never love anyone the way I love Valens. It sounds silly and romantic, I know. But I also know that I shall never be happy without him. My happiness must be worth something."

Her father snorted. "Do you know who you sound like?"

She did not care for riddles and games this morning. Phaedra glared at her father.

"You sound like me when I wanted to marry your mother," he said.

"I thought you were given the choice to marry any eligible woman."

"If the story is told simply, then yes, my father allowed me to choose my wife. I loved your mother from the first time I saw her. I asked her to marry me that very night. The more complex part of the tale is that my father disapproved because her family had no coin."

"Yet you made each other happy."

"We did, unless we did not. I enjoy expensive things, Phaedra."

"I have noticed."

"Expensive tastes and no money do not go together well. I sometimes wonder if the fear of poverty killed your mother."

Her father was in one of his sentimental moods and therefore more likely to give her what she wanted. She pressed her advantage and said, "Just as life in a gilded cage would kill me."

"No need to waste away right here and now. But what of Acestes? I think your mother would have liked him."

"I think Mother would have liked him, too. But what of me? I do not love him, nor will I ever."

"You do not know that. He is very much like Marcus, and you came to love him."

"Acestes *looks* very much like his uncle, I agree. But the two men are wholly different. Marcus focused his entire life on the betterment of Rome. He was a great man and a kind husband. Acestes only wants what he wants, the rest of us be damned."

Her father chewed on the quick of his thumbnail, a nervous act she had never seen from him before. Was he about to rescind his promise to her? Had he accepted Acestes's offer of marriage on Phaedra's behalf without her knowledge, believing that she eventually would capitulate? A red line of blood spread across the base of his nail. He blotted it on the hem of his toga and looked up, his eyes bright and his cheeks ruddy. "I had always heard that Valens was a bastard and knew not his sire. In order to be named an equestrian, he must also have a father."

"At this moment Valens is speaking to his lanista, who I believe will claim him as a son."

"Ah, so that is why Paullus Secundus took him in and trained him well. Valens really is his son."

"As far as you and I and the rest of Rome knows, he is," she said.

"Which means that Valens really is a bastard."

"I will not allow you to argue your way out of keeping your promise, Father. What do you care about his lineage, as long as all appears right in the law?"

"I promised you your choice in husbands," he said finally, "and to consider any and all reasonable offers of marriage. I am a man of my word."

Phaedra jumped up and kissed her father on the cheek. "Thank you, thank you. A million times, thank you."

"It is two million times."

She laughed. "I thank you two million times, then."

"Are you sure you want to give away all that Acestes offers you? The money, the homes, the chance to be a consul's wife? He will be named a provincial governor someday."

He was turning the talk to her future life, but she knew well what was really on his mind.

"Do not worry, Father. You can learn how to manage on two million sesterces. Although you may have to curb your spending."

Her father harrumphed. "At least you have perfect timing. Today is a good day to ask that Valens Secundus be named an equestrian. There is not much other business in the Senate, and everyone will be talking about yesterday's victory."

"Thank you, Father."

"Come with me to the Senate. You will not be allowed inside, but you can hear from the street when I make a motion for your gladiator to become an equestrian."

"Is that wise? I do not want Acestes to suspect that anything's amiss until all is settled."

"We can ride together in a litter. All will be well if you wait in it outside. Then we will go to the games together."

"Terenita!" she called. The maid stepped from a nearby corner. "Please fetch my wrap and then we can be off."

"Yes, my lady," the maid said with a smile.

"I do want to see you happy, but we must make one thing clear," her father said. "Should your gladiator not be allowed to enter the knighthood of Rome, or if he falls in one of his two final matches, we will consider that I have kept my part of our bargain and allowed you to arrange your own marriage. The next time you wed, it will be to a man of my choosing."

"Acestes," she said.

"We are agreed?"

The thought of marrying Acestes made Phaedra ill. No, not ill, but empty. Yet if she and Valens could not be together, then it mattered little who else she might marry. "We are."

She and her father rode together as Terenita walked beside the litter with a small contingent of guards. The ride down the Palatine Hill took too long for Phaedra's liking. She could feel the excitement flushing her face and could not help but smile. Her father ordered the litter to be set down on the uppermost steps. Although the Senate was in session, very few men in white togas hurried past as her father made his way into the Senate building.

From her seat in the litter, she heard Consul Flaccus call the meeting to order and ask for any new business. Then, in his deep voice, he invited the honorable Senator Phaedrus Scaeva Didius to take the floor.

Phaedra held her breath and shut her eyes as she imagined her father limping from his seat at the front of the Senate chamber to stand before the black chairs reserved for the co-consuls. Her father's slow speech with his nasal intonation floated out the open door. "My friends," he began, "my brothers. None of us wants to be here today." A few chuckles followed his remark. "Why? Because we would all rather be at the Forum Boarium just across the way watching the gladiatorial matches fought to honor our good friend and fellow senator, Marcus Rullus Servilia. As you all know, Marcus holds a place of particular sentiment to me because he was also the beloved husband to my daughter, Phaedra."

"He paid a large amount of coin for your beautiful daughter," someone called out.

"A fair trade, I am sure," someone else replied.

More laughter followed.

Would her father really allow her to become a jest? Had she always been that to him? No, she reminded herself. He was keeping his word, trying to win support for Valens in the Senate. Still, she disliked appearing foolish, even if it was as a means to her desired end.

Phaedra's father continued. "When my daughter married Marcus, we entertained you all well with gladiatorial combats. Many of us, me included, saw firsthand the men who would forever be known as the Titans of Rome do battle. Valens Secundus, the Champion of Rome, spent more years than anyone inspiring us all with his feats of valor and bravery. He won his freedom and has now returned to the arena in order to save his sister. We all must agree that this man has exemplified the Roman way of life."

A round of "Hear, hear" answered her father.

Phaedra smiled and began to relax. It was happening.

"Senators. Brothers. Friends. I make a motion that Valens Secundus, paragon of Roman virtue, be admitted into the knighthood of the Roman republic."

Silence. No one in the Senate said a word. Phaedra froze in her seat, listening for even the slightest whisper.

After a moment, someone spoke up. "He is a slave."

"Born a pleb," said her father, "conscripted into the gladiators and proved his worth to once again be a free man by a contest of strength and heroism."

"He needs money," said someone else. "At least half a million sesterces."

"I have it on the highest authority that Valens has more than enough coin to satisfy even you."

Laughter.

"Does he have enough coin to satisfy you, Scaeva?"

"No one has enough coin for him. That is why he wants to marry the daughter to the same fortune Marcus left behind."

Laughter. Lots of laughter. Hilarity. Was this what the all-important Senate of Rome did all day? Make jokes at each other's expense? And where was her father? What was he doing? He should be returning their attention to the matter at hand.

"He needs a family, a clan," another senator said. "I always understood Valens to be a bastard who never knew his father."

"I have it on higher authority that he has known his sire all along," said her father.

"He has to fight two more times. What if he dies in the process?" another senator asked.

"Then we," said her father, "the benevolent members of this Senate, will have given the highest honor to a lowly but brave gladiator. We never have to do anything but enjoy the praise of his admirers."

Phaedra reminded herself that her father did not wish for Valens to die. He was only saying the right thing at the correct time.

Laughter and calls for Senator Scaeva to run for consul followed his remark. Consul Flaccus called for a vote. From her vantage point on the steps, Phaedra heard the overwhelming vote for Valens to become a knight, assuming that Valens was, in fact, claimed by a suitable sire. Once that happened, and it would, he would become an appropriate husband. Now nothing could keep them apart.

"Terenita," she said. "Take word of the vote to Valens at the ludus."

The maid nodded and smiled. "With pleasure, my lady."

Chapter 39

Valens

Valens left the ludus, his stride quick and purposeful. Keeping his head down, he avoided looking at passersby. Today he lacked the time to talk to admirers about his career or yesterday's near defeat. A few whispers of "Is that Valens Secundus? I thought he would be taller" caught his ears. He ignored them all—even those of a woman who chased after him, screaming his name like one possessed. He increased his pace. He had no time for the crazed devotee.

People stopped their work, pointing and laughing. Valens hurried on as the woman continued to run after him. Annoyed with the commotion she was creating, he stopped and turned around.

Holding her long skirts up with one hand and balancing a headscarf with the other, Terenita asked as she approached, breathless, "Have you gone deaf? I have been calling for you since you left the ludus."

"I did not realize it was you," he said.

"Why? Because lovesick women call after you day and night?"

"Not *every* day." Valens laughed and shrugged.

"Ah." The maid was trying to look disapproving, but he could see the rigid lines in her face soften, and some of the hostile bite in her words disappeared. "My mistress sends me with congratulations. The Senate approved your bid into the knighthood of the Roman republic."

Valens gripped Terenita by the shoulders and kissed her on the cheek. When he felt her muscles tense at the familiarity of the gesture, he released his hold and stepped back. "I thank you for bringing me word. Send my thanks and affection to your mistress as well." Fancy, formal language felt false on his tongue, yet Valens thought they were words that befitted an equestrian.

"I will do so. I hope the Fates continue to smile upon you and my mistress," said the maid.

"They have, said Valens. "And tell your mistress that my part of the plan has worked out as well."

By the time he reached his villa, the sun hung halfway up the sky. It beat down on the white paving stones and heated the air. A sheen of sweat clung to his brow and neck. As he approached, Valens looked for the soldiers Phaedra had told him about. They were easy to spot, their bearings too stiff and their gazes too intent. Valens knocked upon the villa's door. The steward opened a window set within and peered out. With a wide smile, he slid the interior bolt free.

"Dominus," he said as Valens entered the villa. "We did not expect to see you so soon."

"Water," he said. The steward filled a pottery cup from the pool in the atrium. Valens drank it in one swallow. He handed it back to the steward twice more before quenching his thirst.

"It is good to see you again, dominus," said the steward.

Valens and the old man grasped wrists. "It is good to be seen."

"We heard that the fight yesterday was not in your favor until the end."

"The ending is all that matters."

"I suppose you are right."

The steward had once been a trainer, and a wily one at that. He could easily distract the soldiers Acestes had sent to watch the villa. "I need you to do something for me," Valens said.

"Anything, dominus."

"There are two men watching the house—soldiers. I need them gone long enough for Antonice to get out of the house and off the Aventine."

"Consider it done," said the steward. "They will not even suspect that she has left for days."

Although Valens ached all over, he allowed himself to smile. "All's the better." Then he added, "Send Antonice and Leto to my tablinum."

Valens turned to go and the steward called after him, "Your back is bleeding."

He looked over his shoulder. Wet, red blood stained his tunic, and the cloth stuck to his back. "Have Leto bring hot water and some towels."

"Might I suggest some salve and a clean tunic?"

"Fine," said Valens. He wanted to sit in the coolness of his tablinum and rest his weary legs for a moment. He took another step forward and stumbled, tripped up on his own stupidity. He had let his shoulder putrefy. He suddenly realized that a fever-filled ache radiated from his back. If not treated aggressively and quickly, it would move on to poison the rest of his body.

Dazed, he moved through the villa. As he took a seat behind his desk, Valens wondered what kind of gladiator he was. The first rule, the most important rule, the only rule worth remembering was that a gladiator's most effective weapon was his body. Ignoring the needs of the body rendered every other tool useless. Lovesick and dumb with lust, he had broken the unbreakable rule, and now Valens would pay with an ineffective weapon.

Antonice burst into the room. She ran to him, wrapping her arms around his wounded shoulder. "You live. We heard of your victory, and you have come home to celebrate."

He returned the embrace, although it pained him all the more. "I have come home, but not to celebrate. You must leave the city. Baro's aunt in Padua has need of a girl to help her with a newborn."

Antonice let go of Valens and moved to the other side of his desk. "I am not a wet nurse."

"It is not that kind of help. I do not know what you will be required to do. You must leave Rome for your own safety."

"You won your match. I am safe for now," she said.

"For now, yes," said Valens. "I need to win twice more or you will be dragged to the arena and executed. If you are not in Rome, then Acestes will have a harder time finding you. If you are hidden away, he might give up looking. If not, I can ask a friend to convince him to grant clemency." How awful to rely on Phaedra to help Antonice if he died. She would have to bargain with Acestes, who by then would be her husband. But Valens saw no other choice.

Antonice stood by a potted palm and traced lines in the leaves.

"Do not sulk," he said. "I am trying to save your life."

"By ruining it?"

"I ask for no thanks," said Valens as he resisted the urge to shake his sister. "But I do not expect an argument from you, either."

"You lock me away for a week and then show up and tell me to leave Rome without telling me why."

Valens breathed in and counted to four. His sister was little more than an angry child with an adult's ability to ruin lives. He exhaled slowly before speaking. "You understand, Antonice. You know why. You would like to blame me as the one who makes you miserable, but you chose poorly and now we all suffer. I have two more bouts ahead of me this week, thanks to your behavior."

Chastened, she nodded. "I am sorry for that," she said, her eyes downcast. "When will I leave?"

"Soon," he said. "The steward will tell you when."

The housekeeper entered with a bowl of steaming water, a swatch of linen, and a small jar on a tray. Over her arm she carried a clean and folded tunic. "The steward said you injured your back, dominus. Might I have a look?"

"Gather your things," he said to Antonice as he stood.

"I want to stay and visit a moment longer. I did not mean for us to quarrel."

"I am sorry, but you really should leave now."

She stamped her foot, the pouting girl suddenly reappearing. "You are always unreasonable."

"I also do not wear a loincloth and need to remove my tunic so Leto can tend my wound."

"That is disgusting," Antonice said as her eyes widened and she rushed from the room.

"Such is the way with young women," said Leto. She drew a low arc in the air. "Their moods swing from one side to the other without cause."

"I am glad you appreciate her." Valens tried to take off his tunic, but he could not lift his arm even to his ear. "My shoulder is worse than I thought."

"Let us have a look, shall we?" Leto helped him undress. She gasped. Valens took that as a bad sign. "Oh, my, and the doctor at the ludus did not stitch this up?"

"I did not see the doctor," he said. Yesterday he had wanted Phaedra—he had let the German wrap his shoulder in rather unclean linen to stop the bleeding and then ignored the trainer's advice to see the physician. Leaving a wound untended was worse than leaving his sword out in the rain.

"The good news, dominus, is that the cut is still open. I need to get out the infection and then clean the wound."

In the distance Valens heard the bells from the forum begin to toll the eleventh hour. "Do what needs to be done," he said, "but hurry."

Leto tended to his shoulder. He redirected his mind from the pain by telling her his plan for getting Antonice from the city. After the steward distracted the soldiers on guard, the housekeeper and his sister were to travel with a hired guide to Capernaum. From there they would hire another guide to take them to Padua, but stop in a small town just before that city. After that, they needed to ask for the location of Baro's family home. Valens would send word if he survived the next two fights. Otherwise, news of his demise would reach them soon enough.

"Do you think it is necessary," asked Leto, "to go first to Capernaum?"

"If they find your Roman guide, he will lead them there. Then General Acestes would have to determine that you had not remained. After that, it will be a matter of finding the next guide. By then another slave uprising may come along to take his attention from my sister." Valens bit off the last word as the housekeeper washed his shoulder with salty water, and the sting took his breath away.

"It will help to kill the bad humors," she said.

"I know. Can you work faster? I am expected back at the ludus."

She wrapped his shoulder with a clean bandage. "I am no medicus, but this will have to do for now."

Valens kissed her plump, dimpled cheek. "Thank you for everything." He slipped the clean tunic over his head. "Take care of my sister."

"Do you want to say good-bye to her?"

"I need to leave now. One last thing—if ever an aristocratic lady named Phaedra comes to you, know that she can be trusted."

"May the gods keep you safe, Valens Secundus," the housekeeper called as he ran out the door. "Because you are doing a bad job without my help."

Valens hurried through the Aventine and returned to the forum. He found Paullus waiting outside the gate of the ludus.

"Where in the name of Hades have you been?" the lanista asked.

"I went to my villa to see Antonice. My shoulder is injured and my housekeeper tended to the wound."

They walked together as two guards made a path for them through the crowd of gathered admirers. "What did the physician at the ludus do for you?"

Valens wiped sweat from his brow.

"You did not see him, did you?" asked Paullus.

"I was busy."

"Doing what?" Paullus asked. "Never mind giving me an answer. You were busy with the senator's daughter."

The sun, a great ball in the sky, fried Valens's skin. He wiped away more sweat and tried to think of something to say.

"You are sick, either with love or fever," said Paullus.

"Or both," said Valens.

They entered the cool stables. Paullus ordered a nearby slave to bring water and inform General Acestes that he wished to speak to the crowd. The same slave returned with two pottery mugs. Ignoring the bits of hay that floated about, Valens drank the water in both mugs. A few moments later another slave, dressed in a finer tunic, approached. "The general invites you to speak to the crowd now, if convenient, as the final fight of the morning has just ended."

"I accept your master's invitation," said Paullus.

Valens and the lanista followed the slave through a warren of stables and indoor pens. In one pen four men and a woman huddled in the corner. Dirty, smelling of vomit and blood, frightened of the upcoming horrors, and yet ready to die, the condemned looked at Valens with already lifeless eyes. He turned away lest he imagine his sister among them.

The well-dressed slave opened a door leading to the arena. Paullus stepped through and Valens followed. The crowd cheered. Their cries of approval were too loud for Valens's liking. Puddles of blood soaked the hard-baked earth. The coppery grit filled his nose, coated his throat, and turned his stomach. He stood still, although the earth underfoot swayed.

Valens looked at the sponsor's box for Phaedra. Acestes and Senator Scaeva stood at the railing, but she was not there. The general held up his hands for silence.

They ignored the gesture and filled the air with a chant. "Valens. Valens. Valens."

Valens gave a little wave and they screamed all the more. He waited a moment before lifting both hands, palms down. The crowd grew so silent that he heard the unmistakable scraping of Paullus's foot through the sand as he fidgeted and waited.

"I understand you wished to make a public announcement, honorable Paullus Secundus," said Acestes. His deep voice carried to every part of the arena, his diction clear and precise so that he could be understood by all. The general wore a silver tunic, and his hair, so perfect, looked to have been arranged by a lady's cosmetics slave. Even Valens admitted that Acestes was an impressive man, and he hated him all the more for it.

"Great and noble General Acestes," said Paullus, "I have come to right a wrong. Many years ago I knew the mother of the man who stands next to me, Valens Secundus. I spent many nights in her arms but knew we could never marry. Nine months later she bore a child, a son, again the man who stands next to me."

"Are you saying that Valens Secundus is your natural son?" asked Acestes.

Paullus paused a moment. "He is. That is why I allowed him to join my ludus and have trained him well."

"Why claim him as your son now?"

"He is injured. He has become ill. In order to save his sister from the arena, he must fight and win two more times."

"In other words, tomorrow might be too late."

"Yes, although I dearly pray that does not happen."

"I have more good news, honorable Paullus Secundus," said Phaedra's father. "Earlier today the Senate voted to name Valens Secundus a knight of the Roman republic."

The crowd went wild. Valens looked into the stands. They chanted his name again. Louder. Stronger. "Valens. Valens. Valens" became the thunder that echoed across the hills.

Paullus leaned into Valens. "This is your moment, my boy."

"No," said Valens. "It is our moment."

He grasped the lanista by the wrist and held both their arms high. He wanted to savor the moment, to drink it in like an expensive wine and swirl it through his mouth.

Acestes looked down from the sponsor's box, his eyes narrowed and full of hate. Valens feared that the general saw through all the lies and understood the complete truth. He also feared that because of this, the general would never let Phaedra go.

Chapter 40

Phaedra

At the end of the day, Acestes accompanied Phaedra and her father to their home. The general lingered, drinking wine and talking politics. As the hour grew later, he accepted the invitation to remain for dinner. Now, as he brought the conversation around to the gladiatorial contests, Phaedra wondered if he ever planned to leave.

"Valens Secundus is without question the hero of the games," Acestes said.

Phaedra wanted to blush with pride and tell the world that he was her hero, now and always. Soon she would be able to, but not now, not yet. Instead she took another long sip of water. She wanted to remain clear of thought, lest she let her secret slip at the wrong moment.

"Valens Secundus is a gladiator," her father said. "It is his way of life to be a hero, if not a legend."

"You will become part of his legend, will you not? You made Valens an equestrian on the same day that his father claimed him as his own. I am sure that story will be told again and again. I do wonder why now. Why at all?" Although Acestes spoke to her father, he watched Phaedra.

She held up her goblet to a slave. "More water."

"You saw the gladiator," said her father. "He is old and tired. I doubt if he will win his match tomorrow. I took advantage of this turn of events. Today I made him a knight. Tomorrow I will mourn his death with the rest of Rome. From then on, I can bask in the thanks and admiration of the plebs for bringing a slave, a bastard, and a gladiator into the higher ranks of society."

"Brilliant move," said Acestes.

Phaedra's father placed his feet on the floor and leaned forward. "I will share with you a secret. To succeed in politics, you must never just think of how your next move will be perceived at the moment you make it."

"Never?"

"You must always think of the consequences of your actions now, later, and even later still."

Was that it? Her father had agreed to nominate Valens into the knighthood not so she and he might marry, but for political gain? Had he kept his promise to her assuming that he would never have to honor it, all the while secure that she would perceive his actions as loving? Or was her father a deal maker to the core, giving Acestes a version of the truth that the general appreciated?

"It appears there is much for this old soldier to learn," said Acestes.

"Together we have what it takes to run the republic, you and I."

Acestes held up his goblet, and the two men toasted each other and their certain success.

"I did not know that I could become any drowsier," said Phaedra. "Constant talk of running the world wears on the nerves. I am off to bed."

"If you could wait a moment," said Acestes, "there is another topic that I would like to discuss. It does not concern you."

He paused and examined his fingernails. "Marcus kept an untidy villa, but very tidy accounts. Well, Scaeva, I want to discuss the debt you owed my uncle and now owe to me. Five million sesterces is quite a bit of money. I wonder when you planned to tell me."

Five million sesterces? Damn her father and his lies and his expensive parties and his well-made clothes—damn them to Hades. No, damn them all to a river of fire and eternal suffering. Five million owed to Marcus and now to Acestes. Yes, when *did* he plan to tell them? Or had he not planned to tell them at all?

"I wanted to wait until we settled the matter of the marriage," her father said.

"Why? So I did not demand Phaedra's hand, or so she did not feel obligated to marry me? Perhaps you did not want me to withdraw my suit because of the debt."

"A bit of all those reasons."

"Did you know of this debt?" Acestes asked Phaedra.

She shook her head, not quite believing what she heard but knowing the truth of it all the same.

"I did not think you did," said Acestes. "Even though your father owes me this money and has played me for a fool, I am still willing to marry you."

Her father's full cheeks grew red and redder still, almost purple. Sweat dripped from his hairline and dampened the fabric under his arms. He looked ill. But he had manipulated her—all of them—to meet his own ends, and Phaedra refused to offer him sympathy now that he had been caught.

She bit off an oath. The gods preserve them all. She had no choice but to marry Acestes. Valens had only two million sesterces, not enough to pay back the debt. Unless he won his other matches, then she would be wealthy in her own right and could easily pay back her father's debt.

"What about running the republic together?" she asked of Acestes. "You will have a hard time courting the voters with a disgraced adviser."

"I can manage. There are many men in Rome happy to share their advice with me. Besides, if we marry, the debt disappears and no one ever need know." Acestes sighed. "I do tire of the games you play with me, Phaedra. I need an answer now."

"Phaedra, forgive me," said her father. "I never meant to hurt you. I wanted to pay back the debt a little at a time. You do not understand the cost of everything. Food. Clothes."

"You were hardly eating porridge three times a day and wearing sackcloth." While arguing with her father kept Phaedra from having to answer Acestes's question, the three of them knew she must accept his offer.

"I know, I know. It is the appearance of wealth that costs so much."

"That is what makes the wealthy special, Father."

"Without the parties and the clothes and the seat in the Senate, I am no one, Phaedra. No one at all."

"Funny," she said as she stood. "I thought you were my father."

Tears blurred her vision and she ran from the room.

"My lady!" Terenita stepped from the shadows and called after Phaedra.

Phaedra ran through the atrium and out the front door. Once in the street, she leaned against the wall of a neighboring villa and sobbed.

"My lady." Terenita placed her hands on Phaedra's shoulders. "You must get off the street. Come back inside."

Phaedra knew that Terenita had heard everything. The maid had broken with expectations and come to Phaedra as a friend, not simply waiting to be ordered as a slave. The gesture and the kindness it implied were not lost on Phaedra, and yet her grief over the betrayal overtook every other emotion until she felt nothing but raw.

"He lied to me," she said. "He told me I could choose my own husband. He helped Valens become a knight, knowing we would never be together. With all this debt, I now must marry Acestes, though I do not love him. I suppose we could sell everything, but then what will be left of us?" Phaedra sobbed. "Terenita, I would be forced to sell you."

"Now, let us return to the villa," said Terenita. "You must work with your father and General Acestes to resolve all the issues, personal and financial both."

Phaedra looked back at her home. The door remained closed. Eventually she would have to face her father and Acestes again, but not now. For the moment she needed time away from them all. "No," Phaedra said. "I will see Valens one last time."

They walked through the darkened streets of Rome without incident. Phaedra thought of the last time she had left her villa without guards, the time she and Valens found each other in the market. How much had changed for her, within her, since that day.

Phaedra needed to tell him that they could never marry. Her father had played everyone false—all of them, including Acestes. He had quietly lied and cheated without making a sound, all the while hoping never to get caught and somehow to appear wise and loving in the end.

The Capitoline Market, empty of vendors and shoppers, stretched out before her. In the distance she saw the ludus. Torches burned at the open gates. Several men huddled in a group with the lanista, Paullus, his mane of white hair unmistakable in the firelight. The men looked familiar, but at a distance Phaedra did not know why. As she approached she recognized them both as the physicians called to Marcus's deathbed. Valens had looked ill today. He had fought poorly the day before, and the cut to his shoulder had been deep. He had claimed that the injury did not bother him, but now she recalled the warmth of his skin last night. In the moment she had thought it was the heat of passion, not illness.

Never once did Phaedra consider that the physicians had come to treat another gladiator. Nor did she care that she tripped over her long gown as she ran across the empty plaza. She could see coins glinting in the torchlight as Paullus paid the physicians. Breathless, Phaedra arrived at the ludus gates as the doctors took their leave.

"I thought about sending for you," Paullus said, confirming what she knew already. "I had not yet found the time. Here you are on your own. I heard that sometimes love can be so strong that the man and woman are connected even when apart."

"How is he?"

A guard opened the heavy gate and Paullus motioned for Phaedra to pass through. "He is alive," he said, "but weak."

"He was not that ill when I saw him today." They walked across the training ground, and Phaedra tried to believe her own words. She knew a body could turn on itself without warning, leaving a person sound one minute and dead the next. She had watched it happen with Marcus. Once his final decline began, it had gathered alarming speed until the inevitable end.

She did not want that for Valens.

"His shoulder is tainted," said Paullus. "The physician at the ludus drained the wound but fears it has spread. It might heal, but not by tomorrow, and that is when he must fight again."

The news came as a shock. Phaedra pressed her hand into the wall and steadied herself.

Another guard unlocked a barred door. "This leads to the barracks. I should forbid you from entering. But both you and Valens are so foolish I doubt anything I say will dissuade you."

"We are the best kind of fools," she said. "Let me enter."

"At least wear this. Shield yourself and save whatever dignity you can." Paullus unfastened his cloak and handed it to Phaedra.

Phaedra took the cloak and draped it over her head and shoulders. What need had she for secrecy? Her life was ruined. Her remaining joy would be her memories of Valens.

She walked past cell after cell. Men, large and well muscled, looked out of barred doors. Some called to her, inviting her to visit them later, while others stared. Realizing why Paullus had given her his cloak, Phaedra wrapped it more tightly around herself and lowered her gaze.

In the last cell at the end of a long and narrow hallway, Valens lay on a small bed pushed into a corner. Torches burned on the wall above him. A fat candle, held steady in a pool of its own dried wax, flickered on a nearby table. A thick gray blanket covered Valens, and still he shivered. Sweat coated his forehead. His damp hair clung to his scalp. The room stank, sweet and rotten.

"Phaedra," he said as she entered the cell. "Is that you?"

She rushed to his bedside and knelt on the floor. Taking his hand in hers, she said, "Here I am."

She pressed her lips to his cheek. It felt too hot. Since Valens might not heal in time to fight, in time to win, she almost hoped the fever killed him in his sleep. Then death might sweep him away to Elysium on a dream. Better that than to be claimed by death on the sunbaked earth of the arena, with only pain, heat, and the screams of a thousand bloodthirsty Romans to comfort him.

"Did they call you to me? Am I so bad that Paullus thinks I will die?"

Phaedra decided to answer the second question and ignore the first. "He says you will heal."

"Then why send for you?"

She did not want Valens to think his injury fatal. At the same time, his ill health prevented her from telling him the real reason that brought her to the ludus. They would never marry. Instead she kissed his lips and said, "I just came."

He chuckled. "I do not know what kind of lover I will be tonight."

"Just looking upon your face brings me more joy than anything in the world."

He smiled and closed his eyes. "I need to ask a favor of you."

"I will do anything you ask."

"If I should fall tomorrow . . ."

The words pierced Phaedra's heart as surely as if she had been run through with a sword. She pressed her fingers to his lips. "Do not speak of such things. It invites bad omens."

He gripped Phaedra's wrist and placed her palm on his chest. His heart beat so fast that she feared it might explode any second. "Bad omens come when you ignore the obvious. I am ill and in no shape to fight. If the poison from my wound does not kill me, then whomever I face on the morrow will."

Hot tears stung her eyes. Her throat tightened and ached. "No."

Valens took Phaedra's hand from his chest and kissed her palm. "I do not have the time or energy to argue. Please listen."

Phaedra wiped tears from her eyes with the edge of Paullus's cloak. Since she had taken him as her lover, Valens had become the very reason she drew breath. Without him she might cease to exist. As the tears ran down her cheeks, she said, "Ask anything of me. I will do whatever you need."

"My sister left Rome this morning. I had to hide her away. She is with the family of a brother gladiator, Baro. They live in Padua. If I die, Acestes will see my contract as unfulfilled and want my sister executed for her crimes. Beg for her life."

"You will not die. You cannot. You have become my light in the darkness. Without you I am lost," said Phaedra.

Valens opened one eye. "I beseech you now to beg for my sister's sake."

There was so much Phaedra wanted to say. She wanted to tell Valens to live for her, to live for them both. She wanted to tell him that she loved him now and always. But her throat closed around the hard kernel of truth. They were not fated to be together. She managed to speak. "I will."

Valens closed his eyes and settled into the pillow. His features slackened and his breath slowed. "Valens," she said as she shook his leg. He could not die as she sat there. She would not let him. "Valens."

He awakened, wide-eyed. "Another favor," he said.

"Anything."

"If Acestes will not show mercy to my sister, then never tell him where she has gone, and send her money, enough for her to live. Will you do that for me?"

"I will," she said.

"Will you sit with me as I sleep?"

Phaedra twined her fingers through his. Soon his breathing slowed but remained steady. The fat candle burned out, leaving a puddle of wax dripping to the floor. She heard a cough by the door and turned to see Paullus.

"The physicians have returned, my lady. Might I escort you to the gates?"

Phaedra stood. Her feet had gone numb and she stumbled as she took her first few steps. The lanista offered his arm and she held it. Remembering the stares and the calls of the other gladiators, Phaedra draped the cloak over her head and shoulders as they left Valens sleeping.

Terenita waited by the gates of the ludus. "She stayed in the kitchen," Paullus said. "My servants and slaves took good care of her."

"Thank you," Phaedra said.

"I offer guards to see you home."

"No, thank you. Guards from your ludus will be recognized, as will I"—she removed the cloak and handed it back to Paullus—"even with this."

"May the gods bless you, my lady."

"They did," she said, "for a short while."

Phaedra walked as if blind up the Palatine Hill. When the street before her villa came into view, a crowd blocked her way.

One man in the mob turned to her and pointed. "There she is," he said.

She tensed, ready to run away.

"Let her through," said the man.

Arms and hands reached out for Phaedra, pulling her gently forward. She saw a multitude of faces, all with the same look of pity in their eyes. People parted as she passed. She approached the door to her villa. A guard she did not recognize knocked twice as Terenita came to stand at her side. Acestes answered the door and wrapped Phaedra in his embrace. He pulled her into the villa and closed the door. With his arm about her shoulder, he led her to the main triclinium. Dozens of candles burned, making the room as bright as day. Her father would not like the expense used to impress no one.

"I am so glad to see you. I have looked everywhere for you."

"Odd," she said. "When I left the villa, no one followed. Not my father. Not you. Forgive me if I find your concern now unconvincing."

"Phaedra, you do not understand. Right after you left, your father felt a severe pain in his arm and a tightening in his chest. He stopped breathing, collapsed, and hit his head."

"Take me to him."

"Not yet," said Acestes. "His body is being cleaned. You may see him once his body is laid out in the atrium."

The possibility was unbelievable. Only the cruel Acestes would joke of such a thing. "Dead? My father cannot be dead."

"He is."

Phaedra slapped Acestes. The pain in her palm transformed her grief into anger. "You killed him for the money he owed you."

"That makes no sense, Phaedra. He will never be able to repay me now, will he?" Acestes pulled her to him again. "I have killed men for less, but trust me when I say I did not kill your father."

She saw the reason in his words. "I will see him now," she said.

Holding her by the hand, Acestes led Phaedra to the atrium. Slaves were situating her father's body, placing pungent herbs on the sofa where he lay. She kissed her father on the forehead. His skin was already cool under her lips. Yes, she had been justified in her anger at him that evening. He had been manipulative at her expense. But he also had been her only parent for so many years, and now all she could think about were their times of closeness and the way he had made her feel safe. Memories came flooding over her. For a moment she was five and sitting on her father's lap as they watched the rain fall in the garden, the loamy scent of wet vegetation hanging in the air. Then she was twelve and twirling through her father's tablinum as she showed him her newest gown. She was seventeen, crying on his shoulder, as her father said he could not allow her to marry a boy she had so fancied at the time, but whose name she could not now recall.

She had kept control of her emotions after Marcus had died, but the death of her father, with Valens ill, was too much. She felt like an urn with thousands of tiny cracks as she collapsed into Acestes's arms. He continued to hold her—the only thing real was the warmth of his embrace. Wave after wave, the grief washed over her, pushing her down. Finally, she had shed her last tear. Her eyes burned. Her throat was raw from sobbing.

With Phaedra bereft and exhausted, Acestes convinced her to return to his villa. Convinced—no, that was not the right word, for convincing someone assumed she had a will of her own. Phaedra was nothing but shards and dust. She let Acestes make the decision for her, thankful, even, that he took charge.

She went to bed in her old chamber and lay down, staring at nothing.

Terenita entered and stood quietly at the foot of the bed. "Is there anything I can bring to you, Lady Phaedra? Something to eat, perhaps?"

Shaking her head, she patted a space beside her on the bed. "Will you sit with me?"

Terenita hesitated. "I could, I suppose, if it is something you would permit." She lowered onto the mattress, her back straight and rigid.

"It is an odd relationship we have, is it not?" asked Phaedra. "In the eyes of the law, you are but a possession, much as I was for my father." Emotions, grief and anger, filled Phaedra, and she sobbed again.

Terenita placed a soft hand on her shoulder. "Cry as much as you need, my lady. It will do you good."

Phaedra wiped her eyes with the corner of her bedcover. "Another favor—call me Phaedra, only Phaedra. Not my lady, nor Lady Phaedra. For this night I would lose titles."

"If you wish." Terenita paused. "Phaedra."

Phaedra clasped the other woman's hands with her own. "No matter what happens to me, I will do all that I can to keep you with me. Without you, Terenita, I would be alone."

"I know," said Terenita. "I know you are loyal and good-hearted."

"Even when I am naive," said Phaedra.

"Even then," said Terenita, giving Phaedra's hands a squeeze. "And also when you are stubborn."

Phaedra smiled. "I am my father's daughter, am I not?"

"You are the best of him, and through you, your actions, and your memories, he will live on," she said.

"That thought brings me much comfort," she said. "Thank you."

"Try to rest, Phaedra," said Terenita. "It will help you face tomorrow with more strength."

Phaedra closed her eyes but did not sleep. She saw only her father. Without him, what would become of her? True, she had been disgusted by his spending. But even at her most exasperated, she loved him.

Who would be her guardian now? As a lone woman in Rome, she had no legal rights. Most likely she would be sent to live with her closest male relative, whoever that might be. What might they do with her? The answer, simple enough, came immediately. It would be another marriage for her. It was with that bleak thought that a black and bottomless sleep claimed her.

Chapter 41

Phaedra

As soon as Phaedra awakened in the morning, the sharp pain of grief sliced through her yet again, laying her soul open. She muffled a sob with a musty pillow. Before her eyes opened, as tears coursed down her cheeks, someone touched her foot. It had to be Terenita, hoping to rouse Phaedra by playing with her toes. It might have worked if she was five annums and her father had not died the night before.

"I am not hungry," said Phaedra, her head still buried in the pillow. "But do fetch me water."

Terenita touched her foot again, this time a little more insistently.

"For the love of all the gods, I just need a glass of water." Phaedra sat up and opened her eyes to look upon a world where her father no longer lived.

Terenita was nowhere to be seen. Instead, the old peacock stood at the foot of her bed, his beady eyes trained on Phaedra's foot. What tasty morsels did he imagine her toes to be? The obvious joy she read in his stare seemed a crime when she felt such unending sadness. Loss. Loneliness. Grief. These would be Phaedra's constant companions, now and always.

"I suppose I need to find water myself," she said to the peacock.

He pecked at her toes again.

She stood up in a whirl of covers and feathers. "You find your own breakfast."

Phaedra slipped on yesterday's dress and ran a brush through her hair. She had no appetite for food. But her throat hurt from crying. Phaedra wandered toward the dining room, and the peacock followed. Its dull and tattered tail trailed behind him like the flag of a defeated army.

She stopped to stroke the short, silky feathers on the top of his head. Did he miss Marcus, or had he even noticed that there was a new master? The peacock and Phaedra were linked, both at someone else's mercy, beholden to them for every kindness and comfort.

She heard male voices coming from the dining room. Her hidden vantage point in the corridor allowed her to see the perfectly dressed Acestes entertaining her father's cousin, a man she had not seen in years. She stopped and listened to their conversation.

"Then there is the debt owed to me by the late senator," Acestes said.

"You must know that I do not have that kind of coin," her father's cousin replied. As her closest living male relative, he was now Phaedra's guardian, inheritor of all that belonged to her father, both good and bad. She moved closer to the dining room, hoping that by staying in the shadows she would be close enough to hear what they were saying while remaining unseen. The peacock had other ideas, however. He strutted into the room, letting out his warbling call.

Acestes turned to the peacock and saw Phaedra as well. "I did not know you were there. How fare you this morning?"

As she stepped into the room, she said, "Not well. Of course I am saddened by the death of my father." She said nothing of the heartbreak over losing her chance at a life with Valens and her worry for his health. "I am also very troubled to know that my father's debt will be passed on to his cousin."

"I have no coin," said her cousin. Sweat dotted his upper lip. "I live on a farm outside of the city. I do not want the Didius family Senate seat. I cannot afford it."

"You have an obligation," said Acestes, "to your dead cousin and his living daughter. If you do not accept responsibility for the family and for Phaedra, who will? Am I to throw her out into the street?"

"She is the widow of your uncle. I say that she and her father's debt are your responsibility."

Acestes opened and closed his mouth, as if he had planned to say one thing and then decided to say another. He appeared to weigh his options and to think through every eventuality. "I suppose I could become Phaedra's guardian. We had spoken of marriage on more than one occasion."

It galled her that her father's death was playing perfectly into Acestes's plan to marry her. "I will leave you both to work out the arrangements," she said. "Good day to you, Cousin. Acestes, might you have someone bring water with lemon to my room?"

"I will send some food as well," he said.

"Grief steals my appetite. I think today I shall just rest."

"You will eat and bathe and be ready for the games in an hour."

"I am in mourning and not going to attend the games today. You cannot ask me to be seen in public."

"I can ask you. If you refuse, then my request will become an order."

"I see," she said. She did see, in so many ways. She was no longer the daughter of an influential senator. She had no personal wealth or family connections. Stripped of her titles, she was no one.

Acestes said, "Do not say, 'I see,' as if I am a monster."

Alone. Vulnerable. Beholden. Phaedra lowered her eyes, taking the stance of the weak and humbled. "As you wish," she said.

Acestes walked to Phaedra. He placed his hand on her shoulder. His touch, both warm and soft, turned her stomach. "I need the people of Rome to see you with me today. You understand?"

"I do not," she said, "but I will do as you ask."

He kissed her on the lips. It took all of her energy to keep from shivering. Phaedra had wanted her first husband, Marcus, to have passion for her, and she had felt keenly disappointed when he had not. With Acestes, lust radiated off him like the heat rising from a noonday street, and his desperate desire left her frightened.

She walked away as soon as the kiss ended, not bothering to say good-bye to her father's cousin. She kept her pace slow and steady in the dining room. Once she was out of sight, she raced through the rest of the villa, never bothering to turn around. She slammed her chamber door and slid to the floor. From the corridor came a light knocking. She wiped her eyes and moved away so it might be opened.

"Enter."

No slave came in with a tray of food. She heard the knocking again.

Each movement pained her. Slowly, she stood and opened the heavy door. From the corridor, the peacock regarded her with his shiny black eyes and strutted into the room. Closing the door, she slid once again to the floor. The peacock pranced upon her lap, turning twice, and sat down. Resting his head upon her leg, they regarded one another. In his look she read the undeniable truth: *We lovely captives must remain together.*

Chapter 42

Phaedra

Phaedra and Acestes arrived at the forum during the middle of the first match of the morning. The noise and the heat and the dust provided scant distraction from her grief. Without her father, the box seats felt empty and too silent. The other guests kept their voices low and made few comments out of deference to his passing.

How ludicrous to attend games the day after her father died. The urge to slap Acestes, to beat upon his chest and demand that he return her to her home, came upon her with such a force that she had to clench her fists to control herself.

Two large gladiators struck at each other with swords. The clanging of steel on steel reverberated in her chest, changing the rhythm of her heart. Phaedra swallowed a hard lump of grief, and tears clouded her vision. The ashes she had used to darken her lashes melted and stung her eyes. She motioned Terenita to her side. "I need a cloth with water."

"Yes, my lady. Anything else?"

Phaedra hesitated. Even with all the sadness it would bring, she needed to know about Valens like she needed the air she breathed. She had been reckless with her behavior before, and now had to be careful lest she lose Acestes's favor. "Find out about my friend," she said in a whisper.

"Your friend?" asked Acestes from the other side of the box. "What friend?"

For the love of the gods, that man missed nothing.

"It is not a friend, precisely," she said. "During these games Valens Secundus has become a favorite of mine. He looked ill yesterday—I wonder if he is able to fight today."

"Ah, yes, you have developed a soft spot for the handsome gladiator, have you not?"

"I never follow the games," she said. "But having a gladiator to cheer for makes them more enjoyable, or at least less difficult to watch."

"He did look horrible," said the former consul, Fimbria. "Shame if old Scaeva and his new equestrian died one day apart."

Phaedra gasped, unable to hold her tears any longer. They spilled over her cheeks.

"I would thank you to hold your tongue," said Acestes. "Can you not see how upsetting you are to Scaeva's daughter?"

"Apologies," the man said.

Phaedra bit her bottom lip and nodded in his direction. She could not bear to look him, or anyone else, in the eye.

"I can provide you with some happier news," said Acestes to the Phaedra. He opened his arms and addressed everyone in the private seats. "I heard that Valens, though ill yesterday, recovered enough and will fight again today. Perhaps he can fulfill his contract and save his sister, after all."

Phaedra wiped her eyes with a wet cloth that Terenita handed to her. The lack of cosmetics left her with nothing to hide behind. Still, she said, "That is happy news."

Acestes stood beside Phaedra and gripped her palm in his own. Hand to hand, they looked like silver and gold. His skin, burnished from the outdoors, and hers, pale from ever avoiding the sun. "You do look drawn," he said. "You may return to the villa to rest and then return for the primus. I would hate for you to miss a chance to see your favorite fight."

It was not a request or suggestion. She had been dismissed and told when to return. A thousand possible responses came to mind, yet there was but one thing for her to say. "Of course."

Guards escorted Phaedra from the arena. She stood next to the litter and looked across the forum. The roofline of the ludus drew her eye, and his name came with an unbidden breath. *Valens.* At least he had recovered. While she feared he would never forgive her for marrying Acestes, perhaps he, of all people, would understand that she no longer had the freedom of choice.

Terenita touched Phaedra's arm. "The litter is over here."

Phaedra paused. If she could just see Valens once more and explain, then maybe he would not hate her. And maybe then she could forgive herself for surrendering to the inevitability of a marriage to Acestes.

"Take me to the villa," she said, regretting her words the moment she uttered them. To her surprise, she found that all of her belongings, which had been at her father's villa the day before, were now waiting in her chamber at Acestes's. *So this is how it is*, she thought. *The cage is filled with beautiful things, and then the door snaps shut.*

Chapter 43

Valens

Valens stood in the damp coolness of the inner maze of the bowels of the Forum Boarium more than a little surprised that he stood at all. After having slept away the morning and most of the afternoon, he was roused by a slave two hours before the fight. His body still ached and his head buzzed. Before Valens was fitted into his kit, the ludus physician had given him syrup made from poppy seeds. Black and thick, it had filled him with sunshine. Grateful to be free of pain, he had found the strength to leave the ludus and come to fight.

In truth, he would have found his strength without the syrup of poppy. He would not have given up, even if the stakes were not as high. He tried to picture his opponent and visualize a win. Yet in his mind he saw nothing save a field of golden wheat. Elysium. Was this his end? At least he had saved his sister. Antonice was well away from Rome by now—perhaps she and Leto had already left Capernaum and at this moment made their way to Padua. Phaedra had sworn to protect his sister and keep Acestes from carrying out the execution. So if Valens died today, then he would die well.

"It is time," said Paullus.

Valens nodded and followed him to the door that led to the arena.

"I am proud to call you my son," said Paullus.

"A man could have no better father."

Paullus smiled broadly and clapped him on his wounded shoulder. Valens winced at the pain and then set it aside.

"Apologies," said Paullus. "I forgot which arm ails you."

"Nothing ails me, not now, not ever. I am Valens Secundus, Equestrian, the Trainer of Champions, Son of Paullus Secundus, and a Titan made flesh."

"A titan made flesh? That is a bit much, even for you." Paullus's eyes twinkled.

Valens ignored him. For his mind had already taken him to the middle of the arena, where the editor held his arm high and proclaimed him victor. And yet he knew that he was not in top form. The illness was still with him. Sloppy and weak, he might not win. He fixed his thoughts on Phaedra—her smile, her spirit, her kisses. Yes, for Phaedra and their love and the life they would live together, he would win.

The heavy wooden door opened and light spilled across the dirt floor. Valens stepped through and raised his arms as the crowd cheered. The editor, a tiny man with a shiny, bald pate, stood in the middle of the sands, baton in hand. The other gladiator, an African almost a head taller than Valens, came out of the other door. Two thick leather straps crossed his chest, and one arm was covered from finger to shoulder in a leather manica. In his other arm he held an oval shield. He wore boots that came to his knees, and a buff-colored skirt of lion skin. An open-faced helmet with a crimson horsehair plume completed his kit. The crowd cheered this man as well.

The applause stunned Valens. He knew nothing of the man he faced—his strengths, his weaknesses, even his name. It had been narrow sighted on his part not to learn anything of his opponent.

The gladiators stood on either side of the editor and waited for him to review the rules, lift his baton, and begin the contest. Before the editor had even finished, the other gladiator struck Valens on the helmet with the flat of his sword. The blow was not meant to harm, but to unhinge. It worked. The second blow came in as quickly and unexpectedly as the first. The tip of the other gladiator's sword connected with Valens's calf.

Valens ignored the pain and the blood, but the momentary inability to move his leg sharpened his attention. The crowd stood and screamed. He heard them despite the throbbing in his head and the clang that reverberated in his ears. The two gladiators circled one another.

Thrust, thrust, block, slice.

Thrust, block, block, thrust.

Valens's sword connected with the other man's arm. He nicked an artery and blood pumped out like a tiny fountain. The gladiator's shield sagged. Valens rushed in, aiming for the soft spot where shoulder and neck became one. For a split second he imagined Phaedra in his arms as he tasted her in the same place he now aimed.

His sword connected, but the tip did not punch through flesh and sinew and bone. Rather it glanced off a leather strap and leaped upward, making a shallow slice on the African's cheek, just missing the eye. He would never get a chance at that eye again.

Focus.

No worries.

No thoughts.

Only actions.

His opponent came at Valens from the left. Wait, wait. Shift right. Turn. Valens stabbed the other man in the side as they passed each other. The movement of the fight became natural, fluid, like a long-practiced dance. They locked swords, each pushing against the other until sweat streamed down their faces and the veins under the skin bulged and pulsed.

The crowd booed their inaction, and the editor separated Valens from his opponent with a swipe of his baton.

They backed away from each other, panting. Valens's leg had gone numb. His arm bled from a wound he did not recall getting. His shoulder throbbed. He had always known he would die in the arena.

He looked to the covered seats, those reserved for Acestes and the rest of the lazy patricians. He wanted to scream and spit and flay them all alive.

This is what you came for, he wanted to say. *To watch men suffer for your twisted pleasure. To see me draw my final breath, then later tell your children of the history you witnessed.*

Instead he saw Phaedra. He forgot all about his numb leg, his infected shoulder, and his bleeding arm.

The other gladiator came at Valens, who stepped to the side. He moved too slowly, and the larger man crashed into his injured leg. Both men tumbled to the ground. Valens saw a blinding flash of white as he heard a crack and felt a bone in his calf snap.

For a moment all was silent, save for the thumping pulse in Valens's ears. Then came the collective gasp from the crowd. He had heard it many times as his opponents fell. It was a sign that everyone knew the fallen would never again rise.

Give up, whispered a voice in the back of his skull. *Give up and let all the pain go.*

He should kneel and take a clean gladiator's death. Let the sword sever his spine and open the front of his throat. He would be in Elysium before his corpse hit the sands.

But no one waited for him in Elysium. Here, in Rome, were the people who mattered.

Phaedra, Paullus, and Baro were his family. If he lived, he would bring back his sister and Leto. They were his reason for rising from bed in the morning. Not the fame, or the coin, or even the notoriety.

He pushed up to his side. Leaning on his hilt, Valens rose to his knees. The other gladiator held his sword with both hands and waited for him to take the position of the doomed.

"No," Valens said as he stood. His injured leg could still bear some weight, although he listed to the side. "If I am to die, then you will have to skewer me to the ground."

With a nod that Valens assumed meant *so be it*, the other gladiator took a step back and lifted his sword and shield. At least his opponent would let Valens die in a fight and not slaughter him in his moment of weakness. Both men nodded at each other. The editor swiped his baton between the two, and the men started to fight again.

Slash, thrust, block, shield, thrust.

He compensated for his broken leg by using his toe to keep steady. In his mind, Valens saw his square. He never left the box and made the other man come to him.

Slash, thrust, shield, shield, turn.

In quick, successive movements, the other gladiator rushed in and withdrew. Valens remained in his square and defended his space. Once more the African tried to move the fight. It did not work. Then the man feigned right, and Valens, anticipating the trick, sliced his opponent's back open. Shiny bits of spine shone through the skin. The African staggered, then lunged for Valens with a wild arc of his sword. The blade passed far to the left.

The man still stood. His eyes rolled back in his head. Blood trailed down his back, collecting into a black puddle at his feet. Valens moved in close and drove his sword into the gladiator's gut. He pulled the blade upward and then free. Entrails pushed out of the gaping wound. The African stumbled forward and clung to Valens's shoulders.

"Sleep well, Brother," said Valens. "You have fought long and hard and deserve a rest."

The gladiator nodded. Or maybe Valens just wanted to think that his opponent had heard the words and accepted the killing. Holding the sword's grip tighter, he slid it across the African's throat. A spray of blood blinded Valens, and the other man slipped to the ground.

Valens let the editor lift his hand and proclaim him victor. Silver coins and rose petals rained down from the stands along with screams and cheers that he imagined even Antonice could hear on the road to Padua.

Acestes came to the rail of his box and stood next to Phaedra. He slowly clapped his hands. "You are, without doubt, the Champion of Rome. It seems as though you have gained the favor of Phaedra as well."

Valens held on to the editor's shoulder to stay upright. "I am honored to have gained the lady's favor," Valens said.

"Perhaps I can convince you to fight at her next wedding, when she marries me. Just like when you fought at her wedding to my uncle."

"You plan to marry her?" As Valens stepped forward, his broken leg buckled. The editor lifted him up by the shoulder, helping him to stand steady again. "Has her father given his permission?"

Phaedra looked away in a gesture Valens took for complicity, if not guilt.

"Her father is dead," said Acestes. "He died last night. I am Phaedra's guardian now, and I have decided to marry her myself."

Senator Scaeva was dead and Phaedra was Acestes's ward? The world he now inhabited was not the same one he had just fought to keep. If Valens had given up during his fight, at least he would have died thinking that one day he would have married Phaedra.

"Nothing to add?" asked Acestes.

Valens stood tall, although every part of his body ached. "I offer you sympathies, my lady."

"Do you not mean that you offer her your sympathies for her father's death and congratulations for her upcoming marriage?" asked Acestes.

"No, I offer her sympathies for them both." Then to the editor, Valens said, "Help me to the door. I should see the physician about this leg." Without being dismissed or asking for permission to leave, he turned his back on Acestes and the elite of Rome. But in truth, he walked away from Phaedra.

Chapter 44

Phaedra

Look at me. Please, for the love of the gods, look at me. Phaedra willed Valens to turn around as he limped from the arena. She wanted him to know and understand that being with Acestes was not her choice. Also, that his announcement of their betrothal had surprised her as well.

Well, perhaps that last bit was not entirely true.

She understood Acestes's need for a lavish production, his desire to have everyone talking about him, and his unblinking focus on becoming first above all. The fact that he had turned their betrothal into a bit of gossip that stole some of Valens's well-deserved acclaim was no surprise.

As Valens hobbled across the sands of the arena, Phaedra tried to force her thoughts into his mind. He never once turned around.

"I think it is all over—for today, at least," said Acestes.

"I think it is," said Phaedra.

Acestes held out his hand. "Allow me to escort you to my litter."

Marcus had never cared to spend much on finery, preferring to hoard his fortune until Phaedra imagined that even his coins grew moldy. Acestes did not seem so afflicted, and he brought her to another newly purchased litter.

A crimson veil hung down over its sides, turning the world ruby red. With Phaedra at one end and Acestes at the other, they reclined on silk pillows and cushions. They rode together in silence, not touching, and yet the heat from his calves radiated all the way to hers.

Each person they passed looked to her like Valens, so Phaedra closed her eyes. Without the sights of the forum to distract her, she envisioned her father and knew that amends would never be made for his betrayal. That the last time they spoke had been with filled with anger consumed Phaedra with guilt. At least her parents were together again in Elysium.

Acestes's hand trailed over the scarlet cushion to rest on her ankle.

Acestes still wanted her, even without a powerful father. She knew that she should be grateful, but even that emotion could not overcome the sadness that enveloped her soul.

"It has been less than two weeks since Marcus died, and now my father. Everything has changed for me and not even a month gone by."

"Even though it has been less than a month, I suppose you know that you are not with child. Your father would have made an issue out of the possible heir."

Marcus had not lain with Phaedra for several months and her courses had come regularly. But she might be carrying Valens's child. For an instant she felt the thrill of possibly having created a life with the man she loved. Then reality took over. Phaedra knew that the Fates would be cruel to the child, whose eyes would be brown, like rich soil, and not gray, like a stormy sky. She prayed that her womb was empty and felt it must be such. Still, she said, "I will have to wait until my time comes again to know whether Marcus's seed took root or not. What an irony that would be, for you to think that you are his heir when all the while I am carrying his child."

"It would matter little, since I plan to marry you myself. Besides, I do not worry about my uncle being amorous with you, much less fertile, in the last month of his life. However, I do worry about the gladiator."

"What gladiator?" asked Phaedra, panicked that Acestes had even the slightest inkling of her relationship with Valens.

"You saw how he reacted to the news of our betrothal. He mocked me in front of Rome. He turned his back on me and walked away without permission. I must wonder why. Has the Champion of Rome also become the Master of Your Bed?"

She could not deny the implication outright. Nor could Phaedra do what she wanted and acknowledge Valens as her lover and the man she loved. Avoiding the question, she said. "I wonder why you immediately think Valens Secundus is upset about me. Correct me if I am wrong, but did you not force him to return to the arena in order to save his sister from execution?"

Acestes opened the sheer curtain and looked into the street. A shaft of pure sunlight bathed him in gold. "I did not force him to do anything. He offered to fight in her stead."

Phaedra hesitated a moment before pressing the advantage she had found. "Valens won today in superb fashion. Wounded shoulder, broken leg, and still he was victorious. You stole his glory by announcing that you planned to marry me. Besides, he is now an equestrian and can turn his back on any of us if he chooses."

"Valens," said Acestes. He let the curtain fall back into place and leaned back on the cushion. "You called him Valens. Not Valens Secundus, or the Champion of Rome. You use his name as though you *know* him. I ask you yet again. *How* do you know Valens Secundus?"

"Stop being crude."

"I knew my uncle," said Acestes, "or feel I understood him as a man. In a way I would not mind if you had taken a lover while married. At least you would have some sexual experience. Although I do not like the idea of a gladiator's cock having been where mine will be going."

Phaedra could not even think about engaging in sex with Acestes. Why did he not see that if she desired him, she would have accepted his offer of a child long ago, or his offer of marriage not long past? "Did you not hear me? Do not be crude."

"Apologies."

Again he traced Phaedra's ankle; this time he traveled higher to her calf. She shifted, pulling her leg from his reach.

"Perhaps my uncle chose wives who did not like sex and therefore suited him."

"You cannot speak to me that way. Get out." She raised her voice and called out, "Stop the litter! The general wishes to walk."

The litter ceased moving.

"You cannot remove me from my own litter," Acestes said.

"Get out." Phaedra threw a pillow. He caught it in midair and placed it behind his head. How she hated him.

Phaedra rose to her knees. "Then I will walk."

"You will do no such thing." Acestes knelt next to her and forced her back into the seat. He handed her a pillow. "If you really cannot stand to be around me, then I can walk to the villa. Besides, riding makes me appear weak to the voters."

"You *are* weak. Get out."

Ignoring the stairs set out for his benefit, Acestes leaped from the litter and laughed. "You are many things, Phaedra. Dull is not one of them."

"Return her to the villa," Acestes said to a guard. "I have business that needs tending. You and you"—he picked two guards—"come with me. Maid," he said to Terenita, "ride with your mistress. I vexed her too much today."

"Yes, my lord," said Terenita as she climbed into the litter. She sat, straight-backed, with her hands clasped over her lap at the far end of the seat.

"Since I am in the litter with you, my lady, might I speak with some frankness?"

"I wish someone would," said Phaedra.

"Why do you bait General Acestes? If he is your guardian and will be your husband, do you not think it wise to be kind to him?"

"My father promised that I could choose my husband if Marcus died," said Phaedra. "Marcus is dead and I have another that I love, so I do not want Acestes."

"Along with Marcus, your father is also dead, and with him any promises he made to you. Perhaps it is time you worried less about love and more about survival."

"How can you suggest such a thing? Why survive if not for love?"

"Beautiful sentiments," said Terenita. "But I am a slave, so survival is all that concerns me."

Phaedra's face flushed and her throat constricted as unshed tears stung her eyes. She knew that her maid had spoken a version of the truth she did not care to hear. She wanted to believe in love. "Have you never loved someone so much that without them you feel that the dawn may not come?"

"I was born a slave, my lady. I have always known that love was not to be my lot in life. Being purchased by your father to care for you was more than I could have ever hoped for."

"But you have been in love. Certainly before you came to me there was another slave or servant whom you fancied."

Terenita's cheeks reddened. How could Phaedra have never known? How could she have never thought to ask? "There was someone. Tell me who he is—I will purchase him on the morrow and then you might be reunited. At least you should be with the one you love."

"Do not concern yourself with me, my lady. The man I once cared for has been dead for many, many years."

"I grieve with you," said Phaedra. The finality of death, all deaths, weighed upon her. A tear leaked from her eye and snaked down her cheek. She bothered not with stopping it, and it dripped from her chin, falling onto her gown. "You must promise me that you will let me know if ever you find a man whom you might love."

Terenita's blush deepened. "I promise."

"I would have you with a good man."

"Valens is a good man. He would have worked very hard to make you happy. Yet I fear for you, my lady. What will become of you if you lose the general's affections?"

That, of course, was the one question that had plagued Phaedra since her father died. "What if Valens wins his final match the day after tomorrow?"

"Is that what this is all about? Marrying your gladiator?" asked Terenita. "If you want to make a choice in who you marry, then choose Acestes. It will still be your choice, even if it is the eventual outcome."

"I will think on what you say." The litter stopped in front of the heavy doors to the villa. She imagined that once she stepped across the threshold, coming out again would not be her decision. What else was she to do? Sleep in the litter? Return to her father's villa, which no doubt belonged to Acestes now? Run to the ludus and beg Valens to overlook everything that had happened?

Although the last option tempted her, she alighted and walked through the doors and told herself that she entered the villa out of strength, not fear. And that what she feared most was not that Valens might never forgive her.

Chapter 45

Valens

The physician fitted flat boards around Valens's broken leg. He applied layers of cloth strips covered in wet plaster that when dried would hold them all in place.

"You must keep the bandage dry," the physician said.

Baro and Paullus insisted on being present as the ludus physician tended to Valens. The four powerful men made the cramped infirmary seem that much smaller. Three narrow beds stood in a line. Valens lay on the one in the middle, and Baro sat on the one closest to the door. Paullus leaned his shoulder against a corner. A small table sat next to each bed. Shelves lined the walls, filled with jars and pots and bundles of herbs tied together.

"No more long soaks in the hot bath for a while," said Baro.

"He can manage," said Paullus. "He is alive. I will speak to General Acestes this evening and try to renegotiate terms. You cannot fight again in two days. If you do, you may never fight again. Perhaps you can pay a fine for your sister's crime. Jupiter knows that you have entertained Rome better than she has been entertained in years."

Baro grinned. "Should I be offended by your comment?"

"You do not let yourself get beaten half to death and then rise from the River Styx."

"Why did you not tell me that Phaedra was betrothed to Acestes?" Valens cared little for the lighthearted banter between the other men. "You must have known yet chose not to tell me. Why?"

Baro picked up a bowl filled with white plaster and spun it between his hands.

"That is not a plaything," said the physician. He took the bowl from Baro and set it on the table. "You need to lie still for four hours and allow the plaster to harden," he said to Valens. "In a few days you will be able to stand and walk with a crutch. The break was clean, so the bones should knit back together. But your career in the arena is over."

"It was over two years ago," said Valens. "And you two"—he pointed at Paullus and Baro—"need to stop ignoring me."

"Do not blame me," said Baro. "This is the first I am hearing of your new lady love."

"Well, *you* knew and you kept quiet," Valens said to the lanista.

Paullus removed a few coins from a bag he wore around his waist and pressed them into the physician's palm. "Thank you for your loyal service. You can take your leave now, but come back in a few hours to check on our patient."

The physician, a good and true servant, refused the coins, but did promise to return. Paullus shut the door as soon as the three men were alone. A square of light from a small window reflected off the floor.

"You will need to learn to hold your tongue, my boy. You may be the strongest of the strong in the arena, but in the ways that matter outside, you are weak." Paullus raked his hands through his hair and sat next to Baro. "I knew nothing of the engagement. I heard that Phaedra's father, Senator Scaeva, died last night. I kept the news from you, true. You had enough worries, and I did not want to give you one more thing to think about while fighting."

Valens snorted. "How very noble of you."

"Stop blaming others and listen to what I have to say. I am trying to save you. With Phaedra you aimed too high. She loves you, I grant you that."

"If she loved me, she would not be marrying someone else."

"Are you really that naive? Phaedra never had a choice in husbands. Fall out of love with her and find someone else. That is the best advice I can give you."

Fall out of love with her? Paullus made it sound as if Valens had any hand in controlling his emotions. Like he could discard his love in the same fashion he discarded fear before stepping into the arena. Actually, when Valens thought of it that way, he supposed he should be able to will himself to stop loving Phaedra. But he knew that would never happen.

"I do not want to."

Paullus sighed with resignation. "You are the most stubborn bastard in the world."

"You do not get to be Champion of Rome twice in a life by being a weakling who is easily dissuaded," said Baro.

Good old Baro. You could always count on him to cut to the real meat of the matter. "Thank you," said Valens.

"Do not thank me. I do not care who claims to be your father or why. You are still an idiot for thinking that you were going to steal General Acestes's bride at the altar."

You could also always count on Baro to take a solid idea and, in a few words, make a mess of it.

"Leave, both of you. I need to rest."

Baro opened his mouth and Paullus raised his hand. "Let us leave him alone. Once his head clears, he will see the wisdom in our words."

"I doubt it," said Valens.

"Rest. Heal. Live," said Baro.

"Get out."

Paullus laid his hand on Baro's shoulder and nodded toward the door. Once the two men had slipped out and he was alone, Valens lay on the bed, gripped with hatred for them both. Then he turned his hate toward Phaedra. He hated her for making him believe that she loved him. He hated her for making him believe in himself. He hated her for making him believe that he could be more than an uneducated slave. The need to strike someone or something boiled within him. The bowl with the plaster still sat on the table next to his bed. He stretched until his fingertips grazed the side, and he pulled it closer. With true aim, he threw it at the wall. Bits of pottery exploded around the room, and thick white paste oozed down the wall, forming a puddle on the floor. With the evidence of his destruction around him, Valens finally closed his eyes and rested.

Chapter 46

Phaedra

Acestes arrived at the villa an hour after Phaedra. She ordered drinks and olives brought to the small dining room while he settled on a sofa. She poured wine and handed it to him.

"This is an unexpected treat," he said, taking the offered goblet. He sat up and patted the upholstery next to him. "Join me."

Phaedra sat with her back so stiff and posture so rigid that her shoulder blades nearly pinched together. He ran his fingers up the side of her neck. She neither moved nor made comment. Had she ever found Acestes appealing? He was handsome, for certain. They were, as he had been quick to point out, the same kind of people. A shared background should count for something toward lifelong happiness, should it not?

"I realize you are being kind to me," she said after he withdrew his hand. "I have nothing to bring to a union now other than myself. And perhaps a lineage for a child."

"Children," said Acestes. "I want you to bear me more than one child. But in truth, you alone are enough for me."

Oh, where was the Phaedra who had longed to hear those words from a young, wealthy, and handsome patrician? If the girl of her youth could be resurrected, then they would both be happy.

"That pleases me," she said. And, strangely, it did please her—as much as anything might please her now.

"I am glad that we are becoming friends. Perhaps I should not have forced you to attend the games this afternoon. Nor should I have announced our marriage without telling you beforehand. The first was cruel and the second must have come as quite a shock. Know this—I love you, Phaedra. I always have and always will want you as mine and mine alone."

Yes, the young Phaedra would have longed to hear Acestes's words of undying adoration. The Phaedra of today saw things differently, especially when he made her sound more like a possession than a person. She rose from the sofa and filled her own goblet with wine. She finished the drink in one long swallow, happy that the floor underneath swayed a little.

She filled the goblet again and took another long drink, finding that the detached feeling it brought suited her. She reclined on the sofa opposite Acestes and ate an olive. At last she had found a moment of peace, even if it had come thanks to the riches of the vineyard.

"There is a jeweler at the door," a slave said. "He says you asked for him, General."

"I did. Show him in." The slave walked away and Acestes turned to Phaedra. "I hate that we quarreled, so I wanted to do something special for you. I hope you do not mind."

Phaedra shrugged and took a sip. She was light-headed and her tongue felt cottony in her mouth. Or maybe that was because her lips were a bit numb. "I do not mind anything." Her voice came out too loudly. "Not at all," she whispered.

Acestes laughed. "I think you have gotten yourself good and drunk. Not a bad thing, really. You needed the release, what with your father's passing." He took the goblet from her. "But let us not make this a habit."

The jeweler, a tall man with dark hair and a hooked nose, stood at the door to the dining room.

"You may enter." Acestes waved the jeweler into the room. "Come in."

Three slaves carrying large wooden boxes followed on the jeweler's heels. Within a few moments, legs had been screwed into the bottom of the boxes and the lids opened to display a variety of necklaces, bracelets, and earrings.

"Choose anything you like," said Acestes.

Phaedra examined the jewelry piece by piece, holding up necklaces and draping bracelets across her wrist. Earrings made up of four tiers of tiny diamonds held together with thin golden wire moved, flowed, and sparkled with each step she took. She tried on a bracelet of white pearls, which on closer inspection, shimmered with the iridescence of a thousand different shades of blue and pink. There also were thick collar necklaces of gold and silver with bronze embellishment.

Phaedra tried on a necklace with a chain of rubies that dropped from the throat, each one larger than the one before.

"I have a bracelet that matches," said the jeweler. "All the loveliest ladies in Alexandria wear necklaces such as these."

"Egypt," Acestes spat. "This is Rome. Our ladies set the trends, not follow them. Show her something else."

"I have one more piece. It is very expensive, very valuable."

"Let us see it then." Acestes poured another goblet of wine and settled back on the sofa.

The jeweler produced a key from the folds of his tunic and unlocked a bottom drawer in the smallest of the three wooden boxes. The jeweler held up for all to see—entwined chains of silver and gold holding a single stone, a deep green emerald the size of a grape.

Acestes stood. His hands trembled and wine sloshed over the cup's rim. "Where did you get this piece?"

"Beautiful, is it not?"

"Where?"

Phaedra tried to speak but could think of nothing to say that would calm the moment.

The jeweler stood taller. "I will not tell you. My clients know of my discretion."

"You are a thief, and if you do not tell me how you came to possess this necklace, I shall have you executed tomorrow. You will be hanged upside down and your gut opened. Then I will release starving lions into the arena, and they will complete the execution by devouring you, piece by piece."

"You have no authority."

"No authority?" Acestes roared. "Who in this city would defy me? You? A peddler?" Acestes threw his drink across the room. Wine, deep and red as blood, came out in an arc as the cup tumbled through the air. It hit the floor with a clang that made Phaedra jump. Suddenly sober, she saw how wrong she had been to underestimate Acestes.

Acestes crossed the room and grabbed the necklace from the jeweler. "Are you willing to trade your life for this?"

"The necklace came to me from a lanista, Paullus Secundus, as a bet on the current games."

"What was the wager?"

"I know not." The jeweler held up his hands in surrender. "Honestly."

Holding the necklace in his hands, Acestes shook his head. "The sneaking and scheming is all too much. I know who placed the bet and why. This came from a senator, did it not?" He pointed to Phaedra. "Your father took this necklace from you, knowing its value, and gave it to the lanista, who then sold it in order to get coin for a wager. Your father was wily, I grant you that, Phaedra."

"I do not believe that is what happened," said the jeweler.

"There is no need to lie to me. I shall not punish you if you are honest."

"My understanding was that the necklace came from a lady," said the jeweler.

Wine rumbled in her stomach, and Phaedra was overcome with the need to retch on the floor. If Acestes were not her guardian, she could walk out the door and never see him again. If he were not in control of her life, she would tell him that he had given her a gift and she could do whatever she pleased with the cursed necklace. If he were not the god who controlled her life, she would have no need to worry. But he was all of that and more, and now Acestes knew that Phaedra had played him false. Or at least that she had not been honest with him. Either way, he now knew, and she doubted that she would ever have the favor of his forgiveness.

"Leave," Acestes said to the jeweler.

"You must return the necklace to me. It is valuable and I paid a fair price for it."

"Leave or I will have you arrested and then executed on the morrow."

"You can do no such thing. There are no charges to be brought."

"The charges will be whatever I say they are," said Acestes, "and by the time anyone has thought to ask questions, the vultures will have long since picked your bones clean."

Without bothering to remove the legs from his makeshift table, the jeweler repacked his boxes and ushered his slaves from the room.

"Why?" Acestes asked. "I just want to know why. Tell me you did this for your father. Tell me that he asked you to bet this necklace so he could make some money and that you loved him so much you agreed."

Phaedra wondered if her younger self would have told Acestes what he wanted to hear, saving them all from the hurt and heartache that accompanied an unpleasant truth. No, that Phaedra had held honesty paramount. Why did she consider lying now? Was she so concerned with self-preservation that she had lost her moral strength? In a way, her honesty honored her father's memory. She could not allow him to be seen as even more manipulative and grasping than he had been.

No, it was finally time for the entire truth.

Phaedra took a deep breath and steadied herself before she spoke. "I used the necklace to bet on Valens Secundus winning all of his fights. I did not do it for the coin or my father, but rather because of my love for the gladiator."

"Valens? You love the gladiator Valens Secundus?"

Phaedra looked out of the open door. Dark had fallen long before. A cool breeze blew in from the garden. She faced Acestes. "I have loved Valens since I first met him."

"You lust for him—it is infatuation," said Acestes. "Not love."

"You are wrong. I do love him. He changes my world. With Valens anything is possible. Even the daughter of a senator can marry for love and not for political alliances or the purity of her blood." Phaedra was shocked by her outburst. She stopped speaking as her heart beat quickly beneath her breast. In her mind, telling Acestes the truth had seemed the best thing to do. But as the last traces of her voice faded away, she knew how wrong she had been.

Hurt and anger twisted Acestes's handsome features into a grimace. His eyes shone with tears that he fought to keep from falling. Phaedra reached out to him, hoping that her touch would offer comfort.

"Do not," he said through clenched teeth, "put your hand upon me."

She let her arm fall to her side, and they watched each other for a moment. Finally, she walked back to the door and looked into the darkened garden. She looked heavenward, hoping to find Polaris. Thick clouds obscured the night sky, and Phaedra saw not a single star.

Carrying a torch, a slave walked by. His footfalls crunched softly on the gravel path that wound through the garden. Aside from that, there were no other sounds. Phaedra waited for Acestes to say something. Perhaps he would strike her without warning. She cared little.

Her father was dead. Valens was lost to her. And her final thin hope of a contented life with Acestes had been ruined by her honesty. She had no one to love, or to love her in return. The Fates had turned their back on her. Perhaps they had cut the thread tethering her to the world, and it was now Acestes's fate to end her life. In a way, she longed for the release of death. She tensed, sensing the moment drawing near.

But there was only silence.

She turned to look and found Acestes gone. In his place were three of Acestes's guards, armed with swords. Phaedra knew they meant to do her harm. For an instant she considered meekly giving in to their plans. But as two of the men grabbed her, she found herself fighting—hitting and kicking—although she knew they barely felt her blows. Her knuckles bled as she continued to punch the stiff leather of their breastplates. Her feet throbbed from landing one too many kicks to the thick greaves that covered their shins. She twisted and turned in their grasp as they pulled her to the door.

She screamed, ordering them to stop at first, and begging them later. There would be no one to help her, save herself. These men had been sent by Acestes to make her sorry for not loving him. By the gods, she was so sorry. Sorry she had ever met him.

Struggling, the guards pulled Phaedra to the atrium. They all stopped as one man unbolted the front door. With everyone's attention on the door, she grabbed one man by the hair. His grip lessened and she wrenched herself free. She tumbled backward with a handful of bloody hair as the man bent double and held his head. She righted herself and traded the clump of hair for a bowl that sat at the edge of the pool. A second guard came at her. She swung out wildly with the bowl. It connected with the guard, just under his chin, and he fell backward.

Scrambling to her feet, she raced to the open door. A strong arm grabbed her around the middle. She bucked and screamed. Bending over, she tried to bite the arm that held her. Another hand grabbed the back of her head. Pain seared through her scalp, and she reached up, trying to loosen the grip. The frame of the door came in so close and fast that Phaedra had no time to react. The single blow stole her senses and left her dizzy and tired. As her world closed in upon itself, she heard the rumbling of wheels over paving stones and smelled the sickly sweet scent of rotting food. *A cart*, she thought. *They have thrown me into a refuse cart.* Then it all became black.

Chapter 47

Valens

A shake to his shoulder awakened Valens. Startled, he grabbed the person who touched him with one hand and lifted his other fist, ready to strike.

"It is me, Paullus."

Valens lowered his raised fist. The lanista held a lone candle, and Valens rubbed his eyes against the glare.

"What time is it?"

"The tenth bell rang not long ago. You know where you are?"

"I remember everything—the fight, my leg, Phaedra, her lies. Your lies." Valens squeezed the lanista's wrist once and let go. "I should break your arm. But I expect I will feel guilty later if I do."

"You are not the first man to lose his love. You will not be the last." Paullus held out his hand. "Break every bone if you think it will make a difference."

It would not. Nothing would. Valens folded his arms across his chest. "You woke me for a reason?"

"General Acestes is here. He wants to renegotiate the terms of your agreement. They sound generous and I think you should accept."

For a moment Valens thought of refusing to see the general. How could he bargain with the man who planned to marry Phaedra? Without her, Valens's life seemed worthless.

Part of Valens felt there was no use in keeping his commitment to Acestes anyway. His next scheduled fight was the day after tomorrow. By then, Antonice and Leto should be safe with Baro's family. What else did he have to live for? When he took to the arena for the last time, he could open his arms and expose his chest, giving his opponent an easy target.

But still . . .

"Bring Acestes to me," he said.

The general came into the infirmary and sat on a stool brought in for him by a slave.

"You fought well," said Acestes. "All of Rome loves you again."

Valens nodded toward his broken leg. "I am not sure that I fought well at all."

"Well, Rome is once again yours."

Valens shrugged. His infected shoulder ached. "I care little for an entire city."

"But you do love a single woman."

Did Acestes know about Phaedra? Well, Valens would not gift the arrogant patrician with a confession. "My sister—of course I love her and would do anything to keep her safe."

"Let us not play games," said Acestes. "I do not speak of your sister. I speak of Phaedra."

Valens let out a long breath. "Paullus said you came to offer different terms for my sister's pardon."

"Do you not care about Phaedra?"

Valens did not like being at such a disadvantage. Acestes knew something, or at least suspected something, about Phaedra. To confess was foolish. But being obstinate was a mistake as well. "She is your future wife. Why would I care about her?"

"I will not marry a woman who loves another and has played me for a fool. She loves you and told me as much tonight. I assume the scheme of making you an equestrian was so you might marry. If so, it was very ingenious."

"Phaedra said all of that to you? What were the circumstances?" Although he was still angry, the idea that Acestes had hurt her in order to get her to speak enraged Valens all the more. Through clenched teeth he said, "If you tortured her, I swear I will kill you and use your rotting skull as a piss pot." Valens struggled to sit up. He lifted his shoulders but nothing else moved.

"I did not harm her. She told me everything freely. She is no longer my guest. Guards have seen her safely away, and she is, as we speak, healthy and whole."

What if Phaedra's engagement to Acestes ended? Well, if he did not live past his next fight, all of his wonderings would be for naught.

Focus.

"I do not want to discuss Phaedra with you anymore," said Valens. "What terms do you offer for my final fight?"

"On the morrow you will conduct the executions."

"That is the lowest form of gladiatorial fighting. There is no combat, no resistance from the condemned, just cold-blooded slaughter."

"The people who must die are guilty of crimes. Thievery, murder, rape. Your mother's killer died in the arena, did he not?"

"He did."

"Do you feel he deserved his fate?"

"He did."

"If the lack of a fight bothers you, kill them as mercifully as you like. Slit their throats." The general drew his thumb across his neck.

"How many executions are scheduled for tomorrow?" Valens asked.

"I do not know. This is my offer. Conduct tomorrow's executions and I will consider that you have kept your part of our bargain."

"You are not a benevolent man, General Acestes. Why offer mercy now?"

"I tire of this all." He opened his hands as if to take in the entire world. "I wish to be rid of you. At the same time, I cannot be seen as the man who killed Valens Secundus, even if it was by forcing you to keep your word. I wanted to marry Phaedra. But she wanted you. That truth injures me. But I also cannot be the husband of a gladiator's mistress. Can you imagine how foolish I would look?" Acestes laughed and shook his head.

Valens sensed that the general was truly weary. Could Acestes be telling the truth?

"Who will fight on the last day?" Valens asked.

"Baro has the final fight."

Valens had few options, given his weakened condition. If he saved his sister by slitting a few more throats, it would be worth it. He would figure out later what to do about Phaedra, if anything.

"I will see you at noon tomorrow," he said to Acestes.

"Good choice," said the general, and without another word, he left.

Valens knew there was more to the plan than met the eye. He tried to stay awake and think of the many ways a manipulative man like Acestes might exact his revenge, but Valens was far too tired to catalog them all.

Chapter 48

Phaedra

Phaedra woke on a floor of dirt with the stink of cow dung thick in the air. Her head throbbed with each beat of her heart. A bruise had risen in the middle of her forehead. She brushed it with her fingers. The pain from the slight touch was so great that she gasped.

She lay still for a moment and let the discomfort pass. Sitting up slowly, Phaedra looked around the room. Two windows, high and long, let in the dull gray light of dawn. Stirred up by her movements, bits of hay and dust floated past. The room was empty—just two windows, a bare floor, four walls of stone, and a thick wooden door.

Phaedra stood and steadied herself on a wall before walking to the door. She tried to lift the latch but found that it had been bolted shut from the outside. She pushed upon the door until she began to feel dizzy. After taking a moment to regain her breath, she called out, demanding to be released. No one heard her. Or if they did, they did not answer her call.

She slumped to the floor. Without a powerful father or husband or suitor, she was no one. Acestes had locked her away in a stable. Did anyone know where she was? Did anyone care? Certainly, Terenita cared. Although as a slave, she could do nothing to help.

Why had she not listened to Terenita's warnings? The maid had clearly seen the misery that Phaedra would bring upon herself. Love for Valens had stolen her judgment. Little good that knowledge would do her now that she was forgotten and alone, perhaps even locked away until she rotted.

From the opposite side of the door, Phaedra heard voices and the sounds of wood on metal as the bolt was disengaged. She moved away, stood, and tried to shake some of the dust from her gown. The door opened and Acestes stepped through.

Her heart began to race. He had come for her, forgiven her. She met Acestes's flint-hard stare. No. There was no forgiveness. He was a formidable enemy, and she was now at the mercy of a merciless man.

The thought of what he might do terrified Phaedra. Her hands trembled, her pulse raced, and her breath caught in her chest. Yet she refused to let him see her distress. "What do you want?" she asked with as much contempt in her voice as she could muster. A wide-eyed look of surprise registered for the span of a second, and then he smirked. Her bravado fooled no one. She was his captive, and powerless. He would do whatever he wanted, and her desires mattered for naught.

Acestes shut the door and leaned his shoulder into the jamb. He held out his hand and examined his outstretched fingers for a moment. "I have but one question for you. Why is it that you could not love me?"

Of all the questions Acestes might have asked her, Phaedra had not expected it to be that one. She looked away, her eyes trailing to the small windows, high in the wall. The sky beyond had turned from soft gray to pale blue. "I do not know," she said finally.

"I would have loved you well."

"Is that why you locked me away in your stable, because you love me?"

"Beautiful Phaedra, you are too naive sometimes. I would find it endearing, were it not so sad. You are in the bowels of the Forum Boarium."

She lost her breath and her head swam. Reaching out, she held fast to the wall as she was crushed by the truth of the matter. "I am to be executed. What are the charges?"

"Adultery," he said, "of course."

The need to remain composed disappeared like the last traces of fog that hung over the Tiber River. "No," she said as she moved toward Acestes, her hands clasped together in prayer and petition. "No. It is not true."

"You slept with that brute, the gladiator. Do not lie to me."

Her head pounded, the rush of her pulse drowning out every other sound. "I was not married to your uncle when we became lovers. You must believe me. I was a widow."

"I came upon the two of you in the garden on the night of your wedding. I spied you from a distance. For propriety's sake I gave you a moment to cover your nakedness before I made myself known."

"No," she said again, hoping to reason with him, "you are mistaken. We embraced, yes. It was wrong of me to stand so close to a man who was not my husband. But we never made love, not then. We did not even kiss that night."

"It is not I who am mistaken," said Acestes. "You are."

As quickly as the panic that enveloped her had arrived, it left. In its wake were stillness and understanding. "You know the truth but do not care. You plan to level a charge of adultery against me and call for my execution."

"It seems as though I was wrong to assume that you are naive."

"Since there is no one who will refute your claim, I will be executed like all women who commit adultery—tied to the back of a bull, thrown about, and gouged until dead."

"I suppose it will be something like that, yes," Acestes said.

"But you are a fool, you know. Rome will not elect a man to be her consul who one day announced his engagement to a woman and the next called for her death. Seasons will pass, but this incident will always stain your name."

Acestes rapped on the door. It opened and he pulled it wide. "That may be," he said. "But I plan to give them something even more interesting to talk about."

With that, he slipped through the door and was gone.

Chapter 49

Valens

Slaves fitted Valens into his kit as best they could. He looked ridiculous, asinine, really—helmet but no faceplate, greaves on one leg, the other one set in a cast, all of this with a bandage entirely visible on his shoulder. Holding his sword in one hand and a crutch in the other, he might have been part of a perverse play depicting the dark side of the gladiatorial games.

This was not theater. Valens was not an actor. The death he would mete out would be all too real. He decided to look upon each of the condemned as his mother's killer. It gave a sense of honor to the slaying of untrained and unarmed people.

With this being the final time he would step into the arena, Valens sent his scant belongings to his villa. He planned to be home not long after noontime. Once his contract was completed, he would send for his sister.

Paullus came to escort Valens to his final fight. "Word has gotten out that you will be in the arena today and that this will be your final time," he said as they walked toward the gates of the ludus.

"Word always gets out in Rome," said Valens. But as the door swung open, giving him a view of the Capitoline Market, he found himself speechless. A huge crowd, maybe twenty deep, had gathered. They did not cheer. No one pressed in on Valens. As always, he tried to focus on creating an inner calm and not on the mob. But their eerie silence bothered him more than when they screamed his name.

At the gates of the Forum Boarium, Valens stopped and turned to face the crowd.

One voice called out, "We love you, Valens."

Then the applause began. Still holding the crutch, Valens raised his good arm. They yelled louder, calling down blessings from every known god and goddess. He pumped his arm once more, this time nearly pitching off-balance. Paullus held him steady.

The love and adoration of the crowd were not the lure for Valens. He had never become entangled in the trap laid by fame. But seeing these people, his people—the plebs and slaves of Rome—moved by his struggles brought out his affection for each person there.

"Gratitude," he said, "to you all." He wished he had other eloquent or wise words. "Gratitude," he said again. He doubted anyone heard him. He could hardly hear himself over the cries of the crowd.

Inside the Forum Boarium, Valens stood at the same door he had on so many other occasions. Often he was nervous before fights, sometimes confident, always focused. Yet today, when called to conduct the executions, a simple task, he trembled. It was not fatigue or pain from his many injuries that caused his shaking. This time, Valens felt fear. The terms Acestes had offered were too generous, too easy. He looked across the raked sands to another door. He knew that the condemned waited behind it. What secrets did it hide?

A lion, perhaps, that had mauled its trainer and needed to die. Perhaps Acestes had lied all along and did know how many executions were to take place that day—there could be a hundred criminals, all armed with swords, who would face Valens at the same time. What if Antonice was one of them? No, he had to believe that she was safely hidden with Baro's family, lest he go insane.

A slave opened the door and Valens limped into the arena. The crowd, silent for a moment, began screaming when they saw him. For the first time in his life, he understood that the power of a gladiator did not come from the number of men he had killed—it came from how he had chosen to live.

Standing at the rail of his reserved box seats, Acestes lifted his hands for quiet. It took less than a minute. The crowd was also anxious to see what final challenge faced Valens.

"Today you see a titan standing before you." Again the crowd cheered and Acestes waited for it to die down. "But we must not forget what brought about his return to the arena. It was the death of a man, a great man. My uncle was a titan in his own right. Not of the arena, but of the Senate and the law. It is because we honor Marcus Rullus Servilia that we have gathered." The crowd cheered this statement as well, but not with the same gusto as when Acestes had named Valens a titan.

"I think it fitting that Valens Secundus is here today, at noon, for the executions rather than fighting tomorrow in the final primus. In fact, I think the gods played a role in making this day a reality as well. Justice lifted her blindfold, and seeing all, brought Valens Secundus to this moment." Acestes paused.

There were no cheers from the crowd. Instead, the confused murmur of many voices asking the same question over and over: *What does this mean?*

Valens strained to see beyond the general and the railing. He stared at each patrician who milled about with a golden goblet in hand. Phaedra was not among them.

"There is only one execution scheduled to take place today." The crowd groaned. "As I said, the gods played a part in this day. Although it is a single execution, I think this will test Rome's champion more than any other combat."

The mob cheered, ecstatic.

Valens tried to yell over their voices. "No. No. No."

"Bring her out," Acestes called.

The door from which the criminals came was opened. She stood at the threshold—a little dirty, a little tattered, but whole and safe. To Valens, she was the most beautiful sight in the world. A guard shoved Phaedra from behind, and she toppled into the arena. Valens hobbled to her and helped her to stand. He pressed his lips into her hair, and she clung tight to him.

To hold her close, to feel her skin next to his—this was a reason to live. Yet that was not his task.

"I refuse to kill her," Valens called out. "She has done nothing wrong."

"Nothing, you say? I say she is guilty of adultery. You have been her lover for four years. I do not blame you for acting on your desire—no man in here does. She was the one who needed to keep her virtue safe. For if a woman commits adultery, it is she who pays with her life."

"You lie," Phaedra said.

"It is the law."

"This is revenge, not justice," said Phaedra. "I am here because I do not want you. How can anyone want you? You are a swine."

"Teach your whore to keep her mouth shut or I will slice out her tongue," said Acestes.

Valens wrapped his arm around Phaedra's waist. "I will not execute her. She did nothing wrong. Yes, we have known each other in an intimate way, but after your uncle died. Never did I lie with her before."

"Of course you answer the charge against Phaedra by claiming her innocence," said Acestes. "She is, as you claim, your lover."

"She is innocent. You have no proof. Where is the proof to this charge?" challenged Valens.

"Proof. Proof. Proof," chanted the crowd.

"I will keep you safe," he said to Phaedra. He knew not how.

"You want proof?" asked Acestes. "I witnessed it all. Remember the night she wed my uncle? You were hired to fight and later invited to stay and enjoy the banquet. I always found it curious that Senator Scaeva hired gladiators to fight at his daughter's wedding. It is not so odd if you think of him as a loving father, manipulated by his daughter. She wanted you there so she could seduce you on her wedding night."

The crowd gasped.

"Untrue," said Valens.

Acestes smiled. "I found you two in the garden. I saw it all."

"You saw nothing because there was nothing to see," said Valens.

The crowd again gasped, not sure whom to believe.

Acestes gripped the rail with fingers that had gone white. "I will make this simple for you. One of you will leave this arena. You choose, Valens Secundus. Will it be her life or yours?"

Chapter 50

Phaedra

For the love of the gods, Acestes was a monster. Under his perfectly sculpted chest beat a rotten heart.

She could not let Valens take his own life. Hers was over. Yesterday she had thought that an unhappy marriage was the worst possible fate. But now she understood that if she lived, Acestes could, and would, do much worse to her than force her into a marriage she did not want.

She lifted Valens's palm to her lips and kissed it. Her testament to their love was to give Valens life. His testament must then be to give her a quick and painless death. She knelt before him as she had seen other defeated gladiators do. She looked down, exposing the back of her neck.

From the sponsor's box came a single scream—"No!"

Terenita stood at the edge, a golden pitcher clenched to her belly. Her hand trembled and water soaked her dun-colored tunic. At least her maid had not been harmed. With Phaedra's death, neither Terenita nor her pain could be used as bargaining chip.

The crowd began to cheer again, so thirsty for blood and drama that they cared not why it was spilled. Their yells took form and became a one-word chant: "Death."

"Do your duty," said Acestes. "Slay her."

"If you want one of us dead, you will have to come into the arena and do it yourself."

The crowd stopped calling for her blood and began a new chant: "Arena. Arena. Arena."

"Do not be a fool. I am not getting into the arena," said Acestes. "I am no gladiator. Nor am I a criminal."

"But you are a coward. All of you are." Valens pointed to the sponsor's reserved seats. "You train men to fight and kill for your amusement. Never once do you do your own killing."

The crowd booed and cried out that Acestes was a coward. Phaedra stood. Acestes had not thought through his plan very well. All of Rome loved Valens Secundus, and to use him poorly had earned the crowd's ire. As much as Rome loved her champion, they loved a fight even more. Acestes's refusal to take part in the combat was unforgivable.

Perhaps Acestes would not have made a very good politician after all.

"End all this now, Acestes," she said. "Let us both go."

"You must be mad if you think I will ever let you go. You toyed with me and let me think we would marry. All the while you were this gladiator's lover. No, you will pay with your life today, or I will make sure you always pay."

"I never loved you, Acestes. I never toyed with you, either. You asked me to marry you, yes. But I never gave you an answer. You presumed and saw what you wanted to see."

Phaedra waited for an outburst from Acestes. When none came, she continued, "You know the charge of adultery is false. There is no law preventing a widow from having a lover. Beyond that, Valens and I planned to marry. That was why my father made him an equestrian, so I could take him as a husband." She raised her voice so all could hear. "Please, Acestes, I beg of you. Let us both go."

"Let them go. Let them go. Let them go," the crowd chanted.

If she learned nothing else today, she learned that the fickle crowd at a gladiatorial game would repeat almost anything, so long as it could become a chant.

Valens squeezed her hand. She looked to where their fingers intertwined, and although his skin held a bronze hue and hers was white as milk, she could not tell at what point he ended and she began.

"Never," said Acestes. Somehow this single word rose over the voices of thousands and silenced them all. "I will never let you go free."

Knowing what she must do, Phaedra knelt again. The lack of panic she felt as her knees pressed into the sand surprised her, as did the clarity and calm that surrounded her. "Then I die today."

"No." Valens tried to pull her up by her arm. What would have been a simple thing for him to do if he were whole and strong now caused him to draw back reflexively in pain. Phaedra slipped easily from his grasp.

"I find it very touching that she sacrifices herself for you," said Acestes. "Now kill her."

Valens dropped his sword, and it landed on the ground with a thud next to Phaedra's feet. "If you want her dead, you need to come down here and kill me first. I know you will not do that. You possess none of the Roman virtue of bravery in the face of adversity."

"I am a general," said Acestes. "I led troops in the Sicilian slave uprising. Few are as brave as I."

"The slaves were farmers who wanted their land back. Soldiers who fight untrained men and women are not brave. They are cowards. And you are their cowardly leader," said Valens.

"Coward. Coward. Coward. Coward." The crowd found a chant they enjoyed, and their volume increased with each round until the ground shook.

"Enough!" cried Acestes. Phaedra could not hear his voice. It was lost in the continual chant, but she read it on his lips. He turned abruptly from his place at the railing and stalked to the back of the reserved box seats before disappearing down a set of stairs, which she knew led to the inside of the cattle market.

What might he do? He could order his guards into the arena to slaughter both her and Valens. That would be a decisive plan, a bold plan, but one that was destined to end Acestes's political career for allowing others to fight his personal battles. Once Acestes understood that his life's goal was virtually destroyed, then he would be very dangerous indeed.

As expected, a door to the arena opened. It was not a group of hired guards who streamed onto the sands with orders of vengeance. Rather, it was Acestes alone, armed with a sword. He wore a tunic of deep blue that shimmered in the light. A slight breeze caught his golden hair and ruffled the ends. The muscles in his arms, taut as ropes, flexed hard as he lifted the sword.

Finally, he had made a brilliant political move. The crowd went hoarse from cheering at the sight of him. It mattered little who Acestes slew today, for by stepping into the arena, he had made himself a hero. Phaedra loved Valens with every fiber of her being, but he was injured and his gladiator's kit covered many more bandages then even the mob could see. He would not be able to defeat Acestes with ease, or maybe at all.

Chapter 51

Valens

The general had lost his mind. Valens realized that his goading had not only ignited the crowd, but had driven Acestes into the arena, crazed as a rabid goat and just as mean. Like all insane adversaries, he was dangerous. The worst part was that the crowd now loved him, too. Well, no, the worst part of all was that Valens could not fight worth a damn today.

"Pick up your sword and fight," said Acestes. "You mislabeled me a coward. Who, other than the bravest of the brave, is willing to face the Champion of Rome?"

"I do not know," Valens mused, playing for time as he tried to develop an unlikely stratagem to defeat Acestes. "The stupidest of the stupid."

The crowd laughed.

"Enough. Get your sword."

Valens's sword lay on the ground near Phaedra's knees. He truly could not bend over, and so he stretched out his fingers to elongate his reach. The crowd laughed at that, too. He reached out again, farther, knowing his awkward stance entertained. "It seems to be a little far today." More laughter. "My love, can you help out?" More laughter still.

Phaedra looked up, wide-eyed.

"The sword, my love. Can you hand me my sword?"

She picked up the blade and stooped as she gave it to Valens. Perhaps she was playing to the crowd, too. Valens hobbled around, taking his time, exaggerating his movements, until he faced Acestes.

The crowd loved the antics and cheered even more.

Acestes did not.

He rushed toward Valens and kicked at Valens's broken leg. A white flash shot through Valens's vision, and then came the pain. The general slammed the pommel of his sword onto Valens's injured shoulder. He fell to the ground, attempting to conceal the agony. As he tumbled, he prayed that Acestes would not take a perverse revenge on Phaedra and his sister.

So, this is it. The ending of his life would be the greatest story ever told about Valens. Generations to come would describe the events of this day. Strangely, it was a small comfort to know that he would not fade into obscurity.

The crowd grew silent. Or maybe Valens was so focused on the final beats of his heart that he heard nothing else.

He might die today, but it was against his nature not to fight.

Action.

Focus.

The general lifted his sword, ready to strike. Valens rocked and reached to the left. Wait, wait. The glinting blade pierced the air as Valens rolled to the right. The tip of Acestes's sword hit the dirt and sank halfway up the shaft. The general pulled his sword free amid booing from the crowd.

Valens considered his next move, but lying on the ground, injured, with no weapon at hand, he had none.

Acestes twirled the sword around his wrist. He lifted it high and roared. Valens tensed and waited for the death blow. It never came. The general staggered backward and walked in a drunken circle. Through a slit in the side of Acestes's tunic, Valens saw blood, and flesh flayed from the muscle. Phaedra stood not far away. Valens's sword drooped in her grasp.

Acestes touched his side. The sight of his blood-covered hand seemed to stun the general momentarily. Then he advanced on Phaedra, twirling his sword with each step. She stepped away from him, stumbling, and dropped the sword. She reached down to pick it up, but Acestes kicked it aside.

"You—how could you betray me? I have loved you long and well." Even in the arena, where every word carried, Acestes spoke so quietly that Valens doubted anyone beyond the three of them heard what was said.

"You have never loved me," Phaedra whispered back. "You want to possess me, to make me a prize like the emerald necklace."

Valens crawled behind them to his sword. He used both hilt and crutch to regain his balance.

Focus.

"I meant to keep you safe because I love you," Acestes said to Phaedra.

"You meant to keep me because you love yourself, and you cannot accept that anyone may feel differently."

Valens lined up, ready to run Acestes through. He disliked killing a distracted man from behind, but he disliked dying much more.

"Behind you!" someone in the crowd yelled.

Acestes turned around.

Now that he faced Acestes, Valens seized the moment, ignored the pain, and, driving through the weakness in his leg, rushed forward and ran his sword into the general's middle. He plunged deeper as hot blood spilled over his hand. Then he dragged the blade upward and pulled his sword free.

Acestes dropped to his knees and fell forward, dead.

Chapter 52

Phaedra

To Phaedra, the noise and the frantic motion in the stands might have only been the buzzing of busy bees. She saw nothing other than Valens, and heard nothing beyond his words. "I love you," he repeated over and over. He stroked the hair away from her face. She untied his helmet and let it fall to the ground. He placed a light kiss on the corner of her mouth.

"I love you, too," she said.

"Are we free?"

Acestes lay without moving. The editor of the games slapped him across the face. There was no response. A figure in a dark hood emerged from one of the doors. He was, she knew, a slave dressed as Charon, the ferryman, meant to take Acestes to the other world. She pressed her face into Valens's shoulder as Charon produced a large hook meant to drag the body away. Once she looked again, both slave and general were gone. A bloody trail in the sand remained as a testament to Acestes's time in the arena.

With the body gone, the editor approached Valens and lifted his hand. The crowd cheered. Phaedra looked into the box seats where she had sat as Acestes's guest. Her people, the elite of Rome, looked down, their eyes narrowed with disgust and perhaps vengeance. Yet she also noted fear. Could Acestes's violent end portend what might happen to them if they challenged the Fates and angered the mob?

The former consul, Fimbria, stepped to the railing. He raised his hands for quiet. "As you all know, it is illegal to kill anyone from the patrician rank, unless that person is also a patrician and the death unavoidable."

The crowd booed and called for Fimbria's death as well.

"Since Valens Secundus was recently named equestrian, and General Acestes freely entered the arena intending harm, there will be many disputes as to the legality of this killing. The Senate will discuss this in the near future."

Phaedra knew from long experience as a senator's daughter that they never would. There was no correct way to rule on the matter, and the mob would be angered whatever the outcome. The Senate would all decide to ignore the matter, never letting it be brought up in session.

"Until then, you are free to go. Phaedra needs to be returned to her guardian."

"Acestes was her guardian," said Valens.

Fimbria stepped away from the railing and conferred with a few other senators. "Then she must go to her closest male relative."

"That is my father's cousin," said Phaedra. "He did not want me, so Acestes agreed to make me his charge."

"If I may," said Valens.

"Please do," said Fimbria, interrupting Valens midsentence. "She is yours for the taking, Valens Secundus. You are both free to go."

Valens leaned on Phaedra as they wound through the darkened corridors of the arena and out into the open spaces of the forum. A crowd gathered, but no one tried to stop them with word or deed.

"So, I am your ward now," she asked. "What do you plan to do with me?"

"Nothing," said Valens. "I want you to do what you want to do and be whoever it pleases you to be. No more, no less."

Did he mean to be rid of her? "You say you love me, but then refuse to keep me?"

"I do love you, and that is why I will allow you to go. If that is what you want."

The freedom to make her own choices settled on Phaedra like a warm blanket on a cold night. She now had the power over her life, as she had always wanted. Wrapping her arm tighter around Valens, Phaedra knew what, and whom, she would choose.

"Valens," a voice called. "Wait."

They turned to see Paullus running toward them. At his side was Terenita.

Phaedra embraced the maid. "What are you doing here? How did you get away?"

Breathing heavily, Terenita straightened her turban. "I just ran. No one in the sponsor's box tried to stop me."

"To whom do you belong?" asked Paullus. "It is a matter we must address quickly, lest you gain your new owner's ire for disappearing."

"No one," said Phaedra as she leveled a steely gaze at Paullus. "This woman belongs to no one. She is a free woman and my aunt. I challenge you to defy me."

"The gods themselves would not be so foolish to either challenge or defy you," Valens said with a laugh.

Paullus chuckled in agreement.

"Oh, Lady Phaedra," said Terenita as her eyes began to water, "I cannot thank you enough."

"No, Aunt, I am not your lady, just your loving niece. You are free to stay with me or see the world on your own. I will give you what I have. You are now free."

"Free," whispered Terenita. "I will think on what you have said, but for now I will stay with you." She paused. "Niece."

"This is all working out rather well," said Paullus as he clasped Valens on the shoulder. "You won, you know."

"I know I won," said Valens. "I was there when the editor named me the victor."

"Not you," said Paullus. "Phaedra, you won your wager."

"What wager?" Valens asked.

Ah, yes, the necklace that had started and ended everything with Acestes. "I bet a rather nice piece of jewelry on you winning all three bouts."

"That is kind of you." Valens kissed her lips. "I am glad I had your support."

"It was stupid of her. The necklace was worth a quarter of a million sesterces, and the odds on you winning all three matches were one hundred and fifty to one."

"I did not realize the odds were so low." Valens was in pain and seemed to be getting more confounded and annoyed by the minute.

"You seem to be missing the point," said Paullus. "Phaedra is now a wealthy woman. She can have anything she wants."

"The question becomes," said Valens, "what do you want, Phaedra?"

With her new wealth came independence. She could go anywhere she chose or buy anything she wanted. Or she could stay at home and buy nothing at all. Yet as her mind wandered to a villa she might buy in Pompeii or a bolt of silk she could purchase, she imagined Valens by her side.

"You." Phaedra pushed up to tiptoe and kissed Valens on the mouth. She tasted his lips and smelled his scent—leather, sweat, and costmary. "I want you. Rich or poor. Famous or obscure. Powerful or humble. I want you."

Valens wrapped his arms around her waist. As he placed his mouth on hers, Phaedra chose this moment to begin her life with the man she loved. Now and always.

ACKNOWLEDGMENTS

We've all heard the saying "It takes a village to raise a child." As the mother of three, I agree. Just as parents need support, so do writers. My writer's journey has taken years, and along the way I've been blessed to receive help from many. There are so many, in fact, that I could never thank everyone personally. But to all my friends who ask, "How's the book going?" I am forever grateful.

A huge thank-you goes to Lisa Burke for your unwavering support, encouragement, and friendship. I don't know what I would do without you. Thanks, also, for reading several drafts of this book and your enlightening and honest feedback.

Thanks to Carol Henry, Betsy Garufi, Judy Goldschmidt, Kim Kunkle, Gary Ingraham, and Jim McCarthy for your help as this book traveled from idea to draft to final copy. Thank you also to Jill Shultz for a final read and your wonderful insights.

An important stop on my writer's journey was Wilkes University, where I received my MA. These acknowledgments would be incomplete without sharing my appreciation for the entire faculty of the Creative Writing program. You all inspire through word, deed, and action. Thanks also to my cohort, who read the opening of this book and helped me find the story. A special thank-you goes to the best mentor in the world, Bev Donofrio. The lessons I learned from you will stay with me always. Another special thanks to Ken Vose and Ross Klavan for being so darn fabulous, and for all the writerly advice you've shared over the years.

Thanks to all the folks in Ithaca Fiction Writers—Virginia, Marie, Doreen, Lisa, Eric, Kara, Barb, Phillip, and Gerda. You all *rock*! I would not be where I am today without you.

Thank you also to my amazing agent, Chris Tomasino, for believing in me and this book. Thanks to Ruth Vandevanter for your help as this book went out into the world. To all the wonderful folks at Montlake, especially Hai-Yen Mura, Irene Billings, Melody Guy, and the entire editorial, art, and marketing teams—thank you!

To Jessica Dubey: For five years you have graciously read every word I've written and listened to every idea that has popped into my head. You've offered me advice, counseling, cosmopolitans, and most important—your friendship. For all that and more, thank you.

I don't know where the next leg of my writer's journey will take me, but I cannot imagine better traveling companions than all of you!

ABOUT THE AUTHOR

Having penned her first book at age eight, Jen Bokal has always been a lover of the written word. In 2003 she decided to turn her avocation into a vocation, and from that time on there has been no looking back. Jen is the author of several short stories, poems, and feature articles. She was also the relationship columnist for *Suite* e-zine from 2005 to 2008. Her first novel, *Celtic Heart*, was published in 2007.

In 2010 Jen graduated from Wilkes University with a master of arts in creative writing. She is a member of the Romance Writers of America.

What Jen enjoys most about writing romance is that the alpha males in her books mostly do what she wants them to do. Having been married to an alpha male herself for twenty years, she knows how rare and wonderful that is. Jen and her manly husband live in upstate New

York with their three beautiful daughters, two aloof cats, and two very spoiled dogs.

Jen invites you to visit her on Facebook at Jennifer D. Bokal Author, or follow her on Twitter @jenbokal.